D0914815

The Masterworks of Literature Series

Sylvia E. Bowman, *Editor*
Indiana University

Deephaven and Other Stories

Deephaven and Other Stories

by SARAH ORNE JEWETT

Edited for the Modern Reader by

Richard Cary

COLBY COLLEGE

The New College and University Press, Inc.
New Haven, CT.

Contents

Introduction

In 1877, the year *Deephaven* was issued in book form, there occurred a number of indicative political, economic, technological, and cultural events. President Hayes was inaugurated, the first gasoline-driven horseless carriage was assembled, Harrington and Hart introduced the cakewalk, federal troops quelled violent strikes by railroad workers, Edison patented the phonograph, the Russo-Turkish War commenced, and Zola's *L'Assommoir* and Ibsen's *Pillars of Society* were published. None of these appeared to touch directly the young author of *Deephaven*, whose chief concern in a world of convulsing values seemed to be whether the royalties from her book would permit "of buying myself a most gallant new horse for riding." A review of her career and a close reading of her quiet chronicles of Maine life, however, dissipate any impression of flippancy.

I

Sarah Orne Jewett—born in South Berwick, Maine, in 1849—was the product of a relatively isolated maritime-rural society in the afterglow of its splendor. The Embargo of 1807 had effectively destroyed the vitality of Maine's shipping enterprise; the Civil War, which made clear the irresistible prospect of cities and factories, further diminished the stature of this essentially agrarian state. The forces of the future were working away from the tiny coastal hamlets and farm communities of Maine. New railroads opened the way for ambitious youths to seek brighter possibilities in manufacturing centers or in the enticing West. Elder citizens accepted doom with a mixture of pride and resignation. By the mid-1870's Maine was largely dependent upon fish, timber, potatoes, and nostalgia for its great seafaring days.

Of all these factors, the girl Sarah had long been aware. If she did not clutch them grimly to heart or express them in doleful tones, it is because the immediate economic effects were not consequential to her as a member of the gentry. Daughter of a well-loved, well-to-do country doctor, whose legacy included the accumulations of several successful seagoing forebears, Miss Jewett came to know and appreciate the innate riches of her region through a route more instructive than the reading of history. As a child, she accompanied her father on his daily rounds along shore and through countryside, absorbing native speech, lore, looks, and habits. She sat in the town's general store, listening to ancient beached captains and upcountry traders. As a young girl, she walked and rode in a wide radius, exploring nature, visiting with aged friends, and cultivating chance acquaintances. Frequent excursions to Boston and other metropolises provided insight into a diametrically different mode of existence—enough insight to establish a basis for the comparisons of past and present, of city and country, which were to inform so much of her work. By the time the first section of *Deephaven* appeared in the *Atlantic Monthly* (September, 1873), Miss Jewett was fully saturated in the essential materials of her art, if not fully matured as an artist.

II

If the influences which shape and direct the sensitivity of a writer can be segregated and classified, it may be said that the prime impulsions toward Miss Jewett's ultimate art were the contemporary rage for local color and her own invulnerable inclination. The two decades following the Civil War saw a remarkable proliferation of local-color literature. Extension of the means of mass transportation brought within general scope areas long untroubled by strangers. The incursion of industrialism and its attendant spirit of standardization posed other threats to bucolic singularity. Partly through eagerness to capitalize on the peculiarities of insulated groups, and partly through a more serious desire to save from extinction the intrinsic virtues of regional differences, writers of disparate abilities lent themselves to portrayals of distinctive characters, customs, dialects, and topographies in the West, the South, the Middle Atlantic, the Midwest, and New England. The short story of local color deluged the periodicals; novels and collections of sketches in the same vein dominated the book market. In this period Miss Jewett, already fixed upon becoming a writer, read voraciously and was unquestionably affected by the trend. Her subsequent remarks about one of the first local-color novels, Harriet Beecher Stowe's *The Pearl of Orr's Island* (discussed below), are seminal revelations.

That Miss Jewett chose to take the view of humanist rather than cartoonist is inherent in her character and status. Happy citizen of a village in which the Jewetts had long been prosperous and respected, she moved about her native environs as assured as a begum, but as inconspicuously as a millhand's daughter. She had entrée to every segment of Maine's tacitly classless society and was equally at home in manor or fish shed. She knew the wards of counties as intimately as she did her fragile, antiquated ladies. It has been suggested that she projects an unreal idyl because she was ignorant of the bleaker sides of New England life. This is untrue. She was thoroughly cognizant of the economic and emotional urgencies that spelled misery for her constituents, and on more than one occasion she pulls aside the veil. The equanimity of her temperament and the security of her social situation generated a preference for the less desolate experiences. Without distorting the fundamental realities of places and people, she overlays the harsher aspects with her indomitable memory of past greatness and goodness. An old and treasured fragment of culture was fast disintegrating, and she wished to preserve some of its essence. In the process, she presses many flowers but gilds few lilies.

In still another sense did her Brahmin upbringing in a remote, almost defunct inland port influence the cast of her mind and the course of her work. Quality and quiet, rather than magnitude or movement, became ingrained as ideals. Unused and uncongenial to action per se, she concentrates upon the small joys and stresses that flicker just below the surface and seldom flare into overt declaration. Dramatic plot and intensity are virtually absent from her prose fiction. *The Tory Lover* (1901), her one belated attempt to turn out a consciously "dynamic" novel, is far below her average of achievement. She could not violate with impunity her governing principle that "a dull little country village is just the place to find the real drama of life."

In the second preface she wrote for *Deephaven* Miss Jewett explicitly signifies her growing fear that country values were incontinently vanishing. The first preface of fifteen lines in the first edition merely dissociates the town of Deephaven and its residents from any positive extant originals. For the limited edition illustrated by Charles and Marcia Woodbury in 1894, Miss Jewett extended her remarks to eight pages. With the confidence of some fifteen years of continued professional success, she admits the inexperience which beset the youthful "imaginer of Deephaven" but, more importantly, calls up the phenomena which prompted her to write the book.

She sees the changes wrought in provincial life as the result of two human currents: the flow to cities of immigrants and rustics seeking broader sources of income; and the reflex flow of vacationers from overcrowded cities, with a curiosity—aroused by the Civil War—about other sections of the country, now made accessible by the new wealth and the outreaching railroads. Some benefits accrued from the initial waves of this second invasion, but gradually the money left behind by tourists and summer boarders brought about less desirable effects: "Tradition and time-honored custom were to be swept away together by the irresistible current. Character and architecture seemed to lose individuality and distinction."

In the face of these losses and the perceptibly widening gulf between city and country people, the aborning authoress took it upon herself to correct the misimpression that native Mainers conformed in type to "the caricatured Yankee of fiction, striped trousers, bell-crowned hat, and all." In her callow fervor for truth and goodwill she adopted the "noble saying of Plato that the best thing that can be done for the people of a state is to make them acquainted with one another." She no doubt counted herself among that "class of country people who preserve the best traditions of culture and of manners, from some divine inborn instinct toward what is simplest and best and purest." And she determined, in the role of redemptive scribe, to devote her whole life to the cause.

In her time, Sarah Jewett published twenty books, most of them collections of previously printed sketches and short stories, some of the latter for children. Five of the books may—granting liberal use of the term—be called novels. There are also a history of the Normans and, posthumously, a volume of verse. Of all her books, *Deephaven* (1877) was the first.

Deephaven

III

The most direct incentive to "writing about people of rustic life just as they were" rose out of Mrs. Stowe's *The Pearl of Orr's Island* (1862), which Sarah read in her thirteenth or fourteenth year. She avows her debt to it in several places; it caused her "to see with new eyes, and to follow eagerly the old shore paths from one gray, weather-beaten house to another." Nevertheless, she instinctively drew away from the book's complicated plot and strenuous tone (which in their way owe something to *Wuthering Heights*), from its self-conscious "literary" style, from the calculated interjections of "quaint" dialect, and from the sentimentalized characters. She taxed Mrs. Stowe for failure to sustain the "noble key to simplicity and harmony," and she set her sights on "a more true and sympathetic rendering." She could not compromise with her subjective vision. After a short term of inept ventures, she settled down to a consistent depiction of life as she saw it—through the softened realism of her gentlewoman's lenses, to be sure, but with a gentlewoman's infrangible honesty.

Other books which may have been instrumental in Miss Jewett's particular bearing are Mrs. Gaskell's *Cranford*, which Helen Denis mentions in "Deephaven Society," and Miss Mitford's *Our Village*, which Whittier likened to Deephaven. Van Wyck Brooks suggests (*New England: Indian Summer*, p. 347) that a statement by Howells' Kitty Ellison in *A Chance Acquaintance* "might well have been the germ of Miss Jewett's stories":

> At any rate, if I were to write a story, I should want to take the slightest sort of plot, and lay the scene in the dullest kind of place, and then bringing out all their possibilities. I'll tell you a book after my own heart: *Details,*—just the history of a week in the life of some young people who happen together in an old New England country-house; nothing extraordinary, little, everyday things told so exquisitely, and all fading naturally away without any particular result, only the full meaning of everything brought out.

This indeed comprises the primary fiber of Miss Jewett's literary cloth, but Brooks's own documentation disproves his point. Kitty's exposition appeared in the *Atlantic Monthly* for

April, 1873; Miss Jewett's Kate Lancaster unfolded her scheme for *Deephaven* in September of the same year. There could hardly have been time enough for Kitty to mold or substantially trim Miss Jewett's intention. Books doubtless engraved themselves upon her mind, but the central concepts developed out of a congenital predilection and a precociously long involvement with her subject matter. What she received from her reading was not inspiration but corroboration. In the year of its publication she wrote, "*Deephaven* is not the result of careful study during one 'summer's vacation,' as some persons have thought, but I could write it because it is the fashion of life with which I have always been familiar."

She never unconditionally denied the imputations that Deephaven resembled Berwick or Newport or other actual Maine communities, but she crisply rejected pinpoint identification: "I don't like to have people say that I mean York when I say Deephaven." She insisted that, while York contained unmistakable elements of Deephaven, she had "made up" her fictive town before she "ever stayed overnight in York." And of all the characters in the book, she would accede that only Miss Chauncey was a real person. On the surface, Miss Jewett was honoring two general persuasions of her time. Romanticism called for support of the psychic function of imagination; Victorianism endorsed literature and life as two separate worlds. In practice, however, she was shackled by neither of these esthetic dogmas. She carves her creative world out of the solid physical world, knits the collective traits of her neighbors into unique but unified individuals, and succeeds in fusing literature and life into one indubitable world.

IV

Deephaven is Miss Jewett's formative and fundamental book. It stands in relation to the rest of her work as the embryo to the adult organism. Written in parts over a period of five years, it is preceded by a score of unrelated stories and poems, and interspersed by a like number, growingly consonant but still peripheral. In "The Shore House" (*Atlantic Monthly*, September, 1873) she reveals with occasional crudities of style and lapses of judgment the instinctual wisdom about place and people, the motifs and attitudes, the subtle lights and shades that were thenceforth to be her hallmarks. These intuitions and techniques she enhances through "Deephaven Cronies" (*Atlantic Monthly,* September, 1875), and "Deephaven Excursions" (*Atlantic Monthly,* September, 1876). She continues to ply them in wider and deeper contexts through some hundred other sketches and stories, and two novels, before the final refinement in her masterpiece, *The Country of the Pointed Firs* (1896).

Deephaven, then, represents the first tentative steps of an artist wakened to the genius within him. In the Jewett canon it may be classified as Fielding's *Joseph Andrews* to his *Tom Jones* or as Huxley's *Antic Hay* to his *Point Counter Point.* The conception of Miss Jewett's work is patent but inadequately realized; the privy truth has become evident but the manner and the craft are not yet capable of emitting it in all its incandescence. A collateral reading of the three magazine pieces which inspired *Deephaven* and the transmuted version which appeared as a volume in 1877 will verify that the process of maturation was already in force. Miss Jewett adroitly bolstered the final presentation through revisions and additions. She modified certain minor details to secure a tauter verisimilitude; pruned some of the extravagances out of her language and that of the natives; eliminated several characters not entirely relevant (the Vibberts) and introduced others (Captain Sands, for instance); and described typical activities such as cunner fishing—all of which give fuller symmetry and density to her emerging construct.

In *Deephaven* Miss Jewett discloses a setting which was to become characteristic as landscape and as symbol in her subsequent minute delineations of Maine life. In center stage is the atrophied fishing village with its gaunt wharves and decaying brigs; over the heads of magnificent evergreens, the vista seaward is one of sunlight and islands; the area inland is pocked with dry, brown roads, untidy fields, and farmhouses askew with age. The physiology of this design proclaims Miss Jewett's convictions about the depredations of time and the possible channel of liberation.

Deephaven is inhabited by people who, with infinitely diverse variations, are met later on the marsh island, in Dulham, Law Lane, Oldfields, Longport, and Dunnet Landing. The prim spinsters, the garrulous captains, the spunky housekeepers, the superannuated ladies, the stricken farmers, the pathetic widows, the lone eccentrics—these return without the brand of stereotype. Sprung from common origins, they savor the same air, voice the same hopes, bend to similar adversities, but remain discernibly different from their predecessors.

Miss Jewett's graph of progress is not an undeflected straight line. The style of her next novel, *A Country Doctor* (1884), lacks the attained facility of *Deephaven,* and the situations are often overburdened by a mood of Gothic crisis. The farm and coast locale is commandingly authentic, but the theme of a woman's struggle between love and a career was in that time more an urban than a rural dilemma. However, the oppositions of past-present and country-city operate prominently in the resolution of the action. Some of the characters are plain manipulations, such as impetuous Dr. Ferris, lifeless George Gerry, and, to lesser degree, the protagonist herself, Nan Prince. These are gratifying-ly counterpoised by the bedrock figures of Marilla Thomas, Mrs. Meeker, the four Dyers, and Captain Parish. The marks of Miss Jewett's nearness to native scenes and persons are certain here, but her advance in art is minimal. She works too hard at sustaining a conventional plot, and she allows the feministic aspirations of the day to obtrude upon the more enduring themes.

Greater grace is to be found in *A Marsh Island* (1885). In this *lentissimo* earth-epic, Miss Jewett merges once and for all into the primal rhythms of the region, transcribing life as it courses unresisted through the hearts and minds of the inhabitants. The plot, commenced with a promise of sharper drama than it ful-fills, is firmly subordinated to the theme of man's salutary affinity with nature. Her descriptions of landscape and the seasonal activities on a salt-hay farm are surpassingly beautiful and have a tone of timelessness upon them. The indigenous characters are strongly drawn—from patriarchal Israel Owen to the sage buffoon Jim Fales. The equivocal love affair between rustic Doris Owen and town-bred Dick Dale personifies the con-trast between country and city, between entity and artifice. In this book Miss Jewett takes momentous strides toward the con-summation of her vision and techniques. She retains the barest shadows of mishap and complication, considered *de rigueur* in the novel of her generation, focusing squarely on the origins of character, and the conduct of heredity and environment upon it.

Deephaven

In this novel she makes her last concessions to formalism and the popular reading audience.

In *The Country of the Pointed Firs* (1896) Miss Jewett arrives at full growth. Every element broached in *Deephaven* is here augmented and brought to highest pitch. She discards all semblance of dramatic action and dramatic continuity. The everyday lot of everyday people, as projected in *Deephaven,* constitutes the backbone of the book. The difference between the two books lies in Miss Jewett's additional familiarity with her subject, her deeper insight, finer appreciation, and more secure artistry. *The Country of the Pointed Firs* is Miss Jewett's acknowledged masterwork and an unparalleled register of life in nineteenth-century rural New England. In the more limited order of local-color fiction it is without cavil the best yet written.

Comedy, tragedy, and just ordinary humdrum unfold in the casual routines of a maritime village and its adjoining farmlands. The air of adolescent excitement brewed in *Deephaven* by Kate and Helen gives way to stabler observations by the summer visitor from the city—and Miss Jewett, too, is now twenty years older. The expression is simpler, purer, and as fluent as the sea whose spell encompasses every thought and move in Dunnet Landing. The characters might have been lifted out of *Deephaven,* except that these have a profounder quality. The retrospective sea captain is here, as is the self-reliant matron and widow, the thinning spinster, the capable, reticent fisherman, the pert eccentric, and the invincible octogenarian. But in *The Country of the Pointed Firs* Almira Todd, her mother, William Blackett, Joanna, Captain Littlepage, Esther Hight, and the Bowden clan are not earth-figures only. With a suggestive power she did not have in 1877, Miss Jewett endows them with distinctly human personalities and then sublimates them into exemplary myth-figures. Their experiences are not isolated events happening accidently; they exude connotations of cycle in a pattern of racial recurrence. Mrs. Todd is superb as an image of both solidity and symbol.

The sense of improvisation which pervades the action of *Deephaven* is less sporadic in *The Country of the Pointed Firs.* No string holds successive incidents together in either novel, but the management of intervals is more skilful in the latter. The scarcity of progressive narrative is hardly noticeable, a tribute to the absorbing interest Miss Jewett imparts to temperate episodes. Neither novel coheres by virtue of Aristotelian unity, but through a marvelous blend of tone, point of view, place, and people. Willa Cather says that Miss Jewett always referred to her "Pointed Fir papers" or "Pointed Fir sketches"; she never regarded them as "stories." *The Country of the Pointed Firs* is the acme of Miss Jewett's early conception in *Deephaven*—the plotless novel. The two, she once told Howells, hold all her real knowledge and dreams, "the very dust of thought and association that made me."

V

It was Howells, then editor of the *Atlantic Monthly*, who induced Miss Jewett to collect the Deephaven sketches and to publish them as a book. The volume appeared in the spring without creating undue critical or popular hubbub, although it was reviewed outside the cultural orbit of Boston and sold well. Despite the spirited statements of several chroniclers, Miss Jewett did not, like Byron, wake up to find herself famous. She was competing against what Hawthorne called "a damned mob of scribbling women" who were turning out floods of tearful domestic tragedies and against the mounting tide of opulent historical romance. *Deephaven* attracted not nearly so large an audience, but its admirably muted quality elicited the praise of her friends, of many critics, and stimulated requests from publishers for her sketches and stories.

Whittier assured the author that he had read his presentation copy "over half a dozen times, and always with gratitude to thee for such a book—so simple, pure, and so true to nature." To this he added the encomium, "I know of nothing better in our literature of the kind," and he distributed copies to a number of his friends, "all of whom appreciate it highly." Howells teasingly admonished her, "Don't be proud, now your book has succeeded so splendidly." And it may be adduced from her response to Mrs. Henry Lee Higginson that the comments of her amateur friends exceeded these in warmth (see Richard Cary, *Sarah Orne Jewett Letters*, 32-34).

Critics in the newspapers and periodicals reacted with less unanimity. In its issue of August 28, 1873, the *Nation* declared the first installment of *Deephaven* in the *Atlantic Monthly* "very agreeable reading . . . which is more like talk than reading, and talk of a very fresh, unaffected kind." Between lengthier studies of A. Mahon's *A Critical History of the Late American War* and F. Robertson's *Notes on Genesis*, the New York *Times* of April 28, 1877, threw some heavy ironic darts at the immobile New England seaport which "now abounds in women, old sailors, and boys," and at the two "well regulated young women [who] do not even need a yachtman with a brown mustache to enliven their summer." It concludes morosely that "if condensed considerably, the book would read well in letters, and at the manuscript stage; it is by some mistake, doubtless, that it got into print at all." Not so caustic was the "Recent Literature" section of the *Atlantic Monthly* for June, 1877; it pointed out the book's "very fresh and delicate quality," its "finely and faithfully done" sketches of "the near-at-hand quaint and picturesque." Attentive to both comic and dismal manifestations, the critic opines that "these are all touched with a hand that holds itself far from every trick of exaggeration, and that subtly delights in the very tint and form of reality." Aside from the brickbats and bouquets, Horace E. Scudder astutely summed up the prevailing resistance to Miss Jewett's tendency. In an 1878 review of her *Play Days* he called for "a more positive story"; "we trust that she will cultivate the power of invention."

Deephaven made enough of an impress on the public to be reissued dozens of times. It was the 1894 large-paper, limited edition illustrated by the Woodburys, however, that incited reexamination of Miss Jewett's accomplishment. She was now an established star, having already fashioned her best work, excluding *The Country of the Pointed Firs* and one story in *The Life of Nancy*. Many journals ignored the book as just another Christmas reprint, and some (like the *Dial* and the *Literary World*) confined themselves to remarking the "holiday attire" of "its all too-shiny paper and its crudely-conceived cover," while lauding the illustrations so "thoroughly true to the scenes and characters the author describes." The *Critic* addressed itself less to ephemera and more to the content, asserting that the passage of time seemed not to affect its veracity: "*Deephaven* is still an accurate picture of the out-of-the-way New England village." In this opinion the London *Athenaeum* generously concurred, awarding thanks to Messrs. Osgood, McIlvaine & Company for restoring the book to circulation.

Again, the *Atlantic Monthly* plucked the most vibrant string. In January, 1894, its anonymous reviewer, contemplating the changes maturity had brought to Miss Jewett's work, cited the "delightfully expressive" figures, landscapes, and interiors in *Deephaven* for "their fine drawing, vividness of portraiture, and reserve of force." Then he laid down the true and significant dictum: "The feeling is the same; it is the art which has become more definite and clear." But in the long run, it remained for Ludwig Lewisohn—not renowned for partiality to the feminine in American literature—to suggest *Deephaven's* definitive niche. With customary abruptness he said, "If *Cranford* is a minor classic, so is *Deephaven*." Most readers of this perceptive revelation of life in the backwater of New England will be disposed to agree.

In the decade when local-color writing was in fullest cry, Miss Jewett's entry was a voice of moderation. She shrank from the excesses which eventually degraded the flamboyant exploiters of sectional mores and topography. She sought to conserve values more imperative than odd costume, distorted dialect, or idiosyncratic behavior. She did not implicate her people in provincial activities which would bring indulgent or scornful smiles to the lips of outlanders. From start to end she did not waver from the purposes outlined in her 1893 preface. The ardency of her desire did not contort the honesty of her rendition. Against the absurdities of its contemporaries, *Deephaven*—though an inchoate work—stands as a trustworthy chapter in the unending recital of the national epic.

VI

In addition to five novels, Miss Jewett published over a hundred sketches and short stories dealing with Maine. Reluctant to submit to mandates of form in the novel, here too she eludes regulation. Within the expanse and variety of arrangement she permits herself, one can trace a metamorphosis of artistic practice and the evolution of a sheerly subjective genre. In these compositions Miss Jewett constantly stretches toward more meaningful matter and earnestly refines the raw edges of her manner. When all is said, she achieves a kind of sketch and a kind of short story expressly her own, couched in a style expressly her own. To generalize succinctly, the sequence of development proceeds from the pure essay to the essay verging on story to the story of incident, lacking action. These short works not only contain inherent and individual merit, they also constitute fertile trying grounds on the uphill road to *The Country of the Pointed Firs.*

The portions of *Deephaven* which appeared in 1873 indicate that the ideas Miss Jewett articulates in the 1893 preface had long been germinating within her. This is confirmed by numerous other sketches written between these dates. "River Driftwood" (1881) is a compendium of topics drawn from observation of neighboring vistas, folk, customs, and history. Miss Jewett's fascination with the mythic and prosaic capacities of her native environs is here given free play. She records visual details, biography, anecdote, reminiscence, traditions, apocrypha, and superstitions. All is lovingly set down, with elucidation and preservation in mind.

In "River Driftwood" Miss Jewett meditates discursively upon man's kinship with nature, and upholds the grandeur of the past against the abasements of the present—two frequent tunes in her repertoire. She restores to palpable life the portraits of Doctor and Madam Hovey, the latter an enfeebled but intrepid great lady who recurs many times in Miss Jewett's writings under other appellations. The texture of expression here illustrates compactly the larger-scale transition she was undergoing. Rather stiffly decorative in the beginning, it gradually slips into the more comfortable idiom of the country. Like Mark Twain on the Mississippi, she drifts down an archetypal river, using it as the hub for a discontinuous series of adventures of the eyes and heart. This radial scheme of departure and return to a conceptive point also underscores her two most able novels, *Deephaven* and *The Country of the Pointed Firs.*

Miss Jewett effects a personal remove from the Addison-Hazlitt-Stevenson species of reflective essay in "The Landscape Chamber" (1887), not her first but perhaps her best hybrid sketch-story. (Two other eminent examples are "An Autumn Holiday" [1880] and "The Courting of Sister Wisby" [1887].) In this peculiar marriage of convenience, she unites elements of the essay and the short story without allotting priority to either.

Most frequently, as in this instance, her *alter ego* sets out willy-nilly for a walk or drive through barely familiar coastal or back-land terrain. She keeps up a lively commentary on the myriad impressions encountered in course. Before long she meets a raconteur or strides by chance into an evolving situation. In either case she is presented with the vital ingredients of a short story, but she evades the commitment by recounting the facts, plaiting them with appropriate atmosphere, and then steadfastly resuming her journey. She is of course exercising her strongest aptitude—psychological penetration of place and people—and scanting her most conspicuous debility: dynamic action.

"The Landscape Chamber" is amply essay and short story, manifestly more the former because it trails off into a resource-less farewell and fails to provide a releasing dénouement. With as much justice it can be argued, from the modern view, that in this very vacuum of resolution lies its power and verity as drama. The irreversible end of the tragedy has been forecast by the somber choreography of events. Discounting superfluous frame-work, "The Landscape Chamber" is "The Fall of the House of Usher" without Poe's bravura tone and livid finale.

Miss Jewett turned out a copious measure of prose pieces which, from any view, may be classified as short stories. Indeed, her first appearance in print, "Jenny Garrow's Lovers" (1868), is a model of the hyperplotted, melodramatic fiction which was then passing as an acceptable reflection of life. Either through inefficacy or an urgency for early publication, she again bowed to popular and critical pressure for "positive story" the next year in "Mr. Bruce." For five years thereafter she wrote little else than tales for children and middling verse. A notable relaxation of reins occurs with "Miss Sidney's Flowers" in 1874. She seems content to let this story run its own route. She suffers a serious relapse in "A Sorrowful Guest" (1879), but tends toward less and less plot until, by the mid-1880's, she is unshakeably ded-icated to character and incident. In the short story, as in the novel, she finally abandons all association with dynamic action.

Not much ever happens in Miss Jewett's best short stories. She approaches a circumstance, assesses it with amazing acuity, then leaves it practically undisturbed, a roiled puddle regaining its surface serenity. Climaxes, when they come, are ripples rather than billows. Her aim is to reveal what is integral in character and situation, not to thrust them toward crucial transformations. A calm sense of eternality permeates her tiny, incisive vignettes. People and events move with classic stateliness and a certainty of renewal. In her repudiation of graphic happenings and diagrammatic plots, she anticipates the contour of the short story fifty years later.

The six stories selected for inclusion in this volume show Miss Jewett at her peak. They demonstrate absolute control over medium, infinitesimal knowledge of the actions and passions of her Maine neighbors, confident depiction of town and country settings and customs, and a persistent realistic base to her generally romantic bent. All also exhibit in advanced stages the techniques, personnel, landscapes, and motifs implanted in *Deephaven* and brought to fruition in *The Country of the Pointed Firs*.

"A White Heron" (1886), rated by most as Miss Jewett's sovereign short story, peers into the predicament of a town-bred child now transposed to the sylvan peace of her grandmother's farm. She has embraced the mysteries of living in nature but is suddenly exposed again to worldly lures. The choice she makes between the values of city and country is the one her creator invariably advocates. The relative worth of primitivism and sophistication is never in question in Miss Jewett's mind. She watches mournfully the deterioration of pioneer heritage in every facet of Maine life, and in this story she allegorizes it brilliantly. "The woman's heart, asleep in the child" pulses to the immemorial rhythms of earth freezing and flourishing, fading, freezing and flourishing again.

The other five stories fall into Miss Jewett's favorite category —exquisite exposition of the ways and days of aging widows or spinsters. Emphasis varies but the effect is uniform. One comes away from each of these convinced of having been privileged to glimpse the inmost labyrinths of female sensibility. For profundity of divulgence they are unexcelled anywhere in American literature. Mostly they raise a day out of the lives of these women and through incident and indirection disclose all that they have ever been and will ever be. The principal differences of one story from another exist in the mood engendered by their respective issues and the tone Miss Jewett applies to each.

"The Town Poor" (1890) treats the plight of two helpless

paupers with dour realism, with pity, and with indignation which stops this side of Pollyanna altruism. Pity, somewhat mixed with derision, animates "The Dulham Ladies" (1886). Miss Jewett takes visibly malicious pleasure in offering these two sweetly foolish old sisters to the mercies of a world which has passed them by and has small tolerance for their oddities. The sympathy Miss Jewett usually extends to her beloved dowagers is here often withdrawn in favor of sly, icy gibes.

The atmosphere of "Miss Tempy's Watchers" (1888) is preternaturally solemn by cause of Tempy Dent's corpse in the north chamber. Optimism is made to invade this gloom gradually, however, as Tempy's two old friends, separated for years by status and attitudes, reinstate—imperceptibly to themselves—a quantum of their youthful fellow-feeling. The power of Tempy's personality, operating from beyond the grave, is a third and living presence in this subtle re-creation of long-dormant emotions.

Comedy dominates the remaining two stories. The combustible humor intrinsic in autumnal courtship is the web upon which "Miss Esther's Guest" (1893) rests. Miss Jewett dallies with the amusing antics of elderly lovers in many places throughout the body of her writings but nowhere with keener fun or more joyous outcome. Miss Porley's attire, Mr. Rill's bullfinch, and the four clarion notes of delighted astonishment in the end are unforgettable crests in a charmingly buoyant story. On the other hand, the humor of "The Guests of Mrs. Timms" (1894) bites with acid sharpness into the encrusted core of social hierarchy and usage. Through a gamut of home visits and the translucent hypocrisies of Mrs. Flagg, Miss Jewett constructs her most intricate and expert social comedy, heaping heartfelt disdain upon the superficialities of a system wherein witches like Mrs. Timms wield the stick and decent Nancy Fell must bear the brunt.

VII

In the sketch, the short story, and the novel Sarah Orne Jewett edged slowly to the left of convention, toward a style and structure indisputably her own. Now and again she strove after conformity, but her productions during these periods were inferior and abortive. She experimented until she became master of undemonstrative form, language, and tone which, together, convey the force of artless understatement. At a time when literary realism was beginning to ride rampant over Victorian decorum, she took a median path between politeness and rashness. In making her own temperament the final arbiter of taste, she conferred upon the literature of her day—and upon posterity—an affect which William James has identified as "that incommunicable cleanness of the salt air when one first leaves town." It is not mere cultism when F. O. Matthiessen ranks Miss Jewett with Emily Dickinson as the two foremost women writers of America.

RICHARD CARY

Colby College
Waterville, Maine

Bibliographical and Textual Note

No verbal alterations or excisions have been made in Miss Jewett's original versions of the present selections. Minor adjustments of punctuation, elimination of hyphens, and realignment of paragraphs have been affected in order to conform more closely with recent American usage.

The text of the novel *Deephaven* is taken from the first edition, published by James R. Osgood & Company, Boston, 1877.

Both sketches and three of the short stories are derived from first appearances in the *Atlantic Monthly:*

"River Driftwood," XLVIII, October 1881; collected in *Country By-Ways*, Boston: Houghton, Mifflin & Company, 1881.

"The Landscape Chamber," LX, November 1887; collected in *The King of Folly Island and Other People*, Boston: Houghton, Mifflin & Company, 1888.

"The Dulham Ladies," LVII, May 1886; collected in *A White Heron and Other Stories*, Boston: Houghton, Mifflin & Company, 1886.

"Miss Tempy's Watchers," LXI, March 1888; collected in *The King of Folly Island and Other People*, 1888.

"The Town Poor," LXVI, July 1890; collected in *Strangers and Wayfarers*, Boston: Houghton, Mifflin & Company, 1890.

The short story, "The Guests of Mrs. Timms," first appeared in the *Century Magazine*, XLVII, February 1894; collected in *The Life of Nancy*, Boston: Houghton, Mifflin & Company, 1895.

"A White Heron" and "Miss Esther's Guest" received initial presentation in the volumes, respectively: *A White Heron and Other Stories*, Boston: Houghton, Mifflin & Company, 1886; and *A Native of Winby and Other Tales*, Boston: Houghton, Mifflin & Company, 1893.

Deephaven

Preface to the 1877 Edition

THIS book is not wholly new, several of the chapters having already been published in the *Atlantic Monthly*.

It has so often been asked if Deephaven may not be found on the map of New England under another name, that, to prevent any misunderstanding, I wish to say, while there is a likeness to be traced, few of the sketches are drawn from that town itself, and the characters will in almost every case be looked for there in vain.

I dedicate this story of out-of-door life and country people first to my father and mother, my two best friends, and also to all my other friends, whose names I say to myself lovingly, though I do not write them here.

S. O. J.

Preface to the 1893 Edition

THE short lifetime of this little book has seen great changes in the conditions of provincial life in New England. Twenty years ago, or a little more, the two heroines whose simple adventures are here described might well have served as types of those pioneers who were already on the eager quest for rural pleasures. Twenty years ago, our fast-growing New England cities, which had so lately been but large towns, full of green gardens and quiet neighborhoods, were just beginning to be overcrowded and uncomfortable in summer. The steady inflow of immigration, and the way in which these cities had drawn to themselves, like masses of quicksilver, much of the best life of the remotest villages, had made necessary a reflex current that set countryward in summer. This presently showed itself to be of unsuspected force and significance: it meant something more than the instinct for green fields and hills and the seashore; crowded towns and the open country were to be brought together in new association and dependence upon each other. It appeared as if a second Harvey had discovered a new and national circulation of vitality along the fast-multiplying railroads that spun their webs to bind together men who had once lived far apart. The civil war, which had given so many citizens of the North their first journey and first knowledge of the world outside their native parishes; the fashion set before the war by those gay Southerners who for the most part filled the few mountain and seashore hotels of the North; the increase of wealth, and of the number of persons who had houses in town and country both,—all these causes brought about great and almost sudden changes in rustic life. Old farmhouses opened their doors to the cheerful gayety of summer; the old jokes about the respective aggressions and ignorances of city and country cousins gave place to new compliments between the summer boarder and his rustic host. It began to appear that neither men nor women of the great towns were any longer stayers-at-home according to the Scripture admonition.

The young writer of these Deephaven sketches was possessed by a dark fear that townspeople and country people would never understand one another, or learn to profit by their new relationship. She may have had the unconscious desire to make some sort of explanation to those who still expected to find the caricatured Yankee of fiction, striped trousers, bell-crowned hat, and all, driving his steady horses along the shady roads. It seemed not altogether reasonable when timid ladies mistook a selectman for a tramp, because he happened to be crossing a field in his shirt sleeves. At the same time, she was sensible of grave wrong and misunderstanding when these same timid ladies were regarded with suspicion, and their kindnesses were believed to come from pride and patronage. There is a noble saying of Plato that the best thing that can be done for the people of a state is to make them acquainted with one another. It was, happily, in the writer's childhood that Mrs. Stowe had written of those who dwelt along the wooded seacoast and by the decaying, shipless harbors of Maine. The first chapters of *The Pearl of Orr's Island* gave the younger author of *Deephaven* to see with new eyes, and to follow eagerly the old shore paths from one gray, weather-beaten house to another where Genius pointed her the way.

In those days, if one had just passed her twentieth year, it was easy to be much disturbed by the sad discovery that certain phases of provincial life were fast waning in New England. Small and old-fashioned towns, of which Deephaven may, by the reader's courtesy, stand as a type, were no longer almost self-subsistent, as in earlier times; and while it was impossible to estimate the value of that wider life that was flowing in from the great springs, many a mournful villager felt the anxiety that came with these years of change. Tradition and time-honored custom were to be swept away together by the irresistible current. Character and architecture seemed to lose individuality and distinction. The new riches of the country were seldom very well spent in those days; the money that the tourist or summer citizen left behind him was apt to be used to sweep away the quaint houses, the roadside thicket, the shady woodland, that had lured him first; and the well-filled purses that were scattered in our country's first great triumphal impulse of prosperity often came into the hands of people who hastened to spoil instead of to mend the best things that their village held. It will remain for later generations to make amends for the sad use of riches after the war, for our injury of what we inherited, for the irreparable loss of certain ancient buildings which would have been twice as interesting in the next century as we are just beginning to be wise enough to think them in this.

That all the individuality and quaint personal characteristics of rural New England were so easily swept away, or are even now dying out, we can refuse to believe. It appears, even, that they are better nourished and shine brighter by contrast than in former years. In rustic neighborhoods there will always be those whom George Sand had in mind when she wrote her delightful preface for *Légendes Rustiques:* "Le paysan est donc, si l'on peut ainsi dire, le seul historien qui nous reste des temps ante-historique. Honneur et profit intellectuel à qui se consacrerait à la recherche de ses traditions merveilleuses de chaque hameau qui rassemblées ou groupées, comparées entre elles et minutieuse-ment disséquées, jetteraient peut-être de grandes lueurs sur la nuit profonde des âges primitifs." There will also exist that other class of country people who preserve the best traditions of culture and of manners, from some divine inborn instinct toward what is simplest and best and purest, who know the best because they themselves are of kin to it. It is as hard to be just to our con-temporaries as it is easy to borrow enchantment in looking at the figures of the past; but while the Judges and Governors and grand ladies of old Deephaven are being lamented, we must not forget to observe that it is Miss Carew and Miss Lorimer who lament them, and who insist that there are no representatives of the ancient charm and dignity of their beloved town. Human nature is the same the world over, provincial and rustic in-fluences must ever produce much the same effects upon char-acter, and town life will ever have in its gift the spirit of the present, while it may take again from the quiet of hills and fields and the conservatism of country hearts a gift from the spirit of the past.

In the Preface to the first edition of *Deephaven* it was ex-plained that Deephaven was not to be found on the map of New

England under another name, and that the characters were seldom drawn from life. It was often asserted to the contrary, while the separate chapters were being published from time to time in the *Atlantic Monthly,* and made certain where the town really was, and the true names of its citizens and pew-holders. Therefore it appeared there were already many "places in America," not "few," that were "touched with the hue of decay." Portsmouth and York and Wells, which were known to the author, Fairhaven and other seacoast towns, which were unknown, were spoken of as the originals of this fictitious village which still exists only in the mind. Strangely enough, the Atlantic Ocean always seems to lie to the west of it rather than to the east, and the landscape generally takes its own way and furnishes impossible landmarks and impressions to the one person who can see it clearly and in large. Some early knowledge of the secret found later in the delightful story of *Peter Ibbetson* appears to have been foreseen, but a lack of experience and a limited knowledge of the wide world outside forced the imaginer of Deephaven to build her dear town of such restricted materials as lay within her grasp. The landscape itself is always familiar to her thought, and far more real than many others which have been seen since with preoccupied or tired eyes.

The writer frankly confesses that the greater part of any value which these sketches may possess is in their youthfulness. There are sentences which make her feel as if she were the grandmother of the author of *Deephaven* and her heroines, those "two young ladies of virtue and honour, bearing an inviolable friendship for each other," as two others, less fortunate, are described in the preface to *Clarissa Harlowe*. She begs her readers to smile with her over those sentences as they are found not seldom along the pages, and so the callow wings of what thought itself to be wisdom and the childish soul of sentiment will still be happy and untroubled.

In a curious personal sense the author repeats her attempt to explain the past and the present to each other. This little book will remind some of those friends who read it first of

"—light that lit the olden days;"

but there are kind eyes, unknown then, that are very dear now, and to these the pages will be new. This Preface must end as the first Preface ended, with a dedication to my father and mother— my two best friends—and then to all my other friends whose names I say to myself lovingly, though I do not write them here.

S. O. J.

Kate Lancaster's Plan

I HAD been spending the winter in Boston, and Kate Lancaster and I had been together a great deal, for we are the best of friends. It happened that the morning when this story begins I had waked up feeling sorry, and as if something dreadful were going to happen. There did not seem to be any good reason for it, so I undertook to discourage myself more by thinking that it would soon be time to leave town, and how much I should miss being with Kate and my other friends. My mind was still disquieted when I went down to breakfast; but beside my plate I found, with a hoped-for letter from my father, a note from Kate. To this day I have never known any explanation of that depression of my spirits, and I hope that the good luck which followed will help some reader to lose fear, and to smile at such shadows if any chance to come.

Kate had evidently written to me in an excited state of mind, for her note was not so trig-looking as usual; but this is what she said:—

> DEAR HELEN,—I have a plan—I think it a most delightful plan —in which you and I are chief characters. Promise that you will say yes; if you do not you will have to remember all your life that you broke a girl's heart. Come round early, and lunch with me and dine with me. I'm to be all alone, and it's a long story and will need a great deal of talking over.
>
> K.

I showed this note to my aunt, and soon went round very much interested. My latchkey opened the Lancasters' door, and I hurried to the parlor, where I heard my friend practising with great diligence. I went up to her, and she turned her head and kissed me solemnly. You need not smile; we are not sentimental girls, and are both much averse to indiscriminate kissing, though I have not the adroit habit of shying in which Kate is proficient.

It would sometimes be impolite in any one else, but she shies so affectionately.

"Won't you sit down, dear?" she said, with great ceremony, and went on with her playing, which was abominable that morning; her fingers stepped on each other, and, whatever the tune might have been in reality, it certainly had a most remarkable incoherence as I heard it then. I took up the new *Littell* and made believe to read it, and finally threw it at Kate; you would have thought we were two children.

"Have you heard that my grand-aunt, Miss Katharine Brandon of Deephaven, is dead?" I knew that she had died in November, at least six months before.

"Don't be nonsensical, Kate!" said I. "What is it you are going to tell me?"

"My grand-aunt died very old, and was the last of her generation. She had a sister and three brothers, one of whom had the honor of being my grandfather. Mamma is sole heir to the family estates in Deephaven, wharf property and all, and it is a great inconvenience to her. The house is a charming old house, and some of my ancestors who followed the sea brought home the greater part of its furnishings. Miss Katharine was a person who ignored all frivolities, and her house was as sedate as herself. I have been there but little, for when I was a child my aunt found no pleasure in the society of noisy children who upset her treasures, and when I was older she did not care to see strangers, and after I left school she grew more and more feeble; I had not been there for two years when she died. Mamma went down very often. The town is a quaint old place which has seen better days. There are high rocks at the shore, and there is a beach, and there are woods inland, and hills, and there is the sea. It might be dull in Deephaven for two young ladies who were fond of gay society and dependent upon excitement, I suppose; but for two little girls who were fond of each other and could play in the boats, and dig and build houses in the sea sand, and gather shells, and carry their dolls wherever they went, what could be pleasanter?"

"Nothing," said I, promptly.

Kate had told this a little at a time, with a few appropriate bars of music between, which suddenly reminded me of the story of a Chinese procession which I had read in one of Marryat's novels when I was a child: "A thousand white elephants richly

caparisoned,—ti-tum tilly-lily," and so on, for a page or two. She
seemed to have finished her story for that time, and while it was
dawning upon me what she meant, she sang a bit from one of
Jean Ingelow's verses:—

> "Will ye step aboard, my dearest,
> For the high seas lie before us?"

and then came over to sit beside me and tell the whole story in
a more sensible fashion.

"You know that my father has been meaning to go to England
in the autumn? Yesterday he told us that he is to leave in a
month and will be away all summer, and mamma is going with
him. Jack and Willy are to join a party of their classmates who
are to spend nearly the whole of the long vacation at Lake
Superior. I don't care to go abroad again now, and I did not like
any plan that was proposed to me. Aunt Anna was here all the
afternoon, and she is going to take the house at Newport, which
is very pleasant and unexpected, for she hates housekeeping.
Mamma thought of course that I would go with her, but I did
not wish to do that, and it would only result in my keeping house
for her visitors, whom I know very little; and she will be much
more free and independent by herself. Beside, she can have any
room if I am not there. I have promised to make her a long visit
in Baltimore next winter instead. I told mamma that I should like
to stay here and go away when I choose. There are ever so many
visits which I have promised; I could stay with you and your
Aunt Mary at Lenox if she goes there, for a while, and I have
always wished to spend a summer in town; but mamma did not
encourage that at all. In the evening papa gave her a letter which
had come from Mr. Dockum, the man who takes care of Aunt
Katharine's place, and the most charming idea came into my
head, and I said I meant to spend my summer in Deephaven.

"At first they laughed at me, and then they said I might go if
I chose, and at last they thought nothing could be pleasanter,
and mamma wishes she were going herself. I asked if she did not
think you would be the best person to keep me company, and she
does, and papa announced that he was just going to suggest my
asking you. I am to take Ann and Maggie, who will be overjoyed,
for they came from that part of the country, and the other
servants are to go with Aunt Anna, and old Nora will come to

take care of this house, as she always does. Perhaps you and I
will come up to town once in a while for a few days. We shall
have such jolly housekeeping. Mamma and I sat up very late
last night, and everything is planned. Mr. Dockum's house is
very near Aunt Katharine's, so we shall not be lonely; though I
know you're no more afraid of that than I. O Helen, won't
you go?"

Do you think it took me long to decide?

Mr. and Mrs. Lancaster sailed the 10th of June, and my Aunt
Mary went to spend her summer among the Berkshire Hills, so
I was at the Lancasters' ready to welcome Kate when she came
home, after having said good-by to her father and mother. We
meant to go to Deephaven in a week, but were obliged to stay in
town longer. Boston was nearly deserted of our friends at the
last, and we used to take quiet walks in the cool of the evening
after dinner, up and down the street, or sit on the front steps in
company with the servants left in charge of the other houses,
who also sometimes walked up and down and looked at us won-
deringly. We had much shopping to do in the daytime, for there
was a probability of our spending many days indoors, and as we
were not to be near any large town, and did not mean to come to
Boston for weeks at least, there was a great deal to be remembered and arranged. We enjoyed making our plans, and deciding
what we should want, and going to the shops together. I think
we felt most important the day we conferred with Ann and
made out a list of the provisions which must be ordered. This
was being housekeepers in earnest. Mr. Dockum happened to
come to town, and we sent Ann and Maggie, with most of our
boxes, to Deephaven in his company a day or two before we were
ready to go ourselves, and when we reached there the house was
opened and in order for us.

On our journey to Deephaven we left the railway twelve miles
from that place, and took passage in a stage-coach. There was
only one passenger beside ourselves. She was a very large, thin,
weather-beaten woman, and looked so tired and lonesome and
good-natured, that I could not help saying it was very dusty; and
she was apparently delighted to answer that she should think
everybody was sweeping, and she always felt, after being in the
cars a while, as if she had been taken all to pieces and left in the

different places. And this was the beginning of our friendship with Mrs. Kew.

After this conversation we looked industriously out of the window into the pastures and pinewoods. I had given up my seat to her, for I do not mind riding backward in the least, and you would have thought I had done her the greatest favor of her life. I think she was the most grateful of women, and I was often reminded of a remark one of my friends once made about some one: "If you give Bessie a half-sheet of letterpaper, she behaves to you as if it were the most exquisite of presents!" Kate and I had some fruit left in our lunch basket, and divided it with Mrs. Kew, but after the first mouthful we looked at each other in dismay. "Lemons with oranges' clothes on, aren't they?" said she, as Kate threw hers out of the window, and mine went after it for company; and after this we began to be very friendly indeed. We both liked the old woman, there was something so straightforward and kindly about her.

"Are you going to Deephaven, dear?" she asked me, and then: "I wonder if you are going to stay long? All summer? Well, that's clever! I do hope you will come out to the Light to see me; young folks 'most always like my place. Most likely your friends will fetch you."

"Do you know the Brandon house?" asked Kate.

"Well as I do the meeting-house. There! I wonder I didn't know from the beginning, but I have been a-trying all the way to settle it who you could be. I've been up country some weeks, stopping with my mother, and she seemed so set to have me stay till strawberry time, and would hardly let me come now. You see she's getting to be old; why, every time I've come away for fifteen years she's said it was the last time I'd ever see her, but she's a dreadful smart woman of her age. 'He' wrote me some o' Mrs. Lancaster's folks were going to take the Brandon house this summer; and so you are the ones? It's a sightly old place; I used to go and see Miss Katharine. She must have left a power of chinaware. She set a great deal by the house, and she kept everything just as it used to be in her mother's day."

"Then you live in Deephaven too?" asked Kate.

"I've been here the better part of my life. I was raised up among the hills in Vermont, and I shall always be a real up-country woman if I live here a hundred years. The sea doesn't come natural to me, it kind of worries me, though you won't find a happier woman than I be, 'longshore. When I was first married 'he' had a schooner and went to the banks, and once he was off on a whaling voyage, and I hope I may never come to so long a three years as those were again, though I was up to mother's. Before I was married he had been 'most everywhere. When he came home that time from whaling, he found I'd taken it so to heart that he said he'd never go off again, and then he got the chance to keep Deephaven Light, and we've lived there seventeen years come January. There isn't great pay, but then nobody tries to get it away from us, and we've got so's to be contented, if it is lonesome in winter."

"Do you really live in the lighthouse? I remember how I used to beg to be taken out there when I was a child, and how I used to watch for the light at night," said Kate, enthusiastically.

So began a friendship which we both still treasure, for knowing Mrs. Kew was one of the pleasantest things which happened to us in that delightful summer, and she used to do so much for our pleasure, and was so good to us. When we went out to the lighthouse for the last time to say good-by, we were very sorry girls indeed. We had no idea until then how much she cared for us, and her affection touched us very much. She told us that she loved us as if we belonged to her, and begged us not to forget her,—as if we ever could!—and to remember that there was always a home and a warm heart for us if she were alive. Kate and I have often agreed that few of our acquaintances are half so entertaining. Her comparisons were most striking and amusing, and her comments upon the books she read—for she was a great reader—were very shrewd and clever, and always to the point. She was never out of temper, even when the barrels of oil were being rolled across her kitchen floor. And she was such a wise woman! This stage ride, which we expected to find tiresome, we enjoyed very much, and we were glad to think, when the coach stopped, and "he" came to meet her with great satisfaction, that we had one friend in Deephaven at all events.

I liked the house from my very first sight of it. It stood behind a row of poplars which were as green and flourishing as the poplars which stand in stately processions in the fields around Quebec. It was an imposing great white house, and the lilacs were tall, and there were crowds of rosebushes not yet out of bloom; and there were box borders, and there were great elms at the side of the house and down the road. The hall door stood wide open, and my hostess turned to me as we went in, with one of her sweet, sudden smiles. "Won't we have a good time, Nelly?" said she. And I thought we should.

So our summer's housekeeping began in most pleasant fashion. It was just at sunset, and Ann's and Maggie's presence made the house seem familiar at once. Maggie had been unpacking for us, and there was a delicious supper ready for the hungry girls. Later in the evening we went down to the shore, which was not very far away; the fresh sea air was welcome after the dusty day, and it seemed so quiet and pleasant in Deephaven.

The Brandon House and the Lighthouse

I DO not know that the Brandon house is really very remark-able, but I never have been in one that interested me in the same way. Kate used to recount to select audiences at school some of her experiences with her Aunt Katharine, and it was popularly believed that she once carried down some indestruct-ible picture-books when they were first in fashion, and the old lady basted them for her to hem round the edges at the rate of two a day. It may have been fabulous. It was impossible to imagine any children in the old place; everything was for grown people; even the stair railing was too high to slide down on. The chairs looked as if they had been put, at the furnishing of the house, in their places, and there they meant to remain. The carpets were particularly interesting, and I remember Kate's pointing out to me one day a great square figure in one, and telling me she used to keep house there with her dolls for lack of a better playhouse, and if one of them chanced to fall outside the boundary stripe, it was immediately put to bed with a cold.

It is a house with great possibilities; it might easily be made charming. There are four very large rooms on the lower floor, and six above, a wide hall in each story, and a fascinating garret over the whole, where were many mysterious old chests and boxes, in one of which we found Kate's grandmother's love letters; and you may be sure the vista of rummages which Mr. Lancaster had laughed about was explored to its very end. The rooms all have elaborate cornices, and the lower hall is very fine, with an archway dividing it, and panellings of all sorts, and a great door at each end, through which the lilacs in front and the old pensioner plum trees in the garden are seen exchanging bows and gestures. Coming from the Lancasters' high city house, it did not seem as if we had to go upstairs at all there, for every step of the stairway is so broad and low, and you come half way to a square landing with an old straight-backed chair in each farther corner; and between them a large, round-topped window, with a cushioned seat, looking out on the garden and the village, the hills far inland, and the sunset beyond all. Then you turn and go up a few more steps to the upper hall, where we used to stay a great deal. There were more old chairs and a pair of remarkable sofas, on which we used to deposit the treasures collected in our wanderings.

The wide window which looks out on the lilacs and the sea was a favorite seat of ours. Facing each other on either side of it are two old secretaries, and one of them we ascertained to be the hiding place of secret drawers, in which may be found valuable records deposited by ourselves one rainy day when we first explored it. We wrote, between us, a tragic "journal" on some yellow, old letter paper we found in the desk. We put it in the most hidden drawer by itself, and flatter ourselves that it will be regarded with great interest some time or other.

Of one of the front rooms, "the best chamber," we stood rather in dread. It is very remarkable that there seem to be no ghost stories connected with any part of the house, particularly this. We are neither of us nervous; but there is certainly something dismal about the room. The huge curtained bed and immense easy chairs, windows, and everything were draped in some old-fashioned kind of white cloth which always seemed to be waving and moving about of itself. The carpet was most singularly colored with dark reds and indescribable grays and browns, and the pattern, after a whole summer's study, could never be followed with one's eye. The paper was captured in a French prize somewhere some time in the last century, and part of the figure was shaggy, and therein little spiders found habitation, and went visiting their acquaintances across the shiny places. The color was an unearthly pink and a forbidding maroon, with dim white spots, which gave it the appearance of having moulded. It made you low-spirited to look long in the mirror; and the great lounge one could not have cheerful associations with, after hearing that Miss Brandon herself did not like it, having seen so many of her relatives lie there dead. There were fantastic china ornaments from Bible subjects on the mantel, and the only picture was one of the Maid of Orleans tied with an unnecessarily strong rope to a very stout stake.

The best parlor we also rarely used, because all the portraits which hung there had for some unaccountable reason taken a violent dislike to us, and followed us suspiciously with their eyes. The furniture was stately and very uncomfortable, and there was something about the room which suggested an invisible funeral.

There is not very much to say about the dining room. It was not specially interesting, though the sea was in sight from one of the windows. There were some old Dutch pictures on the wall, so dark that one could scarcely make out what they were meant to represent, and one or two engravings. There was a huge sideboard, for which Kate had brought down from Boston Miss Brandon's own silver which had stood there for so many years, and looked so much more at home and in place than any other possibly could have looked, and Kate also found in the closet the three great decanters with silver labels chained round their necks, which had always been the companions of the tea service in her aunt's lifetime. From the little closets in the sideboard there came a most significant odor of cake and wine whenever one opened the doors. We used Miss Brandon's beautiful old blue India china which she had given to Kate, and which had been carefully packed all winter. Kate sat at the head and I at the foot of the round table, and I must confess that we were apt to have either a feast or a famine, for at first we often forgot to provide our dinners. If this were the case Maggie was sure to serve us with most derisive elegance, and make us wait for as much ceremony as she thought necessary for one of Mrs. Lancaster's dinner parties.

The west parlor was our favorite room downstairs. It had a great fireplace framed in blue and white Dutch tiles which ingeniously and instructively represented the careers of the good and the bad man; the starting place of each being a very singular cradle in the centre at the top. The last two of the series are very high art: a great coffin stands in the foreground of each, and the virtuous man is being led off by two disagreeable-looking angels, while the wicked one is hastening from an indescribable but unpleasant assemblage of claws and horns and eyes which is rapidly advancing from the distance, open mouthed, and bringing a chain with it.

There was a large cabinet holding all the small curiosities and knickknacks there seemed to be no other place for,—odd china figures and cups and vases, unaccountable Chinese carvings and exquisite corals and seashells, minerals and Swiss woodwork, and articles of *vertu* from the South Seas. Underneath were stored boxes of letters and old magazines; for this was one of the houses where nothing seems to have been thrown away. In one parting we found a parcel of old manuscript sermons, the existence of which was a mystery, until Kate remembered there had been a gifted son of the house who entered the ministry and soon died. The windows had each a pane of stained glass, and on the wide sills we used to put our immense bouquets of field flowers.

There was one place which I liked and sat in more than any other. The chimney filled nearly the whole side of the room, all but this little corner, where there was just room for a very comfortable high-backed cushioned chair, and a narrow window where I always had a bunch of fresh green ferns in a tall champagne glass. I used to write there often, and always sat there when Kate sang and played. She sent for a tuner, and used to successfully coax the long-imprisoned music from the antiquated piano, and sing for her visitors by the hour. She almost always sang her oldest songs, for they seemed most in keeping with everything about us. I used to fancy that the portraits liked our being there. There was one young girl who seemed solitary and forlorn among the rest in the room, who were all middle-aged. For their part they looked amiable, but rather unhappy, as if she had come in and interrupted their conversation. We both grew very fond of her, and it seemed, when we went in the last morning on purpose to take leave of her, as if she looked at us imploringly. She was soon afterward boxed up, and now enjoys society after her own heart in Kate's room in Boston.

There was the largest sofa I ever saw opposite the fireplace; it must have been brought in in pieces, and built in the room. It was broad enough for Kate and me to lie on together, and very high and square; but there was a pile of soft cushions at one end. We used to enjoy it greatly in September, when the evenings were long and cool, and we had many candles, and a fire—and crickets too—on the hearth, and the dear dog lying on the rug. I remember one rainy night, just before Miss Tennant and Kitty Bruce went away; we had a real driftwood fire, and blew out the lights and told stories. Miss Margaret knows so many and tells them so well. Kate and I were unusually entertaining, for we became familiar with the family record of the town, and could recount marvellous adventures by land and sea, and ghost stories by the dozen. We had never either of us been in a society consisting of so many travelled people! Hardly a man but had been the most of his life at sea.

Speaking of ghost stories, I must tell you that once in the summer two Cambridge girls who were spending a week with us unwisely enticed us into giving some thrilling recitals, which nearly frightened them out of their wits, and Kate and I were finally in terror ourselves. We had all been on the sofa in the dark, singing and talking, and were waiting in great suspense after I had finished one of such particular horror that I declared it should be the last, when we heard footsteps on the hall stairs. There were lights in the dining room which shone faintly through the half-closed door, and we saw something white and shapeless come slowly down, and clutched each other's gowns in agony. It was only Kate's dog, who came in and laid his head in her lap and slept peacefully. We thought we could not sleep a wink after this, and I bravely went alone out to the light to see my watch, and, finding it was past twelve, we concluded to sit up all night and to go down to the shore at sunrise, it would be so much easier than getting up early some morning. We had been out rowing and had taken a long walk the day before, and were obliged to dance and make other slight exertions to keep ourselves awake at one time. We lunched at two, and I never shall forget the sunrise that morning; but we were singularly quiet and abstracted that day, and indeed for several days after Deephaven was "a land in which it seemed always afternoon," we breakfasted so late.

As Mrs. Kew had said, there was "a power of china." Kate and I were convinced that the lives of her grandmothers must have been spent in giving tea parties. We counted ten sets of cups, beside quantities of stray ones; and some member of the family had evidently devoted her time to making a collection of pitchers.

There was an escritoire in Miss Brandon's own room, which we looked over one day. There was a little package of letters; ship letters mostly, tied with a very pale and tired-looking blue ribbon. They were in a drawer with a locket holding a faded miniature on ivory and a lock of brown hair, and there were also some dry twigs and bits of leaf which had long ago been bright wild roses, such as still bloom among the Deephaven rocks. Kate said that she had often heard her mother wonder why her aunt never had cared to marry, for she had chances enough doubtless, and had been rich and handsome and finely educated. So there was a sailor lover after all, and perhaps he had been lost at sea and she faithfully kept the secret, never mourning outwardly. "And I always thought her the most matter-of-fact old lady," said Kate; "yet here's her romance, after all." We put the letters outside on a chair to read, but afterwards carefully replaced them, without untying them. I'm glad we did.

There were other letters which we did read, and which interested us very much,—letters from her girl friends written in the boarding-school vacations, and just after she finished school. Those in one of the smaller packages were charming; it must have been such a bright, nice girl who wrote them! They were very few, and were tied with black ribbon, and marked on the outside in girlish writing: "My dearest friend, Dolly McAllister, died September 3, 1809, aged eighteen." The ribbon had evidently been untied and the letters read many times. One began: "My dear, delightful Kitten: I am quite overjoyed to find my father has business which will force him to go to Deephaven next week, and he kindly says if there be no more rain I may ride with him to see you. I will surely come, for if there is danger of spattering my gown, and he bids me stay at home, I shall go galloping after him and overtake him when it is too late to send me back. I have so much to tell you." I wish I knew more about the visit.

Poor Miss Katharine! it made us sad to look over these treasures of her girlhood. There were her compositions and exercise books; some samplers and queer little keepsakes; withered flowers and some pebbles and other things of like value, with which there was probably some pleasant association. "Only think of her keeping them all her days," said I to Kate. "I am continually throwing some relic of the kind away, because I forget why I have it!"

There was a box in the lower part which Kate was glad to find, for she had heard her mother wonder if some such things were not in existence. It held a crucifix and a mass book and some rosaries, and Kate told me Miss Katharine's youngest and favorite brother had become a Roman Catholic while studying in Europe. It was a dreadful blow to the family; for in those days there could have been few deeper disgraces to the Brandon family than to have one of its sons go over to popery. Only Miss Katharine treated him with kindness, and after a time he disappeared without telling even her where he was going, and was only heard from indirectly once or twice afterward. It was a great grief to her. "And mamma knows," said Kate, "that she always had a lingering hope of his return, for one of the last times she saw Aunt Katharine before she was ill she spoke of soon going to be with all the rest, and said, 'Though young Uncle Henry, dear,' —and stopped and smiled sadly; 'you'll think me a very foolish old woman, but I never quite gave up thinking he might come home.'"

Mrs. Kew did the honors of the lighthouse thoroughly on our first visit; but I think we rarely went to see her that we did not make some entertaining discovery. Mr. Kew's nephew, a guileless youth of forty, lived with them, and the two men were of a mechanical turn and had invented numerous aids to housekeeping,—appendages to the stove, and fixtures on the walls for everything that could be hung up; catches in the floor to hold the doors open, and ingenious apparatus to close them; but, above all, a system of barring and bolting for the wide "fore door," which would have disconcerted an energetic battering-ram. After all this work being expended, Mrs. Kew informed us that it was usually wide open all night in summer weather. On the back of this door I discovered one day a row of marks, and asked their significance. It seemed that Mrs. Kew had attempted one summer to keep count of the number of people who inquired about the depredations of the neighbors' chickens.

Mrs. Kew's bedroom was partly devoted to the fine arts. There was a large collection of likenesses of her relatives and friends on the wall, which was interesting in the extreme. Mrs. Kew was always much pleased to tell their names, and her remarks about any feature not exactly perfect were very searching and critical. "That's my oldest brother's wife, Clorinthy Adams that was. She's well featured, if it were not for her nose, and that looks as if it had been thrown at her, and she wasn't particular about having it on firm, in hopes of getting a better one. She sets by her looks, though."

There were often sailing parties that came there from up and down the coast. One day Kate and I were spending the afternoon at the Light; we had been fishing, and were sitting in the doorway listening to a reminiscence of the winter Mrs. Kew kept school at the Four Corners; saw a boatful coming, and all lost our tempers. Mrs. Kew had a lame ankle, and Kate offered to go up with the visitors. There were some girls and young men who stood on the rocks awhile, and then asked us, with much better manners than the people who usually came, if they could see the lighthouse, and Kate led the way. She was dressed that day in a costume we both frequently wore, of gray skirts and blue sailor jacket, and her boots were much the worse for wear. The celebrated Lancaster complexion was rather darkened by the sun. Mrs. Kew expressed a wish to know what questions they would ask her, and I followed after a few minutes. They seemed to have finished asking about the lantern, and to have become personal.

"Don't you get tired staying here?"

"No, indeed!" said Kate.

"Is that your sister downstairs?"

"No, I have no sister."

"I should think you would wish she was. Aren't you ever lonesome?"

"Everybody is, sometimes," said Kate.

"But it's such a lonesome place!" said one of the girls. "I should think you would get work away. I live in Boston. Why, it's so awful quiet! nothing but the water, and the wind, when it blows; and I think either of them is worse than nothing. And only this little bit of a rocky place! I should want to go to walk."

I heard Kate pleasantly refuse the offer of pay for her services, and then they began to come down the steep stairs laughing and chattering with each other. Kate stayed behind to close the doors and leave everything all right, and the girl who had talked the most waited too, and when they were on the stairs just above me, and the others out of hearing, she said, "You're real good to show us the things. I guess you'll think I'm silly, but I do like you ever so much! I wish you would come to Boston. I'm in a real nice store,—H——'s, on Winter Street; and they will want new saleswomen in October. Perhaps you could be at my counter. I'd teach you, and you could board with me. I've got a real comfortable room, and I suppose I might have more things, for I get good pay; but I like to send money home to mother. I'm at my aunt's now, but I am going back next Monday, and if you will tell me what your name is, I'll find out for certain about the place, and write you. My name's Mary Wendell."

I knew by Kate's voice that this had touched her. "You are very kind; thank you heartily," said she; "but I cannot go and work with you. I should like to know more about you. I live in Boston too; my friend and I are staying over in Deephaven for the summer only." And she held out her hand to the girl, whose face had changed from its first expression of earnest good humor to a very startled one; and when she noticed Kate's hand, and a ring of hers, which had been turned round, she looked really frightened.

"O, will you please excuse me?" said she, blushing. "I ought to have known better; but you showed us round so willing, and I never thought of your not living here. I didn't mean to be rude."

"Of course you did not, and you were not. I am very glad you said it, and glad you like me," said Kate; and just then the party called the girl, and she hurried away, and I joined Kate. "Then you heard it all. That was worth having!" said she. "She was such an honest little soul, and I mean to look for her when I get home."

Sometimes we used to go out to the Light early in the morning with the fishermen who went that way to the fishing grounds, but we usually made the voyage early in the afternoon if it were not too hot, and we went fishing off the rocks or sat in the house with Mrs. Kew, who often related some of her Vermont experiences, or Mr. Kew would tell us surprising sea stories and ghost stories like a story-book sailor. Then we would have an unreasonably good supper and afterward climb the ladder to the lantern to see the lamps lighted, and sit there for a while watching the ships and the sunset.

Almost all the coasters came in sight of Deephaven, and the sea outside the light was their grand highway. Twice from the lighthouse we saw a yacht squadron like a flock of great white birds. As for the sunsets, it used to seem often as if we were near the heart of them, for the sea all around us caught the color of the clouds, and though the glory was wonderful, I remember best one still evening when there was a bank of heavy gray clouds in the west shutting down like a curtain, and the sea was silver-colored. You could look under and beyond the curtain of clouds into the palest, clearest yellow sky. There was a little black boat in the distance drifting slowly, climbing one white wave after another, as if it were bound out into that other world beyond. But presently the sun came from behind the clouds, and the dazzling golden light changed the look of everything, and it was the time then to say one thought it a beautiful sunset; while before one could only keep very still, and watch the boat, and wonder if heaven would not be somehow like that far, faint color, which was neither sea nor sky.

When we came down from the lighthouse and it grew late, we would beg for an hour or two longer on the water, and row away in the twilight far out from land, where, with our faces turned from the Light, it seemed as if we were alone, and the sea shoreless; and as the darkness closed round us softly, we watched the stars come out, and were always glad to see Kate's star and my star, which we had chosen when we were children. I used long ago to be sure of one thing,—that, however far away heaven might be, it could not be out of sight of the stars. Sometimes in the evening we waited out at sea for the moonrise, and then we would take the oars again and go slowly in, once in a while singing or talking, but oftenest silent.

My Lady Brandon and the Widow Jim

WHEN it was known that we had arrived in Deephaven, the people who had known Miss Brandon so well, and Mrs. Lancaster also, seemed to consider themselves Kate's friends by inheritance, and were exceedingly polite to us, in either calling upon us or sending pleasant messages. Before the first week had ended we had no lack of society. They were not strangers to Kate, to begin with, and as for me, I think it is easy for me to be contented, and to feel at home anywhere. I have the good fortune and the misfortune to belong to the navy,—that is, my father does,—and my life has been consequently an unsettled one, except during the years of my school life, when my friendship with Kate began.

I think I should be happy in any town if I were living there with Kate Lancaster. I will not praise my friend as I can praise her, or say half the things I might say honestly. She is so fresh and good and true, and enjoys life so heartily. She is so childlike, without being childish; and I do not tell you that she is faultless, but when she makes mistakes she is sorrier and more ready to hopefully try again than any girl I know. Perhaps you would like to know something about us, but I am not writing Kate's biography and my own, only telling you of one summer which we spent together. Sometimes in Deephaven we were between six and seven years old, but at other times we have felt irreparably grown-up, and as if we carried a crushing weight of care and duty. In reality we are both twenty-four, and it is a pleasant age, though I think next year is sure to be pleasanter, for we do not mind growing older, since we have lost nothing that we mourn about, and are gaining so much.

I shall be glad if you learn to know Kate a little in my stories. It is not that I am fond of her and endow her with imagined virtues and graces; no one can fail to see how unaffected she is, or not notice her thoughtfulness and generosity and her delight-

ful fun, which never has a trace of coarseness or silliness. It was
very pleasant having her for one's companion, for she has an
unusual power of winning people's confidence, and of knowing
with surest instinct how to meet them on their own ground. It is
the girl's being so genuinely sympathetic and interested which
makes every one ready to talk to her and be friends with her;
just as the sunshine makes it easy for flowers to grow which the
chilly winds hinder. She is not polite for the sake of seeming
polite, but polite for the sake of being kind, and there is not a
particle of what Hugh Miller justly calls the insolence of condescension about her; she is not brilliantly talented, yet she does
everything in a charming fashion of her own; she is not profound-
ly learned, yet she knows much of which many wise people are
ignorant, and while she is a patient scholar in both little things
and great, she is no less a teacher to all her friends,—dear Kate
Lancaster!

We knew that we were considered Miss Brandon's representatives in Deephaven society, and this was no slight responsibility,
as she had received much honor and respect. We heard again
and again what a loss she had been to the town, and we tried
that summer to do nothing to lessen the family reputation, and to
give pleasure as well as take it, though we were singularly
persistent in our pursuit of a good time. I grew much interested
in what I heard of Miss Brandon, and it seems to me that it is a
great privilege to have an elderly person in one's neighborhood,
in town or country, who is proud, and conservative, and who
lives in stately fashion; who is intolerant of sham and of useless
novelties, and clings to the old ways of living and behaving as
if it were part of her religion.

There is something immensely respectable about the gentle-
women of the old school. They ignore all bustle and flashiness,
and the conceit of the younger people, who act as if at last it had
been time for them to appear and manage this world as it ought
to have been managed before. Their position in modern society
is much like that of the King's Chapel in its busy street in Boston.
It perhaps might not have been easy to approach Miss Brandon,
but I am sure that if I had visited in Deephaven during her lifetime I should have been very proud if I had been asked to take
tea at her house, and should have liked to speak afterward of
my acquaintance with her. It would have been impossible not

to pay her great deference; it is a pleasure to think that she must have found this world a most polite world, and have had the highest opinion of its good manners. *Noblesse oblige:* that is true in more ways than one!

I cannot help wondering if those of us who will be left by and by to represent our own generation will seem to have such superior elegance of behavior; if we shall receive so much respect and be so much valued. It is hard to imagine it. We know that the world gains new refinements and a better culture; but to us there never will be such imposing ladies and gentlemen as these who belong to the old school.

The morning after we reached Deephaven we were busy upstairs, and there was a determined blow at the knocker of the front door. I went down to see who was there, and had the pleasure of receiving our first caller. She was a prim little old woman who looked pleased and expectant, who wore a neat cap and front, and whose eyes were as bright as black beads. She wore no bonnet, and had thrown a little three-cornered shawl, with palm-leaf figures, over her shoulders; and it was evident that she was a near neighbor. She was very short and straight and thin, and so quick that she darted like a pickerel when she moved about. It occurred to me at once that she was a very capable person, and had "faculty," and, dear me, how fast she talked! She hesitated a moment when she saw me, and dropped a fragment of a courtesy. "Miss Lan'k'ster?" said she, doubtfully.

"No," said I, "I'm Miss Denis: Miss Lancaster is at home, though: come in, won't you?"

"O Mrs. Patton!" said Kate, who came down just then. "How very kind of you to come over so soon! I should have gone to see you today. I was asking Mrs. Kew last night if you were here."

"Land o' compassion!" said Mrs. Patton, as she shook Kate's hand delightedly. "Where'd ye s'pose I'd be, dear? I ain't like to move away from Deephaven now, after I've held by the place so long, I've got as many roots as the big ellum. Well, I should know you were a Brandon, no matter where I see you. You've got a real Brandon look; tall and straight, ain't you? It's four or five years since I saw you, except once at church, and once you went by, down to the shore, I suppose. It was a windy day in the spring of the year."

Deephaven

"I remember it very well," said Kate. "Those were both visits of only a day or two, and I was here at Aunt Katharine's funeral, and went away that same evening. Do you remember once I was here in the summer for a longer visit, five or six years ago, and I helped you pick currants in the garden? You had a very old mug."

"Now, whoever would ha' thought o' your rec'lecting that?" said Mrs. Patton. "Yes. I had that mug because it was handy to carry about among the bushes, and then I'd empt' it into the baskets as fast as I got it full. Your aunt always told me to pick all I wanted; she couldn't use 'em, but they used to make sights o' currant wine in old times. I s'pose that mug would be considerable of a curiosity to anybody that wasn't used to seeing it round. My grand'ther Joseph Toggerson—my mother was a Toggerson—picked it up on the long sands in a wad of sea-weed: strange it wasn't broke, but it's tough; I've dropped it on the floor, many's the time, and it ain't even chipped. There's some Dutch reading on it and it's marked 1732. Now I shouldn't ha' thought you'd remembered that old mug, I declare. Your aunt she had a monstrous sight of chiny. She's told me where 'most all of it come from, but I expect I've forgot. My memory fails me a good deal by spells. If you hadn't come down I suppose your mother would have had the chiny packed up this spring,—what she didn't take with her after your aunt died. S'pose she hasn't made up her mind what to do with the house?"

"No," said Kate; "she wishes she could: it is a great puzzle to us."

"I hope you will find it in middling order," said Mrs. Patton, humbly. "Me and Mis' Dockum have done the best we knew,—opened the windows and let in the air and tried to keep it from getting damp. I fixed all the woollens with fresh camphire and tobacco the last o' the winter; you have to be dreadful careful in one o' these old houses, 'less everything gets creaking with moths in no time. Miss Katharine, how she did hate the sight of a moth-miller! There's something I'll speak about before I forget it: the mice have eat the backs of a pile o' old books that's stored away in the west chamber closet next to Miss Katharine's room, and I set a trap there, but it was older'n the ten commandments, that trap was, and the spring's rusty. I guess you'd better get some new ones and set round in different places, 'less the mice'll pester you. There ain't been no chance for 'em to get much of a living 'long through the winter, but they'll be sure to come back quick as they find there's likely to be good board. I see your aunt's cat setting out on the front steps. She never was no great of a mouser, but it went to my heart to see how pleased she looks! Come right back, didn't she? How they do hold to their old haunts!"

"Was that Miss Brandon's cat?" I asked, with great interest. "She has been upstairs with us, but I supposed she belonged to some neighbor, and had strayed in. She behaved as if she felt at home, poor old pussy!"

"We must keep her here," said Kate.

"Mis' Dockum took her after your mother went off, and Miss Katharine's maids," said Mrs. Patton; "but she told me that it was a long spell before she seemed to feel contented. She used to set on the steps and cry by the hour together, and try to get in, to first one door and then another. I used to think how bad Miss Katharine would feel; she set a great deal by a cat, and she took notice of this as long as she did of anything. Her mind failed her, you know. Great loss to Deephaven, she was. Proud woman, and some folks were scared of her; but I always got along with her, and I wouldn't ask for no kinder friend nor neighbor. I've had my troubles, and I've seen the day I was suffering poor, and I couldn't have brought myself to ask town help nohow, but I wish ye'd ha' heared her scold me when she found it out; and she come marching into my kitchen one morning, like a grenadier, and says she, 'Why didn't you send and tell me how sick and poor you are?' says she. And she said she'd ha' been so glad to help me all along, but she thought I had means,—everybody did; and I see the tears in her eyes, but she was scolding me and speaking as if she was dreadful mad. She made me comfortable, and she sent over one o' her maids to see to me, and got the doctor, and a load o' stuff come up from the store, so I didn't have to buy anything for a good many weeks. I got better and so's to work, but she never'd let me say nothing about it. I had a good deal o' trouble, and I thought I'd lost my health, but I hadn't, and that was thirty or forty years ago. There never was nothing going on at the great house that she didn't have me over, sewing or clean- ing or company; and I got so that I knew how she liked to have things done. I felt as if it was my own sister, though I never had one, when I was going over to help lay her out. She used to talk as free to me as she would to Miss Lorimer or Miss Carew. I s'pose ye ain't seen nothing o' them yet? She was a good Christian woman, Miss Katharine was. 'The memory of the just is blessed'; that's what Mr. Lorimer said in his sermon the Sunday after she died, and ther wasn't a blood relation there to hear it. I declare it looked pitiful to see that pew empty that ought to ha' been the mourners' pew. Your mother, Mis' Lancaster, had to go home Saturday, your father was going away sudden to Washington, I've understood, and she come back again the first of the week. There! it didn't make no sort o' difference, p'r'aps nobody thought of it but me. There hadn't been anybody in the pew more than a couple o' times since she used to sit there herself, regular as Sunday come." And Mrs. Patton looked for a minute as if she were going to cry, but she changed her mind upon second thought.

"Your mother gave me most of Miss Katharine's clothes; this cap belonged to her, that I've got on now; it's 'most wore out, but it does for mornings."

"O," said Kate, "I have two new ones for you in one of my trunks! Mamma meant to choose them herself, but she had not time, and so she told me, and I think I found the kind she thought you would like."

"Now I'm sure!" said Mrs. Patton, "if that ain't kind; you don't tell me that Mis' Lancaster thought of me just as she was going off? I shall set everything by them caps, and I'm much obliged to you too, Miss Kate. I was just going to speak of that time you were here and saw the mug; you trimmed a cap for Miss Katharine to give me, real Boston style. I guess that box of cap fixings is up to the top shelf of Miss Katharine's closet now, to the left hand," said Mrs. Patton, with wistful certainty. "She used to make her everyday caps herself, and she had some beautiful materials laid away that she never used. Some folks has laughed at me for being so particular 'bout wearing caps except for best, but I don't know's it's presuming beyond my station, and somehow I feel more respect for myself when I have a good cap on. I can't get over your mother's rec'lecting about me; and she sent me a handsome present o' money this spring for looking after the house. I never should have asked for a cent; it's a pleasure to me to keep an eye on it, out o' respect to your aunt. I was so pleased when I heard you were coming long o' your friend. I like to see the old place open; it was about as bad as having no meeting. I miss seeing the lights, and your aunt was a great hand for lighting up bright; the big hall lantern was lit every night, and she put it out when she went upstairs. She liked to go round same's if it was dry. You see I forget all the time she was sick, and go back to the days when she was well and about the house. When her mind was failing her, and she was upstairs in her room, her eyesight seemed to be lost part of the time, and sometimes she'd tell us to get the lamp and a couple o' candles in the middle o' the day, and then she'd be as satisfied! But she used to take a notion to set in the dark, some nights, and think, I s'pose. I should have forty fits, if I undertook it. That was a good while ago; and do you rec'lect how she used to play the piano? She used to be a great hand to play when she was young."

"Indeed I remember it," said Kate, who told me afterward how her aunt used to sit at the piano in the twilight and play to herself. "She was formerly a skilful musician," said my friend, "though one would not have imagined she cared for music. When I was a child she used to play in company of an evening, and once when I was here one of her old friends asked for a tune, and she laughingly said that her day was over and her fingers were stiff; though I believe she might have played as well as ever then, if she had cared to try. But once in a while when she had been quiet all day and rather sad—I am ashamed that I used to think she was cross—she would open the piano and sit there until late, while I used to be enchanted by her memories of dancing-tunes, and old psalms, and marches and songs. There was one tune which I am sure had a history: there was a sweet wild cadence in it, and she would come back to it again and again, always going through with it in the same measured way. I have remembered so many things about my aunt since I have been here," said Kate, "which I hardly noticed and did not understand when they happened. I was afraid of her when I was a little girl, but I think if I had grown up sooner, I should have enjoyed her heartily. It never used to occur to me that she had a spark of tenderness or of sentiment, until just before she was ill, but I have been growing more fond of her ever since. I might have given her a great deal more pleasure. It was not long after I was through school that she became so feeble, and of course she liked best having mamma come to see her; one of us had to be at home. I have thought lately how careful one ought to be, to be kind and thoughtful to one's old friends. It is so soon too late to be good to them, and then one is always so sorry."

I must tell you more of Mrs. Patton; of course it was not long before we returned her call, and we were much entertained; we always liked to see our friends in their own houses. Her house was a little way down the road, unpainted and gambrel roofed, but so low that the old lilac bushes which clustered round it were as tall as the eaves. The Widow Jim (as nearly every one called her in distinction to the widow Jack Patton, who was a tailoress and lived at the other end of the town) was a very useful person.

I suppose there must be her counterpart in all old New England villages. She sewed, and she made elaborate rugs, and she had a decided talent for making carpets,—if there were one to be made, which must have happened seldom. But there were a great many to be turned and made over in Deephaven, and she went to the Carews' and Lorimers' at housecleaning time or in seasons of great festivity. She had no equal in sickness, and knew how to brew every old-fashioned dose and to make every variety of herb tea, and when her nursing was put to an end by the patient's death, she was commander-in-chief at the funeral, and stood near the doorway to direct the mourning friends to their seats; and I have no reason to doubt that she sometimes even had the immense responsibility of making out the order of the procession, since she had all genealogy and relationship at her tongue's end. It was an awful thing in Deephaven, we found, if the precedence was wrongly assigned, and once we chanced to hear some bitter remarks because the cousins of the departed wife had been placed after the husband's relatives,—"the blood-relations ridin' behind them that was only kin by marriage! I don't wonder they felt hurt!" said the person who spoke; a most unselfish and unassuming soul, ordinarily.

Mrs. Patton knew everybody's secrets, but she told them judiciously if at all. She chattered all day to you as a sparrow twitters, and you did not tire of her; and Kate and I were never more agreeably entertained than when she told us of old times and of Kate's ancestors and their contemporaries; for her memory was wonderful, and she had either seen everything that had happened in Deephaven for a long time, or had received the particulars from reliable witnesses. She had known much trouble, her husband had been but small satisfaction to her, and it was not to be wondered at if she looked upon all proposed marriages with compassion. She was always early at church, and she wore the same bonnet that she had when Kate was a child; it was such a well-preserved, proper black straw bonnet, with discreet bows of ribbon, and a useful lace veil to protect it from the weather.

She showed us into the best room the first time we went to see her. It was the plainest little room, and very dull, and there was an exact sufficiency about its furnishings. Yet there was a certain dignity about it; it was unmistakably a best room, and not a place where one might make a litter or carry one's every-day work. You felt at once that somebody valued the prim old-fashioned chairs, and the two half-moon tables, and the thin carpet, which must have needed anxious stretching every spring to make it come to the edge of the floor. There were some mourning pieces by way of decoration, inscribed with the names of Mrs. Patton's departed friends,—two worked in crewel to the memory of her father and mother, and two paper memorials, with the woman weeping under the willow at the side of a monument. They were all brown with age; and there was a sampler beside, worked by "Judith Beckett, aged ten," and all five were framed in slender black frames and hung very high on the walls. There was a rocking chair which looked as if it felt too grand for use, and considered itself imposing. It tilted far back on its rockers, and was bent forward at the top to make one's head uncomfortable. It need not have troubled itself; nobody would ever wish to sit there. It was such a big rocking chair, and Mrs. Patton was proud of it; always generously urging her guests to enjoy its comfort, which was imaginary with her, as she was so short that she could hardly have climbed into it without assistance.

Mrs. Patton was a little ceremonious at first, but soon recovered herself and told us a great deal which we were glad to hear. I asked her once if she had not always lived at Deephaven. "Here and beyond East Parish," said she. "Mr. Patton,—that was my husband,—he owned a good farm there when I married him, but I come back here again after he died; place was all mortgaged. I never got a cent, and I was poorer than when I started. I worked harder'n ever I did before or since to keep things together, but 'twasn't any kind o' use. Your mother knows all about it, Miss Kate,"—as if we might not be willing to believe it on her authority. "I come back here a widow and destitute, and I tell you the world looked fair to me when I left this house first to go over there. Don't you run no risks, you're better off as you be, dears. But land sakes alive, 'he' didn't mean no hurt! and he set everything by me when he was himself. I don't make no scruples of speaking about it, everybody knows how it was, but I did go through with everything. I never knew what the day would bring forth," said the widow, as if this were the first time she had had a chance to tell her sorrows to a sympathizing audience. She did not seem to mind talking about the troubles of her married life any more than a soldier minds telling the story of his campaigns, and dwells with pride on the worst battle of all.

Her favorite subject always was Miss Brandon, and after a pause she said that she hoped we were finding everything right in the house; she had meant to take up the carpet in the best spare room, but it didn't seem to need it; it was taken up the year before, and the room had not been used since, there was not a mite of dust under it last time. And Kate assured her, with an appearance of great wisdom, that she did not think it could be necessary at all.

"I come home and had a good cry yesterday after I was over to see you," said Mrs. Patton, and I could not help wondering if she really could cry, for she looked so perfectly dried up, so dry that she might rustle in the wind. "Your aunt had been failin' so long that just after she died it was a relief, but I've got so's to forget all about that, and I miss her as she used to be; it seemed as if you had stepped into her place, and you look some as she used to when she was young."

"You must miss her," said Kate, "and I know how much she used to depend upon you. You were very kind to her."

"I sat up with her the night she died," said the widow, with mournful satisfaction. "I have lived neighbor to her all my life except the thirteen years I was married, and there wasn't a week I wasn't over to the great house except I was off to a distance taking care of the sick. When she got to be feeble she always wanted me to 'tend to the cleaning and to see to putting the canopies and curtains on the bedsteads, and she wouldn't trust nobody but me to handle some of the best china. I used to say, 'Miss Katharine, why don't you have some young folks come and stop with you? There's Mis' Lancaster's daughter a-growing up'; but she didn't seem to care for nobody but your mother. You wouldn't believe what a hand she used to be for company in her younger days. Surprisin' how folks alters. When I first rec'lect her much she was as straight as an arrow, and she used to go to Boston visiting and come home with the top of the fashion. She always did dress elegant. It used to be gay here, and she was always going down to the Lorimers' or the Carews' to tea, and they coming here. Her sister was married; she was a good deal older; but some of her brothers were at home. There was your grandfather and Mr. Henry. I don't think she ever got it over,— his disappearing so. There were lots of folks then that's dead and gone, and they used to have their card parties, and old Cap'n Manning—he's dead and gone—used to have 'em all to play whist every fortnight, sometimes three or four tables, and they always had cake and wine handed round, or the cap'n made some punch, like's not, with oranges in it, and lemons; *he* knew how! He was a bachelor to the end of his days, the old cap'n was, but he used to entertain real handsome.

"I rec'lect one night they was a-playin' after the wine was brought in, and he upset his glass all over Miss Martha Lorimer's invisible-green watered silk, and spoilt the better part of two breadths. She sent right over for me early the next morning to see if I knew of anything to take out the spots, but I didn't, though I can take grease out o' most any material. We tried clear alcohol, and saleratus water, and hartshorn, and pouring water through, and heating of it, and when we got through it was worse than when we started. She felt dreadful bad about it, and at last she says, 'Judith, we won't work over it any more, but if you'll give me a day some time or 'nother, we'll rip it up and make a quilt of it.' I see that quilt last time I was in Miss Rebecca's north chamber. Miss Martha was her aunt; you never saw her; she was dead and gone before your day. It was a silk old Cap'n Peter Lorimer, her brother, who left 'em his money, brought home from sea, and she had worn it for best and second best eleven year. It looked as good as new, and she never would have ripped it up if she could have matched it. I said it seemed to be a shame, but it was a curi's figure. Cap'n Manning fetched her one to pay for it the next time he went to Boston. She didn't want to take it, but he wouldn't take no for an answer; he was free-handed, the cap'n was. I helped 'em make it 'long of Mary Ann Simms the dressmaker,—she's dead and gone too,—the time it was made. It was brown, and a beautiful-looking piece, but it wore shiny, and she made a double-gown of it before she died."

Mrs. Patton brought Kate and me some delicious old-fashioned cake with much spice in it, and told us it was made by old Mrs. Chantrey Brandon's receipt which she got in England, that it would keep a year, and she always kept a loaf by her, now that she could afford it; she supposed we knew Miss Katharine had named her in her will long before she was sick. "It has put me beyond fear of want," said Mrs. Patton. "I won't deny that I used to think it would go hard with me when I got so old I couldn't earn my living. You see I never laid up but a little, and it's hard for a woman who comes of respectable folks to be a pauper in her last days; but your aunt, Miss Kate, she thought of it too, and I'm sure I'm thankful to be so comfortable, and to stay in my house, which I couldn't have done, like's not. Miss Rebecca Lorimer said to me after I got news of the will, 'Why, Mis' Patton, you don't suppose your friends would ever have let you want!' And I says, 'My friends are kind,—the Lord bless 'em!—but I feel better to be able to do for myself than to be beholden.'"

After this long call we went down to the post office, and coming home stopped for a while in the old burying ground, which we had noticed the day before; and we sat for the first time on the great stone in the wall, in the shade of a maple tree, where we so often waited afterward for the stage to come with the mail, or rested on our way home from a walk. It was a comfortable perch; we used to read our letters there, I remember.

I must tell you a little about the Deephaven burying ground, for its interest was inexhaustible, and I do not know how much time we may have spent in reading the long epitaphs on the gravestones and trying to puzzle out the inscriptions, which were often so old and worn that we could only trace a letter here and there. It was a neglected corner of the world, and there were straggling sumachs and acacias scattered about the enclosure, while a row of fine old elms marked the boundary of two sides. The grass was long and tangled, and most of the stones leaned one way or the other, and some had fallen flat. There were a few handsome old family monuments clustered in one corner, among which the one that marked Miss Brandon's grave looked so new and fresh that it seemed inappropriate. "It should have been dingy to begin with, like the rest," said Kate one day; "but I think it will make itself look like its neighbors as soon as possible."

There were many stones which were sacred to the memory of men who had been lost at sea, almost always giving the name of the departed ship, which was so kept in remembrance; and one felt as much interest in the ship Starlight, supposed to have foundered off the Cape of Good Hope, as in the poor fellow who had the ill luck to be one of her crew. There were dozens of such inscriptions, and there were other stones perpetuating the fame of Honourable gentlemen who had been members of His Majesty's Council, or surveyor's of His Majesty's Woods, or King's Officers of Customs for the town of Deephaven. Some of the epitaphs were beautiful, showing that tenderness for the friends who had died, that longing to do them justice, to fully acknowledge their virtues and dearness, which is so touching, and so unmistakable even under the stiff, quaint expressions and formal words which were thought suitable to be chiselled on the stones, so soon to be looked at carelessly by the tearless eyes of strangers. We often used to notice names, and learn their history from the old people whom we knew, and in this way we heard many stories which we never shall forget. It is wonderful, the romance and tragedy and adventure which one may find in a quiet old-fashioned country town, though to heartily enjoy the everyday life one must care to study life and character, and must find pleasure in thought and observation of simple things, and have an instinctive, delicious interest in what to other eyes is unflavored dullness.

To go back to Mrs. Patton; on our way home, after our first call upon her, we stopped to speak to Mrs. Dockum, who mentioned that she had seen us going in to the "Widow Jim's."

"Willin' woman," said Mrs. Dockum, "always been respected; got an uncommon facility o' speech. I never saw such a hand to talk, but then she has something to say, which ain't the case with everybody. Good neighbor, does according to her means always. Dreadful tough time of it with her husband, shif'less and drunk all his time. Noticed that dent in the side of her forehead, I s'pose? That's where he liked to have killed her; slung a stone bottle at her."

"*What!*" said Kate and I, very much shocked.

"She don't like to have it inquired about; but she and I were sitting up with 'Manda Damer one night, and she gave me the particulars. I knew he did it, for she had a fit o' sickness afterward. Had sliced cucumbers for breakfast that morning; he was very partial to them, and he wanted some vinegar. Happened to be two bottles in the cellar way; were just alike, and one of 'em was vinegar and the other had sperrit in it at haying time. He takes up the wrong one and pours on quick, and out come the hayseed and flies, and he give the bottle a sling, and it hit her there where you see the scar; might put the end of your finger into the dent. He said he meant to break the bottle ag'in the door, but it went slantwise, sort of. I don't know, I'm sure" (meditatively). "She said he was good-natured; it was early in the mornin', and he hadn't had time to get upset; but he had a high temper naturally, and so much drink hadn't made it much better. She had good prospects when she married him. Six-foot-two and red cheeks and straight as a Noroway pine; had a good property from his father, and his mother come of a good family, but he died in debt; drank like a fish. Yes, 'twas a shame, nice woman; good consistent church-member; always been respected; useful among the sick."

Deephaven Society

It was curious to notice, in this quaint little fishing-village by the sea, how clearly the gradations of society were defined. The place prided itself most upon having been long ago the residence of one Governor Chantrey, who was a rich shipowner and East India merchant, and whose fame and magnificence were almost fabulous. It was a never-ceasing regret that his house should have burned down after he died, and there is no doubt that if it were still standing it would rival any ruin of the Old World.

The elderly people, though laying claim to no slight degree of present consequence, modestly ignored it, and spoke with pride of the grand way in which life was carried on by their ancestors, the Deephaven families of old times. I think Kate and I were assured at least a hundred times that Governor Chantrey kept a valet, and his wife, Lady Chantrey, kept a maid, and that the governor had an uncle in England who was a baronet; and I believe this must have been why our friends felt so deep an interest in the affairs of the English nobility: they no doubt felt themselves entitled to seats near the throne itself. There were formerly five families who kept their coaches in Deephaven; there were balls at the governor's and regal entertainments at other of the grand mansions; there is not a really distinguished person in the country who will not prove to have been directly or indirectly connected with Deephaven.

We were shown the cellar of the Chantrey house, and the terraces, and a few clumps of lilacs, and the grand rows of elms. There are still two of the governor's warehouses left, but his ruined wharves are fast disappearing, and are almost deserted, except by small barefooted boys who sit on the edges to fish for sea perch when the tide comes in. There is an imposing monument in the burying ground to the great man and his amiable consort. I am sure that if there were any surviving relatives of the governor they would receive in Deephaven far more def-

Deephaven

erence than is consistent with the principles of a republican
government; but the family became extinct long since, and I
have heard, though it is not a subject that one may speak of
lightly, that the sons were unworthy their noble descent and
came to inglorious ends.

There were still remaining a few representatives of the old
families, who were treated with much reverence by the rest of
the townspeople, although they were, like the conies of Scripture,
a feeble folk.

Deephaven is utterly out of fashion. It never recovered from
the effects of the embargo of 1807, and a sand bar has been
steadily filling in the mouth of the harbor. Though the fishing
gives what occupation there is for the inhabitants of the place,
it is by no means sufficient to draw recruits from abroad. But
nobody in Deephaven cares for excitement, and if some one once
in a while has the low taste to prefer a more active life, he is
obliged to go elsewhere in search of it, and is spoken of afterward with kind pity. I well remember the Widow Moses said to
me, in speaking of a certain misguided nephew of hers, "I never
could see what could 'a' sot him out to leave so many privileges
and go way off to Lynn, with all them children too. Why, they
lived here no more than a cable's length from the meetin' house!"

There were two schooners owned in town, and 'Bijah Mauley
and Jo Sands owned a trawl. There were some schooners and a
small brig slowly going to pieces by the wharves, and indeed all
Deephaven looked more or less out of repair. All alongshore one
might see dories and wherries and whaleboats, which had been
left to die a lingering death. There is something piteous to me
in the sight of an old boat. If one I had used much and cared
for were past its usefulness, I should say good-by to it, and have
it towed out to sea and sunk; it never should be left to fall to
pieces above highwater mark.

Even the commonest fishermen felt a satisfaction, and seemed
to realize their privilege, in being residents of Deephaven; but
among the nobility and gentry there lingered a fierce pride in
their family and town records, and a hardly concealed contempt
and pity for people who were obliged to live in other parts of
the world. There were acknowledged to be a few disadvantages,
—such as living nearly a dozen miles from the railway,—but, as
Miss Honora Carew said, the tone of Deephaven society had al-

ways been very high, and it was very nice that there had never been any manufacturing element introduced. She could not feel too grateful, herself, that there was no disagreeable foreign population.

"But," said Kate one day, "wouldn't you like to have some pleasant new people brought into town?"

"Certainly, my dear," said Miss Honora, rather doubtfully; "I have always been public spirited; but then, we always have guests in summer, and I am growing old. I should not care to enlarge my acquaintance to any great extent." Miss Honora and Mrs. Dent had lived gay lives in their younger days, and were interested and connected with the outside world more than any of our Deephaven friends; but they were quite contented to stay in their own house, with their books and letters and knitting, and they carefully read *Littell* and "the new magazine," as they called the *Atlantic*.

The Carews were very intimate with the minister and his sister, and there were one or two others who belonged to this set. There was Mr. Joshua Dorsey, who wore his hair in a queue, was very deaf, and carried a ponderous cane which had belonged to his venerated father,—a much taller man than he. He was polite to Kate and me, but we never knew him much. He went to play whist with the Carews every Monday evening, and commonly went out fishing once a week. He had begun the practice of law, but he had lost his hearing, and at the same time his lady love had inconsiderately fallen in love with somebody else; after which he retired from active business life. He had a fine library, which he invited us to examine. He had many new books, but they looked shockingly overdressed, in their fresher bindings, beside the old brown volumes of essays and sermons, and lighter works in many-volume editions.

A prominent link in society was Widow Tully, who had been the much-respected housekeeper of old Captain Manning for forty years. When he died he left her the use of his house and family pew, besides an annuity. The existence of Mr. Tully seemed to be a myth. During the first of his widow's residence in town she had been much affected when obliged to speak of him, and always represented herself as having seen better days and as being highly connected. But she was apt to be ungrammatical when excited, and there was a whispered tradition that she used to keep a toll bridge in a town in Connecticut; though the mystery of her previous state of existence will probably never be solved. She wore mourning for the captain which would have befitted his widow, and patronized the townspeople conspicuously, while she herself was treated with much condescension by the Carews and Lorimers. She occupied, on the whole, much the same position that Mrs. Betty Barker did in Cranford. And, indeed, Kate and I were often reminded of that estimable town. We heard that Kate's aunt, Miss Brandon, had never been appreciative of Mrs. Tully's merits, and that since her death the others had received Mrs. Tully into their society rather more.

It seemed as if all the clocks in Deephaven, and all the people with them, had stopped years ago, and the people had been doing over and over what they had been busy about during the last week of their unambitious progress. Their clothes had lasted wonderfully well, and they had no need to earn money when there was so little chance to spend it; indeed, there were several families who seemed to have no more visible means of support than a balloon. There were no young people whom we knew, though a number used to come to church on Sunday from the inland farms, or "the country," as we learned to say. There were children among the fishermen's families at the shore, but a few years will see Deephaven possessed by two classes instead of the time-honored three.

As for our first Sunday at church, it must be in vain to ask you to imagine our delight when we heard the tuning of a bass viol in the gallery just before service. We pressed each other's hands most tenderly, looked up at the singers' seats, and then trusted ourselves to look at each other. It was more than we had hoped for. There were also a violin and sometimes a flute, and a choir of men and women singers, though the congregation were expected to join in the psalm-singing. The first hymn was

> "The Lord our God is full of might,
> The winds obey his will,"

to the tune of "St. Ann's." It was all so delightfully old-fashioned; our pew was a square pew, and was by an open window looking seaward. We also had a view of the entire congregation, and as we were somewhat early, we watched the people come in, with great interest. The Deephaven aristocracy came with stately step up the aisle; this was all the chance there was for displaying their unquestioned dignity in public.

Many of the people drove to church in wagons that were low and old and creaky, with worn buffalo robes over the seat, and some hay tucked underneath for the sleepy, undecided old horse. Some of the younger farmers and their wives had high, shiny wagons, with tall horsewhips,—which they sometimes brought into church,—and they drove up to the steps with a consciousness of being conspicuous and enviable. They had a bashful look when they came in, and for a few minutes after they took their seats they evidently felt that all eyes were fixed upon them; but after a little while they were quite at their ease, and looked critically at the new arrivals.

The old folks interested us most. "Do you notice how many more old women there are than old men?" whispered Kate to me. And we wondered if the husbands and brothers had been drowned, and if it must not be sad to look at the blue, sunshiny sea beyond the marshes, if the far-away white sails reminded them of some ships that had never sailed home into Deephaven harbor, or of fishing boats that had never come back to land.

The girls and young men adorned themselves in what they believed to be the latest fashion, but the elderly women were usually relics of old times in manner and dress. They wore to church thin, soft silk gowns that must have been brought from over the seas years upon years before, and wide collars fastened with mourning pins holding a lock of hair. They had big black bonnets, some of them with stiff capes, such as Kate and I had not seen before since our childhood. They treasured large rusty lace veils of scraggly pattern, and wore sometimes, on pleasant Sundays, white Chinacrape shawls with attenuated fringes; and there were two or three of these shawls in the congregation which had been dyed black, and gave an aspect of meekness and general unworthiness to the aged wearer, they clung and drooped about the figure in such a hopeless way. We used to notice often the most interesting scarfs, without which no Deephaven woman considered herself in full dress. Sometimes there were red India scarfs in spite of its being hot weather; but our favorite ones were long strips of silk, embroidered along the edges and at the ends with dismal-colored floss in odd patterns. I think there must have been a fashion once, in Deephaven, of working these

Deephaven

scarfs, and I should not be surprised to find that it was many years before the fashion of working samplers came about.

Our friends always wore black mitts on warm Sundays, and many of them carried neat little bags of various designs on their arms, containing a precisely folded pocket handkerchief, and a frugal lunch of caraway seeds or red and white peppermints. I should like you to see, with your own eyes, Widow Ware and Miss Exper'ence Hull, two old sisters whose personal appearance we delighted in, and whom we saw feebly approaching down the street this first Sunday morning under the shadow of the two last members of an otherwise extinct race of parasols.

There were two or three old men who sat near us. They were sailors,—there is something unmistakable about a sailor,—and they had a curiously ancient, uncanny look, as if they might have belonged to the crew of the *Mayflower*, or even have cruised about with the Northmen in the times of Harold Harfager and his comrades. They had been blown about by so many winter winds, so browned by summer suns, and wet by salt spray, that their hands and faces looked like leather, with a few deep folds instead of wrinkles. They had pale blue eyes, very keen and quick; their hair looked like the fine seaweed which clings to the kelp roots and mussel shells in little locks. These friends of ours sat solemnly at the heads of their pews and looked unflinchingly at the minister, when they were not dozing, and they sang with voices like the howl of the wind, with an occasional deep note or two.

Have you never seen faces that seemed old-fashioned? Many of the people in Deephaven church looked as if they must be—if not supernaturally old—exact copies of their remote ancestors. I wonder if it is not possible that the features and expressions may be almost perfectly reproduced. These faces were not modern American faces, but belonged rather to the days of the early settlement of the country, the old colonial times. We often heard quaint words and expressions which we never had known anywhere else but in old books. There was a great deal of sea lingo in use; indeed, we learned a great deal ourselves, unconsciously, and used it afterward to the great amusement of our friends; but there were also many peculiar provincialisms, and among the people who lived on the lonely farms inland we often noticed words we had seen in Chaucer, and studied out at school in our English literature class. Everything in Deephaven was more or less influenced by the sea; the minister spoke oftenest of Peter and his fishermen companions, and prayed most earnestly every Sunday morning for those who go down to the sea in ships. He made frequent allusions and drew numberless illustrations of a similar kind for his sermons, and indeed I am in doubt whether, if the Bible had been written wholly in inland countries, it would have been much valued in Deephaven.

The singing was very droll, for there was a majority of old voices, which had seen their best days long before, and the bass viol was excessively noticeable, and apt to be a little ahead of the time the singers kept, while the violin lingered after. Somewhere on the other side of the church we heard an acute voice which rose high above all the rest of the congregation, sharp as a needle, and slightly cracked, with a limitless supply of breath. It rose and fell gallantly, and clung long to the high notes of "Dundee." It was like the wail of the banshee, which sounds clear to the fated hearer above all other noises. We afterward became acquainted with the owner of this voice, and were surprised to find her a meek widow, who was like a thin black beetle in her pathetic cypress veil and big black bonnet. She looked as if she had forgotten who she was, and spoke with an apologetic whine; but we heard she had a temper as high as her voice, and as much to be dreaded as the equinoctial gale.

Near the church was the parsonage, where Mr. Lorimer lived, and the old Lorimer house not far beyond was occupied by Miss Rebecca Lorimer. Some stranger might ask the question why the minister and his sister did not live together, but you would have understood it at once after you had lived for a little while in town. They were very fond of each other, and the minister dined with Miss Rebecca on Sundays, and she passed the day with him on Wednesdays, and they ruled their separate households with decision and dignity. I think Mr. Lorimer's house showed no signs of being without a mistress, any more than his sister's betrayed the want of a master's care and authority.

The Carews were very kind friends of ours, and had been Miss Brandon's best friends. We heard that there had always been a coolness between Miss Brandon and Miss Lorimer, and that, though they exchanged visits and were always polite, there was a chill in the politeness, and one would never have suspected them of admiring each other at all. We had the whole history of the trouble, which dated back scores of years, from Miss Honora Carew, but we always took pains to appear ignorant of the feud, and I think Miss Lorimer was satisfied that it was best not to refer to it, and to let bygones be bygones. It would not have been true Deephaven courtesy to prejudice Kate against her grand-aunt, and Miss Rebecca cherished her dislike in silence, which gave us a most grand respect for her, since we knew she thought herself in the right; though I think it never had come to an open quarrel between these majestic aristocrats.

Miss Honora Carew and Mr. Dick and their elder sister, Mrs. Dent, had a charmingly sedate and quiet home in the old Carew house. Mrs. Dent was ill a great deal while we were there, but she must have been a very brilliant woman, and was not at all dull when we knew her. She had outlived her husband and her children, and she had, several years before our summer there, given up her own home, which was in the city, and had come back to Deephaven. Miss Honora—dear Miss Honora!—had been one of the brightest, happiest girls, and had lost none of her brightness and happiness by growing old. She had lost none of her fondness for society, though she was so contented in quiet Deephaven, and I think she enjoyed Kate's and my stories of our pleasures as much as we did hers of old times.

We used to go to see her almost every day. "Mr. Dick," as they called their brother, had once been a merchant in the East Indies, and there were quantities of curiosities and most beautiful china which he had brought and sent home, which gave the house a character of its own. He had been very rich and had lost some of his money, and then he came home and was still considered to possess princely wealth by his neighbors. He had a great fondness for reading and study, which had not been lost sight of during his business life, and he spent most of his time in his library. He and Mr. Lorimer had their differences of opinion about certain points of theology, and this made them much fonder of each other's society, and gave them a great deal of pleasure; for after every series of arguments, each was sure that he had vanquished the other, or there were alternate victories and defeats which made life vastly interesting and important.

Miss Carew and Mrs. Dent had a great treasury of old brocades and laces and ornaments, which they showed us one day, and told us stories of the wearers, or, if they were their own, there were always some reminiscences which they liked to talk over with each other and with us. I never shall forget the first evening we took tea with them; it impressed us very much, and yet nothing wonderful happened. Tea was handed round by an old-fashioned maid, and afterward we sat talking in the twilight, looking out at the garden. It was such a delight to have tea served in this way. I wonder that the fashion has been almost forgotten. Kate and I took much pleasure in choosing our teapoys; hers had a mandarin parading on the top, and mine a flight of birds and a pagoda; and we often used them afterward, for Miss Honora asked us to come to tea whenever we liked. "A stupid, common country town" some one dared to call Deephaven in a letter once, and how bitterly we resented it! That was a house where one might find the best society, and the most charming manners and good breeding, and if I were asked to tell you what I mean by the word "lady," I should ask you to go, if it were possible, to call upon Miss Honora Carew.

After a while the elder sister said, "My dears, we always have prayers at nine, for I have to go upstairs early nowadays." And then the servants came in, and she read solemnly the King of glory Psalm, which I have always liked best, and then Mr. Dick read the church prayers, the form of prayer to be used in families. We stayed later to talk with Miss Honora after we had said good night to Mrs. Dent. And we told each other, as we went home in the moonlight down the quiet street, how much we had enjoyed the evening, for somehow the house and the people had nothing to do with the present, or the hurry of modern life. I have never heard that psalm since without its bringing back that summer night in Deephaven, the beautiful quaint old room, and Kate and I feeling so young and worldly, by contrast, the flickering, shaded light of the candles, the old book, and the voices that said Amen.

There were several other fine old houses in Deephaven beside this and the Brandon house, though that was rather the most imposing. There were two or three which had not been kept in repair, and were deserted, and of course they were said to be haunted, and we were told of their ghosts, and why they walked, and when. From some of the local superstitions Kate and I have vainly endeavored ever since to shake ourselves free. There was a most heathenish fear of doing certain things on Friday, and there were countless signs in which we still have confidence. When the moon is very bright and other people grow sentimental, we only remember that it is a fine night to catch hake.

The Captains

I SHOULD consider my account of Deephaven society incomplete
if I did not tell you something of the ancient mariners, who may
be found every pleasant morning sunning themselves like turtles
on one of the wharves. Sometimes there was a considerable
group of them, but the less constant members of the club were
older than the rest, and the epidemics of rheumatism in town were
sadly frequent. We found that it was etiquette to call them each
captain, but I think some of the Deephaven men took the title
by brevet upon arriving at a proper age.

They sat close together because so many of them were deaf,
and when we were lucky enough to overhear the conversation, it
seemed to concern their adventures at sea, or the freight carried
out by the *Sea Duck*, the *Ocean Rover*, or some other Deephaven
ship,—the particulars of the voyage and its disasters and successes being as familiar as the wanderings of the children of
Israel to an old parson. There were sometimes violent alterca-
tions when the captains differed as to the tonnage of some craft
that had been a prey to the winds and waves, dry rot, or
barnacles fifty years before. The old fellows puffed away at
little black pipes with short stems, and otherwise consumed
tobacco in fabulous quantities. It is needless to say that they gave
an immense deal of attention to the weather. We used to wish
we could join this agreeable company, but we found that the
appearance of an outsider caused a disapproving silence, and
that the meeting was evidently not to be interfered with. Once
we were impertinent enough to hide ourselves for a while just
round the corner of the warehouse, but we were afraid or
ashamed to try it again, though the conversation was inconceiv-
ably edifying. Captain Isaac Horn, the eldest and wisest of all,
was discoursing upon some cloth he had purchased once in
Bristol, which the shopkeeper delayed sending until just as they
were ready to weigh anchor.

"I happened to take a look at that cloth," said the captain, in a loud droning voice, "and as quick as I got sight of it, I spoke onpleasant of that swindling English fellow, and the crew, they stood back. I was dreadful high tempered in them days, mind ye; and I had the gig manned. We was out in the stream, just ready to sail. 'Twas no use waiting any longer for the wind to change, and we was going north-about. I went ashore, and when I walks into his shop ye never see a creatur' so wilted. Ye see the miser'ble sculpin thought I'd never stop to open the goods, an' it was a chance I did, mind ye! 'Lor,' says he, grinning and turning the color of a biled lobster, 'I s'posed ye were a standing out to sea by this time.' 'No,' says I, 'and I've got my men out here on the quay a landing that cloth o' yourn, and if you don't send just what I bought and paid for down there to go back in the gig within fifteen minutes, I'll take ye by the collar and drop ye into the dock.' I was twice the size of him, mind ye, and master strong. 'Don't ye like it?' says he, edging round; 'I'll change it for ye, then.' Ter'ble perlite he was. 'Like it?' says I, 'it looks as if it were built of dog's hair and divil's wool, kicked together by spiders; and it's coarser than Irish frieze; three threads to an *armful*,' says I."

This was evidently one of the captain's favorite stories, for we heard an approving grumble from the audience.

In the course of a walk inland we made a new acquaintance, Captain Lant, whom we had noticed at church, and who sometimes joined the company on the wharf. We had been walking through the woods, and coming out to his fields we went on to the house for some water. There was no one at home but the captain, who told us cheerfully that he should be pleased to serve us, though his women folks had gone off to a funeral, the other side of the P'int. He brought out a pitcherful of milk, and after we had drunk some, we all sat down together in the shade. The captain brought an old flag-bottomed chair from the wood-house, and sat down facing Kate and me, with an air of certainty that he was going to hear something new and make some desirable new acquaintances, and also that he could tell something it would be worth our while to hear. He looked more and more like a well-to-do old English sparrow, and chippered faster and faster.

"Queer ye should know I'm a sailor so quick; why, I've been

a-farming it this twenty years; have to go down to the shore and take a day's fishing every hand's turn, though, to keep the old hulk clear of barnacles. There! I do wish I lived nigher the shore, where I could see the folks I know, and talk about what's been a-goin' on. You don't know anything about it, you don't; but it's tryin' to a man to be called 'old Cap'n Lant,' and, so to speak, be forgot when there's anything stirring, and be called gran'ther by clumsy creatur's goin' on fifty and sixty, who can't do no more work today than I can; an' then the women folks keeps a-tellin' me to be keerful and not fall, and as how I'm too old to go out fishing; and when they want to be soft-spoken, they say as how they don't see as I fail, and how wonderful I keep my hearin'. I never did want to farm it, but 'she' always took it to heart when I was off on a v'y'ge, and this farm and some consider'ble means beside come to her from her brother, and they all sot to and give me no peace of mind till I sold out my share of the *Ann Eliza* and come ashore for good. I did keep an eighth of the *Pactolus*, and I was ship's husband for a long spell, but she never was heard from on her last voyage to Singapore. I was the lonesomest man, when I first come ashore, that ever you see.

"Well, you are master hands to walk, if you come way up from the Brandon house. I wish the women was at home. Know Miss Brandon? Why, yes; and I remember all her brothers and sisters, and her father and mother. I can see 'em now coming into meeting, proud as Lucifer and straight as a mast, every one of 'em. Miss Katharine, she always had her butter from this very farm. Some of the folks used to go down every Saturday, and my wife, she's been in the house a hundred times, I s'pose. So you are Hathaway Brandon's grand-daughter?" (to Kate); "why, he and I have been out fishing together many's the time,—he and Chantrey, his next younger brother. Henry, he was a disappointment; he went to furrin parts and turned out a Catholic priest, I s'pose you've heard? I never was to set ag'in Mr. Henry as some folks was. He was the pleasantest spoken of the whole on 'em. You do look like the Brandons; you really favor 'em consider'ble. Well, I'm pleased to see ye, I'm sure."

We asked him many questions about the old people, and found he knew all the family histories and told them with great satisfaction. We found he had his pet stories, and it must have been gratifying to have an entirely new and fresh audience. He was adroit in leading the conversation around to a point where the stories would come in appropriately, and we helped him as much as possible. In a small neighborhood all the people know each other's stories and experiences by heart, and I have no doubt the old captain had been snubbed many times on beginning a favorite anecdote. There was a story which he told us that first day, which he assured us was strictly true, and it is certainly a remarkable instance of the influence of one mind upon another at a distance. It seems to me worth preserving, at any rate; and as we heard it from the old man, with his solemn voice and serious expression and quaint gestures, it was singularly impressive.

"When I was a youngster," said Captain Lant, "I was an orphan, and I was bound out to old Mr. Peletiah Daw's folks, over on the Ridge Road. It was in the time of the last war, and he had a nephew, Ben Dighton, a dreadful high-strung, wild fellow, who had gone off on a privateer. The old man, he set everything by Ben; he would disoblige his own boys any day to please him. This was in his latter days, and he used to have spells of wandering and being out of his head; and he used to call for Ben and talk sort of foolish about him, till they would tell him to stop. Ben never did a stroke of work for him, either, but he was a handsome fellow, and had a way with him when he was good-natured. One night old Peletiah had been very bad all day and was getting quieted down, and it was after supper; we sat round in the kitchen, and he lay in the bedroom opening out. There were some pitch-knots blazing, and the light shone in on the bed, and all of a sudden something made me look up and look in; and there was the old man setting up straight, with his eyes shining at me like a cat's. 'Stop 'em!' says he; '*stop 'em!*' and his two sons run in then to catch hold of him, for they thought he was beginning with one of his wild spells; but he fell back on the bed and began to cry like a baby. 'O, dear me,' says he, 'they've hung him,—hung him right up to the yardarm! O, they oughtn't to have done it; cut him down quick! he didn't think; he means well, Ben does; he was hasty. O my God, I can't bear to see him swing round by the neck! It's poor Ben hung up to the yardarm. Let me alone, I say!' Andrew and Moses, they were holding him with all their might, and they were both hearty men, but he 'most got away from them once or twice, and he screeched and howled like a mad creatur', and then he would cry again like a child. He was worn out after a while and lay back quiet, and said over and over, 'Poor Ben!' and 'hung at the yardarm'; and he told the neighbors next day, but nobody noticed him much, and he seemed to forget it as his mind come back.

"All that summer he was miser'ble, and towards cold weather he failed right along, though he had been a master strong man in his day, and his timbers held together well. Along late in the fall he had taken to his bed, and one day there came to the house a fellow named Sim Decker, a reckless fellow he was too, who had gone out in the same ship with Ben. He pulled a long face when he came in, and said he had brought bad news. They had been taken prisoner and carried into port and put in jail, and Ben Dighton had got a fever there and died.

"'You lie!' says the old man from the bedroom, speaking as loud and f'erce as ever you heard. 'They hung him to the yardarm!'

"'Don't mind him,' says Andrew; 'he's wandering-like, and he had a bad dream along back in the spring; I s'posed he'd forgotten it.' But the Decker fellow he turned pale, and kept talking crooked while he listened to old Peletiah a-scolding to himself. He answered the questions the women folks asked him,—they took on a good deal,—but pretty soon he got up and winked to me and Andrew, and we went out in the yard. He began to swear, and then says he, 'When did the old man have his dream?' Andrew couldn't remember, but I knew it was the night before he sold the gray colt, and that was the 24th of April.

"'Well,' says Sim Decker, 'on the twenty-third day of April Ben Dighton was hung to the yardarm, and I see 'em do it, Lord help him! I didn't mean to tell the women, and I s'posed you'd never know, for I'm all the one of the ship's company you're ever likely to see. We were taken prisoner, and Ben was mad as fire, and they were scared of him and chained him to the deck; and while he was sulking there, a little parrot of a midshipman come up and grinned at him, and snapped his fingers in his face; and Ben lifted his hands with the heavy irons and sprung at him like a tiger, and the boy dropped dead as a stone; and they put the bight of a rope round Ben's neck and slung him right up to the yardarm, and there he swung back and forth until as soon as we dared one of us clim' up and cut the rope and let him go over the ship's side; and they put us in irons for that, curse 'em! How did that old man in there know, and he bedridden here, nigh upon three thousand miles off?" says he. But I guess there wasn't any of us could tell him," said Captain Lant in conclusion. "It's something I never could account for, but it's true as truth.

"I've known more such cases; some folks laughs at me for believing 'em,—'the cap'n's yarns,' they calls 'em,—but if you'll notice, everybody's got some yarn of that kind they do believe, if they won't believe yours. And there's a good deal happens in the world that's mysterious. Now there was Widder Oliver Pinkham, over to the P'int, told me with her own lips that she—" But just here we saw the captain's expression alter suddenly, and looked around to see a wagon coming up the lane. We immediately said we must go home, for it was growing late, but asked permission to come again and hear the Widow Oliver Pinkham story. We stopped, however, to see "the women-folks," and afterward became so intimate with them that we were invited to spend the afternoon and take tea, which invitation we accepted with great pride. We went out fishing, with the captain and "Danny," of whom I will tell you presently. I often think of Captain Lant in the winter, for he told Kate once that he "felt master old in winter to what he did in summer."

He likes reading, fortunately, and we had a letter from him, not long ago, acknowledging the receipt of some books of travel by land and water which we had luckily thought to send him. He gave the latitude and longitude of Deephaven at the beginning of his letter, and signed himself, "Respectfully yours with esteem, Jacob Lant (condemned as unseaworthy)."

Danny

DEEPHAVEN seemed more like one of the lazy little English seaside towns than any other. It was not in the least American. There was no excitement about anything; there were no manufactories; nobody seemed in the least hurry. The only foreigners were a few standard sailors. I do not know when a house or a new building of any kind had been built; the men were farmers, or went outward in boats, or inward in fishwagons, or sometimes mackerel and halibut fishing in schooners for the city markets. Sometimes a schooner came to one of the wharves to load hay or firewood; but Deephaven used to be a town of note, rich and busy, as its forsaken warehouses show.

We knew almost all the fisher people at the shore, even old Dinnett, who lived an apparently desolate life by himself in a hut and was reputed to have been a bloodthirsty pirate in his youth. He was consequently feared by all the children, and for misdemeanors in his latter days avoided generally. Kate talked with him awhile one day on the shore, and made him come up with her for a bandage for his hand which she saw he had hurt badly; and the next morning he brought us a "new" lobster apiece,—fishermen mean that a thing is only not salted when they say it is "fresh." We happened to be in the hall, and received him ourselves, and gave him a great piece of tobacco and (unintentionally) the means of drinking our health. "Bless your pretty hearts!" said he; "may ye be happy, and live long, and get good husbands, and if they ain't good to you may they die from you!"

None of our friends were more interesting than the fishermen. The fish houses, which might be called the business centre of the town, were at a little distance from the old warehouses, farther down the harbor shore, and were ready to fall down in despair. There were some fishermen who lived near by, but most of them were also farmers in a small way, and lived in the village or farther inland. From our eastern windows we could see the moorings, and we always liked to watch the boats go out or come straying in, one after the other, tipping and skimming under the square little sails; and we often went down to the fish houses to see what kind of a catch there had been.

I should have imagined that the sea would become very commonplace to men whose business was carried on in boats, and who had spent night after night and day after day from their boyhood on the water; but that is a mistake. They have an awe of the sea and of its mysteries, and of what it hides away from us. They are childish in their wonder at any strange creature which they find. If they have not seen the sea serpent, they believe, I am sure, that other people have, and when a great shark or blackfish or swordfish was taken and brought in shore, everybody went to see it, and we talked about it, and how brave its conqueror was, and what a fight there had been, for a long time afterward.

I said that we liked to see the boats go out, but I must not give you the impression that we saw them often, for they weighed anchor at an early hour in the morning. I remember once there was a light fog over the sea, lifting fast, as the sun was coming up, and the brownish sails disappeared in the mist, while voices could still be heard for some minutes after the men were hidden from sight. This gave one a curious feeling, but afterward, when the sun had risen, everything looked much the same as usual; the fog had gone, and the dories and even the larger boats were distant specks on the sparkling sea.

One afternoon we made a new acquaintance in this wise. We went down to the shore to see if we could hire a conveyance to the lighthouse the next morning. We often went out early in one of the fishing boats, and after we had stayed as long as we pleased, Mr. Kew would bring us home. It was quiet enough that day, for not a single boat had come in, and there were no men to be seen along shore. There was a solemn company of lobster coops or cages which had been brought in to be mended. They always amused Kate. She said they seemed to her like droll old women telling each other secrets. These were scattered about in different attitudes, and looked more confidential than usual.

Just as we were going away we happened to see a man at work in one of the sheds. He was the fisherman whom we knew least of all; an odd-looking, silent sort of man, more sunburnt and weatherbeaten than any of the others. We had learned to know him by the bright red flannel shirt he always wore, and besides, he was lame; some one told us he had had a bad fall once, on board ship. Kate and I had always wished we could find a chance to talk with him. He looked up at us pleasantly, and when we nodded and smiled, he said "Good day" in a gruff, hearty voice, and went on with his work, cleaning mackerel.

"Do you mind our watching you?" asked Kate.

"No, *ma'am!*" said the fisherman emphatically. So there we stood.

Those fish houses were curious places, so different from any other kind of workshop. In this there was a seine, or part of one, festooned among the cross-beams overhead, and there were snarled fishing lines, and barrows to carry fish in, like wheel-barrows without wheels; there were the queer round lobster nets, and "kits" of salt mackerel, tubs of bait, and piles of clams; and some queer bones, and parts of remarkable fish, and lobster claws of surprising size fastened on the walls for ornament. There was a pile of rubbish down at the end; I dare say it was all use-ful, however,—there is such mystery about the business.

Kate and I were never tired of hearing of the fish that come at different times of the year, and go away again, like the birds; or of the actions of the dogfish which the 'longshoremen hate so bitterly; and then there are such curious legends and traditions, of which almost all fishermen have a store.

"I think mackerel are the prettiest fish that swim," said I presently.

"So do I, miss," said the man, "not to say but I've seen more fancy-looking fish down in southern waters, bright as any flower you ever see; but a mackerel," holding up one admiringly, "why, they're so clean built and trig looking! Put a cod alongside, and he looks as lumbering as an old-fashioned Dutch brig aside a yacht.

"Those are good-looking fish, but they an't made much ac-count of," continued our friend, as he pushed aside the mackerel and took another tub. "They're hake, I s'pose you know. But I forgot,—I can't stop to bother with them now." And he pulled forward a barrow full of small fish, flat and hard, with pointed, bony heads.

Deephaven

"Those are porgies, aren't they?" asked Kate.

"Yes," said the man, "an' I'm going to sliver them for the trawls."

We knew what the trawls were, and supposed that the porgies were to be used for bait; and we soon found out what "slivering" meant, by seeing him take them by the head and cut a slice from first one side and then the other in such a way that the pieces looked not unlike smaller fish.

"It seems to me," said I, "that fishermen always have sharper knives than other people."

"Yes, we do like a sharp knife in our trade; and then we are mostly strong handed."

He was throwing the porgies' heads and back-bones—all that was left of them after slivering—in a heap, and now several cats walked in as if they felt at home, and began a hearty lunch. "What a troop of pussies there is round here," said I; "I wonder what will become of them in the winter,—though, to be sure, the fishing goes on just the same."

"The better part of them don't get through the cold weather," said Danny. "Two or three of the old ones have been here for years, and are so much belonging to Deephaven as the meetin' house; but the rest of them an't to be depended on. You'll miss the young ones by the dozen, come spring. I don't know myself but they move inland in the fall of the year; they're knowing enough, if that's all!"

Kate and I stood in the wide doorway, arm in arm, looking sometimes at the queer fisherman and the porgies, and sometimes out to sea. It was low tide; the wind had risen a little, and the heavy salt air blew toward us from the wet brown ledges in the rocky harbor. The sea was bright blue, and the sun was shining. Two gulls were swinging lazily to and fro; there was a flock of sandpipers down by the water's edge, in a great hurry, as usual.

Presently the fisherman spoke again, beginning with an odd laugh: "I *was* scared last winter! Jack Scudder and me, we were up in the Cap'n Manning storehouse hunting for a half-bar'l of salt the skipper said was there. It was an awful blustering kind of day, with a thin icy rain blowing from all points at once; sea roaring as if it wished it could come ashore and put a stop to everything. Bad days at sea, them are; rigging all froze up. As I

was saying, we were hunting for a half-bar'l of salt, and I laid
hold of a bar'l that had something heavy in the bottom, and tilted
it up, and my eye! there was a stir and a scratch and a squeal,
and out went some kind of a creatur', and I jumped back, not
looking for anything live, but I see in a minute it was a cat; and
perhaps you think it is a big story, but there were eight more in
there, hived in together to keep warm. I car'd 'em up some new
fish that night; they seemed short of provisions. We hadn't been
out fishing as much as common, and they hadn't dared to be
round the fish houses much, for a fellow who came in on a
coaster had a dog, and he used to chase 'em. Hard chance they
had, and lots of 'em died, I guess; but there seem to be some
survivin' relatives, an' al'ays just so hungry! I used to feed them
some when I was ashore. I think likely you've heard that a cat
will fetch you bad luck; but I don't know's that made much
difference to me. I kind of like to keep on the right side of 'em,
too; if ever I have a bad dream there's sure to be a cat in it; but
I was brought up to be clever to dumb beasts, an' I guess it's my
natur'. Except fish," said Danny after a minute's thought; "but
then it never seems like they had feelin's like creatur's that live
ashore." And we all laughed heartily and felt well acquainted.

"I s'pose you misses will laugh if I tell ye I kept a kitty once
myself." This was said rather shyly, and there was evidently a
story, so we were much interested, and Kate said, "Please tell us
about it; was it at sea?"

"Yes, it was at sea; leastways, on a coaster. I got her in a
sing'lar kind of way: it was one afternoon we were lying alongside Charlestown Bridge, and I heard a young cat screeching real
pitiful; and after I looked all round, I see her in the water clutch-
ing on to the pier of the bridge, and some little divils of boys
were heaving rocks down at her. I got into the schooner's tag
boat quick, I tell ye, and pushed off for her, 'n' she let go just
as I got there, 'n' I guess you never saw a more miser'ble-looking
creatur' than I fished out of the water. Cold weather it was. Her
leg was hurt, and her eye, and I thought first I'd drop her overboard again, and then I didn't, and I took her aboard the
schooner and put her by the stove. I thought she might as well
die where it was warm. She eat a little mite of chowder before
night, but she was very slim; but next morning, when I went to
see if she was dead, she fell to licking my finger, and she did

purr away like a dolphin. One of her eyes was out, where a stone had took her, and she never got any use of it, but she used to look at you so clever with the other, and she got well of her lame foot after a while. I got to be ter'ble fond of her. She was just the knowingest thing you ever saw, and she used to sleep alongside of me in my bunk, and like as not she would go on deck with me when it was my watch.

"I was coasting then for a year and eight months, and I kept her all the time. We used to be in harbor consider'ble, and about eight o'clock in the forenoon I used to drop a line and catch her a couple of cunners. Now, it is cur'us that she used to know when I was fishing for her. She would pounce on them fish and carry them off and growl, and she knew when I got a bite,—she'd watch the line; but when we were mackereling she never give us any trouble. She would never lift a paw to touch any of our fish. She didn't have the thieving ways common to most cats. She used to set round on deck in fair weather, and when the wind blew she al'ays kept herself below.

"Sometimes when we were in port she would go ashore awhile, and fetch back a bird or a mouse, but she wouldn't eat it till she come and showed it to me. She never wanted to stop long ashore, though I never shut her up; I always give her her liberty. I got a good deal of joking about her from the fellows, but she was a sight of company. I don' know as I ever had anything like me as much as she did. Not to say as I ever had much of any trouble with anybody, ashore or afloat. I'm a still kind of fellow, for all I look so rough.

"But then, I han't had a home, what I call a home, since I was going on nine years old."

"How has that happened?" asked Kate.

"Well, mother, she died, and I was bound out to a man in the tanning trade, and I hated him, and I hated the trade; and when I was a little bigger I ran away, and I've followed the sea ever since. I wasn't much use to him, I guess; leastways, he never took the trouble to hunt me up.

"About the best place I ever was in was a hospital. It was in foreign parts. Ye see I'm crippled some? I fell from the topsail yard to the deck, and I struck my shoulder, and broke my leg, and banged myself all up. It was to a nuns' hospital where they took me. All of the nuns were Catholics, and they wore big white things on their heads. I don't suppose you ever saw any. Have you? Well, now, that's queer! When I was first there I was scared of them; they were real ladies, and I wasn't used to being in a house, anyway. One of them, that took care of me most of the time, why, she would even set up half the night with me, and I couldn't begin to tell you how good-natured she was, an' she'd look real sorry too. I used to be ugly, I ached so, along in the first of my being there, but I spoke of it when I was coming away, and she said it was alright. She used to feed me, that lady did; and there were some days I couldn't lift my head, and she would rise it on her arm. She give me a little mite of a book, when I come away. I'm not much of a hand at reading, but I always kept it on account of her. She was so pleased when I got so's to set up in a chair and look out of the window. She wasn't much of a hand to talk English. I did feel bad to come away from there; I 'most wished I could be sick a while longer. I never said much of anything either, and I don't know but she thought it was queer, but I am a dreadful clumsy man to say anything, and I got flustered. I don't know's I mind telling you; I was 'most a-crying.

"I used to think I'd lay by some money and ship for there and carry her something real pretty. But I don't rank able-bodied seaman like I used, and it's as much as I can do to get a berth on a coaster; I suppose I might go as cook. I liked to have died with my hurt at that hospital, but when I was getting well it made me think of when I was a mite of a chap to home before mother died, to be laying there in a clean bed with somebody to do for me. Guess you think I'm a good hand to spin long yarns; somehow it comes easy to talk today."

"What became of your cat?" asked Kate, after a pause, during which our friend sliced away at the porgies.

"I never rightfully knew; it was in Salem harbor, and a windy night. I was on deck consider'ble, for the schooner pitched lively, and once or twice she dragged her anchor. I never saw the kitty after she eat her supper. I remember I gave her some milk,—I used to buy her a pint once in a while for a treat; I don't know but she might have gone off on a cake of ice, but it did seem as if she had too much sense for that. Most likely she missed her footing, and fell overboard in the dark. She was marked real pretty, black and white, and kep' herself just as clean! She knew as well as could be when foul weather was coming; she would bother round and act queer; but when the sun was out she would sit round on deck as pleased as a queen. There! I feel bad sometimes when I think of her, and I never went into Salem since without hoping that I should see her. I don't know but if I was a-going to begin my life over again, I'd settle down ashore and have a snug little house and farm it. But I guess I shall do better at fishing. Give me a trig-built topsail schooner painted up nice, with a stripe on her, and clean sails, and a fresh wind with the sun a-shining, and I feel first-rate."

"Do you believe that codfish swallow stones before a storm?" asked Kate. I had been thinking about the lonely fisherman in a sentimental way, and so irrelevant a question shocked me. "I saw he felt slightly embarrassed at having talked about his affairs so much," Kate told me afterward, "and I thought we should leave him feeling more at his ease if we talked about fish for a while." And sure enough he did seem relieved, and gave us his opinion about the codfish at once, adding that he never cared much fôr cod anyway; folks up country bought 'em a good deal, he heard. Give him a haddock right out of the water for his dinner!

"I never can remember," said Kate, "whether it is cod or haddock that have a black stripe along their sides—"

"O, those are haddock," said I; "they say that the Devil caught a haddock once, and it slipped through his fingers and got scorched; so all the haddock had the same mark afterward."

"Well, now, how did you know that old story?" said Danny, laughing heartily; "ye mustn't believe all the old stories ye hear, mind ye!"

"O, no," said we.

"Hullo! There's Jim Toggerson's boat close in shore. She sets low in the water, so he's done well. He and Skipper Scudder have been out deep-sea fishing since yesterday."

Our friend pushed the porgies back into a corner, stuck his knife into a beam, and we hurried down to the shore. Kate and I sat on the pebbles, and he went out to the moorings in a dirty dory to help unload the fish.

We afterward saw a great deal of Danny, as all the men called him. But though Kate and I tried our best and used our utmost skill and tact to make him tell us more about himself, he never did. But perhaps there was nothing more to be told.

The day we left Deephaven we went down to the shore to say good-by to him and to some other friends, and he said, "Goin', are ye? Well, I'm sorry; ye've treated me first-rate; the Lord bless ye!" and then was so much mortified at the way he had said farewell that he turned and fled round the corner of the fish house.

Captain Sands

OLD Captain Sands was one of the most prominent citizens of Deephaven, and a very good friend of Kate's and mine. We often met him, and grew much interested in him before we knew him well. He had a reputation in town for being peculiar and somewhat visionary; but every one seemed to like him, and at last one morning, when we happened to be on our way to the wharves, we stopped at the door of an old warehouse which we had never seen opened before. Captain Sands sat just inside, smoking his pipe, and we said good morning, and asked him if he did not think there was a fog coming in by and by. We had thought a little of going out to the lighthouse. The cap'n rose slowly, and came out so that he could see farther round to the east. "There's some scud coming in a'ready," said he. "None to speak of yet, I don't know's you can see it,—yes, you're right; there's a heavy bank of fog lyin' off, but it won't be in under two or three hours yet, unless the wind backs round more and freshens up. Weren't thinking of going out, were ye?"

"A little," said Kate, "but we had nearly given it up. We are getting to be very weather wise, and we pride ourselves on being quick at seeing fogs." At which the cap'n smiled and said we were consider'ble young to know much about weather, but it looked well that we took some interest in it; most young people were fools about weather, and would just as soon set off to go anywhere right under the edge of a thundershower. "Come in and set down, won't ye?" he added; "it ain't much of a place; I've got a lot of old stuff stowed away here that the women folks don't want up to the house. I'm a great hand for keeping things." And he looked round fondly at the contents of the wide low room.

"I come down here once in a while and let in the sun, and sometimes I want to hunt up something or 'nother; kind of stow-away place, ye see." And then he laughed apologetically, rubbing his hands together, and looking out to sea again as if he wished to appear unconcerned; yet we saw that he wondered if we thought it ridiculous for a man of his age to have treasured up so much trumpery in that cobwebby place. There were some whole oars and the sail of his boat and two or three killicks and painters, not to forget a heap of worn-out oars and sails in one corner and a sailor's hammock slung across the beam overhead, and there were some sailor's chests and the capstan of a ship and innumerable boxes which all seemed to be stuffed full, besides no end of things lying on the floor and packed away on shelves and hanging to rusty big-headed nails in the wall. I saw some great lumps of coral, and large, rough shells, a great hornet's nest, and a monstrous lobster shell. The cap'n had cobbled and tied up some remarkable old chairs for the accommodation of himself and his friends.

"What a nice place!" said Kate in a frank, delighted way which could not have failed to be gratifying.

"Well, no," said the cap'n, with his slow smile, "it ain't what you'd rightly call 'nice,' as I know of: it ain't never been cleared out all at once since I began putting in. There's nothing that's worth anything, either, to anybody but me. Wife, she's said to me a hundred times, 'Why don't you overhaul them old things and burn 'em?' She's al'ays at me about letting the property, as if it were a corner lot in Broadway. That's all women folks know about business!" And here the captain caught himself tripping, and looked uneasy for a minute. "I suppose I might have let it for a fish house, but it's most too far from the shore to be handy— and—well—there are some things here that I set a good deal by."

"Isn't that a swordfish's sword in that piece of wood?" Kate asked presently; and was answered that it was found broken off as we saw it, in the hull of a wreck that went ashore on Blue P'int when the captain was a young man, and he had sawed it out and kept it ever since,—fifty-nine years. Of course we went closer to look at it, and we both felt a great sympathy for this friend of ours, because we have the same fashion of keeping worthless treasures, and we understood perfectly how dear such things may be.

"Do you mind if we look round a little?" I asked doubtfully, for I knew how I should hate having strangers look over my own treasury. But Captain Sands looked pleased at our interest, and said cheerfully that we might overhaul as much as we chose. Kate discovered first an old battered wooden figurehead of a ship,—a woman's head with long curly hair falling over the shoulders. The paint was almost gone, and the dust covered most of what was left: still there was a wonderful spirit and grace, and a wild, weird beauty which attracted us exceedingly; but the captain could only tell us that it had belonged to the wreck of a Danish brig which had been driven on the reef where the lighthouse stands now, and his father had found this on the long sands a day or two afterward.

"That was a dreadful storm," said the captain. "I've heard the old folks tell about it; it was when I was only a year or two old. There were three merchantmen wrecked within five miles of Deephaven. This one was all stove to splinters, and they used to say she had treasure aboard. When I was small I used to have a great idea of going out there to the rocks at low water and trying to find some gold, but I never made out no great." And he smiled indulgently at the thought of his youthful dream.

"Kate," said I, "do you see what beauties these Turk's-head knots are?" We had been taking a course of first lessons in knots from Danny, and had followed by learning some charmingly intricate ones from Captain Lant, the stranded mariner who lived on a farm two miles or so inland. Kate came over to look at the Turk's-heads, which were at either end of the rope handles of a little dark-blue chest.

Captain Sands turned in his chair and nodded approval. "That's a neat piece of work, and it was a first-rate seaman who did it; he's dead and gone years ago, poor young fellow; an I-talian he was, who sailed on the *Ranger* three or four long voyages. He fell from the masthead on the voyage home from Callao. Cap'n Manning and old Mr. Lorimer, they owned the *Ranger*, and when she come into port and they got the news they took it as much to heart as if he'd been some relation. He was smart as a whip, and had a way with him, and the pleasantest kind of a voice; you couldn't help liking him. They found out that he had a mother alive in Port Mahon, and they sent his pay and some money he had in the bank at Riverport out to her by a ship that was going to the Mediterranean. He had some clothes in his chest, and they sold those and sent her the money, —all but some trinkets they supposed he was keeping for her; I rec'lect he used to speak consider'ble about his mother. I shipped one v'y'ge with him before the mast, before I went out mate of the *Daylight*. I happened to be in port the time the *Ranger* got in, an' I see this chist lying round in Cap'n Manning's storehouse, and I offered to give him what it was worth; but we was good friends, and he told me take it if I wanted it, it was no use to him, and I've kept it ever since.

"There are some of his traps in it now, I believe; ye can look." And we took off some tangled codlines and opened the chest. There was only a round wooden box in the till, and in some idle hour at sea the young sailor had carved his initials and an anchor and the date on the cover. We found some sail needles and a palm in this "kit," as the sailors call it, and a little string of buttons with some needles and yarn and thread in a neat little bag, which perhaps his mother had made for him when he started off on his first voyage. Besides these things there was only a fanciful little broken buckle, green and gilt, which he might have picked up in some foreign street, and his protection paper carefully folded, wherein he was certified as being a citizen of the United States, with dark complexion and dark hair.

"He was one of the pleasantest fellows that ever I shipped with," said the captain, with a gruff tenderness in his voice. "Always willin' to do his work himself, and like's not when the other fellows up the rigging were cold, or ugly about something or 'nother, he'd say something that would set them all laughing, and somehow it made you good-natured to see him around. He was brought up a Catholic, I s'pose; anyway, he had some beads, and sometimes they would joke him about 'em on board ship, but he would blaze up in a minute, ugly as a tiger. I never saw him mad about anything else, though he wouldn't stand it if anybody tried to crowd him. He fell from the main-to'-gallant yard to the deck, and was dead when they picked him up. They were off the Bermudas. I suppose he lost his balance, but I never could see how; he was sure-footed, and as quick as a cat. They said they saw him try to catch at the stay, but there was a heavy sea running, and the ship rolled just so's to let him through between the rigging, and he struck the deck like a stone. I don't know's that chest has been opened these ten years,—I declare it carries me back to look at those poor little traps of his. Well, it's the way of the world; we think we're somebody, and we have our day, but it isn't long afore we're forgotten."

The captain reached over for the paper, and taking out a clumsy pair of steel-bowed spectacles, read it through carefully. "I'll warrant he took good care of this," said he. "He was an I-talian, and no more of an American citizen than a Chinese; I wonder he hadn't called himself John Jones, that's the name most of the foreigners used to take when they got their papers. I remember once I was sick with a fever in Chelsea Hospital, and one morning they came bringing in the mate of a Portugee brig on a stretcher, and the surgeon asked what his name was. 'John Jones,' says he. 'O, say something else,' says the surgeon; 'we've got five John Joneses here a'ready, and it's getting to be no name at all.'

"Sailors are great hands for false names; they have a trick of using them when they have any money to leave ashore, for fear their shipmates will go and draw it out. I suppose there are thousands of dollars unclaimed in New York banks, where men have left it charged to their false names; then they got lost at sea or something, and never go to get it, and nobody knows whose it is. They're curious folks, take 'em altogether, sailors is; specially these foreign fellows that wander about from ship to ship. They're getting to be a dreadful low set, too, of late years. It's the last thing I'd want a boy of mine to do,—ship before the mast with one of these mixed crews. It's a dog's life, anyway, and the risks and the chances against you are awful. It's a good while before you can lay up anything, unless you are part owner. I saw all the p'ints a good deal plainer after I quit followin' the sea myself, though I've always been more or less into navigation until this last war come on. I know when I was ship's husband of the *Polly and Susan* there was a young man went out cap'n of her,—her last voyage, and she never was heard from. He had a wife and two or three little children, and for all he was so smart, they would have been about the same as beggars, if I hadn't happened to have his life insured the day I was having the papers made out for the ship. I happened to think of it. Five thousand dollars there was, and I sent it to the widow along with his primage. She hadn't expected nothing, or next to nothing, and she was pleased, I tell ye."

"I think it was very kind in you to think of that, Captain Sands," said Kate. And the old man said, flushing a little, "Well, I'm not so smart as some of the men who started when I did, and some of 'em went ahead of me, but some of 'em didn't, after all. I've tried to be honest, and to do just about as nigh right as I could, and you know there's an old sayin' that a cripple in the right road will beat a racer in the wrong."

The Circus at Denby

KATE and I looked forward to a certain Saturday with as much eagerness as if we had been little schoolboys, for on that day we were to go to a circus at Denby, a town perhaps eight miles inland. There had not been a circus so near Deephaven for a long time, and nobody had dared to believe the first rumor of it, until two dashing young men had deigned to come themselves to put up the big posters on the end of 'Bijah Mauley's barn. All the boys in town came as soon as possible to see these amazing pictures, and some were wretched in their secret hearts at the thought that they might not see the show itself. Tommy Dockum was more interested than any one else, and mentioned the subject so frequently one day when he went blackberrying with us, that we grew enthusiastic, and told each other what fun it would be to go, for everybody would be there, and it would be the greatest loss to us if we were absent. I thought I had lost my childish fondness for circuses, but it came back redoubled; and Kate may contradict me if she chooses, but I am sure she never looked forward to the Easter Oratorio with half the pleasure she did to this "caravan," as most of the people called it.

We felt that it was a great pity that any of the boys and girls should be left lamenting at home, and finding that there were some of our acquaintances and Tommy's who saw no chance of going, we engaged Jo Sands and Leander Dockum to carry them to Denby in two fish wagons, with boards laid across for the extra seats. We saw them join the straggling train of carriages which had begun to go through the village from all alongshore, soon after daylight, and they started on their journey shouting and carousing, with their pockets crammed with early apples and other provisions. We thought it would have been fun enough to see the people go by, for we had had no idea until then how many inhabitants that country held.

We had asked Mrs. Kew to go with us; but she was half an

hour later than she had promised, for, since there was no wind, she could not come ashore in the sailboat, and Mr. Kew had had to row her in in the dory. We saw the boat at last nearly in shore, and drove down to meet it: even the horse seemed to realize what a great day it was, and showed a disposition to friskiness, evidently as surprising to himself as to us.

Mrs. Kew was funnier that day than we had ever known her, which is saying a great deal, and we should not have had half so good a time if she had not been with us; although she lived in the lighthouse, and had no chance to "see passing," which a woman prizes so highly in the country, she had a wonderful memory for faces, and could tell us the names of all Deep-haveners and of most of the people we met outside its limits. She looked impressed and solemn as she hurried up from the water's edge, giving Mr. Kew some parting charges over her shoulder as he pushed off the boat to go back; but after we had convinced her that the delay had not troubled us, she seemed more cheerful. It was evident that she felt the importance of the occasion, and that she was pleased at our having chosen her for company. She threw back her veil entirely, sat very straight, and took immense pains to bow to every acquaintance whom she met. She wore her best Sunday clothes, and her manner was formal for the first few minutes; it was evident that she felt we were meeting under unusual circumstances, and that although we had often met before on the friendliest terms, our having asked her to make this excursion in public required a different sort of behavior at her hands, and a due amount of ceremony and propriety. But this state of things did not last long, as she soon made a remark at which Kate and I laughed so heartily in lighthouse-acquaintance fashion, that she unbent, and gave her whole mind to enjoying herself.

When we came by the store where the post office was kept, we saw a small knot of people gathered round the door, and stopped to see what had happened. There was a forlorn horse standing near, with his harness tied up with fuzzy ends of rope, and the wagon was cobbled together with pieces of board; the whole craft looked as if it might be wrecked with the least jar. In the wagon were four or five stupid-looking boys and girls, one of whom was crying softly. Their father was sick, some one told us. "He was took faint, but he is coming to all right; they have give him something to take: their name is Craper, and they live way over beyond the Ridge, on Stone Hill. They were goin' over to Denby to the circus, and the man was calc'lating to get doctored, but I d' know's he can get so fur; he's powerful slim-looking to me."

Kate and I went to see if we could be of any use, and when we went into the store we saw the man leaning back in his chair, looking ghastly pale, and as if he were far gone in consumption. Kate spoke to him, and he said he was better; he had felt bad all the way along, but he hadn't given up. He was pitiful, poor fellow, with his evident attempt at dressing up. He had the bushiest, dustiest red hair and whiskers, which made the pallor of his face still more striking, and his illness had thinned and paled his rough, clumsy hands. I thought what a hard piece of work it must have been for him to start for the circus that morning, and how kindhearted he must be to have made such an effort for his children's pleasure. As we went out, they stared at us gloomily. The shadow of their disappointment touched and chilled our pleasure.

Somebody had turned the horse so that he was heading toward home, and by his actions he showed that he was the only one of the party who was glad. We were so sorry for the children; perhaps it had promised to be the happiest day of their lives, and now they must go back to their uninteresting home without having seen the great show.

"I am so sorry you are disappointed," said Kate, as we were wondering how the man who had followed us could ever climb into the wagon.

"Heh?" said he, blankly, as if he did not know what her words meant. "What fool has been a-turning o' this horse?" he asked a man who was looking on.

"Why, which way be ye goin'?"

"To the circus," said Mr. Craper, with decision, "where d'ye s'pose? That's where I started for, anyways." And he climbed in and glanced round to count the children, struck the horse with the willow switch, and they started off briskly, while everybody laughed. Kate and I joined Mrs. Kew, who had enjoyed the scene.

"Well, there!" said she, "I wonder the folks in the old North burying ground ain't a-rising up to go to Denby to that caravan!"

We reached Denby at noon; it was an uninteresting town which had grown up around some mills. There was a great commotion in the streets, and it was evident that we had lost much in not having seen the procession. There was a great deal of business going on in the shops, and there were two or three hand organs at large, near one of which we stopped awhile to listen, just after we had met Leander and given the horse into his charge. Mrs. Kew finished her shopping as soon as possible, and we hurried toward the great tents, where all the flags were flying. I think I have not told you that we were to have the benefit of seeing a menagerie in addition to the circus, and you may be sure we went faithfully round to see everything that the cages held.

I cannot truthfully say that it was a good show; it was somewhat dreary, now that I think of it quietly and without excitement. The creatures looked tired, and as if they had been on the road for a great many years. The animals were all old, and there was a shabby great elephant whose look of general discouragement went to my heart, for it seemed as if he were miserably conscious of a misspent life. He stood dejected and motionless at one side of the tent, and it was hard to believe that there was a spark of vitality left in him. A great number of the people had never seen an elephant before, and we heard a thin little old man, who stood near us, say delightedly, "There's the old creatur', and no mistake, Ann 'Liza. I wanted to see him most of anything. My sakes alive, ain't he big!"

And Ann 'Liza, who was stout and sleepy-looking, droned out, "Ye-es, there's consider'ble of him; but he looks as if he ain't got no animation."

Kate and I turned away and laughed, while Mrs. Kew said confidentially, as the couple moved away, "*She* needn't be a-reflectin' on the poor beast. That's Mis Seth Tanner, and there isn't a woman in Deephaven nor East Parish to be named the same day with her for laziness. I'm glad she didn't catch sight of me; she'd have talked about nothing for a fortnight."

There was a picture of a huge snake in Deephaven, and I was just wondering where he could be, or if there ever had been one, when we heard a boy ask the same question of the man whose thankless task it was to stir up the lions with a stick to make them roar. "The snake's dead," he answered good-naturedly. "Didn't you have to dig an awful long grave for him?" asked the boy; but the man said he reckoned they curled him up some, and smiled as he turned to his lions, who looked as if they needed a tonic.

Everybody lingered longest before the monkeys, who seemed to be the only lively creatures in the whole collection; and finally we made our way into the other tent, and perched ourselves on a high seat, from whence we had a capital view of the audience and the ring, and could see the people come in. Mrs. Kew was on the lookout for acquaintances, and her spirits as well as our own seemed to rise higher and higher. She was on the alert, moving her head this way and that to catch sight of people, giving us a running commentary in the meantime. It was very pleasant to see a person so happy as Mrs. Kew was that day, and I dare say in speaking of the occasion she would say the same thing of Kate and me,—for it was such a good time! We bought some peanuts, without which no circus seems complete, and we listened to the conversations which were being carried on around us while we were waiting for the performance to begin.

There were two old farmers whom we had noticed occasionally in Deephaven; one was telling the other, with great confusion of pronouns, about a big pig which had lately been killed. "John did feel dreadful disappointed at having to kill now," we heard him say, "bein' as he had calc'lated to kill along near Thanksgivin' time; there was goin' to be a new moon then, and he expected to get seventy-five or a hundred pound more on to him. But he didn't seem to gain, and me and 'Bijah both told him he'd be better to kill now, while everything was favor'ble, and if he set out to wait something might happen to him, and then I've always held that you can't get no hog only just so fur, and for my part I don't like these great overgrown creatur's. I like well enough to see a hog that'll weigh six hundred, just for the beauty on't, but for my eatin' give me one that'll just rise three. 'Bijah's accurate, and he says he is goin' to weigh risin' five hundred and fifty. I shall stop, as I go home, to John's wife's brother's and see if they've got the particulars yet; John was goin' to get the scales this morning. I guess likely consider'ble many 'll gather there tomorrow after meeting. John didn't calc'late to cut up till Monday."

"I guess likely I'll stop in tomorrow," said the other man; "I like to see a han'some hog. Chester White, you said? Consider them best, don't ye?" But this question never was answered, for the greater part of the circus company in gorgeous trappings came parading in.

The circus was like all other circuses, except that it was shabbier than most, and the performers seemed to have less heart in it than usual. They did their best, and went through with their parts conscientiously, but they looked as if they never had had a good time in their lives. The audience was hilarious, and cheered and laughed at the tired clown until he looked as if he thought his speeches might possibly be funny, after all. We were so glad we had pleased the poor thing; and when he sang a song our satisfaction was still greater, and so he sang it all over again. Perhaps he had been associating with people who were used to circuses. The afternoon was hot, and the boys with Japanese fans and trays of lemonade did a remarkable business for so late in the season; the brass band on the other side of the tent shrieked its very best, and all the young men of the region had brought their girls, and some of these countless pairs of country lovers we watched a great deal, as they "kept company" with more or less depth of satisfaction in each other. We had a grand chance to see the fashions, and there were many old people and a great number of little children, and some families had evidently locked their house door behind them, since they had brought both the dog and the baby.

"Doesn't it seem as if you were a child again?" Kate asked me. "I am sure this is just the same as the first circus I ever saw. It grows more and more familiar, and it puzzles me to think they should not have altered in the least while I have changed so much, and have even had time to grow up. You don't know how it is making me remember other things of which I have not thought for years.

"I was seven years old when I went that first time. Uncle Jack invited me. I had a new parasol, and he laughed because I would hold it over my shoulder when the sun was in my face. He took me into the side shows and bought me everything I asked for, on the way home, and we did not get home until twilight. The rest of the family had dined at four o'clock and gone out for a long drive, and it was such fun to have our dinner by ourselves. I sat at the head of the table in mamma's place, and when Bridget came down and insisted that I must go to bed, Uncle

Jack came softly upstairs and sat by the window, smoking and telling me stories. He ran and hid in the closet when we heard mamma coming up, and when she found him out by the cigar smoke, and made believe scold him, I thought she was in earnest, and begged him off. Yes; and I remember that Bridget sat in the next room, making her new dress so she could wear it to church next day. I thought it was a beautiful dress, and besought mamma to have one like it. It was bright green with yellow spots all over it," said Kate.

"Ah, poor Uncle Jack! he was so good to me! We were always telling stories of what we would do when I was grown up. He died in Canton the next year, and I cried myself ill; but for a long time I thought he might not be dead, after all, and might come home any day. He used to seem so old to me, and he really was just out of college and not so old as I am now. That day at the circus he had a pink rosebud in his buttonhole, and— ah! when have I ever thought of this before!—a woman sat before us who had a stiff little cape on her bonnet like a shelf, and I carefully put peanuts round the edge of it, and when she moved her head they would fall. I thought it was the best fun in the world, and I wished Uncle Jack to ride the donkey; I was sure he could keep on, because his horse had capered about with him one day on Beacon Street, and I thought him a perfect rider, since nothing had happened to him then."

"I remember," said Mrs. Kew, presently, "that just before I was married 'he' took me over to Wareham Corners to a caravan. My sister Hannah and the young man who was keeping company with her went too. I haven't been to one since till today, and it does carry me back same's it does you, Miss Kate. It doesn't seem more than five years ago, and what would I have thought if I had known 'he' and I were going to keep a lighthouse and be contented there, what's more, and sometimes not get ashore for a fortnight; settled, gray-headed old folks! We were gay enough in those days. I know old Miss Sabrina Smith warned me that I'd better think twice before I took up with Tom Kew, for he was a light-minded young man. I speak o' that to him in the wintertime, when he sets reading the almanac half asleep and I'm knitting, and the wind's a-howling and the waves coming ashore on those rocks as if they wished they could put out the light and blow down the lighthouse. We were reflected on a good deal for going to that caravan; some of the old folks didn't think it was improvin'—Well, I should think that man was a trying to break his neck!"

Coming out of the great tent was disagreeable enough, and we seemed to have chosen the worst time, for the crowd pushed fiercely, though I suppose nobody was in the least hurry, and we were all severely jammed, while from somewhere underneath came the wails of a deserted dog. We had not meant to see the side shows, and went carelessly past two or three tents; but when we came in sight of the picture of the Kentucky giantess, we noticed that Mrs. Kew looked at it wistfully, and we immediately asked if she cared anything about going to see the wonder, whereupon she confessed that she never heard of such a thing as a woman's weighing six hundred and fifty pounds, so we all three went in. There were only two or three persons inside the tent, beside a little boy who played the hand organ.

The Kentucky giantess sat in two chairs on a platform, and there was a large cage of monkeys just beyond, toward which Kate and I went at once. "Why, she isn't more than two thirds as big as the picture," said Mrs. Kew, in a regretful whisper; "but I guess she's big enough; doesn't she look discouraged, poor creatur'?" Kate and I felt ashamed of ourselves for being there. No matter if she had consented to be carried round for a show, it must have been horrible to be stared at and joked about day after day; and we gravely looked at the monkeys, and in a few minutes turned to see if Mrs. Kew were not ready to come away, when to our surprise we saw that she was talking to the giantess with great interest, and we went nearer.

"I thought your face looked natural the minute I set foot inside the door," said Mrs. Kew; "but you've—altered some since I saw you, and I couldn't place you till I heard you speak. Why, you used to be spare; I am amazed, Marilly! Where are your folks?"

"I don't wonder you are surprised," said the giantess. "I was a good ways from this when you knew me, wasn't I? But father he run through with every cent he had before he died, and 'he' took to drink and it killed him after awhile, and then I began to grow worse and worse, till I couldn't do nothing to earn a dollar, and everybody was a-coming to see me, till at last I used to ask 'em ten cents apiece, and I scratched along somehow till this man came round and heard of me, and he offered me my keep and good pay to go along with him. He had another giantess before me, but she had begun to fall away consider'ble, so he paid her off and let her go. This other giantess was an awful expense to him, she was such an eater; now I don't have no great of an appetite,"—this was said plaintively,—"and he's raised my pay since I've been with him because we did so well. I took up with his offer because I was nothing but a drag and never will be. I'm as comfortable as I can be, but it's a pretty hard business. My oldest boy is able to do for himself, but he's married this last year, and his wife don't want me. I don't know's I blame her either. It would be something like if I had a daughter now; but there, I'm getting to like travelling first-rate; it gives anybody a good deal to think of."

"I was asking the folks about you when I was up home the early part of the summer," said Mrs. Kew, "but all they knew was that you were living out in New York State. Have you been living in Kentucky long? I saw it on the picture outside."

"No," said the giantess, "that was a picture the man bought cheap from another show that broke up last year. It says six hundred and fifty pounds, but I don't weigh more than four hundred. I haven't been weighed for sometime past. Between you and me I don't weigh so much as that, but you mustn't mention it, for it would spoil my reputation, and might hender my getting another engagement." And then the poor giantess lost her professional look and tone as she said, "I believe I'd rather die than grow any bigger. I do lose heart sometimes, and wish I was a smart woman and could keep house. I'd be smarter than ever I was when I had the chance; I tell you that! Is Tom along with you?"

"No. I came with these young ladies, Miss Lancaster and Miss Denis, who are stopping over to Deephaven for the summer." Kate and I turned as we heard this introduction; we were standing close by, and I am proud to say that I never saw Kate treat anyone more politely than she did that absurd, pitiful creature with the gilt crown and many bracelets. It was not that she said much, but there was such an exquisite courtesy in her manner, and an apparent unconsciousness of there being anything in the least surprising or uncommon about the giantess.

Just then a party of people came in, and Mrs. Kew said good-by reluctantly. "It has done me sights of good to see you," said our new acquaintance; "I was feeling downhearted just before you came in. I'm pleased to see somebody that remembers me as I used to be." And they shook hands in a way that meant a great deal, and when Kate and I said good afternoon the giantess looked at us gratefully, and said, "I'm very much obliged to you for coming in, young ladies."

"Walk in! walk in!" the man was shouting as we came away. "Walk in and see the wonder of the world, ladies and gentlemen, —the largest woman ever seen in America,—the great Kentucky giantess!"

"Wouldn't you have liked to stay longer?" Kate asked Mrs. Kew as we came down the street. But she answered that it would be no satisfaction; the people were coming in, and she would have no chance to talk. "I never knew her very well; she is younger than I, and she used to go to meeting where I did, but she lived five or six miles from our house. She's had a hard time of it, according to her account," said Mrs. Kew. "She used to be a dreadful flighty, high-tempered girl, but she's lost that now, I can see by her eyes. I was running over in my mind to see if there was anything I could do for her, but I don't know as there is. She said the man who hired her was kind. I guess your treating her so polite did her much good as anything. She used to be real ambitious. I had it on my tongue's end to ask her if she couldn't get a few days' leave and come out to stop with me, but I thought just in time that she'd sink the dory in a minute. There! seeing her has took away all the fun," said Mrs. Kew ruefully; and we were all dismal for a while, but at last, after we were fairly started for home, we began to be merry again.

We passed the Craper family whom we had seen at the store in the morning; the children looked as stupid as ever, but the father, I am sorry to say, had been tempted to drink more whiskey than was good for him. He had a bright flush on his cheeks, and he was flourishing his whip, and hoarsely singing some meaningless tune. "Poor creature!" said I, "I should think this day's pleasuring would kill him." "Now, wouldn't you think so?" said Mrs. Kew, sympathizingly; "but the truth is, you couldn't kill one of those Crapers if you pounded him in a mortar."

We had a pleasant drive home, and we kept Mrs. Kew to supper, and afterward went down to the shore to see her set sail for home. Mr. Kew had come in sometime before, and had been waiting for the moon to rise. Mrs. Kew told us that she should have enough to think of for a year, she had enjoyed the day so much; and we stood on the pebbles watching the boat out of the harbor, and wishing ourselves on board, it was such a beautiful evening.

We went to another show that summer, the memory of which will never fade. It is somewhat impertinent to call it a show, and "public entertainment" is equally inappropriate, though we certainly were entertained. It had been raining for two or three days; the Deephavenites spoke of it as "a spell of weather." Just after tea, one Thursday evening, Kate and I went down to the post office. When we opened the great hall door, the salt air was delicious, but we found the town apparently wet through and discouraged; and though it had almost stopped raining just then, there was a Scotch mist, like a snowstorm with the chill taken off, and the Chantrey elms dripped hurriedly, and creaked occasionally in the east wind.

"There will not be a cap'n on the wharves for a week after this," said I to Kate; "only think of the cases of rheumatism!"

We stopped for a few minutes at the Carews', who were as much surprised to see us as if we had been mermaids out of the sea, and begged us to give ourselves something warm to drink, and to change our boots the moment we got home. Then we went on to the post office. Kate went in, but stopped, as she came out with our letters, to read a written notice securely fastened to the grocery door by four large carpet tacks with wide leathers round their necks.

"Dear," said she, exultantly, "there's going to be a lecture to-night in the church,—a free lecture on the Elements of True Manhood. Wouldn't you like to go?" And we went.

We were fifteen minutes later than the time appointed, and were sorry to find that the audience was almost imperceptible. The dampness had affected the antiquated lamps so that those on the walls and on the front of the gallery were the dimmest lights I ever saw, and sent their feeble rays through a small space the edges of which were clearly defined. There were two rather more energetic lights on the table near the pulpit, where the lecturer sat, and as we were in the rear of the church, we could see the yellow fog between ourselves and him. There were fourteen persons in the audience, and we were all huddled together in a cowardly way in the pews nearest the door: three old men, four women, and four children besides ourselves and the sexton, a deaf little old man with a wooden leg.

The children whispered noisily, and soon, to our surprise, the lecturer rose and began. He bowed, and treated us with beautiful deference, and read his dreary lecture with enthusiasm. I wish I could say, for his sake, that it was interesting; but I cannot tell a lie, and it was so long! He went on and on, until it seemed as if I had been there ever since I was a little girl. Kate and I did not dare to look at each other, and in my desperation at feeling her quiver with laughter, I moved to the other end of the pew, knocking over a big hymnbook on the way, which attracted so much attention that I have seldom felt more embarrassed in my life. Kate's great dog rose several times to shake himself and yawn loudly, and then lie down again despairingly.

You would have thought the man was addressing an enthusiastic Young Men's Christian Association. He exhorted with fervor upon our duties as citizens and as voters, and told us a great deal about George Washington and Benjamin Franklin, whom he urged us to choose as our examples. He waited for applause after each of his outbursts of eloquence, and presently went on again, in no wise disconcerted at the silence, and as if he were sure that he would fetch us next time. The rain began to fall again heavily, and the wind wailed around the meeting-house. If the lecture had been upon any other subject it would not have been so hard for Kate and me to keep sober faces; but it was directed entirely toward young men, and there was not a young man there.

The children in front of us mildly scuffled with each other at one time, until the one at the end of the pew dropped a marble, which struck the floor and rolled with a frightful noise down the edge of the aisle where there was no carpet. The congregation instinctively started up to look after it, but we recollected ourselves and leaned back again in our places, while the awed children, after keeping unnaturally quiet, fell asleep, and tumbled against each other helplessly. After a time the man sat down and wiped his forehead, looking well satisfied; and when we were wondering whether we might with propriety come away, he rose again, and said it was a free lecture, and he thanked us for our kind patronage on that inclement night; but in other places which he had visited there had been a contribution taken up for the cause. It would, perhaps, do no harm,—would the sexton—

But the sexton could not have heard the sound of a cannon at that distance, and slumbered on. Neither Kate nor I had any money, except a twenty-dollar bill in my purse, and some coppers in the pocket of her water-proof cloak which she assured me she was prepared to give; but we saw no signs of the sexton's waking, and as one of the women kindly went forward to wake the children, we all rose and came away.

After we had made as much fun and laughed as long as we pleased that night, we became suddenly conscious of the pitiful side of it all; and being anxious that every one should have the highest opinion of Deephaven, we sent Tom Dockum early in the morning with an anonymous note to the lecturer, whom he found without much trouble; but afterward we were disturbed at hearing that he was going to repeat his lecture that evening,—the wind having gone round to the northwest,—and I have no doubt there were a good many women able to be out, and that he harvested enough ten-cent pieces to pay his expenses without our help; though he had particularly told us it was for "the cause," the evening before, and that ought to have been a consolation.

Cunner-Fishing

ONE of the chief pleasures in Deephaven was our housekeeping. Going to market was apt to use up a whole morning, especially if we went to the fish houses. We depended somewhat upon supplies from Boston, but sometimes we used to chase a butcher who took a drive in his old canvas-topped cart when he felt like it, and as for fish, there were always enough to be caught, even if we could not buy any. Our acquaintances would often ask if we had anything for dinner that day, and would kindly suggest that somebody had been boiling lobsters, or that a boat had just come in with some nice mackerel, or that somebody over on the Ridge was calculating to kill a lamb, and we had better speak for a quarter in good season. I am afraid we were looked upon as being in danger of becoming epicures, which we certainly are not, and we undoubtedly roused a great deal of interest because we used to eat mushrooms, which grew in the suburbs of the town in wild luxuriance.

One morning Maggie told us that there was nothing in the house for dinner, and, taking an early start, we went at once down to the store to ask if the butcher had been seen, but finding that he had gone out deep-sea fishing for two days, and that when he came back he had planned to kill a veal, we left word for a sufficient piece of the doomed animal to be set apart for our family, and strolled down to the shore to see if we could find some mackerel; but there was not a fisherman in sight, and after going to all the fish houses we concluded that we had better provide for ourselves.

We had not brought our own lines, but we knew where Danny kept his, and after finding a basket of suitable size, and taking some clams from Danny's bait tub, we went over to the hull of an old schooner which was going to pieces alongside one of the ruined wharves. We looked down the hatchway into the hold, and could see the flounders and sculpin swimming about lazily, and once in a while a little pollock scooted down among them impertinently and then disappeared. "There is that same big flounder that we saw day before yesterday," said I. "I know him because one of his fins is half gone. I don't believe he can get out, for the hole in the side of the schooner isn't very wide, and it is higher up than flounders ever swim. Perhaps he came in when he was young, and was too lazy to go out until he was so large he couldn't. Flounders always look so lazy, and as if they thought a great deal of themselves."

"I hope they will think enough of themselves to keep away from my hook this morning," said Kate, philosophically, "and the sculpin too. I am going to fish for cunners alone, and keep my line short." And she perched herself on the quarter, baited her hook carefully, and threw it over, with a clam shell to call attention. I went to the rail at the side, and we were presently much encouraged by pulling up two small cunners, and felt that our prospects for dinner were excellent. Then I unhappily caught so large a sculpin that it was like pulling up an open umbrella, and after I had thrown him into the hold to keep company with the flounder, our usual good luck seemed to desert us. It was one of the days when, in spite of twitching the line and using all the tricks we could think of, the cunners would either eat our bait or keep away altogether. Kate at last said we must starve unless we could catch the big flounder, and asked me to drop my hook down the hatchway; but it seemed almost too bad to destroy his innocent happiness. Just then we heard the noise of oars, and to our delight saw Cap'n Sands in his dory just beyond the next wharf. "Any luck?" said he. "S'pose ye don't care anything about going out this morning?"

"We are not amusing ourselves; we are trying to catch some fish for dinner," said Kate. "Could you wait out by the red buoy while we get a few more, and then should you be back by noon, or are you going for a longer voyage, Captain Sands?"

"I was going out to Black Rock for cunners myself," said the cap'n. "I should be pleased to take ye, if ye'd like to go." So we wound up our lines, and took our basket and clams and went round to meet the boat. I felt like rowing, and took the oars while Kate was mending her sinker and the cap'n was busy with a snarled line.

"It's pretty hot," said he, presently, "but I see a breeze coming in, and the clouds seem to be thickening; I guess we shall have it cooler 'long towards noon. It looked last night as if we were going to have foul weather, but the scud seemed to blow off, and it was as pretty a morning as ever I see. 'A growing moon chaws up the clouds,' my gran'ther used to say. He was as knowing about the weather as anybody I ever come across; 'most always hit it just about right. Some folks lay all the weather to the moon, accordin' to where she quarters, and when she's in perigee we're going to have this kind of weather, and when she's in apogee she's got to do so and so for sartain; but gran'ther he used to laugh at all them things. He said it never made no kind of difference, and he went by the looks of the clouds and the feel of the air, and he thought folks couldn't make no kind of rules that held good, that had to do with the moon. Well, he did use to depend on the moon some; everybody knows we aren't so likely to have foul weather in a growing moon as we be when she's waning. But some folks I could name, they can't do nothing without having the moon's opinion on it.

"When I went my second voyage afore the mast we was in port ten days at Cadiz, and the ship she needed salting dreadful. The mate kept telling the captain how low the salt was in her, and we was going a long voyage from there, but no, he wouldn't have her salted nohow, because it was the wane of the moon. He was an amazing set kind of man, the cap'n was, and would have his own way on sea or shore. The mate was his own brother, and they used to fight like a cat and dog; they owned most of the ship between 'em. I was slushing the mizzenmast, and heard 'em a disputin' about the salt. The cap'n was a first-rate seaman and died rich, but he was dreadful notional. I know one time we were a lyin' out in the stream all ready to weigh anchor, and everything was in trim, the men were up in the rigging and a fresh breeze going out, just what we'd been waiting for, and the word was passed to take in sail and make everything fast. The men swore, and everybody said the cap'n had had some kind of a warning. But that night it began to blow, and I tell you afore morning we were glad enough we were in harbor. The old *Victor* she dragged her anchor, and the fore-to'-gallant sail and r'yal got loose somehow and was blown out of the bolt-ropes. Most of the canvas and rigging was old, but we had first-rate weather after that, and didn't bend near all the new sail we had aboard, though the cap'n was most afraid we'd come short when we left Boston.

"That was 'most sixty year ago," said the captain, reflectively. "How times does slip away! You young folks haven't any idea. She was a first-rate ship, the old *Victor* was, though I suppose she wouldn't cut much of a dash now 'longside of some of the new clippers.

"There used to be some strange-looking crafts in those days; there was the old brig *Hannah*. They used to say she would sail backwards as fast as forwards, and she was so square in the bows, they used to call her the sugar box. She was master old, the *Hannah* was, and there wasn't a port from here to New Orleans where she wasn't known; she used to carry a master cargo for her size, more than some ships that ranked two hundred and fifty ton, and she was put down for two hundred. She used to make good voyages, the *Hannah* did, and then there was the *Pactolus*; she was just about such another,—you would have laughed to see her. She sailed out of this port for a good many years. Cap'n Wall he told me that if he had her before the wind with a cargo of cotton, she would make a middling good run, but load her deep with salt, and you might as well try to sail a stick of oak timber with a handkerchief. She was a stout-built ship: I shouldn't wonder if her timbers were afloat somewhere yet; she was to some parties out in San Francisco.

"There! everything's changed from what it was when I used to follow the sea. I wonder sometimes if the sailors have as queer works aboard ship as they used. Bless ye! Deephaven used to be a different place to what it is now; there was hardly a day in the year that you didn't hear the shipwrights' hammers, and there was always something going on at the wharves. You would see the folks from up country comin' in with their loads of oak knees and plank, and logs o' rockmaple for keels when there was snow on the ground in wintertime, and the big sticks of timber pine for masts would come crawling along the road with their three and four yoke of oxen all frosted up, the sleds creaking and the snow growling and the men flapping their arms to keep warm, and hallooing as if there wan't nothin' else goin' on in the world except to get them masts to the shipyard. Bless ye! two o' them teams together would stretch from here 'most up to the Widow Jim's place,—no such timber pines nowadays."

"I suppose the sailors are very jolly together sometimes," said Kate, meditatively, with the least flicker of a smile at me. The captain did not answer for a minute, as he was battling with an obstinate snarl in his line; but when he had found the right loop he said, "I've had the best times and the hardest times of my life at sea, that's certain! I was just thinking it over when you spoke. I'll tell you some stories one day or 'nother that'll please you. Land! you've no idea what tricks some of those wild fellows will be up to. Now, saying they fetch home a cargo of wines and they want a drink; they've got a trick so they can get it. Saying it's champagne, they'll fetch up a basket, and how do you suppose they'll get into it?"

Of course we didn't know.

"Well, every basket will be counted, and they're fastened up particular, so they can tell in a minute if they've been tampered with; and neither must you draw the corks if you could get the basket open. I suppose ye may have seen champagne, how it's all wired and waxed. Now, they take a clean tub, them fellows do, and just shake the basket and jounce it up and down till they break the bottles and let the wine drain out; then they take it down in the hold and put it back with the rest, and when the cargo is delivered there's only one or two whole bottles in that basket, and there's a dreadful fuss about its being stowed so foolish." The captain told this with an air of great satisfaction, but we did not show the least suspicion that he might have assisted at some such festivity.

"Then they have a way of breaking into a cask. It won't do to start the bung, and it won't do to bore a hole where it can be seen, but they're up to that: they slip back one of the end hoops and bore two holes underneath it, one for the air to go in and one for the liquor to come out, and after they got all out they want they put in some spigots and cut them down close to the stave, knock back the hoop again, and there ye are, all trig."

"I never should have thought of it," said Kate, admiringly.

"There isn't nothing," Cap'n Sands went on, "that'll hender some masters from cheating the owners a little. Get them off in a foreign port, and there's nobody to watch, and they most of them have a feeling that they ain't getting full pay, and they'll charge things to the ship that she never seen nor heard of. There were two shipmasters that sailed out of Salem. I heard one of 'em tell the story. They had both come into port from Liverpool nigh the same time, and one of 'em, he was dressed up in a handsome suit of clothes, and the other looked kind of poverty struck. 'Where did you get them clothes?' says he. 'Why, to Liverpool,' says the other; 'you don't mean to say you come away without none, cheap as cloth was there?' 'Why, yes,' says the other cap'n, —'I can't afford to wear such clothes as those be, and I don't see how you can, either.' 'Charge 'em to the ship, bless ye; the owners expect it.'

"So the next v'y'ge the poor cap'n he had a nice rig for himself made to the best tailor's in Bristol, and charged it, say ten pounds, in the ship's account; and when he came home the ship's husband he was looking over the papers, and 'What's this?' says he, 'how come the ship to run up a tailor's bill?' 'Why, them's mine,' says the cap'n very meaching. 'I onderstood that there wouldn't be no objection made.' 'Well, you made a mistake,' says the other, laughing; 'guess I'd better scratch this out.' And it wasn't long before the cap'n met the one who had put him up to doing it, and he give him a blowing up for getting him into such a fix. 'Land sakes alive!' says he, 'were you fool enough to set it down in the account? Why, I put mine in, so many bolts of Russia duck.'"

Captain Sands seemed to enjoy this reminiscence, and to our satisfaction, in a few minutes, after he had offered to take the oars, he went on to tell us another story.

"Why, as for cheating, there's plenty of that all over the world. The first v'y'ge I went into Havana as master of the *Deerhound*, she had never been in the port before and had to be measured and recorded, and then pay her tonnage duties every time she went into port there afterward, according to what she was registered on the custom-house books. The inspector he come aboard, and he went below and looked round, and he measured her between decks; but he never offered to set down any figgers, and when we came back into the cabin, says he, 'Yes—yes—good ship! you put one doubloon front of this eye, *so!*' says he, 'an' I not see with him; and you put one more doubloon front of other eye, and how you think I see at all what figger you write?' So I took his book and I set down her measurements and made her out twenty ton short, and he took his doubloons and shoved 'em into his pocket. There, it isn't what you call straight dealing, but everybody done it that dared, and you'd eat up all the profits of a v'y'ge and the owners would just as soon you'd try a little up-country air, if you paid all those dues according to law. Tonnage was dreadful high and wharfage too, in some ports, and they'd get your last cent some way or 'nother if ye weren't sharp.

"Old Cap'n Carew, uncle to them ye see to meeting, did a smart thing in the time of the embargo. Folks got tired of it, and it was dreadful hard times; ships rotting at the wharves, and Deephaven never was quite the same afterward, though the old place held out for a good while before she let go as ye see her now. You'd 'a' had a hard grip on't when I was a young man to make me believe it would ever be so dull here. Well, Cap'n Carew he bought an old brig that was lying over by East Parish, and he began fitting her up and loading her for the West Indies, and the farmers they'd come in there by night from all round the country, to sell salt fish and lumber and potatoes, and glad enough they were, I tell ye. The rigging was put in order, and it wasn't long before she was ready to sail, and it was all kept mighty quiet. She lay up to an old wharf in a cove where she wouldn't be much noticed, and they took care not to paint her any or to attract any attention.

"One day Cap'n Carew was over in Riverport dining out with some gentlemen, and the revenue officer sat next to him, and by and by says he, 'Why won't ye take a ride with me this afternoon? I've had warning that there's a brig loading for the West Indies over beyond Deephaven somewheres, and I'm going over to seize her.' And he laughed to himself as if he expected fun, and something in his pocket beside. Well, the first minute that Cap'n Carew dared, after dinner he slipped out, and he hired the swiftest horse in Riverport and rode for dear life, and told the folks who were in the secret, and some who weren't, what was the matter, and every soul turned to and helped finish loading her and getting the rigging ready and the water aboard; but just as they were leaving the cove—the wind was blowing just right—along came the revenue officer with two or three men, and they come off in a boat and boarded her as important as could be.

"'Won't ye step into the cabin, gentlemen, and take a glass o' wine?' says Cap'n Carew, very polite; and the wind came in fresher,—something like a squall for a few minutes,—and the men had the sails spread before you could say Jack Robi'son, and before those fellows knew what they were about the old brig was a standing out to sea, and the folks on the wharves cheered and yelled. The Cap'n gave the officers a good scare and offered 'em a free passage to the West Indies, and finally they said they wouldn't report at headquarters if he'd let 'em go ashore; so he told the sailors to lower their boat about two miles off Deephaven, and they pulled ashore meek enough. Cap'n Carew had a first-rate run, and made a lot of money, so I have heard it said. Bless ye! every shipmaster would have done just the same if he had dared, and everybody was glad when they heard about it. Dreadful foolish piece of business that embargo was!

"Now I declare," said Captain Sands, after he had finished this narrative, "here I'm a telling stories and you're doin' all the work. You'll pull a boat ahead of anybody, if you keep on. Tom Kew was a-praisin' up both of you to me the other day: says he, 'They don't put on no airs, but I tell ye they can pull a boat well, and swim like fish,' says he. There now, if you'll give me the oars I'll put the dory just where I want her, and you can be getting your lines ready. I know a place here where it's always toler'ble fishing, and I guess we'll get something."

Kate and I cracked our clams on the gunwale of the boat, and cut them into nice little bits of bait with a piece of the shell, and by the time the captain had thrown out the killick we were ready to begin, and found the fishing much more exciting than it had been at the wharf.

"I don't know as I ever see 'em bite faster," said the old sailor, presently; "guess it's because they like the folks that's fishing. Well, I'm pleased. I thought I'd let 'Bijah take some along to Denby in the cart tomorrow if I got more than I could use at home. I didn't calc'late on having such a lively crew aboard. I s'pose ye wouldn't care about going out a little further by and by to see if we can't get two or three haddock?" And we answered that we should like nothing better.

It was growing cloudy, and was much cooler,—the perfection of a day for fishing,—and we sat there diligently pulling in cunners, and talking a little once in a while. The tide was nearly out, and Black Rock looked almost large enough to be called an island. The sea was smooth and the low waves broke lazily among the seaweed-covered ledges, while our boat swayed about on the water, lifting and falling gently as the waves went in shore. We were not a very long way from the lighthouse, and once we could see Mrs. Kew's big white apron as she stood in the doorway for a few minutes. There was no noise except the plash of the low-tide waves and the occasional flutter of a fish in the bottom of the dory. Kate and I always killed our fish at once by a rap on the head, for it certainly saved the poor creatures much discomfort, and ourselves as well, and it made it easier to take them off the hook than if they were flopping about and making us aware of our cruelty.

Suddenly the captain wound up his line and said he thought we'd better be going in, and Kate and I looked at him with surprise. "It is only half past ten," said I, looking at my watch. "Don't hurry in on our account," added Kate, persuasively, for we were having a very good time.

"I guess we won't mind about the haddock. I've got a feelin' we'd better go ashore." And he looked up into the sky and turned to see the west. "I knew there was something the matter; there's going to be a shower." And we looked behind us to see a bank of heavy clouds coming over fast. "I wish we had two pair of oars," said Captain Sands. "I'm afraid we shall get caught."

"You needn't mind us," said Kate. "We aren't in the least afraid of our clothes, and we don't get cold when we're wet; we have made sure of that."

"Well, I'm glad to hear that," said the cap'n. "Women folks are apt to be dreadful scared of a wetting; but I'd just as lief not get wet myself. I had a twinge of rheumatism yesterday. I guess we'll get ashore fast enough. No, I feel well enough today, but you can row if you want to, and I'll take the oars the last part of the way."

When we reached the moorings the clouds were black, and the thunder rattled and boomed over the sea, while heavy spatters of rain were already falling. We did not go to the wharves, but stopped down the shore at the fish houses, the nearer place of shelter. "You just select some of those cunners," said the captain, who was beginning to be a little out of breath, "and then you can run right up and get under cover, and I'll put a bit of old sail over the rest of the fish to keep the fresh water off." By the time the boat touched the shore and we had pulled it up on the pebbles, the rain had begun in good earnest. Luckily there was a barrow lying near, and we loaded that in a hurry, and just then the captain caught sight of a well-known red shirt in an open door, and shouted, "Halloa, Danny! lend us a hand with these fish, for we're nigh on to being shipwrecked." And then we ran up to the fish house and waited awhile, though we stood in the doorway watching the lightning, and there were so many leaks in the roof that we might almost as well have been out of doors. It was one of Danny's quietest days, and he silently beheaded hake, only winking at us once very gravely at something our other companion said.

"There!" said Captain Sands, "folks may say what they have a mind to; I didn't see that shower coming up, and I know as well as I want to that my wife did, and impressed it on my mind. Our house sets high, and she watches the sky and is al'ays a-worrying when I go out fishing for fear something's going to happen to me, 'specially sense I've got to be along in years."

This was just what Kate and I wished to hear, for we had been told that Captain Sands had most decided opinions on dreams and other mysteries, and could tell some stories which were considered incredible by even a Deephaven audience, to whom the marvellous was of everyday occurrence.

"Then it has happened before?" asked Kate. "I wondered why you started so suddenly to come in."

"Happened!" said the captain. "Bless ye, yes! I'll tell you my views about these p'ints one o' those days. I've thought a good deal about 'em by spells. Not that I can explain 'em, nor anybody else, but it's no use to laugh at 'em as some folks do. Cap'n Lant—you know Cap'n Lant?—he and I have talked it over consider'ble, and he says to me, 'Everybody's got some story of the kind they will believe in spite of everything, and yet they won't believe yourn.'"

The shower seemed to be over now, and we felt compelled to go home, as the captain did not go on with his remarks. I hope he did not see Danny's wink. Skipper Scudder, who was Danny's friend and partner, came up just then and asked us if we knew what the sign was when the sun came out through the rain. I said that I had always heard it would rain again next day. "O no," said Skipper Scudder, "the Devil is whipping his wife."

After dinner Kate and I went for a walk through some pine woods which were beautiful after the rain; the mosses and lichens which had been dried up were all freshened and bloom-

ing out in the dampness. The smell of the wet pitch pines was unusually sweet, and we wandered about for an hour or two there,
to find some ferns we wanted, and then walked over toward
East Parish, and home by the long beach late in the afternoon.
We came as far as the boat landing, meaning to go home through
the lane, but to our delight we saw Captain Sands sitting alone
on an old overturned whaleboat, whittling busily at a piece of
dried kelp. "Good evenin'," said our friend, cheerfully. And we
explained that we had taken a long walk and thought we would
rest awhile before we went home to supper. Kate perched herself
on the boat, and I sat down on a ship's knee which lay on the
pebbles.

"Didn't get any hurt from being out in the shower, I hope?"

"No, indeed," laughed Kate, "and we had such a good time.
I hope you won't mind taking us out again some time."

"Bless ye! no," said the captain. "My girl Lo'isa, she that's Mis
Winslow over to Riverport, used to go out with me a good deal,
and it seemed natural to have you aboard. I missed Lo'isa after
she got married, for she was al'ays ready to go anywhere 'long
of father. She's had slim health of late years. I tell 'em she's been
too much shut up out of the fresh air and sun. When she was
young her mother never could pr'vail on her to set in the house
stiddy and sew, and she used to have great misgivin's that Lo'isa
never was going to be capable. How about those fish you caught
this morning? good, were they? Mis Sands had dinner on the
stocks when I got home, and she said she wouldn't fry any 'til
supper time; but I calc'lated to have 'em this noon. I like 'em best
right out o' the water. Little more and we should have got them
wet. That's one of my whims; I can't bear to let fish get
rained on."

"O Captain Sands!" said I, there being a convenient pause,
"you were speaking of your wife just now; did you ask her if she
saw the shower?"

"First thing she spoke of when I got into the house. 'There,'
says she, 'I was afraid you wouldn't see the rain coming in time,
and I had my heart in my mouth when it began to thunder. I
thought you'd get soaked through, and be laid up for a fortnight,'
says she. 'I guess a summer shower won't hurt an old sailor like
me,' says I." And the captain reached for another piece of his
kelp-stalk, and whittled away more busily than ever. Kate took

out her knife and also began to cut kelp, and I threw pebbles in the hope of hitting a spider which sat complacently on a stone not far away, and when he suddenly vanished there was nothing for me to do but to whittle kelp also.

"Do you suppose," said Kate, "that Mrs. Sands really made you know about that shower?"

The captain put on his most serious look, coughed slowly, and moved himself a few inches nearer us, along the boat. I think he fully understood the importance and solemnity of the subject. "It ain't for us to say what we do know or don't, for there's nothing sartain, but I made up my mind long ago that there's something about these p'ints that's myster'ous. My wife and me will be sitting there to home and there won't be no word between us for an hour, and then of a sudden we'll speak up about the same thing. Now the way I view it, she either puts it into my head or I into hers. I've spoke up lots of times about something, when I didn't know what I was going to say when I began, and she'll say she was just thinking of that. Like as not you have noticed it sometimes? There was something my mind was dwellin' on yesterday, and she come right out with it, and I'd a good deal rather she hadn't," said the captain, ruefully. "I didn't want to rake it all over ag'in, I'm sure." And then he recollected himself, and was silent, which his audience must confess to have regretted for a moment.

"I used to think a good deal about such things when I was younger, and I'm free to say I took more stock in dreams and such like than I do now. I rec'lect old Parson Lorimer—this Parson Lorimer's father who was settled here first—spoke to me once about it, and said it was a tempting of Providence, and that we hadn't no right to pry into secrets. I know I had a dream book then that I picked up in a shop in Bristol once when I was in there on the *Ranger,* and all the young folks were beset to get sight of it. I see what fools it made of folks, bothering their heads about such things, and I pretty much let them go: all this stuff about spirit rappings is enough to make a man crazy. You don't get no good by it.

"I come across a paper once with a lot of letters in it from sperits, and I cast my eye over 'em, and I says to myself, 'Well, I always was given to understand that when we come to a futur' state we was goin' to have more wisdom than we can get afore';

but them letters hadn't any more sense to 'em, nor so much as a man could write here without schooling, and I should think that if the letters be all straight, if the folks who wrote 'em had any kind of ambition, they'd want to be movin' back here again. But as for one person's having something to do with another any distance off, why, that's another thing; there ain't any nonsense about that.

"I know it's true just as well as I want to," said the cap'n warming up. "I'll tell ye how I was led to make up my mind about it. One time I waked a man up out of a sound sleep looking at him, and it set me to thinking. First, there wasn't any noise, and then ag'in there wasn't any touch so he could feel it, and I says to myself, 'Why couldn't I ha' done it the width of two rooms as well as one, and why couldn't I ha' done it with my back turned?' It couldn't have been the looking so much as the thinking. And then I car'd it further, and I says 'Why ain't a mile as good as a yard? and it's the thinking that does it,' says I, 'and we've got some faculty or other that we don't know much about. We've got some way of sending our thought like a bullet goes out of a gun and it hits. We don't know nothing except what we see. And some folks is scared, and some more thinks it is all nonsense and laughs. But there's something we haven't got the hang of.'

"It makes me think o' them little black polliwogs that turns into frogs in the fresh-water puddles in the ma'sh. There's a time before their tails drop off and their legs have sprouted out, when they don't get any use o' their legs, and I dare say they're in their way consider'ble; but after they get to be frogs they find out what they're for without no kind of trouble. I guess we shall turn these fac'lties to account some time or 'nother. Seems to me, though, that we might depend on 'em now more than we do."

The captain was under full sail on what we had heard was his pet subject, and it was a great satisfaction to listen to what he had to say. It loses a great deal in being written, for the old sailor's voice and gestures and thorough earnestness all carried no little persuasion. And it was impossible not to be sure that he knew more than people usually do about these mysteries in which he delighted.

"Now, how can you account for this?" said he. "I remember not more than ten years ago my son's wife was stopping at our house, and she had left her child at home while she come away for a rest. And after she had been there two or three days, one morning she was sitting in the kitchen 'long o' the folks, and all of a sudden she jumped out of her chair and ran into the bedroom, and next minute she come out laughing, and looking kind of scared. 'I could ha' taken my oath,' says she, 'that I heard Katy cryin' out 'mother',' says she, 'just as if she was hurt. I heard it so plain that before I stopped to think it seemed as if she were right in the next room. I'm afeard something has happened.' But the folks laughed, and said she must ha' heard one of the lambs. 'No, it wasn't,' says she, 'it was Katy.' And sure enough, just after dinner a young man who lived neighbor to her come riding into the yard post-haste to get her to go home, for the baby had pulled some hot water over on to herself and was nigh scalded to death and cryin' for her mother every minute. Now, who's going to explain that? It wasn't any common hearing that heard that child's cryin' fifteen miles. And I can tell you another thing that happened among my own folks. There was an own cousin of mine married to a man by the name of John Hathorn. He was trading up to Parsonsfield, and business run down, so he wound up there, and thought he'd make a new start. He moved down to Denby, and while he was getting under way, he left his family up to the old place, and at the time I speak of, was going to move 'em down in about a fortnight.

"One morning his wife was fidgeting round, and finally she come downstairs with her bonnet and shawl on, and said somebody must put the horse right into the wagon and take her down to Denby. 'Why, what for, mother?' they says. 'Don't stop to talk,' says she; 'your father is sick, and wants me. It's been a worrying me since before day, and I can't stand it no longer.' And the short of the story is that she kept hurrying 'em faster and faster, and then she got hold of the reins herself, and when they got within five miles of the place the horse fell dead, and she was nigh about crazy, and they took another horse at a farmhouse on the road. It was the spring of the year, and the going was dreadful, and when they got to the house John Hathorn had just died, and he had been calling for his wife up to 'most the last breath he drew. He had been taken sick sudden the day before, but the folks knew it was bad travelling, and that she was a feeble woman to come near thirty miles, and they had no idee he was so bad off. I'm telling you the living truth," said Captain Sands, with an emphatic shake of his head. "There's more folks than me can tell about it, and if you were goin' to keel haul me next minute, and hang me to the yardarm afterward, I couldn't say it different. I was up to Parsonsfield to the funeral; it was just after I quit following the sea. I never saw a woman so broke down as she was. John was a nice man; stiddy and pleasant spoken and straightforward and kind to his folks. He belonged to the Odd Fellows, and they all marched to the funeral. There was a good deal of respect shown him, I tell ye.

"There is another story I'd like to have ye hear, if it's so that you ain't beat out hearing me talk. When I get going I slip along as easy as a schooner wing and wing afore the wind.

"This happened to my own father, but I never heard him say much about it; never could get him to talk it over to any length, best I could do. But gran'ther, his father, told me about it nigh upon fifty times, first and last, and always the same way. Gran'ther lived to be old, and there was ten or a dozen years after his wife died that he lived year and year about with Uncle Tobias's folks and our folks. Uncle Tobias lived over on the Ridge. I got home from my first v'y'ge as mate of the *Daylight* just in time for his funeral. I was disapp'inted to find the old man was gone. I'd fetched him some first-rate tobacco, for he was a great hand to smoke, and I was calc'latin' on his being pleased: old folks like to be thought of, and then he set more by me than by the other boys. I know I used to be sorry for him when I was a little fellow. My father's second wife she was a well-meaning woman, but an awful driver with her work, and she was always making of him feel he wasn't no use. I do' know as she meant to, either. He never said nothing, and he was always just so pleasant, and he was fond of his book, and used to set round reading, and tried to keep himself out of the way just as much as he could.

"There was one winter when I was small that I had the scarlet fever, and was very slim for a long time afterward, and I used to keep along o' gran'ther, and he would tell me stories. He'd been a sailor,—it runs in our blood to foller the sea,—and he'd been wrecked two or three times and been taken by the Algerine pirates. You remind me to tell you sometime about that; and I wonder if you ever heard about old Citizen Leigh, that used to be about here when I was a boy. He was taken by the Algerines once, same's gran'ther, and they was dreadful f'erce just then, and they sent him home to get the ransom money for the crew; but it was a monstrous price they asked, and the owners wouldn't give it to him, and they s'posed likely the men was dead by that time, anyway. Old Citizen Leigh he went crazy, and used to go about the streets with a bundle of papers in his hands year in and year out. I've seen him a good many times. Gran'ther used to tell me how he escaped. I'll remember it for ye some day if you'll put me in mind.

"I git to be mate when I was twenty, and I was as strong a fellow as you could scare up, and darin'!—why, it makes my blood run cold when I think of the reckless things I used to do. I was off at sea after I was fifteen year old, and there wasn't anybody so glad to see me as gran'ther when I came home. I expect he used to be lonesome after I went off, but then his mind failed him quite awhile before he died. Father was clever to him, and he'd get him anything he spoke about; but he wasn't a man to set round and talk, and he never took notice himself when gran'-ther was out of tobacco, so sometimes it would be a day or two. I know better how he used to feel now that I'm getting to be along in years myself, and likely to be some care to the folks before long. I never could bear to see old folks neglected; nice old men and women who have worked hard in their day and been useful and willin'. I've seen 'em many a time when they couldn't help knowing that the folks would a little rather they'd be in heaven, and a good respectable headstone put up for 'em in the burying ground.

"Well, now, I'm sure I've forgot what I was going to tell you. O, yes; about grandmother dreaming about father when he came home from sea. Well, to go back to the first of it, gran'ther never was rugged; he had ship fever when he was a young man, and though he lived to be so old, he never could work hard and never got forehanded; and Aunt Hannah Starbird over at East Parish took my sister to fetch up, because she was named for her, and Melinda and Tobias stayed at home with the old folks, and my father went to live with an uncle over in Riverport, whom he was named for. He was in the West India trade and was well off, and he had no children, so they expected he would do well by father. He was dreadful high tempered. I've heard say he had the worst temper that was ever raised in Deephaven.

"One day he set father to putting some cherries into a bar'l of rum, and went off down to his wharf to see to the loading of a vessel, and afore he come back father found he'd got hold of the wrong bar'l, and had sp'ilt a bar'l of the best Holland gin; he tried to get the cherries out, but that wasn't any use, and he was dreadful afraid of Uncle Matthew, and he run away, and never was heard of from that time out. They supposed he'd run away to sea, as he had a leaning that way, but nobody ever knew for certain; and his mother she 'most mourned herself to death. Gran'ther told me that it got so at last that if they could only know for sure that he was dead it was all they would ask. But it went on four years, and gran'ther got used to it some; though grandmother never would give up. And one morning early, before day, she waked him up, and says she, 'We're going to hear from Matthew. Get up quick and go down to the store!' 'Non-sense,' says he. 'I've seen him,' says grandmother, 'and he's coming home. He looks older, but just the same other ways, and he's got long hair, like a horse's mane, all down over his shoulders.' 'Well, let the dead rest,' says gran'ther; 'you've thought about the boy till your head is turned.' 'I tell you I saw Matthew himself,' says she, 'and I want you to go right down to see if there isn't a letter.'

"And she kept at him till he saddled the horse, and he got down to the store before it was opened in the morning, and he had to wait round, and when the man came over to unlock it he was 'most ashamed to tell what his errand was, for he had been so many times, and everybody supposed the boy was dead. When he asked for a letter, the man said there was none there, and asked if he was expecting any particular one. He didn't get many letters, I s'pose; all his folks lived about here, and people didn't write any to speak of in those days. Gran'ther said he thought he wouldn't make such a fool of himself again, but he didn't say anything, and he waited round awhile, talking to one and an-other who came up, and by and by says the storekeeper, who was reading a newspaper that had just come, 'Here's some news for you, Sands, I do believe! There are three vessels come into Boston harbor that have been out whaling and sealing in the South Seas for three or four years, and your son Matthew's name is down on the list of the crew.' 'I tell ye,' says gran'ther, 'I took that paper, and I got on my horse and put for home, and your grandmother she hailed me, and she said, 'You've heard, haven't you?' before I told her a word."

"Gran'ther he got his breakfast and started right off for Boston, and got there early the second day, and went right down on the wharves. Somebody lent him a boat, and he went out to where there were two sealers laying off riding at anchor, and he asked a sailor if Matthew was aboard. 'Ay, ay,' says the sailor, 'he's down below.' And he sung out for him, and when he come up out of the hold his hair was long, down over his shoulders like a horse's mane, just as his mother saw it in the dream. Gran'ther he didn't know what to say,—it scared him,—and he asked how it happened; and father told how they'd been off sealing in the South Seas, and he and another man had lived alone on an island for months, and the whole crew had grown wild in their ways of living, being off so long, and for one thing had gone without caps and let their hair grow. The rest of the men had been ashore and got fixed up smart, but he had been busy, and had put it off till that morning; he was just going ashore then.

"Father was all struck up when he heard about the dream, and said his mind had been dwellin' on his mother and going home, and he come down to let her see him just as he was and she said it was the same way he looked in the dream. He never would have his hair cut—father wouldn't—and wore it in a queue. I remember seeing him with it when I was a boy; but his second wife didn't like the looks of it, and she come up behind him one day and cut it off with the scissors. He was terrible worked up about it. I never see father so mad as he was that day. Now this is just as true as the Bible," said Captain Sands. "I haven't put a word to it, and gran'ther al'ays told a story just as it was. That woman saw her son; but if you ask me what kind of eyesight it was, I can't tell you, nor nobody else."

Later that evening Kate and I drifted into a long talk about the captain's stories and these mysterious powers of which we know so little. It was somewhat chilly in the house, and we had kindled a fire in the fireplace, which at first made a blaze which lighted the old room royally, and then quieted down into red coals and lazy puffs of smoke. We had carried the lights away, and sat with our feet on the fender, and Kate's great dog was lying between us on the rug. I remember that evening so well;

we could see the stars through the window plainer and plainer as the fire went down, and we could hear the noise of the sea.

"Do you remember in the old myth of Demeter and Persephone," Kate asked me, "where Demeter takes care of the child and gives it ambrosia and hides it in fire, because she loves it and wishes to make it immortal, and to give it eternal youth; and then the mother finds it out and cries in terror to hinder her, and the goddess angrily throws the child down and rushes away? And he had to share the common destiny of mankind, though he always had some wonderful inscrutable grace and wisdom, because a goddess had loved him and held him in her arms. I always thought that part of the story beautiful where Demeter throws off her disguise and is no longer an old woman, and the great house is filled with brightness like lightning, and she rushes out through the halls with her yellow hair waving over her shoulders, and the people would give anything to bring her back again, and to undo their mistake.

"I knew it almost all by heart once," said Kate, "and I am always finding a new meaning in it. I was just thinking that it may be that we all have given to us more or less of another nature, as the child had whom Demeter wished to make like the gods. I believe old Captain Sands is right, and we have these instincts which defy all our wisdom and for which we never can frame any laws. We may laugh at them, but we are always meeting them, and one cannot help knowing that it has been the same through all history. They are powers which are imperfectly developed in this life, but one cannot help the thought that the mystery of this world may be the commonplace of the next."

"I wonder," said I, "why it is that one hears so much more of such things from simple country people. They believe in dreams, and they have a kind of fetichism, and believe so heartily in supernatural causes. I suppose nothing could shake Mrs. Patton's faith in warnings. There is no end of absurdity in it, and yet there is one side of such lives for which one cannot help having reverence; they live so much nearer to nature than people who are in cities, and there is a soberness about country people oftentimes that one cannot help noticing.

"I wonder if they are unconsciously awed by the strength and purpose in the world about them, and the mysterious creative power which is at work with them on their familiar farms. In their simple life they take their instincts for truths, and perhaps they are not always so far wrong as we imagine. Because they are so instinctive and unreasoning, they may have a more complete sympathy with Nature, and may hear her voices when wiser ears are deaf. They have much in common, after all, with the plants which grow up out of the ground and the wild creatures which depend upon their instincts wholly."

"I think," said Kate, "that the more one lives out of doors the more personality there seems to be in what we call inanimate things. The strength of the hills and the voice of the waves are no longer only grand poetical sentences, but an expression of something real, and more and more one finds God himself in the world, and believes that we may read the thoughts that He writes for us in the book of Nature." And after this we were silent for a while, and in the meantime it grew very late, and we watched the fire until there were only a few sparks left in the ashes. The stars faded away and the moon came up out of the sea, and we barred the great hall door and went up stairs to bed. The lighthouse lamp burned steadily, and it was the only light that had not been blown out in all Deephaven.

Mrs. Bonny

I AM sure that Kate Lancaster and I must have spent by far the greater part of the summer out of doors. We often made long expeditions out into the suburbs of Deephaven, sometimes being gone all day, and sometimes taking a long afternoon stroll and coming home early in the evening hungry as hunters and laden with treasure, whether we had been through the pine woods inland or alongshore, whether we had met old friends or made some desirable new acquaintances. We had a fashion of calling at the farmhouses, and by the end of the season we knew as many people as if we had lived in Deephaven all our days. We used to ask for a drink of water; this was our unfailing introduction, and afterward there were many interesting subjects which one could introduce, and we could always give the latest news at the shore. It was amusing to see the curiosity which we aroused.

Many of the people came into Deephaven only on special occasions, and I must confess that at first we were often naughty enough to wait until we had been severely cross-questioned before we gave a definite account of ourselves. Kate was very clever at making unsatisfactory answers when she cared to do so. We did not understand, for some time, with what a keen sense of enjoyment many of those people made the acquaintance of an entirely new person who cordially gave the full particulars about herself; but we soon learned to call this by another name than impertinence.

I think there were no points of interest in that region which we did not visit with conscientious faithfulness. There were cliffs and pebble beaches, the long sands and the short sands; there were Black Rock and Roaring Rock, High Point and East Point, and Spouting Rock; we went to see where a ship had been driven ashore in the night, all hands being lost and not a piece of her left larger than an axe handle; we visited the spot where a ship had come ashore in the fog, and had been left high and dry on the edge of the marsh when the tide went out; we saw where the brig *Methuselah* had been wrecked, and the shore had been golden with her cargo of lemons and oranges, which one might carry away by the wherryful.

Inland there were not many noted localities, but we used to enjoy the woods, and our explorations among the farms, immensely. To the westward the land was better and the people well-to-do; but we went oftenest toward the hills and among the poorer people. The land was uneven and full of ledges, and the people worked hard for their living, at most laying aside only a few dollars each year. Some of the more enterprising young people went away to work in shops and factories; but the custom was by no means universal, and the people had a hungry, discouraged look. It is all very well to say that they knew nothing better, that it was the only life of which they knew anything; there was too often a look of disappointment in their faces, and sooner or later we heard or guessed many stories: that this young man had wished for an education, but there had been no money to spare for books or schooling; and that one had meant to learn a trade, but there must be some one to help his father with the farm work, and there was no money to hire a man to work in his place if he went away. The older people had a hard look, as if they had always to be on the alert and must fight for their place in the world. One could only forgive and pity their petty sharpness, which showed itself in trifling bargains, when one understood how much a single dollar seemed where dollars came so rarely. We used to pity the young girls so much. It was plain that those who knew how much easier and pleasanter our lives were could not help envying us.

There was a high hill half a dozen miles from Deephaven which was known in its region as "the mountain." It was the highest land anywhere near us, and having been told that there was a fine view from the top, one day we went there, with Tommy Dockum for escort. We overtook Mr. Lorimer, the minister, on his way to make parochial calls upon some members of his parish who lived far from church, and to our delight he proposed to go with us instead. It was a great satisfaction to have him for a guide, for he knew both the country and the people more intimately than anyone else.

It was a long climb to the top of the hill, but not a hard one.

The sky was clear, and there was a fresh wind, though we had left none at all at the sea level. After lunch, Kate and I spread our shawls over a fine cushion of mountain cranberry, and had a long talk with Mr. Lorimer about ancient and modern Deephaven. He always seemed as much pleased with our enthusiasm for the town as if it had been a personal favor and compliment to himself. I remember how far we could see, that day, and how we looked toward the far-away blue mountains, and then out over the ocean. Deephaven looked insignificant from that height and distance, and indeed the country seemed to be mostly covered with the pointed tops of pines and spruces, and there were long tracts of maple and beech woods with their coloring of lighter, fresher green.

"Suppose we go down, now," said Mr. Lorimer, long before Kate and I had meant to propose such a thing; and our feeling was that of dismay. "I should like to take you to make a call with me. Did you ever hear of old Mrs. Bonny?"

"No," said we, and cheerfully gathered our wraps and baskets; and when Tommy finally came panting up the hill after we had begun to think that our shoutings and whistling were useless, we sent him down to the horses, and went down ourselves by another path. It led us a long distance through a grove of young beeches; the last year's whitish leaves lay thick on the ground, and the new leaves made so close a roof overhead that the light was strangely purple, as if it had come through a great church window of stained glass. After this we went through some hemlock growth, where, on the lower branches, the pale green of the new shoots and the dark green of the old made an exquisite contrast each to the other. Finally we came out at Mrs. Bonny's.

Mr. Lorimer had told us something about her on the way down, saying in the first place that she was one of the queerest characters he knew. Her husband used to be a charcoal burner and basket maker, and she used to sell butter and berries and eggs, and chokepears preserved in molasses. She always came down to Deephaven on a little black horse, with her goods in baskets and bags which were fastened to the saddle in a mysterious way. She had the reputation of not being a neat housekeeper, and none of the wise women of the town would touch her butter especially, so it was always a joke when she coaxed a new resident or a strange shipmaster into buying her wares; but the old woman always managed to jog home without the freight she had brought.

"She must be very old, now," said Mr. Lorimer; "I have not seen her in a long time. It cannot be possible that her horse is still alive!" And we all laughed when we saw Mrs. Bonny's steed at a little distance, for the shaggy old creature was covered with mud, pine needles, and dead leaves, with half the last year's burdock burs in all Deephaven snarled into his mane and tail and sprinkled over his fur, which looked nearly as long as a buffalo's. He had hurt his leg, and his kind mistress had tied it up with a piece of faded red calico and an end of ragged rope. He gave us a civil neigh, and looked at us curiously. Then an impertinent little yellow-and-white dog, with one ear standing up straight and the other drooping over, began to bark with all his might; but he retreated when he saw Kate's great dog, who was walking solemnly by her side and did not deign to notice him.

Just now Mrs. Bonny appeared at the door of the house, shading her eyes with her hand, to see who was coming. "Landy!" said she, "if it ain't old Parson Lorimer! And who be these with ye?"

"This is Miss Kate Lancaster of Boston, Miss Katharine Brandon's niece, and her friend Miss Denis."

"Pleased to see ye," said the old woman; "walk in and lay off your things." And we followed her into the house. I wish you could have seen her: she wore a man's coat, cut off so that it made an odd short jacket, and a pair of men's boots much the worse for wear; also, some short skirts, beside two or three aprons, the inner one being a dress apron, as she took off the outer ones and threw them into a corner; and on her head was a tight cap, with strings to tie under her chin. I thought it was a nightcap, and that she had forgotten to take it off, and dreaded her mortification if she should suddenly become conscious of it; but I need not have troubled myself, for while we were with her she pulled it on and tied it tighter, as if she considered it ornamental.

There were only two rooms in the house; we went into the kitchen, which was occupied by a flock of hens and one turkey. The latter was evidently undergoing a course of medical treatment behind the stove, and was allowed to stay with us, while the hens were remorselessly hustled out with a hemlock broom. They all congregated on the doorstep, apparently wishing to hear everything that was said.

"Ben up on the mountain?" asked our hostess. "Real sightly place. Goin' to be a master lot o' rosbries; get any down to the shore sence I quit comin'?"

"O yes," said Mr. Lorimer, "but we miss seeing you."

"I s'pose so," said Mrs. Bonny, smoothing her apron complacently; "but I'm getting old, and I tell 'em I'm goin' to take my comfort; sence 'he' died, I don't put myself out no great; I've got money enough to keep me long's I live. Beckett's folks goes down often, and I sends by them for what store stuff I want."

"How are you now?" asked the minister; "I think I heard you were ill in the spring."

"Stirrin', I'm obliged to ye. I wasn't laid up long, and I was so's I could get about most of the time. I've got the best bitters ye ever see, good for the spring of the year. S'pose yer sister, Miss Lorimer, wouldn't like some? she used to be weakly lookin'." But her brother refused the offer, saying that she had not been so well for many years.

"Do you often get out to church nowadays, Mrs. Bonny? I believe Mr. Reid preaches in the schoolhouse sometimes, down by the great ledge; doesn't he?"

"Well, yes, he does; but I don't know as I get much of any good. Parson Reid, he's a worthy creatur', but he never seems to have nothin' to say about foreordination and them p'ints. Old Parson Padelford was the man! I used to set under his preachin' a good deal; I had an aunt living down to East Parish. He'd get worked up, and he'd shut up the Bible and preach the hair off your head, 'long at the end of the sermon. Couldn't understand more nor a quarter part what he said," said Mrs. Bonny, admiringly. "Well, we were a-speaking about the meeting over to the ledge; I don't know's I like them people any to speak of. They had a great revival over there in the fall, and one Sunday I thought's how I'd go; and when I got there, who should be a-prayin' but old Ben Patey,—he always lays out to get converted,—and he kep' it up diligent till I couldn't stand it no longer; and by and by says he, 'I've been a wanderer'; and I up and says, 'Yes, you have, I'll back ye up on that, Ben; ye've wan-

dered around my wood lot and spoilt half the likely young oaks
and ashes I've got, a-stealing your basket stuff.' And the folks
laughed out loud, and up he got and cleared. He's an awful old
thief, and he's no idea of being anything else. I wa'n't a-goin' to
set there and hear him makin' b'lieve to the Lord. If anybody's
heart is in it, I ain't a-goin' to hender 'em; I'm a professor, and I
ain't ashamed of it, weekdays nor Sundays neither. I can't bear
to see folks so pious to meeting, and cheat yer eyeteeth out Monday morning. Well, there! we ain't none of us perfect; even old
Parson Moody was round-shouldered, they say."

"You were speaking of the Becketts just now," said Mr. Lorimer
(after we had stopped laughing, and Mrs. Bonny had settled her
big steel-bowed spectacles, and sat looking at him with an expression of extreme wisdom. One might have ventured to call her
"peart," I think). "How do they get on? I am seldom in this region nowadays, since Mr. Reid has taken it under his charge."

"They get along, somehow or 'nother," replied Mrs. Bonny;
"they've got the best farm this side of the ledge, but they're
dreadful lazy and shiftless, them young folks. Old Mis' Hate-evil
Beckett was tellin' me the other day—she that was Samanthy
Barnes, you know—that one of the boys got fighting, the other
side of the mountain, and come home with his nose broke and a
piece o' one ear bit off. I forgot which ear it was. Their mother
is a real clever, willin' woman, and she takes it to heart, but it's
no use for her to say anything. Mis' Hate-evil Beckett, says she,
'It does make my man feel dreadful to see his brother's folks
carry on so.' 'But there,' says I, 'Mis' Beckett, it's just such things
as we read of; Scriptur' is fulfilled: In the larter days there shall
be disobedient children.'"

This application of the text was too much for us, but Mrs.
Bonny looked serious, and we did not like to laugh. Two or three
of the exiled fowls had crept slyly in, dodging underneath our
chairs, and had perched themselves behind the stove. They were
long-legged, half-grown creatures, and just at this minute one
rash young rooster made a manful attempt to crow. "Do tell!"
said his mistress, who rose in great wrath, "you needn't be so
forth-putting, as I knows on!" After this we were urged to stay
and have some supper. Mrs. Bonny assured us she could pick a
likely young hen in no time, fry her with a bit of pork, and get

us up "a good meat tea"; but we had to disappoint her, as we had some distance to walk to the house where we had left our horses, and a long drive home.

Kate asked if she would be kind enough to lend us a tumbler (for ours was in the basket, which was given into Tommy's charge). We were thirsty, and would like to go back to the spring and get some water.

"Yes, dear," said Mrs. Bonny, "I've got a glass, if it's so's I can find it." And she pulled a chair under the little cupboard over the fireplace, mounted it, and opened the door. Several things fell out at her, and after taking a careful survey she went in, head and shoulders, until I thought that she would disappear altogether; but soon she came back, and reaching in took one treasure after another, putting them on the mantelpiece or dropping them on the floor. There were some bunches of dried herbs, a tin horn, a lump of tallow in a broken plate, a newspaper, and an old boot, with a number of turkey wings tied together, several bottles, and a steel trap, and finally, such a tumbler! which she produced with triumph, before stepping down. She poured out of it on the table a mixture of old buttons and squash seeds, beside a lump of beeswax which she said she had lost, and now pocketed with satisfaction. She wiped the tumbler on her apron and handed it to Kate, but we were not so thirsty as we had been, though we thanked her and went down to the spring, coming back as soon as possible, for we could not lose a bit of the conversation.

There was a beautiful view from the doorstep, and we stopped a minute there. "Real sightly, ain't it?" said Mrs. Bonny. "But you ought to be here and look across the woods some morning just at sunup. Why, the sky is all yaller and red, and them low lands topped with fog! Yes, it's nice weather, good growin' weather, this week. Corn and all the rest of the trade looks first-rate. I call it a forrard season. It's just such weather as we read of, ain't it?"

"I don't remember where, just at this moment," said Mr. Lorimer.

"Why, in the almanac, bless ye!" said she, with a tone of pity in her grum voice; could it be possible he didn't know,—the Deephaven minister!

Deephaven

We asked her to come and see us. She said she had always thought she'd get a chance some time to see Miss Katharine Brandon's house. She should be pleased to call, and she didn't know but she should be down to the shore before very long. She was 'shamed to look so shif'less that day, but she had some good clothes in a chist in the bedroom, and a boughten bonnet with a good cypress veil, which she had when "he" died. She calculated they would do, though they might be old-fashioned, some. She seemed greatly pleased at Mr. Lorimer's having taken the trouble to come to see her. All those people had a great reverence for "the minister." We were urged to come again in "rosbry" time, which was near at hand, and she gave us messages for some of her old customers and acquaintances. "I believe some of those old creatur's will never die," said she; "why, they're getting to be ter'ble old, ain't they, Mr. Lorimer? There! ye've done me a sight of good, and I wish I could ha' found the Bible, to hear ye read a Psalm." When Mr. Lorimer shook hands with her, at leaving, she made him a most reverential courtesy. He was the greatest man she knew; and once during the call, when he was speaking of serious things in his simple, earnest way, she had so devout a look, and seemed so interested, that Kate and I, and Mr. Lorimer himself, caught a new, fresh meaning in the familiar words he spoke.

Living there in the lonely clearing, deep in the woods and far from any neighbor, she knew all the herbs and trees and the harmless wild creatures who lived among them, by heart; and she had an amazing store of tradition and superstition, which made her so entertaining to us that we went to see her many times before we came away in the autumn. We went with her to find some pitcher plants, one day, and it was wonderful how much she knew about the woods, what keen observation she had. There was something so wild and unconventional about Mrs. Bonny that it was like taking an afternoon walk with a good-natured Indian. We used to carry her offerings of tobacco, for she was a great smoker, and advised us to try it, if ever we should be troubled with nerves, or "narves," as she pronounced the name of that affliction.

In Shadow

SOON after we went to Deephaven we took a long drive one day with Mr. Dockum, the kindest and silentest of men. He had the care of the Brandon property, and had some business at that time connected with a large tract of pasture land perhaps ten miles from town. We had heard of the coast road which led to it, how rocky and how rough and wild it was, and when Kate heard by chance that Mr. Dockum meant to go that way, she asked if we might go with him. He said he would much rather take us than "go sole alone," but he should be away until late and we must take our dinner, which we did not mind doing at all.

After we were three or four miles from Deephaven, the country looked very different. The shore was so rocky that there were almost no places where a boat could put in, so there were no fishermen in the region, and the farms were scattered wide apart; the land was so poor that even the trees looked hungry. At the end of our drive we left the horse at a lonely little farmhouse close by the sea. Mr. Dockum was to walk a long way inland through the woods with a man whom he had come to meet, and he told us if we followed the shore westward a mile or two we should find some very high rocks, for which he knew we had a great liking.

It was a delightful day to spend out of doors; there was an occasional whiff of east wind. Seeing us seemed to be a perfect godsend to the people whose nearest neighbors lived far out of sight. We had a long talk with them before we went for our walk. The house was close by the water by a narrow cove, around which the rocks were low, but farther down the shore the land rose more and more, and at last we stood at the edge of the highest rocks of all and looked far down at the sea, dashing its white spray high over the ledges that quiet day. What could it be in winter when there was a storm and the great waves came thundering in?

Deephaven

After we had explored the shore to our hearts' content and were tired, we rested for a while in the shadow of some gnarled pitch pines which stood close together, as near the sea as they dared. They looked like a band of outlaws; they were such wild-looking trees. They seemed very old, and as if their savage fights with the winter winds had made them hard-hearted. And yet the little wild-flowers and the thin green grass blades were growing fearlessly close around their feet; and there were some comfortable birds nests in safe corners of their rough branches.

When we went back to the house at the cove we had to wait some time for Mr. Dockum. We succeeded in making friends with the children, and gave them some candy and the rest of our lunch, which luckily had been even more abundant than usual. They looked thin and pitiful, but even in that lonely place, where they so seldom saw a stranger or even a neighbor, they showed that there was an evident effort to make them look like other children, and they were neatly dressed, though there could be no mistake about their being very poor. One forlorn little soul, with honest gray eyes and a sweet, shy smile, showed us a string of beads which she wore round her neck; there were perhaps two dozen of them, blue and white, on a bit of twine, and they were the dearest things in all her world. When we came away we were so glad that we could give the man more than he asked us for taking care of the horse, and his thanks touched us.

"I hope ye may never know what it is to earn every dollar as hard as I have. I never earned any money as easy as this before. I don't feel as if I ought to take it. I've done the best I could," said the man, with the tears coming into his eyes, and a huskiness in his voice. "I've done the best I could, and I'm willin' and my woman is, but everything seems to have been ag'in' us; we never seem to get forehanded. It looks sometimes as if the Lord had forgot us, but my woman she never wants me to say that; she says He ain't, and that we might be worse off,—but I don't know. I haven't had my health; that's hendered me most. I'm a boat-builder by trade, but the business's all run down; folks buys 'em second-hand nowadays, and you can't make nothing. I can't stand it to foller deep-sea fishing, and—well, you see what my land's wuth. But my oldest boy, he's getting ahead. He pushed off this spring, and he works in a box shop to Boston; a cousin o' his mother's got him the chance. He sent me ten dollars a spell ago and his mother a shawl. I don't see how he done it, but he's smart!"

This seemed to be the only bright spot in their lives, and we admired the shawl and sat down in the house awhile with the mother, who seemed kind and patient and tired, and to have great delight in talking about what one should wear. Kate and I thought and spoke often of these people afterward, and when one day we met the man in Deephaven we sent some things to the children and his wife, and begged him to come to the house whenever he came to town; but we never saw him again, and though we made many plans for going again to the cove, we never did. At one time the road was reported impassable, and we put off our second excursion for this reason and others until just before we left Deephaven, late in October.

We knew the coast road would be bad after the fall rains, and we found that Leander, the eldest of the Dockum boys, had some errand that way, so he went with us. We enjoyed the drive that morning in spite of the rough road. The air was warm, and sweet with the smell of bayberry bushes and pitch pines and the delicious saltness of the sea, which was not far from us all the way. It was a perfect autumn day. Sometimes we crossed pebble beaches, and then went farther inland, through woods and up and down steep little hills; over shaky bridges which crossed narrow salt creeks in the marsh lands. There was a little excitement about the drive, and an exhilaration in the air, and we laughed at jokes forgotten the next minute, and sang, and were jolly enough.

Leander, who had never happened to see us in exactly this hilarious state of mind before, seemed surprised and interested, and became unusually talkative, telling us a great many edifying particulars about the people whose houses we passed, and who owned every wood lot along the road. "Do you see that house over on the p'int?" he asked. "An old fellow lives there that's part lost his mind. He had a son who was drowned off Cod Rock fishing, much as twenty-five years ago, and he's worn a deep path out to the end of the pi'nt where he goes out every hand's turn o' the day to see if he can't see the boat coming in." And Leander looked round to see if we were not amused, and seemed puzzled because we didn't laugh. Happily, his next story was funny.

We saw a sleepy little owl on the dead branch of a pine tree; we saw a rabbit cross the road and disappear in a clump of juniper, and squirrels run up and down trees and along the stone walls with acorns in their mouths. We passed straggling thickets of the upland sumach, leafless, and holding high their ungainly spikes of red berries; there were sturdy barberry bushes along the lonely wayside, their unpicked fruit hanging in brilliant clusters. The blueberry bushes made patches of dull red along the hillsides. The ferns were whitish gray and brown at the edges of the woods, and the asters and goldenrods which had lately looked so gay in the open fields stood now in faded, frost-bitten companies. There were busy flocks of birds flitting from field to field, ready to start on their journey southward.

When we reached the house, to our surprise there was no one in sight and the place looked deserted. We left the wagon, and while Leander went toward the barn, which stood at a little distance, Kate and I went to the house and knocked. I opened the door a little way and said "Hallo!" but nobody answered. The people could not have moved away, for there were some chairs standing outside the door, and as I looked in I saw the bunches of herbs hanging up, and a trace of corn, and the furniture was all there. It was a great disappointment, for we had counted upon seeing the children again. Leander said there was nobody at the barn, and that they must have gone to a funeral; he couldn't think of anything else.

Just now we saw some people coming up the road, and we thought at first that they were the man and his wife coming back; but they proved to be strangers, and we eagerly asked what had become of the family.

"They're dead, both on 'em. His wife she died about nine weeks ago last Sunday, and he died day before yesterday. Funeral's going to be this afternoon. Thought ye were some of her folks from up country, when we were coming along," said the man.

"Guess they won't come nigh," said the woman, scornfully; "'fraid they'd have to help provide for the children. I was half-sister to him, and I've got to take the two least ones."

"Did you say he was going to be buried this afternoon?" asked Kate, slowly. We were both more startled than I can tell.

"Yes," said the man, who seemed much better-natured than his wife. She appeared like a person whose only aim in life was to have things over with. "Yes, we're going to bury at two o'clock. They had a master sight of trouble, first and last."

Leander had said nothing all this time. He had known the man, and had expected to spend the day with him and to get him to go on two miles farther to help bargain for a dory. He asked, in a disappointed way, what had carried him off so sudden.

"Drink," said the woman, relentlessly. "He ain't been good for nothing sence his wife died: she was took with a fever along in the first of August. I'd ha' got up from it!"

"Now don't be hard on the dead, Marthy," said her husband. "I guess they done the best they could. They weren't shif'less, you know; they never had no health; 'twas against wind and tide with 'em all the time." And Kate asked, "Did you say he was your brother?"

"Yes. I was half-sister to him," said the woman, promptly, with perfect unconsciousness of Kate's meaning.

"And what will become of those poor children?"

"I've got the two youngest over to my place to take care on, and the two next them has been put out to some folks over to the cove. I dare say like's not they'll be sent back."

"They're clever child'n, I guess," said the man, who spoke as if this were the first time he had dared take their part. "Don't be ha'sh, Marthy! Who knows but they may do for us when we get to be old?" And then she turned and looked at him with utter contempt. "I can't stand it to hear men folks talking on what they don't know nothing about," said she. "The ways of Providence is dreadful myster'ous," she went on with a whine, instead of the sharp tone of voice which we had heard before. "We've had a hard row, and we've just got our own children off our hands and able to do for themselves, and now here are these to be fetched up."

"But perhaps they'll be a help to you; they seem to be good little things," said Kate. "I saw them in the summer, and they seemed to be pleasant children, and it is dreadfully hard for them to be left alone. It's not their fault, you know. We brought over something for them; will you be kind enough to take the basket when you go home?"

"Thank ye, I'm sure," said the aunt, relenting slightly. "You can speak to my man about it, and he'll give it to somebody that's going by. I've got to walk in the procession. They'll be obliged, I'm sure. I s'pose you're the young ladies that come here right after the Fourth o' July, ain't you? I should be pleased to have you call and see the child'n if you're over this way again. I heard 'em talk about you last time I was over. Won't ye step into the house and see him? He looks real natural," she added. But we said, "No, thank you."

Leander told us he believed he wouldn't bother about the dory that day, and he should be there at the house whenever we were ready. He evidently considered it a piece of good luck that he had happened to arrive in time for the funeral. We spoke to the man about the things we had brought for the children, which seemed to delight him, poor soul, and we felt sure he would be kind to them. His wife shouted to him from a window of the house that he'd better not loiter round, or they wouldn't be half ready when the folks began to come, and we said good-by to him and went away.

It was a beautiful morning, and we walked slowly along the shore to the high rocks and the pitch pine trees which we had seen before; the air was deliciously fresh, and one could take long deep breaths of it. The tide was coming in, and the spray dashed higher and higher. We climbed about the rocks and went down in some of the deep cold clefts into which the sun could seldom shine. We gathered some wild flowers; bits of pimpernel and one or two sprigs of fringed gentian which had bloomed late in a sheltered place, and a pale little bouquet of asters. We sat for a long time looking off to sea, and we could talk or think of almost nothing beside what we had seen and heard at the farmhouse. We said how much we should like to go to that funeral, and we even made up our minds to go back in season, but we gave up the idea: we had no right there, and it would seem as if we were merely curious, and we were afraid our presence would make the people ill at ease, the minister especially. It would be an intrusion.

We spoke of the children, and tried to think what could be done for them: we were afraid they would be told so many times that it was lucky they did not have to go to the poorhouse, and yet we could not help pitying the hard-worked, discouraged woman whom we had seen, in spite of her bitterness. Poor soul! she looked like a person to whom nobody had ever been very kind, and for whom life had no pleasures: its sunshine had never been warm enough to thaw the ice at her heart.

We remembered how we knocked at the door and called loudly, but there had been no answer, and we wondered how we should have felt if we had gone farther into the room and had found the dead man in his coffin, all alone in the house. We thought of our first visit, and what he had said to us, and we wished we had come again sooner, for we might have helped them so much more if we had only known.

"What a pitiful ending it is," said Kate. "Do you realize that the family is broken up, and the children are to be half strangers to each other? Did you not notice that they seemed very fond of each other when we saw them in the summer? There was not half the roughness and apparent carelessness of one another which one so often sees in the country. Theirs was such a little world; one can understand how, when the man's wife died, he was bewildered and discouraged, utterly at a loss. The thoughts of winter, and of the little children, and of the struggles he had already come through against poverty and disappointment were terrible thoughts; and like a boat adrift at sea, the waves of his misery brought him in against the rocks, and his simple life was wrecked."

"I suppose his grandest hopes and wishes would have been realized in a good farm and a thousand or two dollars in safe keeping," said I. "Do you remember that merry little song in *As You Like It*?

> 'Who doth ambition shun
> And loves to live i' the sun,
>   Seeking the food he eats,
>   And pleased with what he gets';

and

> 'Here shall he see
>   No enemy
> But winter and rough weather.'

That is all he lived for, his literal daily bread. I suppose what would be prosperity to him would be miserably insufficient for some other people. I wonder how we can help being conscious, in the midst of our comforts and pleasures, of the lives which are being starved to death in more ways than one."

"I suppose one thinks more about these things as one grows

older," said Kate, thoughtfully. "How seldom life in this world seems to be a success! Among rich or poor only here and there one touches satisfaction, though the one who seems to have made an utter failure may really be the greater conqueror. And, Helen, I find that I understand better and better how unsatisfactory, how purposeless and disastrous, any life must be which is not a Christian life? It is like being always in the dark, and wandering one knows not where, if one is not learning more and more what it is to have a friendship with God."

By the middle of the afternoon the sky had grown cloudy, and a wind seemed to be coming in off the sea, and we unwillingly decided that we must go home. We supposed that the funeral would be all over with, but found we had been mistaken when we reached the cove. We seated ourselves on a rock near the water; just beside us was the old boat, with its killick and painter stretched ashore, where its owner had left it.

There were several men standing around the door of the house, looking solemn and important, and by and by one of them came over to us, and we found out a little more of the sad story. We liked this man, there was so much pity in his face and voice. "He was a real willin', honest man, Andrew was," said our new friend, "but he used to be sickly, and seemed to have no luck, though for a year or two he got along some better. When his wife died, he was sore afflicted, and couldn't get over it, and he didn't know what to do or what was going to become of 'em with winter comin' on, and—well—I may's well tell ye; he took to drink and it killed him right off. I come over two or three times and made some gruel and fixed him up's well's I could, and the little gals done the best they could, but he faded right out, and didn't know anything the last time I see him, and he died Sunday mornin', when the tide begun to ebb. I always set a good deal by Andrew; we used to play together down to the great cove; that's where he was raised, and my folks lived there too. I've got one o' the little gals. I always knowed him and his wife."

Just now we heard the people in the house singing "China," the Deephaven funeral hymn, and the tune suited well that day, with its wailing rise and fall; it was strangely plaintive. Then the funeral exercises were over, and the man with whom we had just been speaking led to the door a horse and rickety wagon, from which the seat had been taken, and when the coffin had been put in he led the horse down the road a little way, and we watched the mourners come out of the house two by two. We heard someone scold in a whisper because the wagon was twice as far off as it need have been. They evidently had a rigid funeral etiquette, and felt it important that everything should be carried out according to rule.

We saw a forlorn-looking kitten, with a bit of faded braid round its neck, run across the road in terror and presently appear again on the stonewall, where she sat looking at the people. We saw the dead man's eldest son, of whom he had told us in the summer with such pride. He had shown his respect for his father as best he could, by a black band on his hat and a pair of black cotton gloves a world too large for him. He looked so sad, and cried bitterly as he stood alone at the head of the people. His aunt was next, with a handkerchief at her eyes, fully equal to the proprieties of the occasion, though I fear her grief was not so heartfelt as her husband's, who dried his eyes on his coat sleeve again and again. There were perhaps twenty of the mourners, and there was much whispering among those who walked last. The minister and some others fell into line, and the procession went slowly down the slope; a strange shadow had fallen over everything.

It was like a November day, for the air felt cold and bleak. There were some great sea fowl high in the air, fighting their way toward the sea against the wind, and giving now and then a wild, far-off ringing cry. We could hear the dull sound of the sea, and at a little distance from the land the waves were leaping high, and breaking in white foam over the isolated ledges.

The rest of the people began to walk or drive away, but Kate and I stood watching the funeral as it crept along the narrow, crooked road. We had never seen what the people called "walking funerals" until we came to Deephaven, and there was something piteous about this; the mourners looked so few, and we could hear the rattle of the wagon wheels. "He's gone, ain't he?" said some one near us. That was it,—*gone*.

Before the people had entered the house, there had been, I am sure, an indifferent, business-like look, but when they came out, all that was changed; their faces were awed by the presence of death, and the indifference had given place to uncertainty. Their neighbor was immeasurably their superior now. Living, he had been a failure by their own low standards; but now, if he could come back, he would know secrets, and be wise beyond anything they could imagine, and who could know the riches of which he might have come into possession?

To Kate and me there came a sudden consciousness of the mystery and inevitableness of death; it was not fear, thank God! but a thought of how certain it was that some day it would be a mystery to us no longer. And there was a thought, too, of the limitation of this present life; we were waiting there, in company with the people, the great sea, and the rocks and fields themselves, on this side the boundary. We knew just then how close to this familiar, everyday world might be the other, which at times before had seemed so far away, out of reach of even our thoughts, beyond the distant stars.

We stayed awhile longer, until the little black funeral had crawled out of sight; until we had seen the last funeral guest go away and the door had been shut and fastened with a queer old padlock and some links of rusty chain. The door fitted loosely, and the man gave it a vindictive shake, as if he thought that the poor house had somehow been to blame, and that after a long desperate struggle for life under its roof and among the stony fields the family must go away defeated. It is not likely that any one else will ever go to live there. The man to whom the farm was mortgaged will add the few forlorn acres to his pasture land, and the thistles which the man who is dead had fought so many years will march in next summer and take unmolested possession.

I think today of that fireless, empty, forsaken house, where the winter sun shines in and creeps slowly along the floor; the bitter cold is in and around the house, and the snow has sifted in at every crack; outside it is untrodden by any living creature's footstep. The wind blows and rushes and shakes the loose window sashes in their frames, while the padlock knocks—knocks against the door.

Miss Chauncey

THE Deephaven people used to say sometimes complacently, that certain things or certain people were "as dull as East Parish." Kate and I grew curious to see that part of the world which was considered duller than Deephaven itself; and as upon inquiry we found that it was not out of reach, one day we went there.

It was like Deephaven, only on a smaller scale. The village—though it is a question whether that is not an exaggerated term to apply—had evidently seen better days. It was on the bank of a river, and perhaps half a mile from the sea. There were a few old buildings there, some with mossy roofs and a great deal of yellow lichen on the sides of the walls next the sea; a few newer houses, belonging to fishermen; some dilapidated fish houses; and a row of fish flakes. Every house seemed to have a lane of its own, and all faced different ways except two fish houses, which stood amiably side by side. There was a church, which we had been told was the oldest in the region. Through the windows we saw the high pulpit and sounding board, and finally found the keys at a house near by; so we went in and looked around at our leisure. A rusty foot stove stood in one of the old square pews, and in the gallery there was a majestic bass viol with all its strings snapped but the largest, which gave out a doleful sound when we touched it.

After we left the church we walked along the road a little way, and came in sight of a fine old house which had apparently fallen into ruin years before. The front entrance was a fine specimen of old-fashioned workmanship, with its columns and carvings, and the fence had been a grand affair in its day, though now it could scarcely stand alone. The long range of outbuildings were falling piece by piece; one shed had been blown down entirely by a late high wind. The large windows had many panes of glass, and the great chimneys were built of the bright red bricks which used to be brought from overseas in the days of the colonies. We noticed the gnarled lilacs in the yard, the wrinkled cinnamon roses, and a flourishing company of French pinks, or "bouncing Bets," as Kate called them.

"Suppose we go in," said I; "the door is open a little way. There surely must be some stories about its being haunted. We will ask Miss Honora." And we climbed over the boards which were put up like pasture bars across the wide front gateway.

"We shall certainly meet a ghost," said Kate.

Just as we stood on the steps the door was pulled wide open; we started back, and, well-grown young women as we are, we have confessed since that our first impulses was to run away. On the threshold there stood a stately old woman who looked surprised at first sight of us, then quickly recovered herself and stood waiting for us to speak. She was dressed in a rusty black satin gown, with scant, short skirt and huge sleeves; on her head was a great black bonnet with a high crown and a close brim, which came far out over her face. "What is your pleasure?" said she; and we felt like two awkward children. Kate partially recóvered her wits, and asked which was the nearer way to Deephaven.

"There is but one road, past the church and over the hill. It cannot be missed." And she bowed gravely, when we thanked her and begged her pardon, we hardly knew why, and came away.

We looked back to see her still standing in the doorway. "Who in the world can she be?" said Kate. And we wondered and puzzled and talked over "the ghost" until we saw Miss Honora Carew, who told us that it was Miss Sally Chauncey.

"Indeed, I know her, poor old soul!" said Miss Honora; "she has such a sad history. She is the last survivor of one of the most aristocratic old colonial families. The Chaunceys were of great renown until early in the present century, and then their fortunes changed. They had always been rich and well educated, and I suppose nobody ever had a gayer, happier time than Miss Sally did in her girlhood, for they entertained a great deal of company and lived in fine style; but her father was unfortunate in business, and at last was utterly ruined at the time of the embargo; then he became partially insane, and died after many years of poverty. I have often heard a tradition that a sailor to whom he had broken a promise had cursed him, and that none of the family had died in their beds or had any good luck since. The East

Parish people seem to believe in it, and it is certainly strange what terrible sorrow has come to the Chaunceys. One of Miss Sally's brothers, a fine young officer in the navy, who was at home on leave, asked her one day if she could get on without him, and she said yes, thinking he meant to go back to sea; but in a few minutes she heard the noise of a pistol in his room, and hurried in to find him lying dead on the floor. Then there was another brother who was insane, and who became so violent that he was chained for years in one of the upper chambers, a dangerous prisoner. I have heard his horrid cries myself, when I was a young girl," said Miss Honora, with a shiver.

"Miss Sally is insane, and has been for many years, and this seems to me the saddest part of the story. When she first lost her reason, she was sent to a hospital, for there was no one who could take care of her. The mania was so acute that no one had the slightest thought that she would recover or even live long. Her guardian sold the furniture and pictures and china, almost everything but clothing, to pay the bills at the hospital, until the house was fairly empty; and then one spring day, I remember it well, she came home in her right mind, and, without a thought of what was awaiting her, ran eagerly into her home. It was a terrible shock, and she never has recovered from it, though after a long illness her insanity took a mild form, and she has always been perfectly harmless. She has been alone many years, and no one can persuade her to leave the old house, where she seems to be contented, and does not realize her troubles; though she lives mostly in the past, and has little idea of the present, except in her house affairs, which seem pitiful to me, for I remember the housekeeping of the Chaunceys when I was a child.

"I have always been to see her, and she usually knows me, though I have been but seldom of late years. She is several years older than I. The town makes her an allowance every year, and she has some friends who take care that she does not suffer, though her wants are few. She is an elegant woman still, and some day, if you like, I will give you something to carry to her, and a message, if I can think of one, and you must go to make her a call. I hope she will happen to be talkative, for I am sure you would enjoy her. For many years she did not like to see strangers, but some one has told me lately that she seems to be pleased if people go to see her."

Deephaven

You may be sure it was not many days before Kate and I claimed the basket and the message, and went again to East Parish. We boldly lifted the great brass knocker, and were dismayed because nobody answered. While we waited, a girl came up the walk and said that Miss Sally lived upstairs, and she would speak to her if we liked. "Sometimes she don't have sense enough to know what the knocker means," we were told. There was evidently no romance about Miss Sally to our new acquaintance.

"Do you think," said I, "that we might go in and look around the lower rooms? Perhaps she will refuse to see us."

"Yes, indeed," said the girl; "only run the minute I speak; you'll have time enough, for she walks slow and is a little deaf."

So we went into the great hall with its wide staircase and handsome cornices and panelling, and then into the large parlor on the right, and through it to a smaller room looking out on the garden, which sloped down to the river. Both rooms had fine carved mantels, with Dutch-tiled fireplaces, and in the cornices we saw the fastenings where pictures had hung,—old portraits, perhaps. And what had become of them? The girl did not know: the house had been the same ever since she could remember, only it would all fall through into the cellar soon. But the old lady was proud as Lucifer, and wouldn't hear of moving out.

The floor in the room toward the river was so broken that it was not safe, and we came back through the hall and opened the door at the foot of the stairs. "Guess you won't want to stop long there," said the girl. Three old hens and a rooster marched toward us with great solemnity when we looked in. The cobwebs hung in the room, as they often do in old barns, in long, gray festoons; the lilacs outside grew close against the two windows where the shutters were not drawn, and the light in the room was greenish and dim.

Then we took our places on the threshold, and the girl went up stairs and announced us to Miss Sally, and in a few minutes we heard her come along the hall.

"Sophia," said she, "where are the gentry waiting?" And just then she came in sight round the turn of the staircase. She wore the same great black bonnet and satin gown, and looked more old-fashioned and ghostly than before. She was not tall, but very erect, in spite of her great age, and her eyes seemed to "look through you" in an uncanny way. She slowly descended the stairs and came toward us with a courteous greeting, and when we had introduced ourselves as Miss Carew's friends she gave us each her hand in a most cordial way and said she was pleased to see us. She bowed us into the parlor and brought us two rickety, straight-backed chairs, which, with an old table, were all the furniture there was in the room. "Sit ye down," said she, herself taking a place in the window seat.

I have seen few more elegant women than Miss Chauncey. Thoroughly at her ease, she had the manner of a lady of the olden times, using the quaint fashion of speech which she had been taught in her girlhood. The long words and ceremonious phrases suited her extremely well. Her hands were delicately shaped, and she folded them in her lap, as no doubt she had learned to do at boarding school so many years before. She asked Kate and me if we knew any young ladies at that school in Boston, saying that most of her intimate friends had left when she did, but some of the younger ones were there still.

She asked for the Carews and Mr. Lorimer, and when Kate told her that she was Miss Brandon's niece, and asked if she had not known her, she said, "Certainly, my dear; we were intimate friends at one time, but I have seen her little of late."

"Do you not know that she is dead?" asked Kate.

"Ah, they say every one is 'dead,' nowadays. I do not comprehend the silly idea!" said the old lady, impatiently. "It is an excuse, I suppose. She could come to see me if she chose, but she was always a ceremonious body, and I go abroad but seldom now; so perhaps she waits my visit. I will not speak uncourteously, and you must remember me to her kindly."

Then she asked us about other old people in Deephaven, and about families in Boston whom she had known in her early days. I think every one of whom she spoke was dead, but we assured her that they were all well and prosperous, and we hoped we told the truth. She asked about the love affairs of men and women who had died old and gray-headed within our remembrance; and finally she said we must pardon her for these tiresome questions, but it was so rarely she saw any one direct from Boston, of whom she could inquire concerning these old friends and relatives of her family.

Something happened after this which touched us both inexpressibly: she sat for some time watching Kate with a bewildered look, which at last faded away, a smile coming in its place. "I think you are like my mother," she said; "did any one ever say to you that you are like my mother? Will you let me see your forehead? Yes; and your hair is only a little darker." Kate had risen when Miss Chauncey did, and they stood side by side. There was a tone in the old lady's voice which brought the tears to my eyes. She stood there some minutes looking at Kate. I wonder what her thoughts were. There was a kinship, it seemed to me, not of blood, only that they both were of the same stamp and rank: Miss Chauncey of the old generation and Kate Lancaster of the new. Miss Chauncey turned to me, saying, "Look up at the portrait and you will see the likeness too, I think." But when she turned and saw the bare wainscoting of the room, she looked puzzled, and the bright flash which had lighted up her face was gone in an instant, and she sat down again in the window seat; but we were glad that she had forgotten. Presently she said, "Pardon me, but I forget your question."

Miss Carew had told us to ask her about her schooldays, as she nearly always spoke of that time to her; and, to our delight, Miss Sally told us a long story about her friends and about her "coming-out party," when boatloads of gay young guests came down from Riverport, and all the gentry from Deephaven. The band from the fort played for the dancing, the garden was lighted, the card tables were in this room, and a grand supper was served. She also remembered what some of her friends wore, and her own dress was a silver-gray brocade with rosebuds of three colors. She told us how she watched the boats go off up river in the middle of the summer night; how sweet the music sounded; how bright the moonlight was; how she wished we had been there at her party.

"I can't believe I am an old woman. It seems only yesterday," said she, thoughtfully. And then she lost the idea, and talked about Kate's great-grandmother, whom she had known, and asked us how she had been this summer.

She asked us if we would like to go upstairs where she had a fire, and we eagerly accepted, though we were not in the least cold. Ah, what a sorry place it was! She had gathered together some few pieces of her old furniture, which half filled one fine room, and here she lived. There was a tall, handsome chest of

drawers, which I should have liked much to ransack. Miss Carew
had told us that Miss Chauncey had large claims against the
government, dating back sixty or seventy years, but nobody
could ever find the papers; and I felt sure that they must be
hidden away in some secret drawer. The brass handles and
trimmings were blackened, and the wood looked like ebony. I
wanted to climb up and look into the upper part of this antique
piece of furniture, and it seemed to me I could at once put my
hand on a package of "papers relating to the embargo."

On a stand near the window was an old Bible, fairly worn out
with constant use. Miss Chauncey was religious; in fact, it was
the only subject about which she was perfectly sane. We saw
almost nothing of her insanity that day, though afterward she
was different. There were days when her mind seemed clear;
but sometimes she was silent, and often she would confuse Kate
with Miss Brandon, and talk to her of long-forgotten plans and
people. She would rarely speak of anything more than a minute
or two, and then would drift into an entirely foreign subject.

She urged us that afternoon to stay to luncheon with her; she
said she could not offer us dinner, but she would give us tea and
biscuit, and no doubt we should find something in Miss Carew's
basket, as she was always kind in remembering her fancies. Miss
Honora had told us to decline, if she asked us to stay; but I
should have liked to see her sit at the head of her table, and to
be a guest at such a lunch party.

Poor creature! it was a blessed thing that her shattered reason
made her unconscious of the change in her fortunes, and in-
capable of comparing the end of her life with its beginning. To
herself she was still Miss Chauncey, a gentlewoman of high
family, possessed of unusual worldly advantages. The remembrance of her cruel trials and sorrows had faded from her mind.
She had no idea of the poverty of her surroundings when she
paced back and forth, with stately steps, on the ruined terraces
of her garden; the ranks of lilies and the conserve roses were
still in bloom for her, and the box borders were as trimly kept as
ever; and when she pointed out to us the distant steeples of
Riverport, it was plain to see that it was still the Riverport of her
girlhood. If the boat landing at the foot of the garden had long
ago dropped into the river and gone out with the tide; if the
maids and men who used to do her bidding were all out of hear-

ing; if there had been no dinner company that day and no guests were expected for the evening,—what did it matter? The twilight had closed around her gradually, and she was alone in her house, but she did not heed the ruin of it or the absence of her friends. On the morrow, life would again go on.

We always used to ask her to read the Bible to us, after Mr. Lorimer had told us how grand and beautiful it was to listen to her. I shall never hear some of the Psalms or some chapters of Isaiah again without being reminded of her; and I remember just now, as I write, one summer afternoon when Kate and I had lingered later than usual, and we sat in the upper room looking out on the river and the shore beyond, where the light had begun to grow golden as the day drew near sunset. Miss Sally had opened the great book at random and read slowly, "In my Father's house are many mansions"; and then, looking off for a moment at a leaf which had drifted into the window recess, she repeated it: "In my Father's house are many mansions; if it were not so, I would have told you." Then she went on slowly to the end of the chapter, and with her hands clasped together on the Bible she fell into a reverie, and the tears came into our eyes as we watched her look of perfect content. Through all her clouded years the promises of God had been her only certainty.

Miss Chauncey died early in the winter after we left Deephaven, and one day when I was visiting Kate in Boston Mr. Lorimer came to see us, and told us about her.

It seems that after much persuasion she was induced to go to spend the winter with a neighbor, her house having become uninhabitable, and she was, beside, too feeble to live alone. But her fondness for her old home was too strong, and one day she stole away from the people who took care of her, and crept in through the cellar, where she had to wade through half-frozen water, and then went upstairs, where she seated herself at a front window and called joyfully to the people who went by, asking them to come in to see her, as she had got home again. After this she was very ill, and one day, when she was half delirious, they missed her, and found her at last sitting on her hall stairway, which she was too feeble to climb. She lived but a short time afterwards, and in her last days her mind seemed perfectly clear. She said over and over again how good God had always been to her, and she was gentle, and unwilling to be a trouble to those who had the care of her.

Mr. Lorimer spoke of her simple goodness, and told us that though she had no other sense of time, and hardly knew if it were summer or winter, she was always sure when Sunday came, and always came to church when he preached at East Parish, her greatest pleasure seeming to be to give money, if there was a contribution. "She may be a lesson to us," added the old minister, reverently; "for, though bewildered in mind, bereft of riches and friends and all that makes this world dear to many of us, she was still steadfast in her simple faith, and was never heard to complain of any of the burdens which God had given her."

Last Days in Deephaven

WHEN the summer was ended, it was no sorrow to us, for we were even more fond of Deephaven in the glorious autumn weather than we had ever been before. Mr. Lancaster was abroad longer than he had intended to be at first, and it was late in the season before we left. We were both ready to postpone going back to town as late as possible; but at last it was time for my friend to re-establish the Boston housekeeping, and to take up the city life again. I must admit we half dreaded it: we were surprised to find how little we cared for it, and how well one can get on without many things which are thought indispensable.

For the last fortnight we were in the house a good deal, because the weather was wet and dreary. At one time there was a magnificent storm, and we went every day along the shore in the wind and rain for a mile or two to see the furious great breakers come plunging in against the rocks. I never had seen such a wild, stormy sea as that; the rage of it was awful, and the whole harbor was white with foam. The wind had blown northeast steadily for days, and it seemed to me that the sea never could be quiet and smooth and blue again, with soft white clouds sailing over it in the sky. It was a treacherous sea; it was wicked; it had all the trembling land in its power, if it only dared to send its great waves far ashore. All night long the breakers roared, and the wind howled in the chimneys, and in the morning we always looked fearfully across the surf and the tossing gray water to see if the lighthouse were standing firm on its rock. It was so slender a thing to hold its own in such a wide and monstrous sea. But the sun came out at last, and not many days afterward we went out with Danny and Skipper Scudder to say good-by to Mrs. Kew. I have been some voyages at sea, but I never was so danced about in a little boat as I was that day. There was nothing to fear with so careful a crew, and we only enjoyed the roughness as we went out and in, though it took much manoeuvring to land us at the island.

It was very sad work to us—saying good-by to our friends, and we tried to make believe that we should spend the next summer in Deephaven, and we meant at any rate to go down for a visit. We were glad when the people said they should miss us, and that they hoped we should not forget them and the old place. It touched us to find that they cared so much for us, and we said over and over again how happy we had been, and that it was such a satisfactory summer. Kate laughingly proposed one evening, as we sat talking by the fire and were particularly contented, that we should copy the Ladies of Llangollen, and remove ourselves from society and its distractions.

"I have thought often, lately," said my friend, "what a good time they must have had, and I feel a sympathy and friendliness for them which I never felt before. We could have guests when we chose, as we have had this summer, and we could study and grow very wise, and what could be pleasanter? But I wonder if we should grow very lazy if we stayed here all the year round; village life is not stimulating, and there would not be much to do in winter,—though I do not believe that need be true; one may be busy and useful in any place."

"I suppose if we really belonged in Deephaven we should think it a hard fate, and not enjoy it half so much as we have this summer," said I. "Our idea of happiness would be making long visits in Boston; and we should be heartbroken when we had to come away and leave our lunch parties, and symphony concerts, and calls, and fairs, the reading club and the childrens' hospital. We should think the people uncongenial and behind the times, and that the Ridge road was stupid and the long sands desolate; while we remembered what delightful walks we had taken out Beacon Street to the three roads, and over the Cambridge Bridge. Perhaps we should even be ashamed of the dear old church for being so out of fashion. We should have the blues dreadfully, and think there was no society here, and wonder why we had to live in such a town."

"What a gloomy picture!" said Kate, laughing. "Do you know that I have understood something lately better than I ever did before,—it is that success and happiness are not things of chance with us, but of choice. I can see how we might so easily have had a dull summer here. Of course it is our own fault if the events of our lives are hindrances; it is we who make them bad or good. Sometimes it is a conscious choice, but oftener unconscious. I suppose we educate ourselves for taking the best of life or the worst, do not you?"

"Dear old Deephaven!" said Kate, gently, after we had been silent a little while. "It makes me think of one of its own ladies, with its clinging to the old fashions and its respect for what used to be respectable when it was young. I cannot make fun of what was once dear to somebody, and which realized somebody's ideas of beauty or fitness. I don't dispute the usefulness of a new, bustling, manufacturing town with its progressive ideas; but there is a simple dignity in a town like Deephaven, as if it tried to be loyal to the traditions of its ancestors. It quietly accepts its altered circumstances, if it has seen better days, and has no harsh feelings toward the places which have drawn away its business, but it lives on, making its old houses and boats and clothes last as long as possible."

"I think one cannot help," said I, "having a different affection for an old place like Deephaven from that which one may have for a newer town. Here—though there are no exciting historical associations and none of the veneration which one has for the very old cities and towns abroad—it is impossible not to remember how many people have walked the streets and lived in the houses. I was thinking today how many girls might have grown up in this house, and that their places have been ours; we have inherited their pleasures, and perhaps have carried on work which they began. We sit in somebody's favorite chair and look out of the windows at the sea, and have our wishes and our hopes and plans just as they did before us. Something of them still lingers where their lives were spent. We are often reminded of our friends who have died; why are we not reminded as surely of strangers in such a house as this,—finding some trace of the lives which were lived among the sights we see and the things we handle, as the incense of many masses lingers in some old cathedral, and one catches the spirit of longing and prayer where so many heavy hearts have brought their burdens and have gone away comforted?"

"When I first came here," said Kate, "it used to seem very sad to me to find Aunt Katharine's little trinkets lying about the house. I have often thought of what you have just said. I heard Mrs. Patton say the other day that there is no pocket in a shroud, and of course it is better that we should carry nothing out of this world. Yet I can't help wishing that it were possible to keep some of my worldly goods always. There are one or two books of mine and some little things which I have had a long time, and of which I have grown very fond. It makes me so sorry to think of their being neglected and lost. I cannot believe I shall forget these earthly treasures when I am in heaven, and I wonder if I shall not miss them. Isn't it strange to think of not reading one's Bible any more? I suppose this is a very low view of heaven, don't you?" And we both smiled.

"I think the next dwellers in this house ought to find a decided atmosphere of contentment," said I. "Have you ever thought that it took us some time to make it your house instead of Miss Brandon's? It used to seem to me that it was still under her management, that she was its mistress; but now it belongs to you, and if I were ever to come back without you I should find you here."

It is bewildering to know that this is the last chapter, and that it must not be long. I remember so many of our pleasures of which I have hardly said a word. There were our guests, of whom I have told you nothing, and of whom there was so much to say. Of course we asked my Aunt Mary to visit us, and Miss Margaret Tennant, and many of our girl friends. All the people we know who have yachts made the port of Deephaven if they were cruising in the neighboring waters. Once a most cheerful party of Kate's cousins and some other young people whom we knew very well came to visit us in this way, and the yacht was kept in the harbor a week or more, while we were all as gay as bobolinks and went frisking about the country, and kept late hours in the sober old Brandon house. My Aunt Mary, who was with us, and Kate's aunt, Mrs. Thorniford, who knew the Carews, and was commander of the yacht party, tried to keep us in order, and to make us ornaments to Deephaven society instead of reproaches and stumbling blocks. Kate's young brothers were with us, waiting until it was time for them to go back to college, and I think there never had been such picnics in Deephaven before, and I fear there never will be again.

We are fond of reading, and we meant to do a great deal of it, as everyone does who goes away for the summer; but I must

Deephaven

confess that our grand plans were not well carried out. Our German dictionaries were on the table in the west parlor until the sight of them mortified us, and finally, to avoid their silent reproach, I put them in the closet, with the excuse that it would be as easy to get them there, and they would be out of the way. We used to have the magazines sent us from town; you would have smiled at the box of books which we carried to Deephaven, and indeed we sent two or three times for others; but I do not remember that we ever carried out that course of study which we had planned with so much interest. We were out of doors so much that there was often little time for anything else.

Kate said one day that she did not care, in reading, to be always making new acquaintances, but to be seeing more of old ones; and I think it a very wise idea. We each have our pet books; Kate carries with her a much-worn copy of *Mr. Rutherford's Children*, which has been her delight ever since she can remember. Sibyl and Chryssa are dear old friends, though I suppose now it is not merely what Kate reads, but what she associates with the story. I am not often separated from Jean Ingelow's *Stories Told to a Child*, that charmingly wise and pleasant little book. It is always new, like Kate's favorite. It is very hard to make a list of the books one likes best, but I remember that we had *The Village on the Cliff*, and *Henry Esmond*, and *Tom Brown at Rugby*, with his more serious ancestor, *Sir Thomas Browne*. I am sure we had *Fenelon*, for we always have that; and there was *Pet Marjorie*, and *Rab*, and *Annals of a Parish*, and *The Life of the Reverend Sydney Smith*; beside Miss Tytler's *Days of Yore*, and *The Holy and Profane State*, by Thomas Fuller, from which Kate gets so much entertainment and profit. We read Mr. Emerson's essays together, out of doors, and some stories which had been our dear friends at school, like *Leslie Goldthwaite*.

There was a very good library in the house, and we both like old books, so we enjoyed that. And we used to read the *Spectator*, and many old-fashioned stories and essays and sermons, with much more pleasure because they had such quaint old brown leather bindings. You will not doubt that we had some cherished volumes of poetry, or that we used to read them aloud to each other when we sat in our favorite corner of the rocks at the shore, or were in the pine woods of an afternoon.

We used to go out to tea, and do a great deal of social visiting, which was very pleasant. Dinner parties were not in fashion, though it was a great attention to be asked to spend the day, which courtesy we used to delight in extending to our friends; and we entertained company in that way often. When we first went out we were somewhat interesting on account of our clothes, which were of later pattern than had been adopted generally in Deephaven. We used to take great pleasure in arraying ourselves on high days and holidays, since when we went wandering on shore, or out sailing or rowing, we did not always dress as befitted our position in the town. Fish scales and blackberry briers so soon disfigure one's clothes.

We became in the course of time learned in all manner of 'longshore lore, and even profitably employed ourselves one morning in going clam digging with old Ben Horn, a most fascinating ancient mariner. We both grew so well and brown and strong, and Kate and I did not get tired of each other at all, which I think was wonderful, for few friendships would bear such a test. We were together always, and alone together a great deal; and we became wonderfully well acquainted. We are such good friends that we often were silent for a long time, when mere acquaintances would have felt compelled to talk and try to entertain each other.

Before we left, the leaves had fallen off all the trees except the oaks, which make in cold weather one of the dreariest sounds one ever hears: a shivering rustle, which makes one pity the tree and imagine it shelterless and forlorn. The sea had looked rough and cold for many days, and the old house itself had grown chilly,—all the world seemed waiting for the snow to come. There was nobody loitering on the wharves, and when we went down the street we walked fast, arm in arm, to keep warm. The houses were shut up as close as possible, and the old sailors did not seem cheery any longer; they looked forlorn, and it was not a pleasant prospect to be so long weather bound in port. If they ventured out, they put on ancient greatcoats, with huge flaps to the pockets and large horn buttons, and they looked contemptuously at the vane, which always pointed to the north or east. It felt like winter, and the captains rolled more than ever as they walked, as if they were on deck in a heavy sea. The rheumatism claimed many victims, and there was one day, it must be confessed, when a biting, icy fog was blown inshore, that Kate and I were willing to admit that we could be as comfortable in town, and it was almost time for sealskin jackets.

In the front yards we saw the flower beds black with frost, except a few brave pansies which had kept green and had bloomed under the tall china-aster stalks, and one day we picked some of these little flowers to put between the leaves of a book and take away with us. I think we loved Deephaven all the more in those last days, with a bit of compassion in our tenderness for the dear old town which had so little to amuse it. So long a winter was coming, but we thought with a sigh how pleasant it would be in the spring.

You would have smiled at the treasures we brought away with us. We had become so fond of even our fishing lines; and this very day you may see in Kate's room two great bunches of Deephaven cat-o'-nine-tails. They were much in our way on the journey home, but we clung affectionately to these last sheaves of our harvest.

The morning we came away our friends were all looking out from door or window to see us go by, and after we had passed the last house and there was no need to smile any longer, we were very dismal. The sun was shining again bright and warm as if the Indian summer were beginning, and we wished that it had been a rainy day.

The thought of Deephaven will always bring to us our long quiet summer days, and reading aloud on the rocks by the sea, the fresh salt air, and the glory of the sunsets; the wail of the Sunday psalm-singing at church, the yellow lichen that grew over the trees, the houses, and the stone walls; our boating and wanderings ashore; our importance as members of society, and how kind everyone was to us both. By and by the Deephaven warehouses will fall and be used for firewood by the fisher people, and the wharves will be worn away by the tides. The few old gentlefolks who still linger will be dead then; and I wonder if some day Kate Lancaster and I will go down to Deephaven for the sake of old times, and read the epitaphs in the burying ground, look out to sea, and talk quietly about the girls who were so happy there one summer long before.

I should like to walk along the beach at sunset, and watch the color of the marshes and the sea change as the light of the sky goes out. It would make the old days come back vividly. We should see the roofs and chimneys of the village, and the great Chantrey elms look black against the sky. A little later the marsh fog would show faintly white, and we should feel it deliciously cold and wet against our hands and faces; when we looked up there would be a star; the crickets would chirp loudly; perhaps some late sea-birds would fly inland. Turning, we should see the lighthouse lamp shine out over the water, and the great sea would move and speak to us lazily in its idle, high-tide sleep.

River Driftwood

At the head of tidewater on the river there is a dam, and above it is a large millpond, where most of the people who row and sail keep their boats all summer long. I like, perhaps once a year, to cruise around the shores of this pretty sheet of water; but I am always conscious of the dam above it and the dam below it, and of being confined between certain limits. I rarely go beyond a certain point on the lower or tide river, as people call it, but I always have the feeling that I can go to Europe, if I like, or anywhere on the high seas; and when I unfasten the boat there is no dam or harbor bar, or any barrier whatever between this and all foreign ports. Far up among the hills the ocean comes, and its tide ebbs and flows.

When the tide goes out, the narrow reaches of the river become rapids, where a rushing stream fights with the ledges and loose rocks, and where one needs a good deal of skill to guide a boat down safely. Where the river is wide, at low tide one can only see the mud flats and broad stretches of green marsh grass. But when the tide is in, it is a noble and dignified stream. There are no rapids and only a slow current, where the river from among the inland mountains flows along, finding its way to the sea, which has come part way to welcome the company of springs and brooks that have answered to its call. A thousand men band themselves together, and they are one regiment; a thousand little streams flow together, and are one river; but one fancies that they do not lose themselves altogether; while the individuality of a river must come mainly from the different characters of its tributaries. The shape of its shores and the quality of the soil it passes over determine certain things about it, but the life of it is something by itself, as the life of a man is separate from the circumstances in which he is placed. There must be the first spring which overflows steadily and makes a brook, which some second spring joins, and the third, and the fourth; and at last there is a great stream, in which the later brooks seem to make little difference. I should like to find the very beginning and headwater of my river. I should be sorry if it were a pond, though somewhere in the ground underneath there would be a spring that kept the secret and was in command and under marching orders to the sea, commissioned to recruit as it went along. Here at the head of tidewater it first meets the sea, and then when the tide is in there is the presence of royalty, or at least its deputies. The river is a grand thing when it is river and sea together; but how one misses the ocean when the tide is out, for in the great place it filled the stream from the hills, after all, looks of little consequence.

The river is no longer the public highway it used to be years ago, when the few roads were rough, and railroads were not even dreamed of. The earliest chapter of its history that I know is that it was full of salmon and other fish, and was a famous fishing ground with the Indians, who were masters of its neighboring country. To tell its whole story one would have to follow the fashion of the old Spanish writers whom Garcilaso de la Vega says he will not imitate, in the first chapter of his *Commentaries of the Yncas,*—that delightful composition of unconscious pathos and majestic lies. When his predecessors in the field of literature wished to write on any subject whatever, he solemnly tells us, they always began with a history of the globe. One cannot help wishing that he had not disdained to follow their example, and had given his theories, which would have been wildly ahead of even the fancies of his time, in general, and full of most amusing little departures from the truth when he came down to details.

But the earliest history of the river can well be ignored; it is but seldom, as yet, that people really care much for anything for its own sake, until it is proved to have some connection with humankind. We are slow to take an interest in the personality of our neighbors who are not men, or dogs, or horses, or at least some creature who can be made to understand a little of our own spoken language. Who is going to be the linguist who learns the first word of an old crow's warning to his mate, or how a little dog expresses himself when he asks a big one to come and rout his troublesome enemy? How much we shall know when the pimpernel teaches us how she makes her prophecies of the weather, and how long we shall have to go to school when people are expected to talk to the trees, and birds, and beasts, in their own language! What tune could it have been that Orpheus and Amphion played, to which the beasts listened, and even the trees and stones followed them to hear? Is it science that will give us back the gift, or shall we owe it to the successors of those friendly old saints who talked with the birds and fishes? We could have schools for them, if we once could understand them, and could educate them into being more useful to us. There would be intelligent swordfish for submarine divers, and we could send swallows to carry messages, and all the creatures that know how to burrow in the earth would bring us the treasures out of it. I should have a larger calling acquaintance than ever out of doors, and my neighbors down river would present me to congenial friends whom as yet I have not discovered.

The gods are always drawing like toward like, and making them acquainted, if Homer may be believed, but we are apt to forget that this is true of any creatures but ourselves. It is not necessary to tame them before they can be familiar and responsive; we can meet them on their own ground, and be surprised to find how much we may have in common. Taming is only forcing them to learn some of our customs; we should be wise if we let them tame us to make use of some of theirs. They share other instincts and emotions with us beside surprise, or suspicion, or fear. They are curiously thoughtful; they act no more from unconscious instinct than we do; at least, they are called upon to decide as many questions of action or direction, and there are many emergencies of life when we are far more helpless and foolish than they.

It is easy to say that other orders of living creatures exist on a much lower plane than ourselves; we know very little about it, after all. They are often gifted in some way that we are not; they may even carry some virtue of ours to a greater height than we do. But the day will come for a more truly universal suffrage than we dream of now, when the meaning of every living thing is understood, and it is given its rights and accorded its true value: for its life is from God's life, and its limits were fixed by him; its material shape is the manifestation of a thought, and to each body there is given a spirit.

The great gulls watch me float along the river, curiously, and sail in the air overhead. Who knows what they say of me when they talk together; and what are they thinking about when they

fly quickly out of sight? Perhaps they know something about me
that I do not know of myself yet; and so may the muskrat, as he
hurries through the water with a little green branch in his mouth
which will make a salad for his supper. He watches me with his
sharp eyes, and whisks into his hole in the sunny side of the
island. I have a respect for him; he is a busy creature, and he
lives well. You might be hospitable and ask me to supper, muskrat! I don't know whether I should care much for you if I were
another muskrat, or you were a human being, but I shall know
you again when I see you by an odd mark in the fur on the top
of your head, and that is something. I suppose the captive
mussels in your den are quaking now at hearing you come in. I
have lost sight of you, but I shall remember where your house is.

I do not think people are thankful enough who live out of the
reach of beasts that would eat them. When one thinks of whole
races of small creatures like the mussels which are the natural and
proper food of others, it seems an awful fact and necessity of
nature; perhaps, however, no more awful than our natural death
appears to us. But there is something distressing about being
eaten, and having one's substance minister to a superior existence! It hurts one's pride. A death that preserves and elevates our
identity is much more consoling and satisfactory; but what can
reconcile a bird to its future as part of the tissues of a cat, going
stealthily afoot, and by nature treacherous? Who can say, however, that our death may not be simply a link in the chain? One
thing is made the prey of another. In some way our present
state ministers to the higher condition to which we are coming.
The grass is made somehow from the ground, and presently that
is turned into beef, and that goes to make part of a human being.
We are not certain what an angel may be; but the life in us now
will be necessary to the making of one by and by.

There is a wise arrangement in this merging and combining.
It makes more room in the world. We must eat our fellows and
be eaten to keep things within a proper limit. If all the orders of
life were self-existing, and if all the springs that make up the
river flowed down to the sea separately and independently, there
would be an awful confusion and chaos still; but this leads one to
think of the transmigration of souls and other puzzling subjects!
I shall have to end with an ignorant discourse about the globe
instead of having begun with it. My river, as I said at first, leads

to the sea, and from any port one can push off toward another sea of boundless speculation and curious wonderings about this world, familiar, and yet so great a mystery.

There are a thousand things to remember and to say about the river, which seems to be of little use in the half dozen miles I know best, after it has made itself of great consequence by serving to carry perhaps a dozen or twenty mills, of one kind and another. Between its dams it has a civilized and subjected look, but below the last falls, at the Landing, it apparently feels itself to be its own master, and serves in no public capacity except to carry a boat now and then, and give the chance for building some weirs, as it offers some good fishing when the alewives and bass come up, with bony and muddy shad, that are about as good to eat as a rain-soaked paper of pins.

I think its chief use is its beauty, and that has never been as widely appreciated as it ought to be. It is the eastern branch of the Piscataqua, which separates the States of Maine and New Hampshire; and I, being a lawless borderer, beg you to follow for a raid on the shores, not for pillaging the farms and cattle-lifting, but to see the trees and their shadows in the water: the high, steep banks where the great pines of Maine thrive, on one hand, and the gently sloping Southern New Hampshire fields fringed with willows and oaks on the other. When you catch sight of a tall lateen sail and a strange, clumsy craft that looks heavy and low in the water, you will like to know that its ancestor was copied from a Nile boat, from which a sensible old sea captain took a lesson in shipbuilding many years ago. The sail is capitally fitted to catch the uncertain wind, which is apt to come in flaws and gusts between the high, irregular banks of the river; and the boat is called a gundalow, but sometimes spelled gondola. One sees them often on the Merrimac and on the Piscataqua and its branches, and the sight of them brings a curiously foreign element into the New England scenery; for I never see the great peaked sail coming round a point without a quick association with the East, with the Mediterranean ports or the Nile itself, with its ruins and its desert and the bright blue sky overhead; with mummies and scarabei and the shepherd kings; with the pyramids and Sphinx—that strange group, so old one shudders at the thought of it—standing clear against the horizon.

A hundred years ago the northern country was covered for the most part with heavy timber, and the chief business at Berwick was receiving this from the lumbermen, and sending it to Portsmouth to be reshipped, or direct to the West Indies, to be bartered for rum and tobacco and molasses, which might be either brought home at once, or sent to Russia, to be exchanged again for iron and sailcloth and cordage. Not forty years ago there were still twenty gundalows sailing from the Landing wharves, while now there are but two, and long after that the packet boat went regularly every other day to Portsmouth. Until the days of the railroads most of the freight came by water, and the packet skippers were important men.

I have always wished to know something more of the history of the quaint little packet storehouse which, until within a year or two, stood in the mill-yard, just below the falls. It was built of heavy timbers, as if it might some day be called upon to resist a battering-ram. The stories were very low, and the upper one projected over the water with a beam, to which was fastened a tackle and fall to hoist and lower the goods. It was a little building, but there was a great air of consequence about it. It was painted a dark red, which the weather had dulled a good deal, and it leaned to one side. Nobody knew how old it was; it was like a little old woman who belonged to a good family, now dead, save herself; and who could remember a great many valuable people and events which everybody else had forgotten. It was the last of the warehouses that used to stand on the river banks, and I was sorry when it was pulled down. The old wharves have almost disappeared, too, though their timbers can still be seen here and there.

It sometimes takes me a whole afternoon to go two miles down the river. There are many reasons why I should stop every now and then under one bank or another; to look up through the trees at the sky, or at their pictures in the water; or to let the boat lie still, until one can watch the little fish come back to their playground on the yellow sand and gravel; or to see the frogs, that splashed into the water at my approach, poke their heads out a little way to croak indignantly, or raise a loud note such as Scotch bagpipers drive out of the pipes before they start a tune. The swallows dart like bats along the surface of the water after insects, and I see a drowned white butterfly float by, and reach out for it; it looks so frail and little in the river. When the cardinal flowers are in bloom I go from place to place until I have gathered a deckload; and as I push off the boat it leaves the grass bent down, and the water-mint that was crushed sends a delicious fragrance after me, and I catch at a piece and put a leaf in my mouth, and row away lazily to get a branch of oak or maple leaves to keep the sun off my flowers.

Cardinals are quick to wilt, and hang their proud heads wearily. They keep royal state in the shade, and one imagines that the other flowers and all the weeds at the water's edge take care to bow to them as often as the wind comes by, and pay them honor. They are like fine court ladies in their best gowns, standing on the shore. Perhaps they are sending messages down the river and across the seas, or waiting to hear some news. They make one think of Whittier's highborn Amy Wentworth and her sailor lover, for they seem like flowers from a palace garden that are away from home masquerading and waiving ceremony, and taking the country air. They wear a color that is the sign of high ecclesiastical rank, and the temper of their minds would make them furies if they fought for church and state. They are no radicals; they are tories and aristocrats; they belong to the old nobility among flowers. It would be a pity if the rank marsh grass overran them, or if the pickerel weed should wade ashore to invade them and humble their pride.

They are flowers that after all one should not try to put into vases together. They have, like many other flowers, too marked an individuality, and there is more pleasure to be taken from one tall and slender spire of blossoms by itself, just as it is pleasanter to be alone with a person one admires and enjoys. To crowd some flowers together you lose all delight in their shape and beauty; you only have the pleasure of the mass of color or of their perfume; and there are enough bright flowers and fragrant flowers that are only beautiful in masses. To look at some flowers huddled together and losing all their grace and charm is like trying to find companionship and sympathy by looking for a minute at a crowd of people. But there is a low trait of acquisitiveness in human nature. I pick cardinal flowers by the armful, and nothing less than a blue-and-white ginger pot full of daisies is much satisfaction.

But to most people one tree, or flower, or river is as good as

another, and trees and flowers and rivers are to be found without trouble, while there are some who would never know who
has lived beside my river unless it were told here. That says at
once that their fame at best is provincial, except for peppery
little Captain John Paul Jones, who gathered the ship's company
of the *Ranger* from these neighboring farms. Old people, who
died not many years ago, remembered him as he walked on the
wharves at Portsmouth, with his sword point scratching the
ground; a little wasp of a fellow, with a temper like a blaze of
the gunpowder whose smoke he loved. One can imagine him
scrambling up the shore here to one of the old farmhouses, as
short as a boy; but as tall as a grenadier, in his pride and dignity;
and marching into the best room, in all the vainglory and
persuasiveness of his uniform, to make sure of a good fellow
whose looks he liked, and whom he promised to send home a
gallant hero, with his sea chest full of prize money. And afterward he would land again at one of the stately old colonial mansions that used to stand beside the river, at the Wallingford
house by Madam's Cove, or at the Hamilton house, and be received with befitting ceremony.

There were many fine houses in this region in old times, but
only one still lingers,—this same Hamilton house,—which seems
to me unrivaled for the beauty of its situation, and for a certain
grand air which I have found it hard to match in any house I
have ever seen. It is square and gray, with four great chimneys,
and many dormer windows in its high-peaked roof; it stands on
a point below which the river is at its widest. The rows of poplars
and its terraced garden have fallen and been spoiled by time,
but a company of great elms stand guard over it, and the sunset
reddens its windows, and the days of the past seem to have
come back, when one is near it, its whole aspect is so remote
from the spirit of the present. Inside there are great halls and
square rooms with carved woodwork, arched windows and
mahogany window seats, and fireplaces that are wide enough
almost for a seat in the chimney corner. In the country about I
have heard many a tradition of the way this house was kept; of
the fine ladies and gentlemen, and the great dinner-parties, and
the guests who used to come up the river from Portsmouth, and
go home late in the moonlight evening at the turn of the tide.
In those days the wharves that are fast being washed away

were strong enough, and there were warehouses and storehouses and piles of timber all along the river. The builder of the house was a successful man, who made a great fortune in the lucky West India trade of his time; he was poor to begin with, but everything prospered steadily with his business interests, and one owes him a debt of gratitude for leaving so fine a house to delight our eyes.

A little way up the shore there was formerly a shipyard, and I know of four ships that were built there much less than fifty years ago. My grandfather was part owner of them, and their names, with those of other ships, have been familiar to me from my babyhood. It is amusing that the ships of a family concerned in navigation seem to belong to it and to be part of it, as if they were children who had grown up and gone wandering about the world. Long after some familiar craft has changed owners even, its fortunes are affectionately watched, and to know that a ship has been spoken at sea gives a good deal of pleasure beside the assurance that the cargo is so far on its way to market at Canton or Bombay.

I remember wondering why the smooth green bank, where the dandelions were so thick in spring, should be called the shipyard by my family, and even why any one should call that corner of the town the Lower Landing, since nothing ever seemed to land, unless it were the fleets that children built from chips and shingles. It is a lovely, quiet place, and I often think of an early summer morning when I was going down river in a rowboat. The dandelions were sprinkled all over the short green grass, and high on the shore, under a great elm, were two wandering young musicians. They had evidently taken the wrong road, and discovered that this was a long lane that led only to the great house on the point and to the water's edge. They must have been entertained, for they seemed very cheerful; one played a violin, and the other danced. It was like a glimpse of sunshiny, idle Italy: the sparkling river and the blue sky, the wide green shores and the trees, and the great gray house, with its two hall doors standing wide open, the lilacs in bloom, and no noise or hurry,—a quiet place, that the destroying left hand of progress had failed to touch.

One day I was in one of the upper rooms of the Hamilton house in a dormer window, and I was amused at reading the nonsense some young girl had written on the wall. The view was beautiful, and I thought she must have sat there with her work, or have watched the road or the river for some one whom she wished to see coming. There were sentimental verses, written at different times. She seemed to have made a sort of scrapbook of the bit of wall, and she had left me the date, which was very kind of her; so I knew that it was 1802, and in the summer, that she used to sit there in her favorite perch. This is one of her verses that I remember:—

> "May you be blest with all that Heaven may send,
> Long life, good health, much pleasure in a friend;
> May you in every clime most happy be,
> And when far distant often think of me."

It was very pleasant to catch this glimpse of girlhood in the old house. I wondered how she liked life as she grew older, and if the lover—if that were a lover—did think often enough of her, and come back to her at last from the distant climes. She could have wished him nothing better than much pleasure in a friend.

I do not know the history of many members of the family; Colonel Hamilton and his consort are buried under a heavy monument in the Old Fields burying ground, and at the end of the long epitaph is the solemn announcement that Hamilton is no more. It would be a strange sight if one of his heavily-laden little ships came up the river now; but I like to think about those days, and how there might have happened to be some lumbermen from far inland, who were delighted to gossip with the sailors and carry back up into the country the stories of their voyage.

When the French prisoners of war came into Portsmouth, I have heard old people say that there was a great excitement, and as the ships came in they looked like gardens, for the Frenchmen had lettuces for salads, and flowers growing in boxes that were fastened on the decks; and it was amusing to hear of these prisoners being let out on parole about the country towns, in Eliot and Newington and Kittery, and all up and down the river. Perhaps more than one of them found their way to the hospitable families in Berwick and were entertained as became their rank and fortunes. In an old house in Eliot there is a little drawing made by one of these men, and I have an exquisite little watercolor painting of a carnation, with the quaintly written request that charming Sally will sometimes think of the poor Ribère, who will never forget her. It is all that is left of what must have been a tender friendship between this gallant young Frenchman and my grandmother. I found it once among her copy-books, and letters from her girl friends, and love letters from my grandfather which he sent home to her from sea. She was very young when the poor Ribère was so sorry to part from her, for she married at eighteen (and died at twenty-five). I knew very little about her until I found in the garret the little brass-nailed trunk that had kept her secrets for me. I am sure she often made one of the company that used to come up the river to take tea and go home by moonlight. She was a beautiful girl, and everybody was fond of her. The poor Ribère sat beside her in the boat, I have no doubt; and perhaps it was in the terraced garden with the rows of poplars round it, that she picked the flower he painted, and no doubt he carried it away with him when he was set free again, and was not a prisoner of war any longer.

There was formerly a bright array of clerical talent in the river towns, and it was most amusing to listen to the anecdotes which the old people of the last generation delighted to tell of the ministers. Not to speak of the well-known Portsmouth divines, and of Dr. Stevens, of Kittery Point, there was the Reverend Mr. Litchfield, of Kittery, who was called the fisher parson, and his neighbor, Parson Chandler, who might have been called the farmer parson, for he was a celebrated tiller of the soil, and his example was a great blessing to the members of his Eliot parish. The fields there slope to the south and west, and the grass grows green sooner than anywhere else in the region, and the fruits of the earth grow and ripen quickly. He taught his neighbors to improve upon the old fashions of agriculture.

An old friend of mine told me that once he was driving from Portsmouth to Berwick, in his early manhood, with Daniel Webster for company, and when they passed this clergyman's house Mr. Webster said that he should be perfectly satisfied if he could be as great a man as Parson Chandler; and judging from the stories of his wisdom and eloquence, the young lawyer's was no mean ambition.

Mr. Litchfield spent much of his time on week days in the apostolic business of catching fish; and he was a man of rare wit and drollery, with a sailor-like serenity and confidence in everything's coming out right at last, and a true mariner's readiness and intentness when there was work to be done. Once, at a conference in Portsmouth, the preacher failed to come, and some one had to furnish a sermon in his place. It fell to Mr. Litchfield's share; and old Dr. Buckminster said, when the discourse was ended,—it being extemporaneous and very eloquent,—"My friends, the fisher parson beats us all!"

It is interesting to find that many of the clergymen of that day seem to have been uncommonly practical men. One fancies that they all preached the better because much of their time was spent in a way that brought them in close contact with people's everyday lives. It was no ideal human nature, studied from sermons and theological works, and classified and doomed at the recommendation of the old divines. One can believe that it was not abstract generalities of a state of sinfulness so much as particular weakness and shortcomings that they condemned from their pulpits. Parson Litchfield could preach gallantly at some offender who stole from and lied about his lobster pots when he took his text from Ananias and Sapphira, and Parson Chandler could be most impressive and ready with illustration when he chose the parable of the sower for the subject of his discourse.

In Berwick there was a grave and solemn little man, whom all his great parish long remembered admiringly. The church where the whole town centred was at the Old Fields, and it ought to be standing yet, but I do not know that anything is left of it but a bit of paper I found one day, on which is written the names of the men who built it and the sums of money and bundles of shingles or pieces of timber that each contributed.

I do not know why this should have been so superstitious a neighborhood, but there seems to have been a great deal of trouble from ghosts, and it was the duty of the ministers to drive them away, or to "lay" them, as they called it then. An old man told me once that the parsons made a great secret of it. They met together in a room, which nobody was allowed to enter; so whether it was a service with mysterious rites, or they only joked together, and thought it well to keep up the reverence in the rustic mind for the power of the priesthood, nobody knows to this day.

There is still standing at the Landing a house that has always been said to be haunted. Its ghost was laid properly, but she

seems to have risen again defiantly. It formerly stood very near
the shore of the little harbor, if one may give that name to what
was simply the head of navigation on the river. The family who
built and owned it first all died long ago, but I never go by the
house without thinking of its early history in those days, when
the court end of the little town was next the river, and the old
elms shaded the men who were busy with their trading and shipping, and the women who kept up a stately fashion of living indoors, and walked proudly to and fro in the streets dressed in
strange stuffs that had been brought home to them from across
the seas.

There was a fine set of people in the little town, and Berwick
held its head very high, and thought some of the neighboring
towns of little consequence that have long since outgrown it and
looked down upon it in their turn. It even has given up its place
as the head of the family of villages into which the original town-
ship has been divided. It is only South Berwick now; but I like to
call it Berwick here, as it has a right to be called, for it was the
oldest settlement, and the points of the compass should have
been given to the newer centres of civilization which were its
offshoots.

The oldest houses are, with one or two exceptions, by far the
finest ones, and the one of which I have spoken still keeps up as
well as it can the pride as well as the name of its first owner.
One cannot help being interested in this man, who was one of
the earlier physicians of the town, and also had a hand in the
business that was connected with the river. I have heard that he
came from Plymouth in Massachusetts and was a minister's son,
but if ever a man's heart gloried in the good things of this life it
was his, and there was not a trace of Puritan asceticism in his
character. His first house was the finest in town, and stood at the
head of some terraces that still remain, bordered with rows of
elms, and overlooked the river; but that was burnt, and afterward
replaced by another, which was for some mysterious reason
built at the foot of the terraces near the water.

The doctor was said to be a very handsome man, and he
dressed uncommonly well, delighting himself with fine broad-
cloth cloaks with red linings and silk facings, and his visits to his
admiring patients were paid on horseback, as was the custom
then, but he always rode an excellent horse, and dashed about

the country in great splendor. He made an elaborate will, entailing his property in English fashion. He waited to see how much General Lord or the other rich men of the town would pay toward any subscription, and then exceeded the most generous. He even asked how much the richest man in the town was taxed, and paid of his own accord a larger sum than he, and somehow contrived to keep up year after year this appearance of great wealth, and expected and received great deference; though those who knew him best were sure he must be poor, the pride that went with it forbade familiarity and sympathy alike.

There has always been a tradition that his first wife came to her death by foul means, and there is a dislike to the house, which seems never to be occupied for any length of time, even after all these years. The people in the neighborhood believe, as I have said, that it is haunted, and I have often heard stories of the strange cries, and the footsteps that sometimes follow you if you go up the hall stairs in the dark. The doctor himself died suddenly, though he has often been seen since in a grand brocade dressing-gown and close velvet cap.

His business affairs had naturally become a good deal tangled, but no one knew how much so until after his death. For several years he had been in the habit of carrying back and forth a little padlocked box when he went to Portsmouth, which was supposed to hold money and valuable papers; but when this was brought home from the bank, and broken open, it was found to contain only blank bits of paper.

His wife, whom the old people in town still remember, must have had a hard time of it in the house on the wharf after she was left a widow; but she was still the *grande dame,* and when she went into society her old laces and silks and her fine manners made her the queen of her company. She gave no sigh of disappointment at her altered fortunes, and as long as the doctor lived and after he died, she was as serenely magnificent and untroubled as he. The Guard could die, but it never surrendered, and the old prestige was kept up bravely. She lived alone, and might sometimes have needed many of the good things of life, for all one knows; but she was always well dressed, and kept up all possible forms of state, and was rigorous in observing all rules of etiquette. By way of doing a great favor to one of her neighbors, she allowed a stranger the use of one of her rooms for a short time, and this person used to hear a bell ring in the morning, after which Madam Hovey would move about in her room; then she would go downstairs, breakfast being apparently announced; and so on, through the day. There was often a bell heard tinkling in the parlor; she would apologize for opening the outer door herself, and when the lodger called the mistress of the house was always quite at liberty, and seemed to have been awaiting guests in her parlor, with a bit of lace to mend in her fingers, or some silk knitting, as if she occupied her leisure with such dainty trifles. It was some time before the lodger discovered, to her amazement, that there was not a servant under the roof to do my lady's bidding, but that she still kept up the old customs of the house. Poor soul! it was not all silly pretense.

If I were to spend a night (which the saints forbid!) in that beloved mansion where she lived in solitary majesty for so many years, I should not expect to be the guest of the proud doctor's first companion whose death is shrouded in mystery, who cries dismally and walks to and fro in the night, to beg for pity and help. I should look over my shoulder for the lady in the high turban, with a red India shawl around her shoulders, who stood so straight, and used to walk up the aisle to her seat in church on Sunday as if she were a duchess. The cries and the steps behind me would be most annoying, but Madam Hovey, if she also haunts her house, would receive me elegantly. One can imagine her alone in her house at night, with the jar of the river falls and the wind rattling her windows, fearful of her future, and of the poverty and misery old age held in its shaking hands for her. But she carried a brave face in the daylight, however troubled she may have been under the stars, and she gave to the townspeople the best of lessons in behavior; for she was always gracious and courteous, and fine in her own manners, a high-bred lady, who had been in her day a most apt scholar of the old school.

My cruises down the river rarely reach beyond High Point, or Pine Point, or the toll bridge; but one is tempted to linger there late for the sake of the beautiful view. The salt grass is a dazzling green, if the time is early summer and the tide is partly out, and from the bridge to the Hamilton house the river is very wide. The fine old house faces you, and at its right there is a mountain, which is a marked feature in the landscape on a clear day, when it looks far away and blue in the distance. The great tops of the Hamilton elms look round and heavy against the sky, and the shores of the river are somewhat irregular, running out in points which are for the most part heavily wooded, and form backgrounds of foliage for each other. Being at different angles, the light and shade of each are distinct, and make a much finer coloring and outline than could be if the line of the shore were unbroken by so many bays and inlets.

It is very pleasant to push the boat ashore in one of these covers, for in the little ravines that lead down to them there are crowds of ferns and wild flowers, and it is easy to find exactly the place for a little feast at supper time. I know many a small harbor on the eastern shore, where a willow or a birch stands out in front of the dark evergreens, and at one place an oak reaches its long branches far out over the water; and when you are once under its shade, and watch the sunset grow bright and then fade away again, or see the boats go round the point from the wide bay into the narrow reach of the river about it, and listen to the bells ringing in the village or in some town farther away, you hate to think you must take the oars again, and go out into the twilight or the bright sunshine of the summer afternoon.

I miss very much some poplars which stood on the western shore, opposite the great house, and which were not long since cut down. They were not flourishing, but they were like a little procession of a father and mother and three or four children out for an afternoon walk, coming down through the field to the river. As you rowed up or down they stood up in bold relief against the sky, for they were on high land. I was deeply attached to them, and in the spring, when I went down river for the first time, they always were covered with the first faint green mist of their leaves, and it seemed as if they had been watching for me, and thinking that perhaps I might go by that afternoon.

On a spring day how the bobolinks sing, and the busy birds that live along the shores go flitting and chirping and whistling about the world! A great fish hawk drops through the air, and you can see the glitter of the unlucky fish he has seized as he goes off again. The fields and trees have a tinge of green that they will keep only for a few days, until the leaves and grass blades are larger and stronger; and where the land has been plowed its color is as beautiful as any color that can be found the world over, and the long shining brown furrows grow warm lying in the sun. The farmers call to each other and to their horses as they work; the fresh breeze blows from the southwest, and the frogs are cheerful, and the bobolinks grow more and more pleased with themselves every minute, and sing their tunes, which are meant to be sung slower and last longer, as if the sweet notes all came hurrying out together.

And in the summer, when the days are hot and long, there is nothing better than the glory of the moonlighted nights, when the shrill cries of the insects fill all the air, and the fireflies are everywhere, and a whiff of saltness comes up with the tide. In October the river is bright steel color and blue. The ducks rise and fly away from the coves in the early morning, and the oaks and maples dress themselves as they please, as if they were tired of wearing plain green, like everybody else, and were going to be gay and set a new fashion in the cooler weather. You no longer drift lazily with the current, but pull your boat as fast as you can, and are quick and strong with the oars. And in the winter the river looks cold and dead, the wind blows up and down between the hills, and the black pines and hemlocks stare at each other across the ice, which cracks and creaks loudly when the tide comes up and lifts it.

How many men have lived and died on its banks, but the river is always young. How many sailors have gone down to the sea along its channel, and from what strange countries have the ships come in and brought them home again up this crooked highway! A harbor, even if it is a little harbor, is a good thing, since adventurers come into it as well as go out, and the life in it grows strong, because it takes something from the world, and has something to give in return. Not the sheltering shores of England, but the inhospitable low coasts of Africa and the dangerous islands of the southern seas, are left unvisited. One sees the likeness between a harborless heart and a harborless country, where no ships go and come; and since no treasure is carried away no treasure is brought in.

From this inland town of mine there is no seafaring any more, and the shipwright's hammers are never heard now. It is only a station on the railways, and it has, after all these years, grown so little that it is hardly worth while for all the trains to stop. It is busy and it earns its living and enjoys itself, but it seems to me that its old days were its better days. It builds cheaper houses, and is more like other places than it used to be. The people of fifty years ago had some things that were better than ours, even if they did not hear from England by telegraph, or make journeys in a day or two that used to take a week. The old elms and pines look strong yet, though once in a while one blows over or is relentlessly cut down. The willows by the river are cropped and cropped again. The river itself never grows old; though it rushes and rises high in the spring, it never dries up in the autumn; the little white sails flit over it in pleasant weather, like fluttering moths round the track of sunlight on the water; one troop of children after another steals eagerly down to its forbidden shores to play.

The Landscape Chamber

I

I WAS tired of ordinary journeys, which involved either the loneliness and discomfort of fashionable hotels, or the responsibilities of a guest in busy houses. One is always doing the same things over and over; I now promised myself that I would go in search of new people and new scenes, until I was again ready to turn with delight to my familiar occupations. So I mounted my horse one morning, without any definite plan of my journey, and rode eastward, with a business-like haversack strapped behind the saddle. I only wished that the first day's well-known length of road had been already put behind me. One drawback to a woman's enjoyment of an excursion of this sort is the fact that when she is out of the saddle she is uncomfortably dressed. But I compromised matters as nearly as possible by wearing a short corduroy habit, light both in color and weight, and putting a linen blouse and belt into my pack, to replace the stiff habit-waist. The wallet on the saddle held a flat drinking-cup, a bit of chocolate, and a few hard biscuit, for provision against improbable famine. Autumn would be the best time for such a journey, if the evenings need not be so often spent in stuffy rooms, with kerosene lamps for company. This was early summer, and I had long days in which to amuse myself. For a book I took a much-beloved small copy of *The Sentimental Journey*.

After I left my own neighborhood, I was looked at with curious eyes. I was now and then recognized with surprise, but oftener viewed with suspicion, as if I were a criminal escaping from justice. The keepers of the two country taverns at which I rested questioned me outright until I gave a reassuring account of myself. Through the middle of the day I let the horse stand unsaddled in the shade, by the roadside, while I sat near, leaning against the broad trunk of a tree, and ate a bit of luncheon, or slept, or read my book, or strolled away up the shore of a brook or to the top of a hill.

On the third or fourth day I left my faithful companion so long that he grew restless, and at last fearful, as petted horses will. The silence and strangeness of the place and my disappearance frightened him. When I returned, I found that the poor creature had twisted a forward shoe so badly that I could neither pull it off altogether, nor mount again. There was nothing to do but to lead him slowly to some farmhouse, where I could get assistance; so on went the saddle, and away we plodded together sadly along the dusty road. The horse looked at me with anxious eyes, and was made fretful by the difficulty of the projecting shoe. I should have provided myself with some pincers, he seemed to tell me; the foot was aching from the blows I had given it with a rough-edged stone in trying to draw the tenacious nails. It was all my fault, having left him in such a desolate place, fastened to a tree that grew against a creviced ledge of rock. We were both a little sulky at this mischance so early in the careless expedition.

The sea was near, and the salt marshes penetrated deep into the country, like abandoned beds of rivers winding inland among the pine woods and upland pastures. The higher land separated these marshes, like a succession of low promontories trending seaward, and the road climbed and crossed over from one low valley to another. There had been no houses for some distance behind us. I knew that there was a village with a good tavern a few miles ahead; so far, indeed, that I had planned to reach it at sundown. I began to feel very tired, and the horse tossed his head more and more impatiently, resenting my anxious, dragging hold upon the rein close at his mouth. There was nobody to be seen; the hills became steeper, the unshaded strips of marshland seemed hotter, and I determined at last to wait until some traveler appeared who could give us assistance. Perhaps the blacksmith himself might be out adventuring that afternoon.

We halted by some pasture bars in the shade of an old cider-apple tree, and I threw the bridle over a leaning post in the unsteady fence; and there the horse and I waited, and looked at each other reproachfully. It was some time before I discovered a large rusty nail lying in the short grass, within reach of my hand. My pocketknife was already broken, because I had tried to use it for a lever, and this was just what I needed. I quickly caught up the disabled hoof again, and with careful prying the tough nails loosed their hold at last, and the bent shoe dropped with a clink. The horse gave a whinny of evident relief, and seemed to respect me again, and I was ready to mount at once; in an instant life lost its depressing aspect. "Keep your feet out of clefts now!" I said joyfully, with a friendly stroke of the good creature's neck and tangled mane, and a moment afterward we were back in the stony road. Alas, the foot had been strained, and our long halt had only stiffened it. I was mounted on three feet, not four. Nothing was to be done but to go forward, step by step, to the faraway village, or to any friendly shelter this side of it.

The afternoon was waning: sometimes I rode, sometimes I walked; those three miles of marsh and hill seemed interminable. At last I saw the chimneys of a house; the horse raised his head high, and whinnied loud and long.

These chimneys were most reassuring; being high and square, they evidently belonged to a comfortable house of the last century, and my spirits rose again. The country was still abandoned by human beings. I had seen no one since noon, but the road was little used, and was undoubtedly no longer the main highway of that region. I wondered what impression I should make in such a migratory guise. The saddle and its well-stuffed haversack and my own dustiness amused me unexpectedly, and I understood for the first time that the rest and change of this solitary excursion had done me much good. I was no longer listless and uninterested, but ready for adventure of any sort. It had been a most sensible thing to go wandering alone through the country. But now the horse's ankle was swollen. I grew anxious again, and looked at the chimneys with relief. Presently I came in sight of the house.

It was disappointing, for the first view gave an impression of dreariness and neglect. The barn and straggling row of outbuildings were leaning this way and that, mossy and warped; the blinds of the once handsome house were broken; and everything gave evidence of unhindered decline from thrift and competence to poverty and ruin. A good colonial mansion, I thought, abandoned by its former owners, and tenanted now by some shiftless outcasts of society, who ask but meagre comfort, and are indifferent to the decencies of life. Full of uncertainty, I went along the approach to the barn, noticing, however, with surprise that the front yard had been carefully tended; there were some dark crimson roses in bloom, and broken lines of box which had been carefully clipped at no remote period. Nobody was in sight. I went to the side door, and gave a knock with my whip at arm's length, for the horse was eager to reach the uninviting, hungry-looking stable.

Some time elapsed before my repeated summons were answered; then the door slowly opened, and a woman just this side of middle age stood before me, waiting to hear my errand. She had a pathetic look, as if she were forced by circumstances to deny all requests, however her own impulses might lead her toward generosity. I was instantly drawn toward her, in warm sympathy: the blooming garden was hers; she was very poor. I would plead my real fatigue, and ask for a night's lodging, and perhaps my holiday might also give her pleasure. But a curious hardness drew her face into forbidding angles, even as her sweet and womanly eyes watched me with surprised curiosity.

"I should be very sorry to take the horse any further today," said I, after stating my appealing case. "I will give you as little trouble as possible." At this moment the haggard face of an elderly man peered at me over her shoulder.

"We don't keep tavern, young lady," he announced in an unexpectedly musical, low voice, "but since your horse is"—

"I am ready to pay you any price you ask," I interrupted impatiently; and he gave me an eager look, and then came to the outer step, ignoring both his daughter and me, as he touched the horse with real kindliness. "'Tis a pretty creature!" he said admiringly, and at once stooped stiffly down to examine the lifted foot. I explained the accident in detail, grateful for such intelligent sympathy, while he stroked the lamed ankle.

"There's no damage done," he assured me presently, looking up with transient self-forgetfulness. "A common liniment will do; there's a bottle in the house, but 'twill cost you something," and his face clouded again.

I turned to the daughter, who gave me a strange, appealing look. Her eyes begged me entreatingly, "Give him his own way"; her firm-set mouth signified her assent to the idea that I had no right to demand favors.

"Do what you think best," I said, "at your own price. I shall be very grateful to you"; and having come to this understanding, the father and I unbuckled the saddle girths, while the daughter stood watching us. The old man led the limping horse across the green dooryard to a weather-beaten stable, talking to him in a low tone. The creature responded by unusual docility. I even saw him, though usually so suspicious and fretful with strangers, put his head close to his leader's shoulder with most affectionate impulse. I gathered up my belongings,—my needments, as somebody had called them, after Spenser's fashion, in the morning,—and entered the door.

II

Along the byways and in the elder villages of New England stand many houses like this, from which life and vigor have long been ebbing, until all instincts of self-preservation seem to have departed. The commonplace, thrifty fears of increasing damage from cracks, or leaks, or falling plaster no longer give alarm; as age creeps through the human frame, pilfering the pleasures of enthusiasm and activity one by one, so it is with a decaying house. The old man's shrewd eyes alone seemed unrelated to his surroundings. What sorrow or misfortune had made him accept them? I wondered, as I stared about the once elegant room. Nothing new had been brought to it for years; the leather-bound books in the carved secretary might have belonged to his grandfather. The floor was carpetless and deeply worn; the faded paper on the walls and the very paint looked as old as he. The pinch of poverty could nowhere be much sharper than here, but the exquisite cleanness and order of the place made one ignore the thought of poverty in its common aspect, for all its offensive and repulsive qualities were absent.

I sat down in a straight-backed mahogany chair, feeling much relieved, and not without gratitude for this unexpected episode. The hostess left me alone. I was glad enough to have the long day shortened a little, and to find myself in this lonely, mysterious house. I was pleased by the thought that the price of my food and lodging would be very welcome, and I grew more and more eager to know the history of my new friends. I have never been conscious of a more intense desire to make myself harmonious, or to win some degree of confidence. And when the silence of the old sitting room grew tiresome I went out to the stable, whence my host had not returned, and was quite reconciled at finding that I was looked upon by him, at least, merely as an appendage to my four-footed companion.

The old man regarded me with indifference, and went on patiently rubbing the horse's foot. I was silent after having offered to take his place and being contemptuously refused. His clothes were curiously old and worn, patched bravely, and an embroidery of careful darns. The color of them was not unlike the dusty gray of long-neglected cobwebs. There was unusual delicacy and refinement in his hands and feet, and I was sure, from the first glance at my new friends and the first sound of their voices, that they had inherited gentle blood, though such an inheritance had evidently come through more than one generation to whom had been sternly denied any approach to luxury or social advantage. I have often noticed in country villages the descendants of those clergymen who once ruled New England sternly and well, and while they may be men and women of undeveloped minds, without authority and even of humble circumstances, they yet bear the mark of authority and dignified behavior, like silver and copper coins with a guinea stamp.

I was more and more oppressed by the haunting sense of poverty, for I saw proofs everywhere that the inhabitants of the old house made no practical protest against its slow decay. The woman's share of work was performed best, as one might see by their mended clothes; but the master's domain was hopelessly untended, not only as to the rickety buildings, but in the land itself, which was growing wild bushes at its own sweet will, except for a rough patch near the house, which had been dug and planted that year. Was this brooding, sad old man discouraged by life? Did he say to himself, "Let things be; they will last my time"? I found myself watching his face with intense interest, but I did not dare to ask questions, and only stood and watched him. The sad mouth of the man might have been a den from which stinging wild words could assail a curious stranger. I was afraid of what he might say to me, yet I longed to hear him speak.

The summer day was at its close. I moved a step forward, to get away from the level sunbeams which dazzled my eyes, and ventured to give some news about myself and the lonely journey that had hitherto brought me such pleasure. The listener looked up with sincere attention, which made me grow enthusiastic at once, and I described my various experiences, and especially the amusing comments which I had heard upon my mode of traveling about the country. It amazed me to think that I was within sixty miles of home and yet a foreigner.

At last I asked a trivial question about some portion of the scenery, which was pleasantly answered. The old man's voice was singularly sweet and varied in tone, the exact reverse of a New Englander's voice of the usual rural quality. I was half startled at seeing my horse quickly turn his head to look at the speaker, as if with human curiosity equal to my own. I felt a thrill of vague apprehension. I was unwise enough for a moment to dread taking up my residence in this dilapidated mansion; a creeping horror, such as one feels at hearing footsteps behind one in a dark, strange place, made me foolishly uneasy, as I stood looking off across the level country through the golden light of closing day, beyond the marshes and beyond the sand dunes to the sea. What had happened to this uncanny father and daughter, that they were contented to let the chances of life slip by untouched, while their ancestral dwelling gradually made itself ready to tumble about their ears?

I could see that the horse's foot was much better already, and I watched with great sympathy the way that the compassionate, patient fingers touched and soothed the bruised joint. But I saw no sign of any other horse in the stable, save a few stiffened, dusty bits of harness hung on a high peg in the wall; and as I looked at these, and renewed my wonder that such a person should have no horse of his own, especially at such a distance from any town, the old man spoke again.

"Look up at that bit of dry skin over the harnesses," said he. "That was the pretty ear of the best mare that ever trod these roads. She leaped the stable-yard gate one day, caught her foot in a rope, and broke her neck. She was like those swallows one minute, and the next she was a heap of worthless flesh, a heavy thing to be dragged away and hidden in the earth." His voice failed him suddenly, poor old fellow; it told me that he had suffered cruel sorrows that made this loss of a pleasure almost unbearable. So far life had often brought me success, and I had gained a habit of expecting my own enterprises to be lucky. I stood appalled before this glimpse of a defeated life and its long procession of griefs.

Presently the master of the place went into the house, and returned with a worn wooden trencher of bits of hard bread and some meal. The hungry creature in the stall whinnied eagerly, and nestled about, while our host ascended the broken stairway to the stable loft; and after waiting for some time, I heard the rustle of an armful of hay which came down into the crib. I looked that way, and was not surprised, when I noticed the faded, dusty dryness of it, to see my dainty beast sniff at it with disappointment, and look round at me inquiringly. The old man joined me, and I protested hastily against such treatment of my favorite.

"Cannot we get somebody to bring some better hay, and oats enough for a day or two, if you are unprovided?" I asked.

"The creature must not be overfed," he said grudgingly, with a new harsh tone. "You will heat the foot, and we must keep the beast quiet. Anything will serve tonight; tomorrow he can graze all day, and keep the foot moving gently; next day, he can be shod."

"But there is danger in giving him green grass," I suggested. "This is too rich pasturage about the house; surely you know enough of horses to have learned that. He will not be fit to ride, either. If I meant to give him a month of pasture, it would be another thing. No; send somebody for at least an armful of decent hay. I will go myself. Are there houses near?"

The old man had gone into the stall, and was feeding the hungry horse from the trencher. I was startled to see him snatch back two or three bits of the bread and put them into his pocket, as if, with all his fondness for the horse and a sincere desire to make him comfortable, he nevertheless grudged the food. I became convinced that the poor soul was a miser. He certainly played the character exactly, and yet there was an appealing look in his eyes, which, joined with the tones of his voice, made me sure that he fought against his tyrannous inclinations. I wondered irreverently if I should be killed that night, after the fashion of traditional tavern robberies, for the sake of what might be found in my pocket, and sauntered toward the house. It remained to be proved whether the daughter was the victim or the upholder of her father's traits.

I had the satisfaction of finding that the daughter was just arranging a table for supper. As I passed the wide-open door of a closet, I was tempted to look in by the faint ancient odor of plum cakes and Madeira wine which escaped; but I never saw a barer closet than that, or one that looked hungrier in spite of the lingering fragrance of hospitality. It gave me a strange feeling as if there were a still subtler link with the past, and some invisible presence would have me contrast the house's former opulence with its present meagreness.

When we sat at table I was not surprised to find, on a cloth that was half covered with darns and patches, some pieces of superb old English silver and delicate china. The fare was less than frugal, but was nobly eked out with a dish of field strawberries, as if Nature had come to the rescue. Cream there was none, nor sugar, nor even tea or butter. I had an aching sense of the poverty of the family, and curiously questioned in my own mind how far they found it possible to live without money. There was some thin, crisp corn bread, which had been baked in the morning, or whenever there had last been a fire. It was very good. Perhaps my entertainers even gathered their own salt from the tide pools, to flavor the native corn. Look where I would, I could see nothing for which money had been lately spent; here was a thing to be wondered at in this lavish America, and I pushed back my chair at last, while I was still half hungry, from a dread that there would be nothing for breakfast unless I saved it then.

The father and daughter were very agreeable, I must confess: they talked with me about my journey now, and my plans, as if they were my personal friends, and the strange meal was full of pleasure, after all. What had brought a lady and gentleman to such a pass?

After supper the daughter disappeared for a time, busy with her household cares; a little later the father went out of the stable and across the fields, before I could call to him or offer my company. He walked with a light, quick step, like an Indian, as if he were used to taking journeys on foot. I found myself uncommonly tired; the half illness which had fettered me seemed to have returned, after the unusual anxiety and weariness of the afternoon, and I longed to go to bed and to sleep. I had been interested in much that my entertainers had said of the early history of that part of the country, and while we sat at the table I had begun to look forward to a later evening talk, but almost before daylight faded I was forced to go to bed.

My hostess led me through a handsome empty hall, of the wide and stately colonial type, to a comfortable upper room, furnished with a gloomy-looking curtained bedstead and heavy mahogany furniture of the best old fashion. It seemed as if the room had been long unused, and also as if the lower part of the house were in a much worse state of disrepair and threadbareness than this. But the two large windows stood open to the fading sky and sweet country air, and I bade my hostess good-night cheerfully. She lingered to see if I were comfortable; it was the first time I had been alone with her. "You can see that we are not used to entertaining company," she whispered, reddening with sensitiveness, and smiling apologetically. "Father has kept everybody away for so many years that I rarely have any one to speak to, or anything to do but to keep the poor old house clean. Father means to be kind, but he"—and she turned away, much embarrassed by my questioning look—"he has a monomania; he inherits it from my grandfather. He fears want, yet seems to have no power to provide against it. We are poor, God knows, yet we have resources; or had them once," she added, sorrowfully. "It was the horse that made him willing to let you in. He loves horses, yet he has long denied himself even that useful pleasure."

"But surely he ought to be controlled," I urged. "You must have suffered."

"I know all that you are eager to say," she replied; "but I promised my dear mother to be patient with him. It will not be long now; he is very feeble. I have a horror that this habit of parsimony has rooted itself too deeply in my own life to be shaken off. You will hear mockery enough of us among the farmers."

"You surely have friends?"

"Only at a distance," said she, sadly. "I fear that they are no longer friends. I have *you*," she added, turning to me quickly, in a pathetic way that made me wish to put my arms about her. "I have been longing for a friendly face. Yes, it is very hard," and she drearily went out of the door, and left me alone with the dim light of the sky outside, the gloomy shadows of the room within. I tried to fancy some clue to the weird misery of this poverty-stricken household, as I lay down; but I fell asleep very soon, and slept all night, without even a dream.

III

Daylight brought a new eagerness and a less anxious curiosity about my strange entertainers. I opened my eyes in broad sunlight. I was puzzled by the unfamiliar India-cotton hangings of the great bedstead; then I caught sight of my dusty habit and my riding cap and whip, near by. I instantly resolved that even if I found my horse in the restored condition there was every reason to expect, I would make this house my headquarters for as long time as its owners would keep me, or I could content myself. I would try to show some sisterly affection to the fast-aging woman who was so enslaved by her father's delusions. I had come out in search of adventure; it would be a difficult task to match my present surroundings.

I listened for the sound of footsteps or voices from below, but it was still very early, and I looked about the long-untenanted room with deliberate interest and scrutiny. As I changed my position a little, I caught sight of a curious old painting on the large oval panel above the empty fireplace. The colors were dull, the drawing was quaintly conventional, and I recognized the subject, though not immediately. The artist had pleased himself by making a study of the old house itself, and later, as I dressed, I examined it in detail.

From the costume of the figures I saw that it must have been painted more than a hundred years before. In astonishing contrast to the present condition, it appeared like a satirical show of the house's possibilities. Servants held capering steeds for gay gentlemen to mount, and ladies walked together in fine attire down the garden alleys of the picture. Once a hospitable family had kept open house behind the row of elms, and once the follies of the world and the fashions of brilliant, luxurious life had belonged to this decayed and withering household. I wondered if the miserly old man, to whose strangely sweet and compelling voice I had listened the evening before, could bear to look at this picture, and acknowledge his unlikeness to his prosperous ancestors.

It was well for me that the keeping of hens is comparatively inexpensive, for I breakfasted comfortably, and was never so heartily rejoiced at the vicinity of a chicken coop. My proposal to stay with my new friends for a few days met with no opposition from either host or hostess; and again, as I looked in their pinched and hopeless faces, I planned some secret excuses for making a feast of my own, or a happy holiday. The fields and hills of the old picture were still unchanged, but what ebb and flow of purpose, of comfort, of social condition, had enriched and impoverished the household!

"Where did she sleep?" asked the master of the house, suddenly, with a strange, suspicious glance at his daughter.

"In the landscape chamber," the pale woman said, without lifting her eyes to his, though she grew whiter and thinner as she spoke.

I looked at him instinctively to see his eyes blaze with anger, and expected a torrent of abuse, because he was manifestly so much displeased. Nothing was said, but with a feeling of uneasiness we left the table, and I went out to the kitchen with my new friend.

"There is no reason why I should not have put you into the landscape chamber," she told me instantly. "It is a fancy of my father's. I had aired that room thoroughly in the morning, but the front guest chambers have been closed for some time."

"Who painted the strange old picture?" I asked. "Some member of the family?" But I was answered that it was the work of a Frenchman, who was captured in wartime, and paroled under the care of her great-grandfather.

"He must have had a gay visit," I suggested, "if he has left a faithful picture of the house as he saw it."

"The house used to be like that always," was the faint response, and the speaker hesitated, as if she considered whether we did right in discussing her family history; then she turned quickly away. "I believe we are under some miserable doom. Father will be sure to tell you so, at any rate," she added, with an effort at gayety. "He thinks that he fights against it, but I always say that he was cowardly, and accepted it," and she sighed wearily.

I looked at her with fresh surprise and conjecture. I forgot for the time this great, busy, prosaic world of which we were both a part, and I felt as if I had lost a score of years for each day's journey, and had gone backward into the past. New England holds many strange households within its borders, but there could not be another which approached this. The very air of the

house oppressed me, and I strayed out into the beautiful wide
fields, and found my spirits rising again at once. I turned at last
to look back at the group of gray buildings in the great level
landscape. They were such a small excrescence upon the fruitful
earth, those roofs which covered awful stagnation and hindrance
of the processes of spiritual life and growth. What power could
burst the bonds, and liberate the man and woman I had left
from a mysterious tyranny?

I was bareheaded, and the morning grew very hot. I went
toward a group of oaks, to shelter myself in the shade, and found
the ancient burying place of the family. There were numerous
graves, but none were marked except the oldest. There was a
group of rude but stately stones, with fine inscriptions, yet
curiously enough the latest of them bore a date soon after the
beginning of the century; all the more recent graves were low
and unmarked in any way. The family fortunes had waned long
ago, perhaps; I might be wronging the present master of the
house, though I remembered what had been said to me of some
mysterious doom.

I could not help thinking of my new acquaintances most in-
tently, and was startled at the sound of footsteps. I saw the old
man, muttering and bending his head until he could see nothing
but the ground at his feet. He only picked up some dead branches
that had fallen from the oaks, and went away toward the house
again; always looking at the ground, as if he expected to find
something. It came to my mind with greater distinctness that he
was a miser, poor only by his own choice; and I indignantly resolved to urge the daughter to break her allegiance to him for a
time, to claim her own and set herself free. But the miser had no
cheerful sense of his hoards, no certainty of a munificence which
was more to him than any use of it; there was a look upon his
face as of a preying conscience within, a gnawing reptile of
shame and guilt and evil memory. Had he sacrificed all sweet
family life and natural ties to his craving for wealth? I watched
the bent and hungry figure out of sight.

When I reached the house again, I went through the open
door to the wide hall, and gained my landscape chamber without being seen by any one. I was tired and dizzy with the unusual
heat, and, quickly drawing the close shutters, I threw myself on
the bed to rest. All the light in the room came from the shaded

hall; there was absolute silence, except some far-off country sounds of birds high in air or lowing cattle. The house itself was still as a tomb.

I went to sleep, but it was not sound sleep. I grew heavy and tired with my own weight. I heard soft footsteps coming up the stairs; someone stopped as if to listen outside the wide-open door; then the gray, shadowy figure of the old man stood just within, and his eyes peering about the room. I was behind the curtains; one had been unfastened, and hid me from his sight at first, but as he took one step forward he saw me, lying asleep. He bent over me, until I felt my hair stir with his breath, but I did not move. His presence was not frightful, strange to say; I felt as if I were only dreaming. I opened my eyes a little as he went away, apparently satisfied, to the closet door, and unlocked it, starting and looking at me anxiously as the key turned in the lock. Then he disappeared. I had a childish desire to shut him in and keep him prisoner, for reasons that were not clear to myself. Whether he only wished to satisfy himself that a concealed treasure was untouched I do not know, but presently he came out, and carefully locked the door again, and went away on tiptoe. I fancied that he lingered before the picture above the chimney place, and wondered if his conscience pricked him as he acknowledged the contrast between past and present. Then he groaned softly, and went out.

My heart began to beat very fast. I sprang up and tried to lock the door into the hall. My enthusiasm about spending a few days in this dismal place suddenly faded out, for I could not bear the thought that the weird old man was free to prowl about at his own sad will. But as I stood undecided in my doorway, a song sparrow perched on the sill of the wide hall window, and sang his heart away in a most cheerful strain. There was something so touching and appealing in the contrast that I felt a wistful clutch at my throat, while I smiled, as one does when tears are coming like April showers to one's eyes.

Without thinking what I did, I went back into the room, threw open the shutters again, and stood before the dingy landscape. How the horses pranced up to the door, and how fine the ladies were in their hoop petticoats and high feathers! I imagined that the picture had been a constant rebuke to the dwellers in the house through their wasting lives and failing fortunes. In every human heart, said I, there is such a picture of the ideal life,—the high possibilities and successes, the semblance of duties done and of spiritual achievements. It forever measures our incompleteness by its exact likeness to that completeness which we would not fight hard enough to win. But as I looked up at the panel, the old landscape became dim, and I knew that it was only because a cloud was hiding the sun; yet I was glad to leave the shadows of the room, and to hurry down the wide stairway.

I saw nothing of the daughter, though I searched for her, and even called her, through the house. When I reached the side door, I found her father crossing the yard, and wondered if he would show any consciousness of our having so lately met. He stood still and waited for me, and my first impulse made me ask, "What did you want just now? I was not asleep when you were in my room; you frightened me."

"Do not be afraid," he answered, with unexpected patience. "You must take us as you find us. It is a sad old house, but you need not be afraid; we are much more afraid of you!" and we both smiled amiably.

"But your daughter," said I; "I have been asking her to come away for a time, to visit me or take a journey. It would be much better for you both; and she needs a change and a little pleasuring. God does not mean that we shall make our lives utterly dismal." I was afraid, and did not dare to meet the old man's eyes after I had spoken so plainly.

He laughed coldly, and glanced at his mended coat sleeve.

"What do you know about happiness? You are too young," said he. "At your age I thought I knew the world. What difference would it make if the old place here were like the gay ghost of it in our landscape chamber? The farmers would be jealous of our luxury; reverence and respect would be turned into idle curiosity. This quiet countryside would be disgraced by such a flaunting folly. No, we are very comfortable, my child and I; you must not try to disturb us," and he looked at me with a kind of piteous suspicion.

There was a large block of stone under one of the old elms, which had been placed there long ago for a mounting-block, and here we seated ourselves. As I looked at my companion, he seemed like a man unused to the broad light of day. I fancied that a prisoner, who had just ended many years of dungeon life, would wear exactly such a face. And yet it was such a lovely summer day of a joyful world, if he would only take or make it so. Alas, he matched the winter weather better. I could not bear to think of the old house in winter!

"Who is to blame?" said the old man suddenly, in a strange, eager tone which startled me, and made me shrink away from him. "We are in bondage. I am a generous-hearted man, yet I can never follow my own impulses. I longed to give what I had with a lavish hand, when I was younger, but some power restrained me. I have grown old while I tried to fight it down. We are all in prison while we are left in this world,—that is the truth; in prison for another man's sin." For the first time I understood that he was not altogether sane. "If there were an ancestor of mine, as I have been taught, who sold his soul for wealth, the awful price was this, that he lost the power of using it. He was greedy for gain, and now we cannot part with what we have, even for common comfort. His children and his children's children have suffered for his fault. He has lived in the hell of watching us from generation to generation; seeing our happiness spoiled, our power of usefulness wither away. Wherever he is, he knows that we are all misers because he was miserly, and stamped us with the mark of his own base spirit. He has watched his descendants shrivel up and disappear one by one, poor and ungenerous in God's world. We fight against the doom of it, but it wins at last. Thank God, there are only two of us left."

I had sprung to my feet, frightened by the old man's vehemence. I could not help saying that God meant us to be free and unconquered by any evil power; the gray, strange face looked blindly at me, and I could not speak again. This was the secret of the doom, then. I left the old man crying, while I hurried away to find the mistress of the desolate house, and appealed to her to let me send a companion for her father, who could properly care for him here, or persuade him to go away to some place where he would forget his misery among new interests and scenes. She herself must not be worn out by his malady of unreason.

But I only dashed my sympathy against the rock of her hopelessness. "I think we shall all disappear some night in a winter storm, and the world will be rid of us,—father and the house and

The Landscape Chamber

I, all three," she said, with bitter dreariness, and turned to her work again.

Early that evening, I said good-by to my new friends, for the horse was sound, and not to be satisfied by such meagre stabling. Our host seemed sorry to let the creature go, and stood stroking him affectionately after I had mounted. "How the famous old breed holds its own!" he said wistfully. "I should like to have seen the ancestor who has stamped his likeness so unmistakably on all his descendants."

"But among human beings," I could not resist saying, "there is freedom, thank God! We can climb to our best possibilities, and outgrow our worst inheritance."

"No, no!" cried the old man bitterly. "You are young and fortunate. Forget us, if you can; we are of those who have no hope in a world of fate."

I looked back again and again, as I rode away. It was a house of shadows and strange moods, and I was glad when I had fairly left it behind me; yet I look forward to seeing it again. I well remember the old man's clutch at the money I offered him, and the kiss and the bunch of roses that the daughter gave to me. But late that evening I was not sorry to shut myself into my prosaic room at a village hotel, rather than try to sleep again behind the faded figured curtains of the landscape chamber.

A White Heron

I

THE woods were already filled with shadows one June evening, just before eight o'clock, though a bright sunset still glimmered faintly among the trunks of the trees. A little girl was driving home her cow, a plodding, dilatory, provoking creature in her behavior, but a valued companion for all that. They were going away from the western light, and striking deep into the dark woods, but their feet were familiar with the path, and it was no matter whether their eyes could see it or not.

There was hardly a night the summer through when the old cow could be found waiting at the pasture bars; on the contrary, it was her greatest pleasure to hide herself away among the high huckleberry bushes, and though she wore a loud bell she had made the discovery that if one stood perfectly still it would not ring. So Sylvia had to hunt for her until she found her, and call Co'! Co'! with never an answering Moo, until her childish patience was quite spent. If the creature had not given good milk and plenty of it, the case would have seemed very different to her owners. Besides, Sylvia had all the time there was, and very little use to make of it. Sometimes in pleasant weather it was a consolation to look upon the cow's pranks as an intelligent attempt to play hide and seek, and as the child had no playmates she lent herself to this amusement with a good deal of zest. Though this chase had been so long that the wary animal herself had given an unusual signal of her whereabouts, Sylvia had only laughed when she came upon Mistress Moolly at the swamp side, and urged her affectionately homeward with a twig of birch leaves. The old cow was not inclined to wander farther, she even turned in the right direction for once as they left the pasture, and stepped along the road at a good pace. She was quite ready to be milked now, and seldom stopped to browse.

Sylvia wondered what her grandmother would say because they were so late. It was a great while since she had left home at half past five o'clock, but everybody knew the difficulty of making this errand a short one. Mrs. Tilley had chased the hornéd torment too many summer evenings herself to blame any one else for lingering, and was only thankful as she waited that she had Sylvia, nowadays, to give such valuable assistance. The good woman suspected that Sylvia loitered occasionally on her own account; there never was such a child for straying about out of doors since the world was made! Everybody said that it was a good change for a little maid who had tried to grow for eight years in a crowded manufacturing town, but, as for Sylvia herself, it seemed as if she never had been alive at all before she came to live at the farm. She thought often with wistful compassion of a wretched dry geranium that belonged to a town neighbor.

"'Afraid of folks,'" old Mrs. Tilley said to herself, with a smile, after she had made the unlikely choice of Sylvia from her daughter's houseful of children, and was returning to the farm. "'Afraid of folks,' they said! I guess she won't be troubled no great with 'em up to the old place!" When they reached the door of the lonely house and stopped to unlock it, and the cat came to purr loudly, and rub against them, a deserted pussy, indeed, but fat with young robins, Sylvia whispered that this was a beautiful place to live in, and she never should wish to go home.

The companions followed the shady woodroad, the cow taking slow steps, and the child very fast ones. The cow stopped long at the brook to drink, as if the pasture were not half a swamp, and Sylvia stood still and waited, letting her bare feet cool themselves in the shoal water, while the great twilight moths struck softly against her. She waded on through the brook as the cow moved away, and listened to the thrushes with a heart that beat fast with pleasure. There was a stirring in the great boughs overhead. They were full of little birds and beasts that seemed to be wide-awake, and going about their world, or else saying goodnight to each other in sleepy twitters. Sylvia herself felt sleepy as she walked along. However, it was not much farther to the house, and the air was soft and sweet. She was not often in the woods so late as this, and it made her feel as if she were a part of the gray shadows and the moving leaves. She was just thinking how long it seemed since she first came to the farm a year ago, and wondering if everything went on in the noisy town just the same as when she was there; the thought of the great red-faced boy who used to chase and frighten her made her hurry along the path to escape from the shadow of the trees.

Suddenly this little woods girl is horror stricken to hear a clear whistle not very far away. Not a bird's whistle, which would have a sort of friendliness, but a boy's whistle, determined, and somewhat aggressive. Sylvia left the cow to whatever sad fate might await her, and stepped discreetly aside into the bushes, but she was just too late. The enemy had discovered her, and called out in a very cheerful and persuasive tone, "Halloa, little girl, how far is it to the road?" and trembling Sylvia answered almost inaudibly, "A good ways."

She did not dare to look boldly at the tall young man, who carried a gun over his shoulder, but she came out of her bush and again followed the cow, while he walked alongside.

"I have been hunting for some birds," the stranger said kindly, "and I have lost my way, and need a friend very much. Don't be afraid," he added gallantly. "Speak up and tell me what your name is, and whether you think I can spend the night at your house, and go out gunning early in the morning."

Sylvia was more alarmed than before. Would not her grandmother consider her much to blame? But who could have foreseen such an accident as this? It did not appear to be her fault, and she hung her head as if the stem of it were broken, but managed to answer "Sylvy," with much effort when her companion again asked her name.

Mrs. Tilley was standing in the doorway when the trio came into view. The cow gave a loud moo by way of explanation.

"Yes, you'd better speak up for yourself, you old trial! Where'd she tuck herself away this time, Sylvy?" Sylvia kept an awed silence; she knew by instinct that her grandmother did not comprehend the gravity of the situation. She must be mistaking the stranger for one of the farmer lads of the region.

The young man stood his gun beside the door, and dropped a heavy game-bag beside it; then he bade Mrs. Tilley good-evening, and repeated his wayfarer's story, and asked if he could have a night's lodging.

"Put me anywhere you like," he said. "I must be off early in the morning, before day; but I am very hungry, indeed. You can give me some milk at any rate, that's plain."

"Dear sakes, yes," responded the hostess, whose long slumbering hospitality seemed to be easily awakened. "You might fare better if you went out on the main road a mile or so, but you're welcome to what we've got. I'll milk right off, and you make yourself at home. You can sleep on husks or feathers," she proffered graciously. "I raised them all myself. There's good pasturing for geese just below here towards the ma'sh. Now step round and set a plate for the gentleman, Sylvy!" And Sylvia promptly stepped. She was glad to have something to do, and she was hungry herself.

It was a surprise to find so clean and comfortable a little dwelling in this New England wilderness. The young man had known the horrors of its most primitive housekeeping, and the dreary squalor of that level of society which does not rebel at the companionship of hens. This was the best thrift of an old-fashioned farmstead, though on such a small scale that it seemed like a hermitage. He listened eagerly to the old woman's quaint talk, he watched Sylvia's pale face and shining gray eyes with ever growing enthusiasm, and insisted that this was the best supper he had eaten for a month; then, afterward, the new-made friends sat down in the doorway together while the moon came up.

Soon it would be berry time, and Sylvia was a great help at picking. The cow was a good milker, though a plaguy thing to keep track of, the hostess gossiped frankly, adding presently that she had buried four children, so that Sylvia's mother, and a son (who might be dead) in California were all the children she had left. "Dan, my boy, was a great hand to go gunning," she explained sadly. "I never wanted for pa'tridges or gray squer'ls while he was to home. He's been a great wand'rer, I expect, and he's no hand to write letters. There, I don't blame him, I'd ha' seen the world myself if it had been so I could.

"Sylvia takes after him," the grandmother continued affectionately, after a minute's pause. "There ain't a foot o' ground she don't know her way over, and the wild creatur's counts her one o' themselves. Squer'ls she'll tame to come an' feed right out o' her hands, and all sorts o' birds. Last winter she got the jay birds to bangeing here, and I believe she'd 'a' scanted herself of her own meals to have plenty to throw out amongst 'em, if I hadn't kep' watch. Anything but crows, I tell her, I'm willin' to help support,—though Dan he went an' tamed one o' them that did seem to have reason same as folks. It was round here a good spell after he went away. Dan an' his father they didn't hitch,— but he never held up his head ag'in after Dan had dared him an' gone off."

The guest did not notice this hint of family sorrows in his eager interest in something else.

"So Sylvy knows all about birds, does she?" he exclaimed, as he looked round at the little girl who sat, very demure but increasingly sleepy, in the moonlight. "I am making a collection of birds myself. I have been at it ever since I was a boy." (Mrs. Tilley smiled.) "There are two or three very rare ones I have been hunting for these five years. I mean to get them on my own ground if they can be found."

"Do you cage 'em up?" asked Mrs. Tilley doubtfully, in response to this enthusiastic announcement.

"Oh, no, they're stuffed and preserved, dozens and dozens of them," said the ornithologist, "and I have shot or snared every one myself. I caught a glimpse of a white heron three miles from here on Saturday, and I have followed it in this direction. They have never been found in this district at all. The little white heron, it is," and he turned again to look at Sylvia with the hope of discovering that the rare bird was one of her acquaintances.

But Sylvia was watching a hop toad in the narrow footpath.

"You would know the heron if you saw it," the stranger continued eagerly. "A queer tall white bird with soft feathers and long thin legs. And it would have a nest perhaps in the top of a high tree, made of sticks, something like a hawk's nest."

Sylvia's heart gave a wild beat; she knew that strange white bird, and had once stolen softly near where it stood in some bright green swamp grass, away over at the other side of the woods. There was an open place where the sunshine always seemed strangely yellow and hot, where tall, nodding rushes grew, and her grandmother had warned her that she might sink in the soft black mud underneath and never be heard of more. Not far beyond were the salt marshes and beyond those was the sea, the sea which Sylvia wondered and dreamed about, but never had looked upon, though its great voice could often be heard above the noise of the woods on stormy nights.

"I can't think of anything I should like so much as to find that heron's nest," the handsome stranger was saying. "I would give ten dollars to anybody who could show it to me," he added desperately, "and I mean to spend my whole vacation hunting for it if need be. Perhaps it was only migrating, or had been chased out of its own region by some bird of prey."

Mrs. Tilley gave amazed attention to all this, but Sylvia still watched the toad, not divining, as she might have done at some calmer time, that the creature wished to get to its hole under the doorstep, and was much hindered by the unusual spectators at that hour of the evening. No amount of thought, that night, could decide how many wished-for treasures the ten dollars, so lightly spoken of, would buy.

The next day the young sportsman hovered about the woods, and Sylvia kept him company, having lost her first fear of the friendly lad, who proved to be most kind and sympathetic. He told her many things about the birds and what they knew and where they lived and what they did with themselves. And he gave her a jackknife, which she thought as great a treasure as if she were a desert islander. All day long he did not once make her troubled or afraid except when he brought down some unsuspecting singing creature from its bough. Sylvia would have liked him vastly better without his gun; she could not understand why he killed the very birds he seemed to like so much. But as the day waned, Sylvia watched the young man with loving admiration. She had never seen anybody so charming and delightful; the woman's heart, asleep in the child, was vaguely thrilled by a dream of love. Some premonition of that great power stirred and swayed these young foresters who traversed the solemn woodlands with soft-footed silent care. They stopped to listen to a bird's song; they pressed forward again eagerly, parting the branches,—speaking to each other rarely and in whispers; the young man going first and Sylvia following, fascinated, a few steps behind, with her gray eyes dark with excitement.

She grieved because the longed-for white heron was elusive, but she did not lead the guest, she only followed, and there was no such thing as speaking first. The sound of her own unquestioned voice would have terrified her,—it was hard enough to answer yes or no when there was need of that. At last evening began to fall, and they drove the cow together, and Sylvia smiled with pleasure when they came to the place where she heard the whistle and was afraid only the night before.

II

Half a mile from home, at the farther edge of the woods, where the land was highest, a great pine tree stood, the last of its generation. Whether it was left for a boundary mark, or for what reason, no one could say; the woodchoppers who had felled its mates were dead and gone long ago, and a whole forest of sturdy trees, pines and oaks and maples, had grown again. But the stately head of this old pine towered above them all and made a landmark for sea and shore miles and miles away. Sylvia knew it well. She had always believed that whoever climbed to the top of it could see the ocean; and the little girl had often laid her hand on the great rough trunk and looked up wistfully at those dark boughs that the wind always stirred, no matter how hot and still the air might be below. Now she thought of the tree with a new excitement, for why, if one climbed it at break of day, could not one see all the world, and easily discover whence the white heron flew, and mark the place, and find the hidden nest?

What a spirit of adventure, what wild ambition! What fancied triumph and delight and glory for the later morning when she could make known the secret! It was almost too real and too great for the childish heart to bear.

All night the door of the little house stood open, and the whippoorwills came and sang upon the very step. The young sportsman and his old hostess were sound asleep, but Sylvia's great design kept her broad awake and watching. She forgot to think of sleep. The short summer night seemed as long as the winter darkness, and at last when the whippoorwills ceased, and she was afraid the morning would after all come too soon, she stole out of the house and followed the pasture path through the woods, hastening toward the open ground beyond, listening with a sense of comfort and companionship to the drowsy twitter of a

A White Heron

half-awakened bird, whose perch she had jarred in passing. Alas,
if the great wave of human interest which flooded for the first
time this dull little life should sweep away the satisfactions of an
existence heart to heart with nature and the dumb life of the
forest!

There was the huge tree asleep yet in the paling moonlight,
and small and hopeful Sylvia began with utmost bravery to
mount to the top of it, with tingling, eager blood coursing the
channels of her whole frame, with her bare feet and fingers, that
pinched and held like bird's claws to the monstrous ladder reaching up, up, almost to the sky itself. First she must mount the
white oak tree that grew alongside, where she was almost lost
among the dark branches and the green leaves heavy and wet
with dew; a bird fluttered off its nest, and a red squirrel ran to
and fro and scolded pettishly at the harmless housebreaker.
Sylvia felt her way easily. She had often climbed there, and
knew that higher still one of the oak's upper branches chafed
against the pine trunk, just where its lower boughs were set close
together. There, when she made the dangerous pass from one
tree to the other, the great enterprise would really begin.

She crept out along the swaying oak limb at last, and took the
daring step across into the old pine tree. The way was harder
than she thought; she must reach far and hold fast, the sharp dry
twigs caught and held her and scratched her like angry talons,
the pitch made her thin little fingers clumsy and stiff as she went
round and round the tree's great stem, higher and higher upward. The sparrows and robins in the woods below were beginning to wake and twitter to the dawn, yet it seemed much lighter
there aloft in the pine tree, and the child knew that she must
hurry if her project were to be of any use.

The tree seemed to lengthen itself out as she went up, and to
reach farther and farther upward. It was like a great mainmast
to the voyaging earth; it must truly have been amazed that morning through all its ponderous frame as it felt this determined
spark of human spirit creeping and climbing from higher branch
to branch. Who knows how steadily the least twigs held themselves to advantage this light, weak creature on her way! The
old pine must have loved his new dependent. More than all the
hawks, and bats, and moths, and even the sweet-voiced thrushes,

was the brave, beating heart of the solitary gray-eyed child. And the tree stood still and held away the winds that June morning while the dawn grew bright in the east.

Sylvia's face was like a pale star, if one had seen it from the ground, when the last thorny bough was past, and she stood trembling and tired but wholly triumphant, high in the treetop. Yes, there was the sea with the dawning sun making a golden dazzle over it, and toward that glorious east flew two hawks with slow-moving pinions. How low they looked in the air from that height when before one had only seen them far up, and dark against the blue sky. Their gray feathers were as soft as moths; they seemed only a little way from the tree, and Sylvia felt as if she too could go flying away among the clouds. Westward, the woodlands and farms reached miles and miles into the distance; here and there were church steeples, and white villages; truly it was a vast and awesome world.

The birds sang louder and louder. At last the sun came up bewilderingly bright. Sylvia could see the white sails of ships out at sea, and the clouds that were purple and rose-colored and yellow at first began to fade away. Where was the white heron's nest in the sea of green branches, and was this wonderful sight and pageant of the world the only reward for having climbed to such a giddy height? Now look down again, Sylvia, where the green marsh is set among the shining birches and dark hemlocks; there where you saw the white heron once you will see him again; look, look! a white spot of him like a single floating feather comes up from the dead hemlock and grows larger, and rises, and comes close at last, and goes by the landmark pine with steady sweep of wing and outstretched slender neck and crested head. And wait! wait! do not move a foot or a finger, little girl, do not send an arrow of light and consciousness from your two eager eyes, for the heron has perched on a pine bough not far beyond yours, and cries back to his mate on the nest, and plumes his feathers for the new day!

The child gives a long sigh a minute later when a company of shouting catbirds comes also to the tree, and vexed by their fluttering and lawlessness the solemn heron goes away. She knows his secret now, the wild, light, slender bird that floats and wavers, and goes back like an arrow presently to his home

A White Heron

in the green world beneath. Then Sylvia, well satisfied, makes her perilous way down again, not daring to look far below the branch she stands on, ready to cry sometimes because her fingers ache and her lamed feet slip. Wondering over and over again what the stranger would say to her, and what he would think when she told him how to find his way straight to the heron's nest.

"Sylvy, Sylvy!" called the busy old grandmother again and again, but nobody answered, and the small husk bed was empty, and Sylvia had disappeared.

The guest waked from a dream, and remembering his day's pleasure hurried to dress himself that it might sooner begin. He was sure from the way the shy little girl looked once or twice yesterday that she had at least seen the white heron, and now she must really be persuaded to tell. Here she comes now, paler than ever, and her worn old frock is torn and tattered, and smeared with pine pitch. The grandmother and the sportsman stand in the door together and question her, and the splendid moment has come to speak of the dead hemlock tree by the green marsh.

But Sylvia does not speak after all, though the old grandmother fretfully rebukes her, and the young man's kind appealing eyes are looking straight in her own. He can make them rich with money; he has promised it, and they are poor now. He is so well worth making happy, and he waits to hear the story she can tell.

No, she must keep silence! What is it that suddenly forbids her and makes her dumb? Has she been nine years growing, and now, when the great world for the first time puts out a hand to her, must she thrust it aside for a bird's sake? The murmur of the pine's green branches is in her ears, she remembers how the white heron came flying through the golden air and how they watched the sea and the morning together, and Sylvia cannot speak; she cannot tell the heron's secret and give its life away.

Dear loyalty, that suffered a sharp pang as the guest went away disappointed later in the day, that could have served and followed him and loved him as a dog loves! Many a night Sylvia heard the echo of his whistle haunting the pasture path as she came home with the loitering cow. She forgot even her sorrow at the sharp report of his gun and the piteous sight of thrushes and sparrows dropping silent to the ground, their songs hushed and their pretty feathers stained and wet with blood. Were the birds better friends than their hunter might have been,—who can tell? Whatever treasures were lost to her, woodlands and summer time, remember! Bring your gifts and graces and tell your secrets to this lonely country child!

The Dulham Ladies

To be leaders of society in the town of Dulham was as satisfactory to Miss Dobin and Miss Lucinda Dobin as if Dulham were London itself. Of late years, though they would not allow themselves to suspect such treason, the most ill-bred of the younger people in the village made fun of them behind their backs, and laughed at their treasured summer mantillas, their mincing steps, and the shape of their parasols.

They were always conscious of the fact that they were the daughters of a once eminent Dulham minister; but beside this unanswerable claim to the respect of the First Parish, they were aware that their mother's social position was one of superior altitude. Madam Dobin's grandmother was a Greenaple, of Boston. In her younger days she had often visited her relatives, the Greenaples and Hightrees, and in seasons of festivity she could relate to a select and properly excited audience her delightful experiences of town life. Nothing could be finer than her account of having taken tea at Governor Clovenfoot's on Beacon Street in company with an English lord, who was indulging himself in a brief vacation from his arduous duties at the Court of St. James.

"He exclaimed that he had seldom seen in England so beautiful and intellectual a company of ladies," Madam Dobin would always say in conclusion. "He was decorated with the blue ribbon of the Knights of the Garter." Miss Dobin and Miss Lucinda thought for many years that this famous blue ribbon was tied about the noble gentleman's leg. One day they even discussed the question openly; Miss Dobin placing the decoration at his knee, and Miss Lucinda locating it much lower down, according to the length of the short gray socks with which she was familiar.

"You have no imagination, Lucinda," the elder sister replied impatiently. "Of course, those were the days of smallclothes and long silk stockings!"—whereat Miss Lucinda was rebuked, but not persuaded.

"I wish that my dear girls could have the outlook upon society which fell to my portion," Madam Dobin sighed, after she had set these ignorant minds to rights, and enriched them by communicating the final truth about the blue ribbon. "I must not chide you for the absence of opportunities, but if our cousin Harriet Greenaple were only living you would not lack enjoyment or social education."

Madam Dobin has now been dead a great many years. She seemed an elderly woman to her daughters some time before she left them; later they thought that she had really died comparatively young, since their own years had come to equal the record of hers. When they visited her tall white tombstone in the orderly Dulham burying ground, it was a strange thought to both the daughters that they were older women than their mother had been when she died. To be sure, it was the fashion to appear older in her day,—they could remember the sober effect of really youthful married persons in cap and frisette; but, whether they owed it to the changed times or to their own qualities, they felt no older themselves than ever they had. Beside upholding the ministerial dignity of their father, they were obliged to give a lenient sanction to the ways of the world for their mother's sake; and they combined the two duties with reverence and impartiality.

Madam Dobin was, in her prime, a walking example of refinements and courtesies. If she erred in any way, it was by keeping too strict watch and rule over her small kingdom. She acted with great dignity in all matters of social administration and etiquette, but, while it must be owned that the parishioners felt a sense of freedom for a time after her death, in their later years they praised and valued her more and more, and often lamented her generously and sincerely.

Several of her distinguished relatives attended Madam Dobin's funeral, which was long considered the most dignified and elegant pageant of that sort which had ever taken place in Dulham. It seemed to mark the close of a famous epoch in Dulham history, and it was increasingly difficult forever afterward to keep the tone of society up to the old standard. Somehow, the distinguished relatives had one by one disappeared, though they all had excellent reasons for the discontinuance of their visits. A few had left this world altogether, and the family circle of the Green-

aples and Hightrees was greatly reduced in circumference. Sometimes, in summer, a stray connection drifted Dulham-ward, and
was displayed to the townspeople (not to say paraded) by the
gratified hostesses. It was a disappointment if the guest could not
be persuaded to remain over Sunday and appear at church.

When household antiquities became fashionable, the ladies
remarked a surprising interest in their corner cupboard and best
chairs, and some distant relatives revived their almost forgotten
custom of paying a summer visit to Dulham. They were not long
in finding out with what desperate affection Miss Dobin and
Miss Lucinda clung to their mother's wedding china and other
inheritances, and were allowed to depart without a single tea-
cup. One graceless descendant of the Hightrees prowled from
garret to cellar, and admired the household belongings diligently,
but she was not asked to accept even the dislocated cherry-wood
footstool that she had discovered in the far corner of the parsonage pew.

Some of the Dulham friends had long suspected that Madam
Dobin made a social misstep when she chose the Reverend
Edward Dobin for her husband. She was no longer young when
she married, and though she had gone through the wood and
picked up a crooked stick at last, it made a great difference that
her stick possessed an ecclesiastical bark. The Reverend Edward
was, moreover, a respectable graduate of Harvard College, and
to a woman of her standards a clergyman was by no means
insignificant. It was impossible not to respect his office, at any
rate, and she must have treated him with proper veneration for
the sake of that, if for no other reason, though his early advantages had been insufficient, and he was quite insensible to
the claims of the Greenaple pedigree, and preferred an Indian
pudding to pie crust that was, without exaggeration, half a
quarter high. The delicacy of Madam Dobin's touch and preference in everything, from hymns to cookery, was quite lost upon
this respected preacher, yet he was not without pride or complete confidence in his own decisions.

The Reverend Mr. Dobin was never very enlightening in his
discourses, and was providentially stopped short by a stroke of
paralysis in the middle of his clerical career. He lived on and on
through many dreary years, but his children never accepted the
fact that he was a tyrant, and served him humbly and patiently.

He fell at last into a condition of great incapacity and chronic trembling, but was able for nearly a quarter of a century to be carried to the meetinghouse from time to time to pronounce farewell discourses. On high days of the church he was always placed in the pulpit, and held up his shaking hands when the benediction was pronounced, as if the divine gift were exclusively his own, and the other minister did but say empty words. Afterward, he was usually tired and displeased and hard to cope with, but there was always a proper notice taken of these too often recurring events.

For old times' sake and for pity's sake and from natural goodness of heart, the elder parishioners rallied manfully about the Reverend Mr. Dobin; and whoever his successor or colleague might be, the Dobins were always called the minister's folks, while the active laborer in that vineyard was only Mr. Smith or Mr. Jones, as the case might be. At last the poor old man died, to everybody's relief and astonishment; and after he was properly preached about and lamented, his daughters, Miss Dobin and Miss Lucinda, took a good look at life from a new standpoint, and decided that now they were no longer constrained by home duties they must make themselves a great deal more use to the town.

Sometimes there is such a household as this (which has been perhaps too minutely described), where the parents linger until their children are far past middle age, and always keep them in a too childish and unworthy state of subjection. The Misses Dobin's characters were much influenced by such an unnatural prolongation of the filial relationship, and they were amazingly slow to suspect that they were not so young as they used to be. There was nothing to measure themselves by but Dulham people and things. The elm trees were growing yet, and many of the ladies of the First Parish were older than they, and called them perhaps too familiarly, the Dobin girls. These elderly persons seemed really to be growing old, and Miss Lucinda lamented the change in society; she thought it a freak of nature and too sudden blighting of earthly hopes that several charming old friends of her mother's were no longer living. They were advanced in age when Miss Lucinda was a young girl, though time and space are but relative, after all.

Their influence upon society would have made a great difference in many ways. Certainly, the new parishioners, who had often enough been instructed to pronounce their pastor's name as if it were spelled with one "b," would not have boldly returned again and again to their obnoxious habit of saying Dobbin. Miss Lucinda might carefully speak to the neighbor and newcomers of "my sister, Miss Do-bin"; only the select company of intimates followed her lead, and at last there was something humiliating about it, even though many persons spoke of them only as "the ladies."

"The name was originally *D'Aubigne,* we think," Miss Lucinda would say coldly and patiently, as if she had already explained this foolish mistake a thousand times too often. It was like the sorrows in many a provincial château in the Reign of Terror. The ladies looked on with increasing dismay at the retrogression in society. They felt as if they were a feeble garrison, to whose lot it had fallen to repulse a noisy, irreverent mob, an increasing band of marauders who would overthrow all land marks of the past, all etiquette and social rank.

The new minister himself was a round-faced, unspiritual-looking young man, whom they would have instinctively ignored if he had not been a minister. The new people who came to Dulham were not like the older residents, and they had no desire to be taught better. Little they cared about the Greenaples or the Hightrees; and once, when Miss Dobin essayed to speak of some detail of her mother's brilliant opportunities in Boston high life, she was interrupted, and the newcomer who sat next her at the parish sewing society began to talk about something else. We cannot believe that it could have been the tea party at Governor Clovenfoot's which the rude creature so disrespectfully ignored, but some persons are capable of showing any lack of good taste.

The ladies had an unusual and most painful sense of failure, as they went home together that evening. "I have always made it my object to improve and interest the people at such times; it would seem so possible to elevate their thoughts and direct them into higher channels," said Miss Dobin sadly. "But as for that Woolden woman, there is no use in casting pearls before swine!"

Miss Lucinda murmured an indignant assent. She had a secret suspicion that the Woolden woman had heard the story in question oftener than had pleased her. She was but an ignorant creature; though she had lived in Dulham twelve or thirteen years, she was no better than when she came. The mistake was in treating sister Harriet as if she were on a level with the rest of the company. Miss Lucinda had observed more than once, lately, that her sister sometimes repeated herself, unconsciously, a little oftener than was agreeable. Perhaps they were getting a trifle dull; toward spring it might be well to pass a few days with some of their friends, and have a change.

"If I have tried to do anything," said Miss Dobin in an icy tone, "it has been to stand firm in my lot and place, and to hold the standard of cultivated mind and elegant manners as high as possible. You would think it had been a hundred years since our mother's death, so completely has the effect of her good breeding and exquisite hospitality been lost sight of, here in Dulham. I could wish that our father had chosen to settle in a larger and more appreciative place. They would like to put us on the shelf, too. I can see that plainly."

"I am sure we have our friends," said Miss Lucinda anxiously, but with a choking voice. "We must not let them think we do not mean to keep up with the times, as we always have. I do feel as if perhaps—our hair"—

And the sad secret was out at last. Each of the sisters drew a long breath of relief at this beginning of a confession.

It was certain that they must take some steps to retrieve their lost ascendency. Public attention had that evening been called to their fast-disappearing locks, poor ladies; and Miss Lucinda felt the discomfort most, for she had been the inheritor of the Hightree hair, long and curly, and chestnut in color. There used to be a waviness about it, and sometimes pretty escaping curls, but these were gone long ago. Miss Dobin resembled her father, and her hair had not been luxuriant, so that she was less changed by its absence than one might suppose. The straightness and thinness had increased so gradually that neither sister had quite accepted the thought that other persons would particularly notice their altered appearance.

They had shrunk, with the reticence born of close family association, from speaking of the cause even to each other, when they made themselves pretty little lace and dotted muslin caps. Breakfast caps, they called them, and explained that these were universally worn in town; the young Princess of Wales originated them, or at any rate adopted them. The ladies offered no apology

The Dulham Ladies

for keeping the breakfast caps on until bedtime, and in spite of them a forward child had just spoken loud and shrill an untimely question in the ears of the for once silent sewing society. "Do Miss Dobbineses wear them great caps because their bare heads is cold?" the little beast had said; and everybody was startled and dismayed.

Miss Dobin had never shown better her good breeding and valor, the younger sister thought.

"No, little girl," replied the stately Harriet, with a chilly smile. "I believe that our headdresses are quite in the fashion for ladies of all ages. And you must remember that it is never polite to make such personal remarks." It was after this that Miss Dobin had been reminded of Madam Somebody's unusual headgear at the evening entertainment in Boston. Nobody but the Woolden woman could have interrupted her under such trying circumstances.

Miss Lucinda, however, was certain that the time had come for making some effort to replace her lost adornment. The child had told an unwelcome truth, but had paved the way for further action, and now was the time to suggest something that had slowly been taking shape in Miss Lucinda's mind. A young grandnephew of their mother and his bride had passed a few days with them, two or three summers before, and the sisters had been quite shocked to find that the pretty young woman wore a row of frizzes, not originally her own, over her smooth forehead. At the time, Miss Dobin and Miss Lucinda had spoken severely with each other of such bad taste, but now it made a great difference that the wearer of the frizzes was not only a relative by marriage and used to good society, but also that she came from town, and might be supposed to know what was proper in the way of toilet.

"I really think, sister, that we had better see about having some—arrangements, next time we go anywhere," Miss Dobin said unexpectedly, with a slight tremble in her voice, just as they reached their own door. "There seems to be quite a fashion for them nowadays. For the parish's sake we ought to recognize"— and Miss Lucinda responded with instant satisfaction. She did not like to complain, but she had been troubled with neuralgic pains in her forehead on suddenly meeting the cold air. The sisters felt a new bond of sympathy in keeping this secret with and for each other; they took pains to say to several acquaintances that they were thinking of going to the next large town to do a few errands for Christmas.

A bright, sunny morning seemed to wish the ladies good fortune. Old Hetty Downs, their faithful maidservant and protector, looked after them in affectionate foreboding. "Dear sakes, what devil's wiles may be played on them blessed innocents afore they're safe home again!" she murmured, as they vanished round the corner of the street that led to the railway station.

Miss Dobin and Miss Lucinda paced discreetly side by side down the main street of Westbury. It was nothing like Boston, of course, but the noise was slightly confusing, and the passers-by sometimes roughly pushed against them. Westbury was a consequential manufacturing town, but a great convenience at times like this. The trifling Christmas gifts for their old neighbors and Sunday-school scholars were purchased and stowed away in their neat Fayal basket before the serious commission of the day was attended to.

Here and there, in the shops, disreputable frizzes were displayed in unblushing effrontery, but no such vulgar shopkeeper merited the patronage of the Misses Dobin. They pretended not to observe the unattractive goods, and went their way to a low, one-storied building on a side street, where an old tradesman lived. He had been useful to the minister while he still remained upon the earth and had need of a wig, sandy in hue and increasingly sprinkled with gray, as if it kept pace with other changes of existence.

But old Paley's shutters were up, and a bar of rough wood was nailed firmly across the one that had lost its fastening and would rack its feeble hinges in the wind. Old Paley had always been polite and bland; they really had looked forward to a little chat with him; they had heard a year or two before of his wife's death, and meant to offer sympathy. His business of hairdressing had been carried on with that of parasol and umbrella mending, and the condemned umbrella which was his sign cracked and swung in the rising wind, a tattered skeleton before the closed door.

The ladies sighed and turned away; they were beginning to feel tired; the day was long, and they had not met with any pleasures yet. "We might walk up the street a little further," suggested Miss Lucinda; "that is, if you are not tired," as they stood hesitating on the corner after they had finished a short discussion of Mr. Paley's disappearance. Happily it was only a few minutes before they came to a stop together in front of a new, shining shop, where smirking waxen heads all in a row were decked with the latest fashions of wigs and frizzes. One smiling fragment of a gentleman stared so straight at Miss Lucinda with his black eyes that she felt quite coy and embarrassed, and was obliged to feign not to be conscious of his admiration. But Miss Dobin, after a brief delay, boldly opened the door and entered; it was better to be sheltered in the shop than exposed to public remark as they gazed in at the windows. Miss Lucinda felt her heart beat and her courage give out; she, coward-like, left the transaction of their business to her sister, and turned to contemplate the back of the handsome model. It was a slight shock to find that he was not so attractive from this point of view. The wig he wore was well made all round, but his shoulders were roughly finished in a substance that looked like plain plaster of Paris.

"What can I have ze pleasure of showing you young ladies?" asked a person who advanced; and Miss Lucinda faced about to discover a smiling, middle-aged Frenchman, who rubbed his hands together and looked at his customers, first one and then the other, with delightful deference. He seemed a very civil, nice person, the young ladies thought.

"My sister and I were thinking of buying some little arrangements to wear above the forehead," Miss Dobin explained, with pathetic dignity; but the Frenchman spared her any further words. He looked with eager interest at the bonnets, as if no lack had attracted his notice before. "Ah, yes. *Je comprends;* ze high foreheads are not now ze mode. Je prefer them, moi, yes, yes, but ze ladies must accept ze fashion; zay must now cover ta forehead with ze frizzes, ze bangs, you say. As you wis', as you wis'!" and the tactful little man, with many shrugs and merry gestures at such girlish fancies, pulled down one box after another.

It was a great relief to find that this was no worse, to say the least, than any other shopping, though the solemnity and secrecy of the occasion were infringed upon by the great supply of "arrangements" and the loud discussion of the color of some crimps a noisy girl was buying from a young saleswoman the other side of the shop.

Miss Dobin waved aside the wares which were being displayed for her approval. "Something—more simple, if you please," —she did not like to say "older."

"But these are *très simple*," protested the Frenchman. "We have nothing younger"; and Miss Dobin and Miss Lucinda blushed, and said no more. The Frenchman had his own way; he persuaded them that nothing was so suitable as some conspicuous forelocks that matched their hair as it used to be. They would have given anything rather than leave their breakfast caps at home, if they had known that their proper winter bonnets must come off. They hardly listened to the wig merchant's glib voice as Miss Dobin stood revealed before the merciless mirror at the back of the shop.

He made everything as easy as possible, the friendly creature, and the ladies were grateful to him. Beside, now that the bonnet was on again, there was a great improvement in Miss Dobin's appearance. She turned to Miss Lucinda, and saw a gleam of delight in her eager countenance. "It really is very becoming. I like the way it parts over your forehead," said the younger sister, "but if it were long enough to go behind the ears"—"*Non, non*," entreated the Frenchman. "To make her the old woman at once would be cruelty!" And Lucinda, who was wondering how well she would look in her turn, succumbed promptly to such protestations. Yes, there was no use in being old before their time. Dulham was not quite keeping pace with the rest of the world in these days, but they need not drag behind everybody else, just because they lived there.

The price of the little arrangements was much less than the sisters expected, and the uncomfortable expense of their reverend father's wigs had been, it was proved, a thing of the past. Miss Dobin treated her polite Frenchman with great courtesy; indeed, Miss Lucinda had more than once whispered to her to talk French, and as they were bowed out of the shop the gracious *Bong-sure* of the elder lady seemed to act like the sting of a shower bath, and bring down an awesome torrent of foreign words upon the two guileless heads. It was impossible to reply; the ladies bowed again, however, and Miss Lucinda caught a last smile from the handsome wax countenance in the window. He appeared to regard her with fresh approval, and she departed down the street with mincing steps.

The Dulham Ladies

"I feel as if anybody might look at me now, sister," said gentle Miss Lucinda. "I confess, I have really suffered sometimes, since I knew I looked so distressed."

"Yours is lighter than I thought it was in the shop," remarked Miss Dobin, doubtfully, but she quickly added that perhaps it would change a little. She was so perfectly satisfied with her own appearance that she could not bear to dim the pleasure of any-one else. The truth remained that she never would have let Lucinda choose that particular arrangement if she had seen it first in a good light. And Lucinda was thinking exactly the same of her companion.

"I am sure we shall have no more neuralgia," said Miss Dobin. "I am sorry we waited so long, dear," and they tripped down the main street of Westbury, confident that nobody would suspect them of being over thirty. Indeed, they felt quite girlish, and unconsciously looked sideways as they went along, to see their satisfying reflections in the windows. The great panes made excellent mirrors, with not too clear or lasting pictures of these comforted passers-by.

The Frenchman in the shop was making merry with his assistants. The two great frisettes had long been out of fashion; he had been lying in wait with them for two unsuspecting country ladies, who could be cajoled into such a purchase.

"Sister," Miss Lucinda was saying, "you know there is still an hour to wait before our train goes. Suppose we take a little longer walk down the other side of the way"; and they strolled slowly back again. In fact, they nearly missed the train, naughty girls! Hetty would have been so worried, they assured each other, but they reached the station just in time.

"Lutie," said Miss Dobin, "put up your hand and part it from your forehead; it seems to be getting out of place a little"; and Miss Lucinda, who had just got breath enough to speak, returned the information that Miss Dobin's was almost covering her eyebrows. They might have to trim them a little shorter; of course it could be done. The darkness was falling; they had taken an early dinner before they started, and now they were tired and hungry after the exertion of the afternoon, but the spirit of youth flamed afresh in their hearts, and they were very happy. If one's heart remains young, it is a sore trial to have the outward appearance entirely at variance. It was the ladies' nature to be girlish, and they found it impossible not to be grateful to the flimsy, ineffectual disguise which seemed to set them right with the world. The old conductor, who had known them for many years, looked hard at them as he took their tickets, and, being a man of humor and compassion, affected not to notice anything remarkable in their appearance. "You ladies never mean to grow old, like the rest of us," he said gallantly, and the sisters fairly quaked with joy.

"Bless us!" the obnoxious Mrs. Woolden was saying, at the other end of the car. "There's the old maid Dobbinses, and they've bought 'em some bangs. I expect they wanted to get thatched in a little before real cold weather; but don't they look just like a pair o' poodle dogs."

The little ladies descended wearily from the train. Somehow they did not enjoy a day's shopping as much as they used. They were certainly much obliged to Hetty for sending her niece's boy to meet them, with a lantern; also for having a good warm supper ready when they came in. Hetty took a quick look at her mistresses, and returned to the kitchen. "I knew somebody would be foolin' of 'em," she assured herself angrily, but she had to laugh. Their dear, kind faces were wrinkled and pale, and the great frizzes had lost their pretty curliness, and were hanging down, almost straight and very ugly, into the ladies' eyes. They could not tuck them under their caps, as they were sure might be done.

Then came a succession of rainy days, and nobody visited the rejuvenated household. The frisettes looked very bright chestnut by the light of day, and it must be confessed that Miss Dobin took the scissors and shortened Miss Lucinda's half an inch, and Miss Lucinda returned the compliment quite secretly, because each thought her sister's forehead lower than her own. Their dear gray eyebrows were honestly displayed, as if it were the fashion not to have them match with wigs. Hetty at last spoke out, and begged her mistresses, as they sat at breakfast, to let her take the frizzes back and change them. Her sister's daughter worked in that very shop, and, though in the workroom, would be obliging. Hetty was sure.

But the ladies looked at each other in pleased assurance, and then turned together to look at Hetty, who stood already a little apprehensive near the table, where she had just put down a plateful of smoking drop cakes. The good creature really began to look old.

"They are worn very much in town," said Miss Dobin. "We think it was quite fortunate that the fashion came in just as our hair was growing a trifle thin. I dare say we may choose those that are a shade duller in color when these are a little past. Oh, we shall not want tea this evening, you remember, Hetty. I am glad there is likely to be such a good night for the sewing circle." And Miss Dobin and Miss Lucinda nodded and smiled.

"Oh, my sakes alive!" the troubled handmaiden groaned. "Going to the circle, be they, to be snickered at! Well, the Dobbin girls they was born, and the Dobbin girls they will remain till they die; but if they ain't innocent Christian babes to those that knows 'em well, mark me down for an idjit myself! They believe them front pieces has set the clock back forty year or more, but if they're pleased to think so, let 'em!"

Away paced the Dulham ladies, late in the afternoon, to grace the parish occasion, and face the amused scrutiny of their neighbors. "I think we owe it to society to observe the fashions of the day," said Miss Lucinda. "A lady cannot afford to be unattractive. I feel now as if we were prepared for anything!"

Miss Tempy's Watchers

THE time of year was April; the place was a small farming town in New Hampshire, remote from any railroad. One by one the lights had been blown out in the scattered houses near Miss Tempy Dent's; but as her neighbors took a last look out of doors, their eyes turned with instinctive curiosity toward the old house where a lamp burned steadily. They gave a little sigh. "Poor Miss Tempy!" said more than one bereft acquaintance; for the good woman lay dead in her north chamber, and the lamp was a watcher's light. The funeral was set for the next day, at one o'clock.

The watchers were two of the oldest friends, Mrs. Crowe and Sarah Ann Binson. They were sitting in the kitchen, because it seemed less awesome than the unused best room, and they beguiled the long hours by steady conversation. One would think that neither topics nor opinions would hold out, at that rate, all through the long spring night; but there was a certain degree of excitement just then, and the two women had risen to an unusual level of expressiveness and confidence. Each had already told the other more than one fact that she had determined to keep secret; they were again and again tempted into statements that either would have found impossible by daylight. Mrs. Crowe was knitting a blue yarn stocking for her husband; the foot was already so long that it seemed as if she must have forgotten to narrow it at the proper time. Mrs. Crowe knew exactly what she was about, however; she was of a much cooler disposition than Sister Binson, who made futile attempts at some sewing, only to drop her work into her lap whenever the talk was most engaging.

Their faces were interesting,—of the dry, shrewd, quick-witted New England type, with thin hair twisted neatly back out of the way. Mrs. Crowe could look vague and benignant, and Miss Binson was, to quote her neighbors, a little too sharp-set; but the world knew that she had need to be, with the load she must carry of supporting an inefficient widowed sister and six unpromising and unwilling nieces and nephews. The eldest boy was at last placed with a good man to learn the mason's trade. Sarah Ann Binson, for all her sharp, anxious aspect, never defended herself, when her sister whined and fretted. She was told every week of her life that the poor children never would have had to lift a finger if their father had lived, and yet she had kept her steadfast way with the little farm, and patiently taught the young people many useful things, for which, as everybody said, they would live to thank her. However pleasureless her life appeared to outward view, it was brimful of pleasure to herself.

Mrs. Crowe, on the contrary, was well-to-do, her husband being a rich farmer and an easy-going man. She was a stingy woman, but for all that she looked kindly; and when she gave away anything, or lifted a finger to help anybody, it was thought a great piece of beneficence, and a compliment, indeed, which the recipient accepted with twice as much gratitude as double the gift that came from a poorer and more generous acquaintance. Everybody liked to be on good terms with Mrs. Crowe. Socially she stood much higher than Sarah Ann Binson.

They were both old schoolmates and friends of Temperance Dent, who had asked them, one day, not long before she died, if they would not come together and look after the house, and manage everything, when she was gone. She may have had some hope that they might become closer friends in this period of intimate partnership, and that the richer woman might better understand the burdens of the poorer. They had not kept the house the night before; they were too weary with their care of their old friend, whom they had not left until all was over.

There was a brook which ran down the hillside very near the house, and the sound of it was much louder than usual. When there was silence in the kitchen, the busy stream had a strange insistence in its wild voice, as if it tried to make the watchers understand something that related to the past.

"I declare, I can't begin to sorrow for Tempy yet. I am so glad to have her at rest," whispered Mrs. Crowe. "It is strange to set here without her, but I can't make it clear that she has gone. I feel as if she had got easy and dropped off to sleep, and I'm more scared about waking her up than knowing any other feeling."

"Yes," said Sarah Ann, "it's just like that, ain't it? But I tell you we are goin' to miss her worse than we expect. She's helped me through with many a trial, has Temperance. I ain't the only one who says the same, neither."

These words were spoken as if there were a third person listening; somebody beside Mrs. Crowe. The watchers could not rid their minds of the feeling that they were being watched themselves. The spring wind whistled in the window crack, now and then, and buffeted the little house in a gusty way that had a sort of companionable effect. Yet, on the whole, it was a very still night, and the watchers spoke in a half whisper.

"She was the freest-handed woman that ever I knew," said Mrs. Crowe, decidedly. "According to her means, she gave away more than anybody. I used to tell her 'twa'nt right. I used really to be afraid that she went without too much, for we have a duty to ourselves."

Sister Binson looked up in a half-amused, unconscious way, and then recollected herself.

Mrs. Crowe met her look with a serious face. "It ain't so easy for me to give as it is for some," she said simply, but with an effort which was made possible only by the occasion. "I should like to say, while Tempy is laying here yet in her own house, that she has been a constant lesson to me. Folks are too kind, and shame me with thanks for what I do. I ain't such a generous woman as poor Tempy was, for all she had nothin' to do with, as one may say."

Sarah Binson was much moved at this confession, and was even pained and touched by the unexpected humility. "You have a good many calls on you"— she began, and then left her kind little compliment half finished.

"Yes, yes, but I've got means enough. My disposition's more of a cross to me as I grow older, and I made up my mind this morning that Tempy's example should be my pattern henceforth." She began to knit faster than ever.

" 'Tain't no use to get morbid: that's what Tempy used to say herself," said Sarah Ann, after a minute's silence. "Ain't it strange to say 'used to say'?" and her own voice choked a little. "She never did like to hear folks git goin' about themselves."

" 'Twas only because they're apt to do it so as other folks say 'twan't so, an' praise 'em up," humbly replied Mrs. Crowe, "and that ain't my object. There wa'n't a child but what Tempy set herself to work to see what she could do to please it. One time my brother's folks had been stopping here in the summer, from Massachusetts. The children was all little, and they broke up a sight of toys, and left 'em when they were going away. Tempy come right up after they rode by, to see if she couldn't help me set the house to rights, and she caught me just as I was going to fling some of the clutter into the stove. I was kind of tired out, starting 'em off in season. 'Oh, give me them!' says she, real pleading; and she wropped 'em up and took 'em home with her when she went, and she mended 'em up and stuck 'em together, and made some young one or other happy with every blessed one. You'd thought I'd done her the biggest favor. 'No thanks to me. I should ha' burnt 'em, Tempy,' says I."

"Some of 'em came to our house, I know," said Miss Binson. "She'd take a lot o' trouble to please a child, 'stead o' shoving of it out o' the way, like the rest of us when we're drove."

"I can tell you the biggest thing she ever gave, and I don't know's there's anybody left but me to tell it. I don't want it forgot," Sarah Binson went on, looking up at the clock to see how the night was going. "It was that pretty-faced Trevor girl, who taught the Corners school, and married so well afterward, out in New York State. You remember her, I dare say?"

"Certain," said Mrs. Crowe, with an air of interest.

"She was a splendid scholar, folks said, and give the school a great start; but she'd overdone herself getting her education, and working to pay for it, and she all broke down one spring, and Tempy made her come and stop with her awhile,—you remember that? Well, she had an uncle, her mother's brother, out in Chicago, who was well off and friendly, and used to write to Lizzie Trevor, and I dare say make her some presents; but he was a lively, driving man, and didn't take time to stop and think about his folks. He hadn't seen her since she was a little girl. Poor Lizzie was so pale and weakly that she just got through the term o' school. She looked as if she was just going straight off in a decline. Tempy, she cosseted her up awhile, and then, next thing folks knew, she was tellin' round how Miss Trevor had gone to see her uncle, and meant to visit Niagary Falls on the way, and stop over night. Now I happened to know, in ways I won't dwell on to explain, that the poor girl was in debt for her schoolin' when she come here, and her last quarter's pay had just squared it off at last, and left her without a cent ahead, hardly; but it had fretted her thinking of it, so she paid it all; they might have dunned her that she owed it to. An' I taxed Tempy about the girl's goin' off on such a journey till she owned up, rather 'n have Lizzie blamed, that she'd given her sixty dollars, same's if she was rolling in riches, and sent her off to have a good rest and vacation."

"Sixty dollars!" exclaimed Mrs. Crowe. "Tempy only had ninety dollars a year that came in to her; rest of her livin' she got by helpin' about, with what she raised off this little piece o' ground, sand one side an' clay the other. An' how often I've heard her tell, years ago, that she'd rather see Niagary than any other sight in the world!"

The women looked at each other in silence; the magnitude of the generous sacrifice was almost too great for their comprehension.

"She was just poor enough to do that!" declared Mrs. Crowe at last, in an abandonment of feeling. "Say what you may, I feel humbled to the dust," and her companion ventured to say nothing. She never had given away sixty dollars at once, but it was simply because she never had it to give. It came to her very lips to say in explanation, "Tempy was so situated"; but she checked herself in time, for she would not break in upon her own loyal guarding of her dependent household.

"Folks say a great deal of generosity, and this one's being public sperited, and that one freehanded about giving," said Mrs. Crowe, who was a little nervous in the silence. "I suppose we can't tell the sorrow it would be to some folks not to give, same's 'twould be to me not to save. I seem kind of made for that, as if 'twas what I'd got to do. I should feel sights better about it if I could make it evident what I was savin' for. If I had a child, now, Sarah Ann," and her voice was a little husky,—"if I had a child, I should think I was heapin' of it up because he was the one trained by the Lord to scatter it again for good. But here's Crowe and me, we can't do anything with money, and both of us like to keep things same's they've always been. Now Priscilla Dance was talking away like a mill clapper, week before last. She'd think I would go right off and get one o' them new-fashioned gilt-and-white papers for the best room, and some new furniture, an' a marble-top table. And I looked at her, all struck up. 'Why,' says I, 'Priscilla, that nice old velvet paper ain't hurt a mite. I shouldn't feel 'twas my best room without it. Dan'el says 'tis the first thing he can remember rubbin' his little baby fingers on to it, and how splendid he thought them red roses was.' I maintain," continued Mrs. Crowe stoutly, "that folks wastes sights o' good money doin' just such foolish things. Tearin' out the insides o' meetin'houses, and fixin' the pews different; 'twas good enough as 'twas with mendin'; then times come, an' they want to put it all back same's 'twas before."

This touched upon an exciting subject to active members of that parish. Miss Binson and Mrs. Crowe belonged to opposite parties, and had at one time come as near hard feelings as they could, and yet escape them. Each hastened to speak of other things, and to show her untouched friendliness.

"I do agree with you," said Sister Binson, "that few of us know what use to make of money, beyond everyday necessities. You've seen more o' the world than I have, and know what's expected. When it comes to taste and judgment about such things, I ought to defer to others"; and with this modest avowal the critical moment passed when there might have been an improper discussion.

In the silence that followed, the fact of their presence in a house of death grew more clear than before. There was something disturbing in the noise of a mouse gnawing at the dry boards of a closet wall near by. Both the watchers looked up anxiously at the clock; it was almost the middle of the night, and the whole world seemed to have left them alone with their solemn duty. Only the brook was awake.

"Perhaps we might give a look upstairs now," whispered Mrs. Crowe, as if she hoped to hear some reason against their going just then to the chamber of death; but Sister Binson rose, with a serious and yet satisfied countenance, and lifted the small lamp from the table. She was much more used to watching than Mrs. Crowe, and much less affected by it. They opened the door into a small entry with a steep stairway; they climbed the creaking stairs, and entered the cold upper room on tiptoe. Mrs. Crowe's heart began to beat very fast as the lamp was put on a high bureau, and made long, fixed shadows about the walls. She went hesitatingly toward the solemn shape under its white drapery, and felt a sense of remonstrance as Sarah Ann gently, but in a business-like way, turned back the thin sheet.

"Seems to me she looks pleasanter and pleasanter," whispered

Sarah Ann Binson impulsively, as they gazed at the white face with its wonderful smile. "Tomorrow 'twill all have faded out. I do believe they kind of wake up a day or two after they die, and it's then they go." She replaced the light covering, and they both turned quickly away; there was a chill in this upper room.

" 'Tis a great thing for anybody to have got through, ain't it?" said Mrs. Crowe softly, as she began to go down the stairs on tiptoe. The warm air from the kitchen beneath met them with a sense of welcome and shelter.

"I don't know why it is, but I feel as near again to Tempy down here as I do up there," replied Sister Binson. "I feel as if the air was full of her, kind of. I can sense things, now and then, that she seems to say. Now I never was one to take up with no nonsense of sperits and such, but I declare I felt as if she told me just now to put some more wood into the stove."

Mrs. Crowe preserved a gloomy silence. She had suspected before this that her companion was of a weaker and more credulous disposition than herself. " 'Tis a great thing to have got through," she repeated, ignoring definitely all that had last been said. "I suppose you know as well as I that Tempy was one that always feared death. Well, it's all put behind her now; she knows what 'tis." Mrs. Crowe gave a little sigh, and Sister Binson's quick sympathies were stirred toward this other old friend, who also dreaded the great change.

"I'd never like to forgit almost those last words Tempy spoke plain to me," she said gently, like the comforter she truly was. "She looked up at me once or twice, that last afternoon after I come to set by her, and let Mis' Owen go home; and I says, 'Can I do anything to ease you, Tempy?' and the tears come into my eyes so I couldn't see what kind of a nod she give me. 'No, Sarah Ann, you can't, dear,' says she; and then she got her breath again, and says she, looking at me real meanin', 'I'm only a-gettin' sleepier and sleepier; that's all there is,' says she, and smiled up at me kind of wishful, and shut her eyes. I knew well enough all she meant. She'd been lookin' out for a chance to tell me, and I don' know's she ever said much afterwards."

Mrs. Crowe was not knitting; she had been listening too eagerly. "Yes, 'twill be a comfort to think of that sometimes," she said, in acknowledgment.

"I know that old Dr. Prince said once, in evenin' meetin', that he'd watched by many a dyin' bed, as we well knew, and enough o' his sick folks had been scared o' dyin' their whole lives through; but when they come to the last, he'd never seen one but was willin', and most were glad, to go. ' 'Tis as natural as bein' born or livin' on,' he said. I don't know what had moved him to speak that night. You know he wa'n't in the habit of it, and 'twas the monthly concert of prayer for foreign missions anyways," said Sarah Ann; "but 'twas a great stay to the mind to listen to his words of experience."

"There never was a better man," responded Mrs. Crowe, in a really cheerful tone. She had recovered from her feeling of nervous dread, the kitchen was so comfortable with lamplight and firelight; and just then the old clock began to tell the hour of twelve with leisurely whirring strokes.

Sister Binson laid aside her work, and rose quickly and went to the cupboard. "We'd better take a little to eat," she explained. "The night will go fast after this. I want to know if you went and made some o' your nice cupcake, while you was home to-day?" she asked, in a pleased tone; and Mrs. Crowe acknowledged such a gratifying piece of thoughtfulness for this humble friend who denied herself all luxuries. Sarah Ann brewed a generous cup of tea, and the watchers drew their chairs up to the table presently, and quelled their hunger with good country appetites. Sister Binson put a spoon into a small, old-fashioned glass of preserved quince, and passed it to her friend. She was almost familiar with the house, and played the part of hostess. "Spread some o' this on your bread and butter," she said to Mrs. Crowe. "Tempy wanted me to use some three or four times, but I never felt to. I know she'd like to have us comfortable now, and would urge us to make a good supper, poor dear."

"What excellent preserves she did make!" mourned Mrs. Crowe. "None of us has got her light hand at doin' things tasty. She made the most o' everything, too. Now, she only had that one old quince tree down in the far corner of the piece, but she'd go out in the spring and tend to it, and look at it so pleasant, and kind of expect the old thorny thing into bloomin'."

"She was just the same with folks," said Sarah Ann. "And she'd never git more'n a little apernful o' quinces, but she'd have every mite o' goodness out o' those, and set the glasses up onto her best-room closet shelf, *so* pleased. 'Twa'n't but a week ago tomorrow mornin' I fetched her a little taste o' jelly in a teaspoon; and she says 'Thank ye,' and took it, an' the minute she tasted it she looked up at me as worried as could be. 'Oh, I don't want to eat that,' says she. 'I always keep that in case o' sickness.' 'You're goin' to have the good o' one tumbler yourself,' says I. 'I'd just like to know who's sick now, if you ain't!' An' she couldn't help laughin', I spoke up so smart. Oh, dear me, how I shall miss talkin' over things with her! She always sensed things, and got just the p'int you meant."

"She didn't begin to age until two or three years ago, did she?" asked Mrs. Crowe. "I never saw anybody keep her looks as Tempy did. She looked young long after I begun to feel like an old woman. The doctor used to say 'twas her young heart, and I don't know but what he was right. How she did do for other folks! There was one spell she wasn't at home a day to a fort-night. She got most of her livin' so, and that made her own potatoes and things last her through. None o' the young folks could get married without her, and all the old ones was disappointed if she wa'n't round when they was down with sickness and had to go. An' cleanin', or tailorin' for boys, or rug hookin',— there was nothin' but what she could do as handy as most. 'I do love to work,'—ain't you heard her say that twenty times a week?"

Sarah Ann Binson nodded, and began to clear away the empty plates. 'We may want a taste o' somethin' more towards mornin',' she said. "There's plenty in the closet here; and in case some comes from a distance to the funeral, we'll have a little table spread after we get back to the house."

"Yes, I was busy all the mornin'. I've cooked up a sight o' things to bring over," said Mrs. Crowe. "I felt 'twas the last I could do for her."

They drew their chairs near the stove again, and took up their work. Sister Binson's rocking chair creaked as she rocked; the brook sounded louder than ever. It was more lonely when nobody spoke, and presently Mrs. Crowe returned to her thoughts of growing old.

"Yes, Tempy aged all of a sudden. I remember I asked her if she felt as well as common, one day, and she laughed at me good. There, when Dan'el begun to look old, I couldn't help feeling as if somethin' ailed him, and like as not 'twas somethin' he was goin' to git right over, and I dosed him for it stiddy, half of one summer."

"How many things we shall be wanting to ask Tempy!" exclaimed Sarah Ann Binson, after a long pause. "I can't make up my mind to doin' without her. I wish folks could come back just once, and tell us how 'tis where they've gone. Seems then we could do without 'em better."

The brook hurried on, the wind blew about the house now and then; the house itself was a silent place, and the supper, the warm fire, and an absence of any new topics for conversation made the watchers drowsy. Sister Binson closed here eyes first, to rest them for a minute; and Mrs. Crowe glanced at her compassionately, with a new sympathy for the hard-worked little woman. She made up her mind to let Sarah Ann have a good rest, while she kept watch alone; but in a few minutes her own knitting was dropped, and she, too, fell asleep.

Overhead, the pale shape of Tempy Dent, the outworn body of that generous, loving-hearted, simple soul, slept on also in its white raiment. Perhaps Tempy herself stood near, and saw her own life and its surroundings with new understanding. Perhaps she herself was the only watcher.

Later, by some hours, Sarah Ann Binson woke with a start. There was a pale light of dawn outside the small windows. Inside the kitchen, the lamp burned dim. Mrs. Crowe awoke, too.

"I think Tempy'd be the first to say 'twas just as well we both had some rest," she said, not without a guilty feeling.

Her companion went to the outer door, and opened it wide. The fresh air was none too cold, and the brook's voice was not nearly so loud as it had been in the midnight darkness. She could see the shapes of the hills, and the great shadows that lay across the lower country. The east was fast growing bright.

" 'Twill be a beautiful day for the funeral," she said, and turned again, with a sigh, to follow Mrs. Crowe up the stairs. The world seemed more and more empty without the kind face and helpful hands of Tempy Dent.

The Town Poor

MRS. WILLIAM TRIMBLE and Miss Rebecca Wright were driving along Hampden east road, one afternoon in early spring. Their progress was slow. Mrs. Trimble's sorrel horse was old and stiff, and the wheels were clogged by clay mud. The frost was not yet out of the ground, although the snow was nearly gone, except in a few places on the north side of the woods, or where it had drifted all winter against a length of fence.

"There must be a good deal o' snow to the nor'ard of us yet," said weatherwise Mrs. Trimble. "I feel it in the air; 'tis more than the ground damp. We ain't goin' to have real nice weather till the up-country snow's all gone."

"I heard say yesterday that there was good sleddin' yet, all up through Parsley," responded Miss Wright. "I shouldn't like to live up in them northern places. My cousin Ellen's husband was a Parsley man, an' he was obliged, as you may have heard, to go up north to his father's second wife's funeral; got back day before yesterday. 'Twas about twenty-one miles, an' they started on wheels; but when they'd gone nine or ten miles, they found 'twas no sort o' use, an' left their wagon an' took a sleigh. The man that owned it charged 'em four an' six, too. I shouldn't have thought he would; they told him they was goin' to a funeral; an' they had their own buffaloes an' everything."

"Well, I expect it's a good deal harder scratchin', up that way; they have to git money where they can; the farms is very poor as you go north," suggested Mrs. Trimble kindly. "'Tain't none too rich a country where we be, but I've always been grateful I wa'n't born up to Parsley."

The old horse plodded along, and the sun, coming out from the heavy spring clouds, sent a sudden shine of light along the muddy road. Sister Wright drew her large veil forward over the high rim of her bonnet. She was not used to driving, or to being much in the open air; but Mrs. Trimble was an active business woman, and looked after her own affairs herself, in all weathers. The late Mr. Trimble had left her a good farm, but not much

ready money, and it was often said that she was better off in the
end than if he had lived. She regretted his loss deeply, however;
it was impossible for her to speak of him, even with intimate
friends, without emotion, and nobody had ever hinted that this
emotion was insincere. She was most warmhearted and generous,
and in her limited way played the part of Lady Bountiful in the
town of Hampden.

"Why, there's where the Bray girls lives, ain't it?" she exclaimed, as, beyond a thicket of witch hazel and scrub oak, they
came in sight of a weather-beaten, solitary farmhouse. The barn
was too far away for thrift or comfort, and they could see long
lines of light through the shrunken boards as they came nearer.
The fields looked both stony and sodden. Somehow, even Parsley itself could be hardly more forlorn.

"Yes'm," said Miss Wright, "that's where they live now, poor
things. I know the place, though I ain't been up here for years.
You don't suppose, Mis' Trimble—I ain't seen the girls out to
meetin' all winter. I've re'lly been covetin' "—

"Why, yes, Rebecca, of course we could stop," answered Mrs.
Trimble heartily. "The exercises was over earlier'n I expected,
an' you're goin' to remain over night long o' me, you know.
There won't be no tea till we git there, so we can't be late. I'm in
the habit o' sendin' a basket to the Bray girls when any o' our
folks is comin' this way, but I ain't been to see 'em since they
moved up here. Why, it must be a good deal over a year ago.
I know 'twas in the late winter they had to make the move. 'Twas
cruel hard, I must say, an' if I hadn't been down with my pleurisy
fever I'd have stirred round an' done somethin' about it. There
was a good deal o' sickness at the time, an'—well, 'twas kind o'
rushed through, breakin' of 'em up, an' lots o' folks blamed the
selec'men; but when 'twas done, 'twas done, an' nobody took
hold to undo it. Ann an' Mandy looked same's ever when they
come to meetin', 'long in the summer,—kind o' wishful, perhaps.
They've always sent me word they was gittin' on pretty comfortable."

"That would be their way," said Rebecca Wright. "They never
was any hand to complain, though Mandy's less cheerful than
Ann. If Mandy'd been spared such poor eyesight, an' Ann hadn't
got her lame wrist that wa'n't set right, they'd kep' off the town
fast enough. They both shed tears when they talked to me about

havin' to break up, when I went to see 'em before I went over to brother Asa's. You see we was brought up neighbors an' went to school together, the Brays an' me. 'Twas a special Providence brought us home this road, I've been so covetin' a chance to git to see 'em. My lameness hampers me."

"I'm glad we come this way, myself," said Mrs. Trimble.

"I'd like to see just how they fare," Miss Rebecca Wright continued. "They give their consent to goin' on the town because they knew they'd got to be dependent, an' so they felt 'twould come easier for all than for a few to help 'em. They acted real dignified an' right-minded, contrary to what most do in such cases, but they was dreadful anxious to see who would bid 'em off, town-meeting day; they did so hope 'twould be somebody right in the village. I just sat down an' cried good when I found Abel Janes's folks had got hold of 'em. They always had the name of bein' slack an' poor spirited, an' they did it just for what they got out o' the town. The selectmen this last year ain't what we have had. I hope they've been considerate about the Bray girls."

"I should have be'n more considerate about fetchin' of you up," apologized Mrs. Trimble. "I've got my horse, an' you're lame footed; 'tis too far for you to come. But time does slip away with busy folks, an' I forgit a good deal I ought to remember."

"There's nobody more considerate than you be," protested Miss Rebecca Wright.

Mrs. Trimble made no answer, but took out her whip and gently touched the sorrel horse, who walked considerably faster, but did not think it worth while to trot. It was a long, roundabout way to the house, farther down the road and up a lane.

"I never had any opinion of the Bray girls' father, leavin' 'em as he did," said Mrs. Trimble.

"He was much praised in his time, though there was always some said his early life hadn't been up to the mark," explained her companion. "He was a great favorite of our then preacher, the Reverend Daniel Longbrother. They did a good deal for the parish, but they did it their own way. Deacon Bray was one that did his part in the repairs without urging. You know 'twas in his time the first repairs was made, when they got out the old soundin' board an' them handsome square pews. It cost an awful sight o' money, too. They hadn't done payin' up that debt when they set to to alter it again an' git the walls frescoed. My grandmother was one that always spoke her mind right out, an' she was dreadful opposed to breakin' up the square pews where she'd always set. They was countin' up what 'twould cost in parish meetin', an' she riz right up an' said 'twouldn't cost nothin' to let 'em stay, an' there wa'n't a house carpenter left in the parish that could do such nice work, an' time would come when the great-grandchildren would give their eyeteeth to have the old meetin' house look just as it did then. But haul the inside to pieces they would and did."

"There come to be a real fight over it, didn't there?" agreed Mrs. Trimble soothingly. "Well, 'twa'n't good taste. I remember the old house well. I come here as a child to visit a cousin o' mother's, an' Mr. Trimble's folks was neighbors, an' we was drawed to each other then, young's we was. Mr. Trimble spoke of it many's the time,—the first time he ever see me, in a leghorn hat with a feather; 'twas one that mother had, an' pressed over."

"When I think of them old sermons that used to be preached in that old meetin' house of all, I'm glad it's altered over, so's not to remind folks," said Miss Rebecca Wright, after a suitable pause. "Them old brimstone discourses, you know, Mis' Trimble. Preachers is far more reasonable, nowadays. Why, I set an' thought, last Sabbath, as I listened, that if old Mr. Longbrother an' Deacon Bray could hear the difference they'd crack the ground over 'em like pole beans, an' come right up 'longside their headstones."

Mrs. Trimble laughed heartily, and shook the reins three or four times by way of emphasis. "There's no gitting round you," she said, much pleased. "I should think Deacon Bray would want to rise, anyway, if 'twas so he could, an' knew how his poor girls was farin'. A man ought to provide for his folks he's got to leave behind him, specially if they're women. To be sure, they had their little home; but we've seen how, with all their in-dustrious ways, they hadn't means to keep it. I s'pose he thought he'd got time enough to lay by, when he give so generous in collections; but he didn't lay by, an' there they be. He might have took lessons from the squirrels; even them little wild creatur's makes them their winter hoards, an' men folks ought to know enough if squirrels does. 'Be just before you are generous'; that's what was always set for the B's in the copybooks, when I was to school, and it often runs through my mind."

"'As for man, his days are as grass,'—that was for A; the two go
well together," added Miss Rebecca Wright soberly. "My good
gracious, ain't this a starved-lookin' place? It makes me ache to
think them nice Bray girls has to brook it here."

The sorrel horse, though somewhat puzzled by an unexpected
deviation from his homeward way, willingly came to a stand by
the gnawed corner of the dooryard fence, which evidently served
as hitching place. Two or three ragged old hens were picking
about the yard, and at last a face appeared at the kitchen window, tied up in a handkerchief, as if it were a case of toothache.
By the time our friends reached the side door next this window,
Mrs. Janes came disconsolately to open it for them, shutting it
again as soon as possible, though the air felt more chilly inside
the house.

"Take seats," said Mrs. Janes briefly. "You'll have to see me just
as I be. I have been suffering these four days with the ague, and
everything to do. Mr. Janes is to court, on the jury. 'Twas in-
convenient to spare him. I should be pleased to have you lay off
your things."

Comfortable Mrs. Trimble looked about the cheerless kitchen,
and could not think of anything to say; so she smiled blandly
and shook her head in answer to the invitation. "We'll just set a
few minutes with you, to pass the time o' day, an' then we must go
in an' have a word with the Miss Brays, bein' old acquaintance.
It ain't been so we could git to call on 'em before. I don't know's
you're acquainted with Miss R'becca Wright. She's been out of
town a good deal."

"I heard she was stopping over to Plainfields with her brother's
folks," replied Mrs. Janes, rocking herself with irregular motion,
as she sat close to the stove. "Got back some time in the fall, I
believe?"

"Yes'm," said Miss Rebecca, with an undue sense of guilt and
conviction. "We've been to the installation over to the East Parish,
an' thought we'd stop in; we took this road home to see if 'twas
any better. How is the Miss Brays gittin' on?"

"They're well's common," answered Mrs. Janes grudgingly. "I
was put out with Mr. Janes for fetchin' of 'em here, with all I've
got to do, an' I own I was kind o' surly to 'em 'long to the first
of it. He gits the money from the town, an' it helps him out; but
he bid 'em off for five dollars a month, an' we can't do much for

'em at no such price as that. I went an' dealt with the selec'men, an' made 'em promise to find their firewood an' some other things extra. They was glad to git rid o' the matter the fourth time I went, an' would ha' promised 'most anything. But Mr. Janes don't keep me half the time in ovenwood, he's off so much; an' we was cramped o' room, any way. I have to store things up garrit a good deal, an' that keeps me trampin' right through their room. I do the best for 'em I can, Mis' Trimble, but 'tain't so easy for me as 'tis for you, with all your means to do with."

The poor woman looked pinched and miserable herself, though it was evident that she had no gift at house or home keeping. Mrs. Trimble's heart was wrung with pain, as she thought of the unwelcome inmates of such a place; but she held her peace bravely, while Miss Rebecca again gave some brief information in regard to the installation.

"You go right up them back stairs," the hostess directed at last. "I'm glad some o' you church folks has seen fit to come an' visit 'em. There ain't been nobody here this long spell, an' they've aged a sight since they come. They always send down a taste out of your baskets, Mis' Trimble, an' I relish it. I tell you. I'll shut the door after you, if you don't object. I feel every draught o' cold air."

"I've always heard she was a great hand to make a poor mouth. Wa'n't she from somewheres up Parsley way?" whispered Miss Rebecca, as they stumbled in the half-light.

"Poor meechin' body, wherever she come from," replied Mrs. Trimble, as she knocked at the door.

There was silence for a moment after this unusual sound; then one of the Bray sisters opened the door. The eager guests stared into a small, low room, brown with age, and gray, too, as if former dust and cobwebs could not be made wholly to disappear. The two elderly women who stood there looked like captives. Their withered faces wore a look of apprehension, and the room itself was more bare and plain than was fitting to their evident refinement of character and self-respect. There was an uncovered small table in the middle of the floor, with some crackers on a plate; and, for some reason or other, this added a great deal to the general desolation.

But Miss Ann Bray, the elder sister, who carried her right arm in a sling, with piteously drooping fingers, gazed at the visitors with radiant joy. She had not seen them arrive. The one window gave only the view at the back of the house, across the fields, and their coming was indeed a surprise. The next minute she was laughing and crying together. "Oh, sister!" she said, "if here ain't our dear Mis' Trimble!—an' my heart o' goodness, 'tis 'Becca Wright, too! What dear good creatur's you be! I've felt all day as if somethin' good was goin' to happen, an' was just sayin' to myself 'twas most sundown now, but I wouldn't let on Mandany I'd give up hope quite yet. You see, the scissors stuck in the floor this very mornin', an' it's always a reliable sign. There, I've got to kiss ye both again!"

"I don't know where we can all set," lamented sister Mandana. "There ain't but the one chair an' the bed; t'other chair's too rickety; an' we've been promised another these ten days; but first they've forgot it, an' next Mis' Janes can't spare it,—one excuse an' another. I'm goin' to git a stump o' wood an' nail a board on to it, when I can git outdoor again," said Mandana, in a plaintive voice. "There, I ain't goin' to complain o' nothin', now you've come," she added; and the guests sat down, Mrs. Trimble, as was proper, in the one chair.

"We've sat on the bed many's the time with you, 'Becca, an' talked over our girl nonsense, ain't we? You know where 'twas, —in the little back bedroom we had when we was girls, an' used to peek out at our beaux through the strings o' mornin'-glories," laughed Ann Bray delightedly, her thin face shining more and more with joy. "I brought some o' them mornin'-glory seeds along when we come away, we'd raised 'em so many years; an' we got 'em started all right, but the hens found 'em out. I declare I chased them poor hens, foolish as 'twas; but the mornin'-glories I'd counted on a sight to remind me o' home. You see, our debts was so large, after my long sickness an' all, that we didn't feel 'twas right to keep back anything we could help from the auction."

It was impossible for anyone to speak for a moment or two; the sisters felt their own uprooted condition afresh, and their guests for the first time really comprehended the piteous contrast between that neat little village house, which now seemed a palace of comfort, and this cold, unpainted upper room in the remote Janes farmhouse. It was an unwelcome thought to Mrs. Trimble that the well-to-do town of Hampden could provide no better

The Town Poor

for its poor than this, and her round face flushed with resentment and the shame of personal responsibility. "The girls shall be well settled in the village before another winter, if I pay their board myself," she made an inward resolution, and took another almost tearful look at the broken stove, the miserable bed, and the sisters' one hair-covered trunk, on which Mandana was sitting. But the poor place was filled with a golden spirit of hospitality.

Rebecca was again discoursing eloquently of the installation; it was so much easier to speak of general subjects, and the sisters had evidently been longing to hear some news. Since the late summer they had not been to church, and presently Mrs. Trimble asked the reason.

"Now, don't you go to pouring out our woes, Mandy!" begged little old Ann, looking shy and almost girlish, and as if she insisted upon playing that life was still all before them and all pleasure. "Don't you go to spoilin' their visit with our complaints! They know well's we do that changes must come, an' we'd been so wonted to our home things that this come hard at first; but then they felt for us, I know just as well's can be. 'Twill soon be summer again, an' 'tis real pleasant right out in the fields here, when there ain't too hot a spell. I've got to know a sight o' new singin' birds since we come."

"Give me the folks I've always known," sighed the younger sister, who looked older than Miss Ann, and less even-tempered. "You may have your birds, if you want 'em. I do re'lly long to go to meetin' an' see folks go by up the aisle. Now, I will speak of it, Ann, whatever you say. We need, each of us, a pair o' good stout shoes an' rubbers,—ours are all wore out; an' we've asked an' asked, an' they never think to bring 'em, an'"—

Poor old Mandana, on the trunk, covered her face with her arms and sobbed aloud. The elder sister stood over her, and patted her on the thin shoulder like a child, and tried to comfort her. It crossed Mrs. Trimble's mind that it was not the first time one had wept and the other had comforted. The sad scene must have been repeated many times in that long, drear winter. She would see them forever after in her mind as fixed as a picture, and her own tears fell fast.

"You didn't see Mis' Janes's cunning little boy, the next one to the baby, did you?" asked Ann Bray, turning round quickly at last, and going cheerfully on with the conversation. "Now, hush,

Mandy, dear; they'll think you're childish! He's a dear, friendly little creatur', an' likes to stay with us a good deal, though we feel's if 'twas too cold for him, now we are waitin' to get us more wood."

"When I think of the acres o' woodland in this town!" groaned Rebecca Wright. "I believe I'm goin' to preach next Sunday, 'stead o' the minister, an' I'll make the sparks fly. I've always heard the saying, 'What's everybody's business is nobody's business,' an' I've come to believe it."

"Now, don't you, 'Becca. You've happened on a kind of a poor time with us, but we've got more belongings than you see here, an' a good large cluset, where we can store those things there ain't room to have about. You an' Miss Trimble have happened on a kind of poor day, you know. Soon's I git me some stout shoes an' rubbers, as Mandy says, I can fetch home plenty o' little dry boughs o' pine; you remember I was always a great hand to roam in the woods? If we could only have a front room, so 't we could look out on the road an' see the passin', an' was shod for meetin', I don't know's we should complain. Now we're just goin' to give you what we 've got, an' make out with a good welcome. We make more tea 'n we want in the mornin', an' then let the fire go down, since 't has been so mild. We've got a *good* cluset" (disappearing as she spoke), "an' I know this to be good tea, 'cause it's some o' yourn, Mis' Trimble. An' here are our sprigged chiny cups that R'becca knows by sight, if Mis' Trimble don't. We kep' out four of 'em, an' put the even half dozen with the rest of the auction stuff. I've often wondered who'd get 'em, but I never asked, for fear 'twould be somebody that would distress us. They was mother's, you know."

The four cups were poured, and the little table pushed to the bed, where Rebecca Wright still sat, and Mandana, wiping her eyes, came and joined her. Mrs. Trimble sat in her chair at the end, and Ann trotted about the room in pleased content for a while, and in and out of the closet, as if she still had much to do; then she came and stood opposite Mrs. Trimble. She was very short and small, and there was no painful sense of her being obliged to stand. The four cups were not quite full of cold tea, but there was a clean old tablecloth folded double, and a plate with three pairs of crackers neatly piled, and a small—it must be owned, a very small—piece of hard white cheese. Then, for a treat, in a glass dish, there was a little preserved peach, the last—Miss Rebecca knew it instinctively—of the household stores brought from their old home. It was very sugary, this bit of peach; and as she helped her guests and sister Mandy, Miss Ann Bray said, half unconsciously, as she often had said with less reason in the old days, "Our preserves ain't so good as usual this year; this is beginning to candy." Both the guests protested, while Rebecca added that the taste of it carried her back, and made her feel young again. The Brays had always managed to keep one or two peach trees alive in their corner of a garden. "I've been keeping this preserve for a treat," said her friend. "I'm glad to have you eat some, 'Becca. Last summer I often wished you was home an' could come an' see us, 'stead o' being away off to Plainfields."

The crackers did not taste too dry. Miss Ann took the last of the peach on her own cracker; there could not have been quite a small spoonful, after the others were helped, but she asked them first if they would not have some more. Then there was a silence, and in the silence a wave of tender feeling rose high in the hearts of the four elderly women. At this moment the setting sun flooded the poor plain room with light; the unpainted wood was all of a golden-brown, and Ann Bray, with her gray hair and aged face, stood at the head of the table in a kind of aureole. Mrs. Trimble's face was all a-quiver as she looked at her; she thought of the text about two or three being gathered together, and was half afraid.

"I believe we ought to 've asked Mis' Janes if she wouldn't come up," said Ann. "She's real good feelin', but she's had it very hard, an' gits discouraged. I can't find that she's ever had anything real pleasant to look back to, as we have. There, next time we'll make a good heartenin' time for her too."

The sorrel horse had taken a long nap by the gnawed fence rail, and the cool air after sundown made him impatient to be gone. The two friends jolted homeward in the gathering darkness, through the stiffening mud, and neither Mrs. Trimble nor Rebecca Wright said a word until they were out of sight as well as out of sound of the Janes house. Time must elapse before they could reach a more familiar part of the road and resume conversation on its natural level.

"I consider myself to blame," insisted Mrs. Trimble at last. "I haven't no words of accusation for nobody else, an' I ain't one to take comfort in calling names to the board o' selec'*men*. I make no reproaches, an' I take it all on my own shoulders; but I'm goin' to stir about me, I tell you! I shall begin early tomorrow. They're goin' back to their own house,—it's been standin' empty all winter,—an' the town's goin' to give 'em the rent an' what firewood they need; it won't come to more than the board's payin' out now. An' you an' me 'll take this same horse an' wagon, an' ride an' go afoot by turns, an' git means enough together to buy back their furniture an' whatever was sold at that plaguy auction; an' then we'll put it all back, an' tell 'em they've got to move to a new place, an' just carry 'em right back again where they come from. An' don't you never tell, R'becca, but here I be a widow woman, layin' up what I make from my farm for nobody knows who, an' I'm goin' to do for them Bray girls all I'm a mind to. I should be sca't to wake up in heaven, an' hear anybody there ask how the Bray girls was. Don't talk to me about the town o' Hampden, an' don't ever let me hear the name o' town poor! I'm ashamed to go home an' see what's set out for supper. I wish I'd brought 'em right along."

"I was goin' to ask if we couldn't git the new doctor to go up an' do somethin' for poor Ann's arm," said Miss Rebecca. "They say he's very smart. If she could get so's to braid straw or hook rugs again, she'd soon be earnin' a little somethin'. An' maybe he could do somethin' for Mandy's eyes. They did use to live so neat an' ladylike. Somehow I couldn't speak to tell 'em there that 'twas I bought them six best cups an' saucers, time of the auction; they went very low, as everythin' else did, an' I thought I could save it some other way. They shall have 'em back an' welcome. You're real wholehearted, Mis' Trimble. I expect Ann 'll be sayin' that her father's child'n wa'n't goin' to be left desolate, an' that all the bread he cast on the waters's comin' back through you."

"I don't care what she says, dear creatur'!" exclaimed Mrs. Trimble. "I'm full o' regrets I took time for that installation, an' set there seepin' in a lot o' talk this whole day long, except for its kind of bringin' us to the Bray girls. I wish to my heart 'twas tomorrow mornin' a'ready, an' I a-startin' for the selec'*men*."

Miss Esther's Guest

I

Old Miss Porley put on her silk shawl, and arranged it carefully over her thin shoulders, and pinned it with a hand that shook a little as if she were much excited. She bent forward to examine the shawl in the mahogany-framed mirror, for there was a frayed and tender spot in the silk where she had pinned it so many years. The shawl was very old; it had been her mother's, and she disliked to wear it too often, but she never could make up her mind to go out into the street in summer, as some of her neighbors did, with nothing, over her shoulders at all. Next she put on her bonnet and tried to set it straight, allowing for a wave in the looking glass that made one side of her face appear much longer than the other; then she drew on a pair of well-darned silk gloves; one had a wide crack all the way up the back of the hand, but they were still neat and decent for everyday wear, if she were careful to keep her left hand under the edge of the shawl. She had discussed the propriety of drawing the raveled silk together, but a thick seam would look very ugly, and there was something accidental about the crack.

Then, after hesitating a few moments, she took a small piece of folded white letter-paper from the table and went out of the house, locking the door and trying it, and stepped away bravely down the village street. Everybody said, "How do you do, Miss Porley?" or "Good-mornin', Esther." Every one in Daleham knew the good woman; she was one of the unchanging persons, always to be found in her place, and always pleased and friendly and ready to take an interest in old and young. She and her mother, who had early been left a widow, had been for many years the village tailoresses and makers of little boys' clothes. Mrs. Porley had been dead three years, however, and her daughter "Easter," as old friends called our heroine, had lived quite alone. She was made very sorrowful by her loneliness, but she never could be persuaded to take anybody to board: she could not bear to think of anyone's taking her mother's place.

It was a warm summer morning, and Miss Porley had not very far to walk, but she was still more shaky and excited by the time she reached the First Church parsonage. She stood at the gate undecidedly, and, after she pushed it open a little way, she drew back again, and felt a curious beating at her heart and a general reluctance of mind and body. At that moment the minister's wife, a pleasant young woman with a smiling, eager face, looked out of the window and asked the tremulous visitor to come in. Miss Esther straightened herself and went briskly up the walk; she was very fond of the minister's wife, who had only been in Daleham a few months.

"Won't you take off your shawl?" asked Mrs. Wayton affectionately; "I have just been making gingerbread, and you shall have a piece as soon as it cools."

"I don't know's I ought to stop," answered Miss Esther, flushing quickly. "I came on business; I won't keep you long."

"Oh, please stay a little while," urged the hostess. "I'll take my sewing, if you don't mind; there are two or three things that I want to ask you about."

"I've thought and flustered a sight over taking this step," said good old Esther abruptly. "I had to conquer a sight o' reluctance, I must say. I've got so used to livin' by myself that I sha'n't know how to consider another. But I see I ain't got common feelin' for others unless I can set my own comfort aside once in a while. I've brought you my name as one of those that will take one o' them city folks that needs a spell o' change. It come straight home to me how I should be feeling it by this time, if my lot had been cast in one o' them city garrets that the minister described so affecting. If 't hadn't been for kind consideration somewheres, mother an' me might have sewed all them pleasant years away in the city that we enjoyed so in our own home, and our garding to step right out into when our sides set in to ache. And I ain't rich, but we was able to save a little something, and now I'm eatin' of it all up alone. It come to me I should like to have somebody take a taste out o' mother's part. Now, don't you let 'em send me no rampin' boys like them Barnard's folks had come last year, that vexed dumb creatur's so; and I don't know how to cope with no kind o' men folks or strange girls, but I should know how to do for a woman that's getting well along in years, an' has come to feel kind o' spent. Perhaps we ain't no right to pick an' choose, but I should know best how to make that sort comfortable on 'count of doin' for mother and studying what she preferred."

Miss Esther rose with quaint formality and put the folded paper, on which she had neatly written her name and address, into Mrs. Wayton's hand. Mrs. Wayton rose soberly to receive it, and then they both sat down again.

"I'm sure that you will feel more than repaid for your kindness, dear Miss Esther," said the minister's wife. "I know one of the ladies who have charge of the arrangements for the Country Week, and I will explain as well as I can the kind of guest you have in mind. I quite envy her; I have often thought, when I was busy and tired, how much I should like to run along the street and make you a visit in your dear old-fashioned little house."

"I should be more than pleased to have you, I'm sure," said Miss Esther, startled into a bright smile and forgetting her anxiety. "Come any day, and take me just as I am. We used to have a good deal o' company years ago, when there was a number o' mother's folks still livin' over Ashfield way. Sure as we had a pile o' work on hand and was hurrying for dear life an' limb, a wagonload would light down at the front gate to spend the day an' have an early tea. Mother never was one to get flustered same's I do 'bout everything. She was a lovely cook, and she'd fill 'em up an' cheer 'em, and git 'em off early as she could, an' then we'd be kind o' waked up an' spirited ourselves, and would set up late sewin' and talkin' the company over, an' I'd have things saved to tell her that had been said while she was out o' the room. I make such a towse over everything myself, but mother was waked right up and felt pleased an' smart, if anything unexpected happened. I miss her more every year," and Miss Esther gave a great sigh. "I s'pose 'twa'n't reasonable to expect that I could have her to help me through with old age, but I'm a poor tool, alone."

"Oh, no, you mustn't say that!" exclaimed the minister's wife. "Why, nobody could get along without you. I wish I had come to Daleham in time to know your mother too."

Miss Esther shook her head sadly. "She would have set everything by you and Mr. Wayton. Now I must be getting back in case I'm wanted, but you let 'em send me somebody right away, while my bush beans is so nice. An' if any o' your little boy's clothes wants repairin', just give 'em to me; 'twill be a real pleasant thing to set a few stitches. Or the minister's; ain't there something needed for him?"

Mrs. Wayton was about to say no, when she became conscious of the pleading old face before her. "I'm sure you are most kind, dear friend," she answered, "and I do have a great deal to do. I'll bring you two or three things tonight that are beyond my art, as I go to evening meeting. Mr. Wayton frayed out his best coat sleeve yesterday, and I was disheartened, for we had counted upon his not having a new one before the fall."

" 'Twould be mere play to me," said Miss Esther, and presently she went smiling down the street.

II

The Committee for the Country Week in a certain ward of Boston were considering the long list of children, and mothers with babies, and sewing women, who were looking forward, some of them for the first time in many years, to a country holiday. Some were to go as guests to hospitable, generous farmhouses that opened their doors willingly now and then to tired city people; for some persons board could be paid.

The immediate arrangements of that time were settled at last, except that Mrs. Belton, the chairman, suddenly took a letter from her pocket. "I had almost forgotten this," she said; "it is another place offered in dear quiet old Daleham. My friend, the minister's wife there, writes me a word about it: 'The applicant desires especially an old person, being used to the care of an aged parent and sure of her power of making such a one comfortable, and she would like to have her guest come as soon as possible.' My friend asks me to choose a person of some refinement,—'one who would appreciate the delicate simplicity and quaint ways of the hostess.' "

Mrs. Belton glanced hurriedly down the page. "I believe that's all," she said. "How about that nice old sewing woman, Mrs. Connolly, in Bantry Street?"

"Oh, no!" some one entreated, looking up from her writing. "Why isn't it just the place for my old Mr. Rill, the dear old Englishman who lives alone up four flights in Town Court and has the bullfinch. He used to engrave seals, and his eyes gave out, and he is so thrifty with his own bit of savings and an atom of a pension. Someone pays his expenses to the country, and this sounds like a place he would be sure to like. I've been watching for the right chance."

"Take it, then," said the busy chairman, and there was a little more writing and talking, and then the committee meeting was over which settled Miss Esther Porley's fate.

III

The journey to Daleham was a great experience to Mr. Rill. He was a sensible old person, who knew well that he was getting stiffer and clumsier than need be in his garret, and that, as certain friends had said, a short time spent in the country would cheer and invigorate him. There had been occasional propositions that he should leave his garret altogether and go to the country to live, or at least to the suburbs of the city. He could not see things close at hand so well as he could take a wide outlook, and as his outlook from the one garret window was a still higher brick wall and many chimneys, he was losing a great deal that he might have had. But so long as he was expected to take an interest in the unseen and unknown he failed to accede to any plans about the country home, and declared that he was well enough in his high abode. He had lost a sister a few years before who had been his mainstay, but with his hands so well used to delicate work he had been less bungling in his simple household affairs than many another man might have been. But he was very lonely and was growing anxious; as he was rattled along in the train toward Daleham he held the chirping bullfinch's cage fast with both hands, and said to himself now and then, "This may lead to something; the country air smells very good to me."

The Daleham station was not very far out of the village, so that Miss Esther Porley put on her silk shawl and bonnet and everyday gloves just before four o'clock that afternoon, and went to meet her Country Week guest. Word had come the day before that the person for Miss Porley's would start two days in advance of the little company of children and helpless women, and since this message had come from the parsonage Miss Esther had worked diligently, late and early, to have her house in proper order. Whatever her mother had liked was thought of and provided. There were going to be rye shortcakes for tea, and there were some sprigs of thyme and sweet balm in an old-fashioned wine glass on the keeping-room table; mother always said they were so freshening. And Miss Esther had taken out a little shoulder shawl and folded it over the arm of the rocking chair by the window that looked out into the small garden where the London pride was in full bloom, and the morning glories had just begun to climb. Miss Esther was sixty-four herself, but still looked upon age as well in the distance.

She was always a prompt person, and had some minutes to wait at the station; then the time passed and the train was late. At last she saw the smoke far in the distance, and her heart began to sink. Perhaps she would not find it easy to get on with the old lady, and—well it was only for a week, and she had thought it right and best to take such a step, and now it would soon be over.

The train stopped, and there was no old lady at all.

Miss Esther had stood far back to get away from the smoke and roar,—she was always as afraid of the cars as she could be,—but as they moved away she took a few steps forward to scan the platform. There was no black bonnet with a worn lace veil, and no old lady with a burden of bundles; there were only the station master and two or three men, and an idle boy or two, and one clean-faced, bent old man with a bird cage in one hand and an old carpetbag in the other. She thought of the rye short-cakes for supper and all that she had done to make her small home pleasant, and her fire of excitement suddenly fell into ashes.

The old man with the bird cage suddenly turned toward her. "Can you direct me to Miss Esther Porley's?" said he.

"I can," replied Miss Esther, looking at him with curiosity.

"I was directed to her house," said the pleasant old fellow, "by Mrs. Belton, of the Country Week Committee. My eyesight is poor. I should be glad if anybody would help me to find the place."

"You step this way with me, sir," said Miss Esther. She was afraid that the men on the platform heard every word they said, but nobody took particular notice, and off they walked down the road together. Miss Esther was enraged with the Country Week Committee.

"*You* were sent to—Miss Porley's?" she asked grimly, turning to look at him.

"I was, indeed," said Mr. Rill.

"I am Miss Porley, and I expected an old lady," she managed to say, and they both stopped and looked at each other with apprehension.

"I do declare!" faltered the old seal cutter anxiously. "What had I better do, ma'am? They most certain give me your name. Maybe you could recommend me somewheres else, an' I can get home tomorrow if 'tain't convenient."

They were standing under a willow tree in the shade; Mr. Rill took off his heavy hat,—it was a silk hat of bygone shape; a golden robin began to sing, high in the willow, and the old bullfinch twittered and chirped in the cage. Miss Esther heard some footsteps coming behind them along the road. She changed color; she tried to remember that she was a woman of mature years and considerable experience.

"'Tain't a mite o' matter, sir," she said cheerfully. "I guess you'll find everything comfortable for you"; and they turned, much relieved, and walked along together.

"That's Lawyer Barstow's house," she said calmly, a minute afterward, "the handsomest place in town, we think 'tis," and Mr. Rill answered politely that Daleham was a pretty place; he had not been out of the city for so many years that everything looked beautiful as a picture.

IV

Miss Porley rapidly recovered her composure, and bent her energies to the preparing of an early tea. She showed her guest to the snug bedroom under the low gambrel roof, and when she apologized for his having to go upstairs, he begged her to remember that it was nothing but a step to a man who was used to four long flights. They were both excited at finding a proper nail for the birdcage outside the window, though Miss Esther said that she should love to have the pretty bird downstairs where they could see it and hear it sing. She said to herself over and over that if she could have her long-lost brother come home from sea, she should like to have him look and behave as gentle and kind as Mr. Rill. Somehow she found herself singing a cheerful hymn as she mixed and stirred the shortcakes. She could not help wishing that her mother were there to enjoy this surprise, but it did seem very odd, after so many years, to have a man in the house. It had not happened for fifteen years, at least, when they had entertained Deacon Sparks and wife, delegates from the neighboring town of East Wilby to the County Conference.

The neighbors did not laugh at Miss Esther openly or cause her to blush with self-consciousness, however much they may have discussed the situation and smiled behind her back. She took the presence of her guest with delighted simplicity, and the country week was extended to a fortnight, and then to a month. At last, one day Miss Esther and Mr. Rill were seen on their way to the railroad station, with a large bundle apiece beside the carpetbag, though someone noticed that the bullfinch was left behind. Miss Esther came back alone, looking very woebegone and lonely, and if the truth must be known, she found her house too solitary. She looked into the woodhouse where there was a great store of kindlings, neatly piled, and her water pail was filled to the brim, her garden paths were clean of weeds and swept, and yet everywhere she looked it seemed more lonely than ever. She pinned on her shawl again and went along the street to the parsonage.

"My old lady's just gone," she said to the minister's wife. "I was so lonesome I could not stay in the house."

"You found him a very pleasant visitor, didn't you, Miss Esther?" asked Mrs. Wayton, laughing a little.

"I did so; he wa'n't like other men,—kind and friendly and fatherly, and never stayed round when I was occupied, but entertained himself down street considerable, an' was as industrious as a bee, always asking me if there wa'n't something he could do about house. He and a sister some years older used to keep house together, and it was her long sickness used up what they'd saved, and yet he's got a little somethin', and there are friends he used to work for, jewelers, a big firm, that gives him somethin' regular. He's goin' to see,"—and Miss Esther blushed crimson,—"he's goin' to see if they'd be willin' to pay it just the same if he come to reside in Daleham. He thinks the air agrees with him here."

"Does he indeed?" inquired the minister's wife, with deep interest and a look of amusement.

"Yes'm," said Miss Esther simply; "but don't you go an' say nothin' yet. I don't want folks to make a joke of it. Seems to me if he does feel to come back, and remains of the same mind he went away, we might be judicious to take the step"—

"Why, Miss Esther!" exclaimed the listener.

"Not till fall,—not till fall," said Miss Esther hastily. "I ain't going to count on it too much anyway. I expect we could get along; there's considerable goodness left in me, and you can always work better when you've got somebody beside yourself to work for. There, now I've told you I feel as if I was blown away in a gale."

"Why, I don't know what to say at such a piece of news!" exclaimed Mrs. Wayton again.

"I don't know's there's anything *to* say," gravely answered Miss Esther. "But I did laugh just now coming in the gate to think what a twitter I got into the day I fetched you that piece of paper."

"Why, I must go right and tell Mr. Wayton!" said the minister's wife.

"Oh, don't you, Mis' Wayton; no, no!" begged Miss Esther, looking quite coy and girlish. "I really don't know's it's quite settled,—it don't seem's if it could be. I'm going to hear from him in the course of a week. But I suppose *he* thinks it's settled; he's left the bird."

The Guests of Mrs. Timms

MRS. PERSIS FLAGG stood in her front doorway taking leave of Miss Cynthia Pickett, who had just been making a long call. They were not intimate friends. Miss Pickett always came formally to the front door and rang when she paid her visits, but, the week before, they had met at the county conference, and had been sent to the same house for entertainment, and so had deepened and renewed the pleasures of acquaintance.

It was an afternoon in early June; the syringa bushes were tall and green on each side of the stone doorsteps, and were covered with their lovely white and golden flowers. Miss Pickett broke off the nearest twig, and held it before her prim face as she talked. She had a pretty childlike smile that came and went suddenly, but her face was not one that bore the marks of many pleasures. Mrs. Flagg was a tall, commanding sort of person, with an air of satisfaction and authority.

"Oh, yes, gather all you want," she said stiffly, as Miss Pickett took the syringa without having asked beforehand; but she had an amiable expression, and just now her large countenance was lighted up by pleasant anticipation.

"We can tell early what sort of a day it's goin' to be," she said eagerly. "There ain't a cloud in the sky now. I'll stop for you as I come along, or if there should be anything unforeseen to detain me, I'll send you word. I don't expect you'd want to go if it wa'n't so that I could?"

"Oh my sakes, no!" answered Miss Pickett, discreetly, with a timid flush. "You feel certain that Mis' Timms won't be put out? I shouldn't feel free to go unless I went 'long o' you."

"Why, nothin' could be plainer than her words," said Mrs. Flagg in a tone of reproval. "You saw how she urged me, an' had over all that talk about how we used to see each other often when we both lived to Longport, and told how she'd been thinkin' of writin', and askin' if it wa'n't so I should be able to come over and stop three or four days as soon as settled weather come, because she couldn't make no fire in her best chamber on account of the chimbley smokin' if the wind wa'n't just right. You see how she felt toward me, kissin' of me comin' and goin'? Why, she even asked me who I employed to do over my bonnet, Miss Pickett, just as interested as if she was a sister; an' she remarked she should look for us any pleasant day after we all got home, an' were settled after the conference."

Miss Pickett smiled, but did not speak, as if she expected more arguments still.

"An' she seemed just about as much gratified to meet with you again. She seemed to desire to meet you again very particular," continued Mrs. Flagg. "She really urged us to come together an' have a real good day talkin' over old times—there, don't le' 's go all over it again! I've always heard she'd made that old house of her aunt Bascom's where she lives look real handsome. I once heard her best parlor carpet described as being an elegant carpet, different from any there was round here. Why, nobody couldn't be more cordial, Miss Pickett; you ain't goin' to give out just at the last?"

"Oh, no!" answered the visitor, hastily; "no, 'm! I want to go full as much as you do, Mis' Flagg, but you see I never was so well acquainted with Mis' Cap'n Timms, an' I always seem to dread putting myself for'ard. She certain was very urgent, an' she said plain enough to come any day next week, an' here 'tis Wednesday, though of course she wouldn't look for us either Monday or Tuesday. 'Twill be a real pleasant occasion, an' now we've been to the conference it don't seem near so much effort to start."

"Why, I don't think nothin' of it," said Mrs. Flagg, proudly. "We shall have a grand good time, goin' together an' all, I feel sure."

Miss Pickett still played with her syringa flower, tapping her thin cheek, and twirling the stem with her fingers. She looked as if she were going to say something more, but after a moment's hesitation she turned away.

"Good afternoon, Mis' Flagg," she said formally, looking up with a quick little smile; "I enjoyed my call; I hope I ain't kep' you too late; I don't know but what it's 'most tea time. Well, I shall look for you in the mornin'."

"Good afternoon, Miss Pickett; I'm glad I was in when you

came. Call again, won't you?" said Mrs. Flagg. "Yes; you may expect me in good season," and so they parted. Miss Pickett went out at the neat clicking gate in the white fence, and Mrs. Flagg a moment later looked out of her sitting-room window to see if the gate were latched, and felt the least bit disappointed to find that it was. She sometimes went out after departure of a guest, and fastened the gate herself with a loud rebuking sound. Both of these Woodville women lived alone, and were very precise in their way of doing things.

II

The next morning dawned clear and bright, and Miss Pickett rose even earlier than usual. She found it most difficult to decide which of her dresses would be best to wear. Summer was still so young that the day had all the freshness of spring, but when the two friends walked away together along the shady street, with a chorus of golden robins singing high overhead in the elms, Miss Pickett decided that she had made a wise choice of her second-best black silk gown, which she had just turned again and freshened. It was neither too warm for the season nor too cool, nor did it look overdressed. She wore her large cameo pin, and this, with a long watch chain, gave an air of proper mural decoration. She was a straight, flat little person, as if, when not in use, she kept herself, silk dress and all, between the leaves of a book. She carried a noticeable parasol with a fringe, and a small shawl, with a pretty border, neatly folded over her left arm. Mrs. Flagg always dressed in black cashmere, and looked, to hasty observers, much the same one day as another; but her companion recognized the fact that this was the best black cashmere of all, and for a moment quailed at the thought that Mrs. Flagg was paying such extreme deference to their prospective hostess. The visit turned for a moment into an unexpectedly solemn formality, and pleasure seemed to wane before Cynthia Pickett's eyes, yet with great courage she never slackened a single step. Mrs. Flagg carried a somewhat worn black leather handbag, which Miss Pickett regretted; it did not give the visit that casual and unpremeditated air which she felt to be more elegant.

"Sha'n't I carry your bag for you?" she asked timidly. Mrs. Flagg was the older and more important person.

The Guests of Mrs. Timms

"Oh, dear me, no," answered Mrs. Flagg. "My pocket's so remote, in case I should desire to sneeze or anything, that I thought 'twould be convenient for carrying my handkerchief and pocketbook; an' then I just tucked in a couple o' glasses o' my crab-apple jelly for Mis' Timms. She used to be a great hand for preserves of every sort, an' I thought 'twould be a kind of an attention, an' give rise to conversation. I know she used to make excellent drop-cakes when we was both residin' to Longport; folks used to say she never would give the right receipt, but if I get a real good chance, I mean to ask her. Or why can't you, if I start talkin' about receipts—why can't you say, sort of innocent, that I have always spoken frequently of her drop-cakes, an' ask for the rule? She would be very sensible to the compliment, and could pass it off if she didn't feel to indulge us. There, I do so wish you would!"

"Yes, 'm," said Miss Pickett, doubtfully; "I'll try to make the opportunity. I'm very partial to drop-cakes. Was they flour or rye, Mis' Flagg?"

"They was flour, dear," replied Mrs. Flagg, approvingly; "crisp an' light as any you ever see."

"I wish I had thought to carry somethin' to make it pleasant," said Miss Pickett, after they had walked a little farther; "but there, I don't know's 'twould look just right, this first visit, to offer anything to such a person as Mis' Timms. In case I ever go over to Baxter again I won't forget to make her some little present, as nice as I've got. 'Twas certain very polite of her to urge me to come with you. I did feel very doubtful at first. I didn't know but she thought it behooved her, because I was in your company at the conference, and she wanted to save my feelin's, and yet expected I would decline. I never was well acquainted with her; our folks wasn't well off when I first knew her; 'twas before Uncle Cap'n Dyer passed away an' remembered mother an' me in his will. We couldn't make no han'some companies in them days, so we didn't go to none, an' kep' to ourselves; but in my grandmother's time, mother always said, the families was very friendly. I shouldn't feel like goin' over to pass the day with Mis' Timms if I didn't mean to ask her to return the visit. Some don't think o' these things, but mother was very set about not bein' done for when she couldn't make no return."

" 'When it rains porridge hold up your dish,' " said Mrs. Flagg;

but Miss Pickett made no response beyond a feeble "Yes, 'm," which somehow got caught in her pale-green bonnet strings.

"There, 'tain't no use to fuss too much over all them things," proclaimed Mrs. Flagg, walking along at a good pace with a fine sway of her skirts, and carrying her head high. "Folks walks right by an' forgits all about you; folks can't always be going through with just so much. You'd had a good deal better time, you an' your ma, if you'd been freer in your ways; now don't you s'pose you would? 'Tain't what you give folks to eat so much as 'tis makin' 'em feel welcome. Now, there's Mis' Timms; when we was to Longport she was dreadful methodical. She wouldn't let Cap'n Timms fetch nobody home to dinner without lettin' of her know, same's other cap'ns' wives had to submit to. I was thinkin', when she was so cordial over to Danby, how she'd softened with time. Years do learn folks somethin'! She did seem very pleasant an' desirous. There, I am so glad we got started; if she'd gone an' got up a real good dinner today, an' then not had us come till tomorrow, 'twould have been real too bad. Where any body lives alone such a thing is very tryin'."

"Oh, so 'tis!" said Miss Pickett. "There, I'd like to tell you what I went through with year before last. They come an' asked me one Saturday night to entertain the minister, that time we was having candidates—"

"I guess we'd better step along faster," said Mrs. Flagg, suddenly. "Why, Miss Pickett, there's the stage comin' now! It's dreadful prompt, seems to me. Quick! there's folks awaitin' an' I sha'n't get to Baxter in no state to visit Mis' Cap'n Timms if I have to ride all the way there backward!"

III

The stage was not full inside. The group before the store proved to be made up of spectators, except one man, who climbed at once to a vacant seat by the driver. Inside there was only one person, after two passengers got out, and she preferred to sit with her back to the horses, so that Mrs. Flagg and Miss Pickett settled themselves comfortably in the coveted corners of the back seat. At first they took no notice of their companion, and spoke to each other in low tones, but presently something attracted the attention of all three and engaged them in conversation.

"I never was over this road before," said the stranger. "I s'pose you ladies are well acquainted all along."

"We have often traveled it in past years. We was over this part of it last week goin' and comin' from the county conference," said Mrs. Flagg in a dignified manner.

"What persuasion?" inquired the fellow traveler, with interest.

"Orthodox," said Miss Pickett, quickly, before Mrs. Flagg could speak. "It was a very interestin' occasion; this other lady an' me stayed through all the meetin's."

"I ain't Orthodox," announced the stranger, waiving any interest in personalities. "I was brought up amongst the Freewill Baptists."

"We're well acquainted with several of that denomination in our place," said Mrs. Flagg, not without an air of patronage. "They've never built 'em no church; there ain't but a scattered few."

"They prevail where I come from," said the traveler. "I'm goin' now to visit with a Freewill lady. We was to a conference together once, same's you an' your friend, but 'twas a State conference. She asked me to come some time an' make her a good visit, and I'm on my way now. I didn't seem to have nothin' to keep me to home."

"We're all goin' visitin' today, ain't we?" said Mrs. Flagg, sociably; but no one carried on the conversation.

The day was growing very warm; there was dust in the sandy road, but the fields of grass and young growing crops looked fresh and fair. There was a light haze over the hills, and birds were thick in the air. When the stage horses stopped to walk, you could hear the crows caw, and the bobolinks singing, in the meadows. All the farmers were busy in their fields.

"It don't seem but little ways to Baxter, does it?" said Miss Pickett, after a while. "I felt we should pass a good deal o' time on the road, but we must be pretty near half-way there a'ready."

"Why, more 'n half!" exclaimed Mrs. Flagg. "Yes; there's Beckett's Corner right ahead, an' the old Beckett house. I haven't been on this part of the road for so long that I feel kind of strange. I used to visit over here when I was a girl. There's a nephew's widow owns the place now. Old Miss Susan Beckett willed it to him, an' he died; but she resides there an' carries on the farm, an unusual smart woman, everybody says. Ain't it pleasant here, right out among the farms!"

"Mis' Beckett's place, did you observe?" said the stranger, leaning forward to listen to what her companions said. "I expect that's where I'm goin'—Mis' Ezra Beckett's?"

"That's the one," said Miss Pickett and Mrs. Flagg together, and they both looked out eagerly as the coach drew up to the front door of a large old yellow house that stood close upon the green turf of the roadside.

The passenger looked pleased and eager, and made haste to leave the stage with her many bundles and bags. While she stood impatiently tapping at the brass knocker, the stage driver landed a large trunk, and dragged it toward the door across the grass. Just then a busy-looking middle-aged woman made her appearance, with floury hands and with a look as if she were prepared to be somewhat on the defensive.

"Why, how do you do, Mis' Beckett?" exclaimed the guest. "Well, here I be at last. I didn't know's you thought I was ever comin'. Why, I do declare, I believe you don't recognize me, Mis' Beckett."

"I believe I don't," said the self-possessed hostess. "Ain't you made some mistake, ma'am?"

"Why, don't you recollect we was together that time to the State conference, an' you said you should be pleased to have me come an' make you a visit some time, an' I said I would certain. There, I expect I look more natural to you now."

Mrs. Beckett appeared to be making the best possible effort, and gave a bewildered glance, first at her unexpected visitor, and then at the trunk. The stage driver, who watched this encounter with evident delight, turned away with reluctance. "I can't wait all day to see how they settle it," he said, and mounted briskly to the box, and the stage rolled on.

"He might have waited just a minute to see," said Miss Pickett, indignantly, but Mrs. Flagg's head and shoulders were already far out of the stage window—the house was on her side. "She ain't got in yet," she told Miss Pickett, triumphantly. "I could see 'em quite a spell. With that trunk, too! I do declare, how inconsiderate some folks is!"

" 'Twas pushin' an acquaintance most too far, wa'n't it?" agreed

Miss Pickett. "There, 'twill be somethin' laughable to tell Mis' Timms. I never see anything more divertin'. I shall kind of pity that woman if we have to stop an' git her as we go back this afternoon."

"Oh, don't let's forgit to watch for her," exclaimed Mrs. Flagg, beginning to brush off the dust of travel. "There, I feel an excellent appetite, dont you? And we ain't got more 'n three or four miles to go, if we have that. I wonder what Mis' Timms is likely to give us for dinner; she spoke of makin' a good many chicken pies, an' I happened to remark how partial I was to 'em. She felt above most of the things we had provided for us over to the conference. I know she was always counted the best o' cooks when I knew her so well to Longport. Now, don't you forget, if there's a suitable opportunity, to inquire about the drop-cakes," and Miss Pickett, a little less doubtful than before, renewed her promise.

IV

"My gracious, won't Mis' Timms be pleased to see us! It's just exactly the day to have company. And ain't Baxter a sweet pretty place?" said Mrs. Flagg, as they walked up the main street. "Cynthy Pickett, now ain't you proper glad you come? I felt sort o' calm about it part o' the time yesterday, but I ain't felt so like a girl for a good while. I do believe I'm goin' to have a splendid time."

Miss Pickett glowed with equal pleasure as she paced along. She was less expansive and enthusiastic than her companion, but now that they were fairly in Baxter, she lent herself generously to the occasion. The social distinction of going away to spend a day in company with Mrs. Flagg was by no means small. She arranged the folds of her shawl more carefully over her arm so as to show the pretty palmleaf border, and then looked up with great approval to the row of great maples that shaded the broad sidewalk. "I wonder if we can't contrive to make time to go an' see old Miss Nancy Fell?" she ventured to ask Mrs. Flagg. "There ain't a great deal o' time before the stage goes at four o'clock; 'twill pass quickly, but I should hate to have her feel hurt. If she was one we had visited often at home, I shouldn't care so much, but such folks feel any little slight. She was a member of our church; I think a good deal of that."

"Well, I hardly know what to say," faltered Mrs. Flagg, coldly. "We might just look in a minute; I shouldn't want her to feel hurt."

"She was one that always did her part, too," said Miss Pickett, more boldly. "Mr. Cronin used to say that she was more generous with her little than many was with their much. If she hadn't lived in a poor part of the town, and so been occupied with a different kind of people from us, 'twould have made a difference. They say she's got a comfortable little home over here, an' keeps house for a nephew. You know she was to our meeting one Sunday last winter, and 'peared dreadful glad to see her, too. I don't know as you were out."

"She always wore a friendly look," said Mrs. Flagg, indulgently. "There, now, there's Mis' Timms's residence; it's handsome, ain't it, with them big spruce trees? I expect she may be at the window now, an' see us as we come along. Is my bonnet on straight, an' everything? The blinds looks open in the room this way; I guess she's to home fast enough."

The friends quickened their steps, and with shining eyes and beating hearts hastened forward. The slightest mists of uncertainty were now cleared away; they gazed at the house with deepest pleasure; the visit was about to begin.

They opened the front gate and went up the short walk, noticing the pretty herringbone pattern of the bricks, and as they stood on the high steps Cynthia Pickett wondered whether she ought not to have worn her best dress, even though there was lace at the neck and sleeves, and she usually kept it for the most formal of tea parties and exceptional parish festivals. In her heart she commended Mrs. Flagg for that familiarity with the ways of a wider social world which had led her to wear the very best among her black cashmeres.

"She's a good while coming to the door," whispered Mrs. Flagg, presently. "Either she didn't see us, or else she's slipped upstairs to make some change, an' is just goin' to let us ring again. I've done it myself sometimes. I'm glad we come right over after her urgin' us so; it seems more cordial than to keep her expectin' us. I expect she'll urge us terribly to remain with her over night."

"Oh, I ain't prepared," began Miss Pickett, but she looked pleased. At that moment there was a slow withdrawal of the bolt inside, and a key was turned, the front door opened, and

The Guests of Mrs. Timms

Mrs. Timms stood before them with a smile. Nobody stopped to think at that moment what kind of smile it was.

"Why, if it ain't Mis' Flagg," she exclaimed politely, "an' Miss Pickett too! I am surprised!"

The front entry behind her looked well furnished, but not exactly hospitable; the stairs with their brass rods looked so clean and bright that it did not seem as if anybody had ever gone up or come down. A cat came purring out, but Mrs. Timms pushed her back with a determined foot, and hastily closed the sitting-room door. Then Miss Pickett let Mrs. Flagg precede her, as was becoming, and they went into a darkened parlor, and found their way to some chairs, and seated themselves solemnly.

" 'Tis a beautiful day, ain't it?" said Mrs. Flagg, speaking first. "I don't know's I ever enjoyed the ride more. We've been having a good deal of rain since we saw you at the conference, and the country looks beautiful."

"Did you leave Woodville this morning? I thought I hadn't heard you was in town," replied Mrs. Timms, formally. She was seated just a little too far away to make things seem exactly pleasant. The darkness of the best room seemed to retreat somewhat, and Miss Pickett looked over by the door where there was a pale gleam from the side lights in the hall, to try to see the pattern of the carpet; but her effort failed.

"Yes, 'm," replied Mrs. Flagg to the question. "We left Woodville about half-past eight, but it is quite a ways from where we live to where you take the stage. The stage does come slow, but you don't seem to mind it such a beautiful day."

"Why, you must have come right to see me first!" said Mrs. Timms, warming a little as the visit went on. "I hope you're going to make some stop in town. I'm sure it was very polite of you to come right an' see me; well, it's very pleasant, I declare. I wish you'd been in Baxter last Sabbath; our minister did give us an elegant sermon on faith an' works. He spoke of the conference, and gave his views on some o' the questions that came up, at Friday evenin' meetin'; but I felt tired after getting home, an' so I wasn't out. We feel very much favored to have such a man amon'st us. He's building up the parish very considerable. I understand the pew rents come to thirty-six dollars more this quarter than they did last."

"We also feel grateful in Woodville for our pastor's efforts," said Miss Pickett, but Mrs. Timms turned her head away sharply, as if the speech had been untimely, and trembling Miss Pickett had interrupted.

"They're thinking here of raisin' Mr. Barlow's salary another year," the hostess added; "a good many of the old parishioners have died off, but every one feels to do what they can. Is there much interest among the young people in Woodville, Mis' Flagg?"

"Considerable at this time, ma'am," answered Mrs. Flagg, without enthusiasm, and she listened with unusual silence to the subsequent fluent remarks of Mrs. Timms.

The parlor seemed to be undergoing the slow processes of a winter dawn. After a while the three women could begin to see one another's faces, which aided them somewhat in carrying on a serious and impersonal conversation. There were a good many subjects to be touched upon, and Mrs. Timms said everything that she should have said, except to invite her visitors to walk upstairs and take off their bonnets. Mrs. Flagg sat [in] her parlor chair as if it were a throne, and carried her banner of self-possession as high as she knew how, but toward the end of the call even she began to feel hurried.

"Won't you ladies take a glass of wine an' a piece of cake after your ride?" inquired Mrs. Timms, with an air of hospitality that almost concealed the fact that neither cake nor wine was anywhere to be seen; but the ladies bowed and declined with particular elegance. Altogether it was a visit of extreme propriety on both sides, and Mrs. Timms was very pressing in her invitation that her guests should stay longer.

"Thank you, but we ought to be going," answered Mrs. Flagg, with a little show of ostentation, and looking over her shoulder to be sure that Miss Pickett had risen too. "We've got some little ways to go," she added with dignity. "We should be pleased to have you call an' 'see us in case you have occasion to come to Woodville," and Miss Pickett faintly seconded the invitation. It was in her heart to add, "Come any day next week," but her courage did not rise so high as to make the words audible. She looked as if she were ready to cry; her usual smile had burnt itself out into gray ashes; there was a white appealing look about her mouth. As they emerged from the dim parlor and stood at the open front door, the bright June day, the golden-green trees, almost blinded their eyes. Mrs. Timms was more smiling and cordial than ever.

"There, I ought to have thought to offer you fans; I am afraid you was warm after walking," she exclaimed, as if to leave no stone of courtesy unturned. "I have so enjoyed meeting you again, I wish it was so you could stop longer. Why, Mis' Flagg, we haven't said one word about old times when we lived to Longport. I've had news from there, too, since I saw you; my brother's daughter-in-law was here to pass the Sabbath after I returned."

Mrs. Flagg did not turn back to ask any questions as she stepped stiffly away down the brick walk. Miss Pickett followed her, raising the fringed parasol; they both made ceremonious little bows as they shut the high white gate behind them. "Good-by," said Mrs. Timms, finally, as she stood in the door with her set smile; and as they departed she came out and began to fasten up a rosebush that climbed a narrow white ladder by the steps.

"Oh, my goodness alive!" exclaimed Mrs. Flagg, after they had gone some distance in aggrieved silence, "if I haven't gone and forgotten my bag! I ain't goin' back, whatever happens. I expect she'll trip over it in that dark room and break her neck!"

"I brought it; I noticed you'd forgotten it," said Miss Pickett, timidly, as if she hated to deprive her companion of even that slight consolation.

"There, I'll tell you what we'd better do," said Mrs. Flagg, gallantly: "we'll go right over an' see poor old Miss Nancy Fell; 'twill please her about to death. We can say we felt like goin' somewhere today, an' 'twas a good many years since either one of us had seen Baxter, so we come just for the ride, an' to make a few calls. She'll like to hear all about the conference; Miss Fell was always one that took a real interest in religious matters."

Miss Pickett brightened, and they quickened their step. It was nearly twelve o'clock, they had breakfasted early, and now felt as if they had eaten nothing since they were grown up. An awful feeling of tiredness and uncertainty settled down upon their once buoyant spirits.

"I can forgive a person," said Mrs. Flagg, "but when I'm done with 'em, I'm done."

V

"I do declare, 'twas like a scene in Scriptur' to see that poor goodhearted Nancy Fell run down her walk to open the gate for us!" said Mrs. Persis Flagg later that afternoon, when she and Miss Pickett were going home in the stage. Miss Pickett nodded her head approvingly.

"I had a good sight better time with her than I should have had at the other place," she said with fearless honesty. "If I'd been Mis' Cap'n Timms, I'd made some apology or just passed us the compliment. If it wa'n't convenient, why couldn't she just tell us so after all her urgin' and sayin' how she should expect us?"

"I thought then she'd altered from what she used to be," said Mrs. Flagg. "She seemed real sincere an' open away from home. If she wa'n't prepared today, 'twas easy enough to say so; we was reasonable folks, an' should have gone away with none but friendly feelin's. We did have a grand good time with Nancy. She was as happy to see us as if we'd been queens."

"'Twas a real nice little dinner," said Miss Pickett, gratefully. "I thought I was goin' to faint away just before we got to the house, and I didn't know how I should hold out if she undertook to do anything extra, and keep us a-waitin'; but there, she just made us welcome, simple-hearted, to what she had. I never tasted such dandelion greens, an' that nice little piece o' pork and new biscuit, why, they was just splendid. She must have an excellent good cellar, if 'tis such a small house. Her potatoes was truly remarkable for this time o' year. I myself don't deem it necessary to cook potatoes when I'm goin' to have dandelion greens. Now, didn't it put you in mind of that verse in the Bible that says, 'Better is a dinner of herbs where love is'? An' how desirous she'd been to see somebody that could tell her some particulars about the conference!"

"She'll enjoy tellin' folks about our comin' over to see her. Yes, I'm glad we went; 'twill be of advantage every way, an' our bein' of the same church an all, to Woodville. If Mis' Timms hears of our bein' here, she'll see we had reason, an' knew of a place to go. Well, I needn't have brought this old bag!"

Miss Pickett gave her companion a quick resentful glance, which was followed by one of triumph directed at the dust that was collecting on the shoulders of the best black cashmere; then she looked at the bag on the front seat, and suddenly felt illuminated with the suspicion that Mrs. Flagg had secretly made preparations to pass the night in Baxter. The bag looked plump, as if it held much more than the pocketbook and the jelly.

Mrs. Flagg looked up with unusual humility. "I did think about that jelly," she said, as if Miss Pickett had openly reproached her. "I was afraid it might look as if I was tryin' to pay her for her kindness."

"Well, I don't know," said Cynthia; "I guess she'd been pleased. She'd thought you just brought her over a little present: but I do' know as 'twould been any good to her after all; she'd thought so much of it, comin' from you, that she'd kep' it till 'twas all candied." But Mrs. Flagg didn't look exactly pleased by this unexpected compliment, and her fellow traveler colored with confusion and a sudden feeling that she had shown undue forwardness.

Presently they remembered the Beckett house, to their great relief, and, as they approached, Mrs. Flagg reached over and took her handbag from the front seat to make room for another passenger. But nobody came out to stop the stage, and they saw the unexpected guest sitting by one of the front windows comfortably swaying a palm-leaf fan, and rocking to and fro in calm content. They shrank back into their corners, and tried not to be seen. Mrs. Flagg's face grew very red.

"She got in, didn't she?" said Miss Pickett, snipping her words angrily, as if her lips were scissors. Then she heard a cry, and bent forward to see Mrs. Beckett herself appear in the front doorway, very smiling and eager to stop the stage.

The driver was only too ready to stop his horses. "Got a passenger for me to carry back, ain't ye?" said he, facetiously. "Them's the kind I like; carry both ways, make somethin' on a double trip," and he gave Mrs. Flagg and Miss Pickett a friendly wink as he stepped down over the wheel. Then he hurried toward the house, evidently in a hurry to put the baggage on; but the expected passenger still sat rocking and fanning at the window.

"No, sir; I ain't got any passengers," exclaimed Mrs. Beckett, advancing a step or two to meet him, and speaking very loud in her pleasant excitement. "This lady that come this morning wants her large trunk with her summer things that she left to the depo' in Woodville. She's very desirous to git into it, so don't you go an' forgit; ain't you got a book or somethin', Mr. Ma'sh? Don't you forgit to make a note of it; there's her check, an' we've kep' the number in case you should mislay it or anything. There's things in the trunk she needs; you know how you overlooked stoppin' to the milliner's for my bunnit last week."

"Other folks disremembers things as well's me," grumbled Mr. Marsh. He turned to give the passengers another wink more familiar than the first, but they wore an offended air, and were looking the other way. The horses had backed a few steps, and the guest at the front window had ceased the steady motion of her fan to make them a handsome bow, and been puzzled at the lofty manner of their acknowledgment.

"Go 'long with your foolish jokes, John Ma'sh!" Mrs. Beckett said cheerfully, as she turned away. She was a comfortable, hearty person, whose appearance suggested the beauties of hospitality. The driver climbed to his seat, chuckling, and drove away with the dust flying after the wheels.

"Now, she's a friendly sort of a woman, that Mis' Beckett," said Mrs. Flagg, unexpectedly, after a few moments of silence, when she and her friend had been unable to look at each other. "I really ought to call over an' see her some o' these days, knowing her husband's folks as well as I used to, an' visitin' of 'em when I was a girl." But Miss Pickett made no answer.

"I expect it was all for the best, that woman's comin'," suggested Mrs. Flagg again, hopefully. "She looked like a willing person who would take right hold. I guess Mis' Beckett knows what she's about, and must have had her reasons. Perhaps she thought she'd chance it for a couple o' weeks anyway, after the lady 'd come so fur, an' bein' one o' her own denomination. Hayin' 'll be here before we know it. I think myself, gen'rally speakin', 'tis just as well to let anybody know you're comin'."

"Them seemed to be Mis' Cap'n Timms's views," said Miss Pickett in a low tone; but the stage rattled a good deal, and Mrs. Flagg looked up inquiringly, as if she had not heard.